THE FLEETING YEARS

THE FLEETING YEARS

Connie Monk

Severn House Large Print
London & New York

This first large print edition published 2015
in Great Britain and the USA by
SEVERN HOUSE PUBLISHERS LTD of
19 Cedar Road, Sutton, Surrey, England, SM2 5DA.
First world regular print edition published 2015 by
Severn House Publishers Ltd., London and New York.

British Library Cataloguing in Publication Data

Monk, Connie author.
   The fleeting years.
   1. Married people–Fiction. 2. Motion picture actors and
   actresses–Fiction. 3. Women violinists–Fiction.
   4. Large type books.
   I. Title
   823.9'14-dc23

   ISBN-13: 9780727872777

Typeset by Palimpsest Book Production Ltd.,
Falkirk, Stirlingshire, Scotland.

Printed digitally in the USA.

One

Putting the telephone receiver back with a firm click and with an almost imperceptible toss of her head, Zina turned away. That's when she caught a glimpse of herself in the long mirror, the sight a taunting reminder of the care she had taken to get ready for such a special occasion. With her tawny-brown, curly hair cut almost boyishly short, her slim, petite figure shown off to perfection by the lightweight suit she had bought for the occasion, making the best of herself meant an end result that would turn heads. For this, their tenth wedding anniversary, they had planned to meet in time for lunch at the French Horn, where they would spend one night, just as they had the first night of their honeymoon before they'd flown off to the sunshine of Corfu. How young she had been, young and certain of a golden future. But even in their wildest dreams neither had imagined the success the years would bring. Success? For Peter, yes, enormous success. But how can it truly be measured? By fame and fortune or by growing ever closer together and sharing their daily lives? Ought she to forget her own interests and ambitions, simply make a safe and unchanging background for his full and demanding life? She

1

couldn't do that, and why should he expect her to?

Turning from the mirror, she sat on the edge of the bed with her back to her half-packed weekend case. Just a casual phone call to say he couldn't get away. If it had meant as much to him as it had to her, then surely he could have insisted he couldn't work today. If he'd stayed in the theatre she would have understood he had a commitment. But for one day, surely his presence wasn't needed in every scene. In her disappointment she gave full rein to her resentment. She clung to the thought of the letter that had arrived the previous morning and her mouth set in a firmer line. She, too, had a life, she wasn't simply an appendage to be housed and provided for, living in his shadow.

'I'm here,' she heard her mother's voice followed by the click as she shut the front door which Zina had left on the latch when she'd gone upstairs to get ready, filled then with every bit as much eager anticipation as she had been when she'd dressed for her wedding a decade ago. 'I came a bit early so that you knew there was nothing to worry about. Are you all dressed and beautiful?'

Jenny Beckham was a younger-than-her-years looking woman in her early fifties. After more than thirty years of a really happy marriage she had lost her husband in a motoring accident, something that might have crushed a lesser spirit. Only in her solitary moments did she let herself acknowledge the emptiness of her life, but that was *her* secret. Her cheerful willingness to give her time to the affairs of Myddlesham, the nearby village where she lived, and be prepared to take care of her twin grandchildren, kept her very active. She belonged to the Art Society, the Photographic Club, the Horticultural Society and served on the Parish Council where, in the views of some of the members, she cheered up the meetings simply by her presence. A pretty woman with the kind of looks that age wouldn't mar; by no means classically beautiful but with bright, dark blue eyes, a tip-tilted nose and a mouth that always appeared to be on the verge of a smile. With her trim figure and quick movements she was a delightful sight whether dressed smartly or, as on that May morning, in slacks, a check shirt and sandals.

Zina punched her clenched fists together as if to give herself courage, then stood up as she called in reply, 'Change of plans, Mum. Peter phoned that he can't get away. He'll be on the set all day. Come on up.'

Her bright voice didn't fool Jenny.

'If there's a fortune to be made from that film' she said as she came into the bedroom, 'then it'll be on *his* account because of all the starstruck young girls who'll be paying good money to sit drooling in a dark cinema and dreaming of their idol. Do you know, that young girl at the bakers told me the other day that she had seen *In the Wake of the Storm* four times and has his picture on her bedroom wall. There seemed something vaguely indecent about *your* husband being on her wall. Anyway, you can't tell me that if he'd said it was important for him not to be on set

3

today they wouldn't have pandered to him. Of course they would.'

'It's his anniversary too . . .' Zina found herself defending him. 'He was looking forward to it. He'd booked the room at the French Horn and everything.'

'Well, here we are at ten o'clock in the morning, the twins both in school for the day and you looking like something out of a fashion mag. So what are we going to do about it?'

It was impossible for Zina's spirits not to take a momentary leap upwards.

'Oh Mum, what would I do without you?'

'You'd do very well, my sweet,' came Jenny's brisk reply. 'Now then, are you going to get out of your fancy attire or am I going home to get decked up? What shall it be? Town, coast or country?'

'Let's go to that pub on the edge of Exmoor where we used to go with Dad, I forget its name. Let's go there, have a drink then leave the car while we walk like we used to; then we could go back for a pub lunch? It's such a gorgeous day.' Somehow Zina managed to force enthusiasm into her voice.

'Sounds like heaven to me.' Jenny played along. Then, the excitement gone from her tone as she even took herself by surprise, saying, 'Funny the way life goes, isn't it?' But her mask of pleasure was quickly back in place. 'I'll wait downstairs while you get out of your smart gear.'

Ten minutes later she was at the wheel as they headed towards Exmoor. She wanted to believe she was glad of the choice of venue, surely if anything could ease the disappointment Zina had

4

had about her anniversary celebrations, then it must be found in the glorious countryside she had known and loved all her life. Jenny asked herself if she was being unfair in mistrusting her son-in-law? Perhaps he really hadn't been able to come away from the shooting on this special day. But it was more than that which worried her; it was something under the surface, which she tried to believe must be in her imagination. Ten years ago on that sunny May morning when darling Richard had so proudly armed their daughter up the aisle, he had had such faith in the rightness of the joining together of these two people. Six years older than Zina, Peter had been a member of the Marley Players – albeit a leading member and one who drew the audience wherever the repertory company was booked for a six-week season. At that time, it had been Zina's career that had held promise. She had recently left music college with high expectations of her future as a solo violinist. Now Jenny took her eyes off the road just for a second as she drove and glanced at her daughter. Was she happy in her marriage? Did pride in *his* achievement make up for the loss in their close day-to-day union and the end of her hopes as a professional musician? To be fair, he had never become changed by fame, but had he ever considered there was anyone who mattered except himself?

'Somewhere along here we turn right, don't we, Mum?'

'Yes, five minutes and we'll be there. Richard's favourite haunt.' She said it in her usual bright voice, something Zina accepted as normal.

They were greeted by the landlord like long-lost friends, something that helped to make Zina forget her disappointment at the way the day had turned out. With a little more perception she might have guessed what was hidden behind her mother's bright manner. As it was, she took it for granted that Jenny was trying to make up to her for the changes in the planned day and she went out of her way to respond.

They walked, then back at the inn they had a steak and kidney pie lunch, everything according to plan. Zina reminded her mother of previous occasions when they had followed these same tracks when she had been home from music college and there had been three of them, not even suspecting that Jenny was torn between indulging her desire to rekindle times gone and being swamped by the void left in her life. For both of them there was an underlying current of emotion and they were thankful when, just after four o'clock, they arrived outside the children's preparatory school to pick them up.

'They've gone, Mrs Marchand,' one of the twins' classmates called as she passed the car. 'They came out ages ago, five minutes or more. I saw them walking down the drive. I had to go back to get my French homework book and I took ages to find it.'

'They must have started off home on their own,' Jenny said. 'We shall pass them on their way.'

But they didn't. And when they arrived home at Newton House there was no sign of them. Calling out their names through the house brought no answer, so while Zina scoured the large

6

garden, expecting they must be hiding and probably giggling behind a clump of bushes somewhere, Jenny went back to the gate. If either of the children had had a few pence on them, she was sure they would probably have been in the sweet shop when the car went by.

That's when Peter's red open-top vintage sports car appeared at speed, showing no sign that he was about to slow down to turn in at the gate. Instead he came to a halt so suddenly that, but for their recently fitted safety belts, his two young passengers would have been thrown forward off the back seat, something that to them was sheer delight. That was what was so special about being with *him*; he wasn't like other grown-ups. Anyone else would have slowed down so that they stopped without a bump. The twins beamed at each other in a silent message of understanding.

'Mother-in-law,' he called to Jenny with a smile that told her he had no suspicion of her misgivings about him, 'what are you doing wandering in the lane?'

'Looking for the children,' Jenny replied in an unfamiliarly cool voice. 'We were told at the school they had left before we arrived.'

He grinned, turning to give a saucy wink to the nine-year-olds behind him. 'I got there first. We've been adventuring, eh kids?'

'Yep,' Fiona, the more self-assured, answered, returning the wink to her father. 'Dad took us to get some buns and feed the swans.'

'And some ice creams to feed ourselves,' Tommy put in.

'A pity you didn't think to phone Zina and tell

7

her you could get away after all.' Even without looking at her, Peter would have known that his mother-in-law was tight lipped.

'Sorry, Mother-in-law.' Peter words were an apology; his exaggeratedly contrite expression making it clear that it was no such thing.

'You see, Gran, we were so excited to see Dad waiting at the gate that we didn't think of *anything else*. Was Mum worried about us?' That was Tommy, the gentler, more thoughtful of the two. In character, as in appearance, they were poles apart and yet there was an uncanny closeness between them; they seemed to read each other's thoughts.

'And probably still is. She's hunting in the garden in the hope you're just playing the fool and hiding from her.'

'I'll climb out, Dad. I'll run and find her.' Already climbing out as he spoke, Tommy ran up the drive shouting for his mother as Peter leant across and opened the front passenger door.

'In you hop, Mother-in-law. Then I'll know I'm forgiven.'

As Jenny settled into the seat by his side and he turned into the drive she gave him a quick glance. It seemed to her that life was a joke to him, put there for his amusement; and yet, even with her misgivings, she could understand the spell he cast on Zina. Perhaps his charm stemmed from the fact that no matter how his life had changed with the trappings of fame, nothing altered his personality.

As soon as Zina heard Tommy's shout she hurried to the front of the house, a house that at one time would have been beyond her wildest dreams. Modernized and with every comfort, it was a large Georgian building standing in grounds of some three acres, mostly grass and woodland. Even if fame had brought no change to Peter's personality, it certainly had to their lifestyle.

Jenny didn't want to watch the moment of greeting between husband and wife. Why was it she felt so uncomfortable about their relationship? Surely he was no different now from the young actor who had swept Zina off her feet. Was it that the abandoned dreams of her daughter's career were in the forefront of her mind and that was why it hurt to see her doing no more than lead the Myddlesham Symphony Orchestra (something of a misnomer, for although it was based in Myddlesham village with rehearsals in the church hall, the players came from as far afield as Exeter, Torquay and even Cullompton, all of them keen amateurs) or playing solos for local charity concerts? How could Zina not care? And yet she showed no regret; her world seemed to start and end with Peter and the family. It hurt to see the sudden radiance on her face as Peter opened his arms to her with an exaggerated flourish.

'I'm not coming back inside,' Jenny called to them. 'I'll have time to smarten myself up and go to the Parish Council meeting this evening. Now that you're going to be home I'll withdraw my apologies and turn up as usual. Bye my dears, have a lovely evening.' And while Zina and Peter were still in that first embrace she was already getting into her car.

Driving away she was overcome with a rare moment of self-pity. She wasn't proud of the tears that stung her eyes. For all her filling every crowded hour, the family were her life; they had to be now that Richard had gone. Yet, had they even noticed her sudden change of plans for the evening? Did it matter to them that she had nothing better to do with the remaining hours of the day than to sit around a table discussing whether or not to recommend to the planning department that they should reject an application for a new house in the garden of number three Bickley Road or where the signs should be fixed warning the villagers of the penalties of allowing their dogs to foul the pavements? However, she blinked away her unshed tears. Then voicing her thoughts aloud she said, 'Better stop and fill the tank before I put the car to bed,' as with a look of determination she drove into the forecourt of the filling station. Not even to herself did she admit that she disliked filling the petrol tank now that Wilkins Garage had been modernized. It was something she couldn't get used to, remembering how it used to be when she and Richard would sit in the car while an attendant put the petrol in the tank then washed the windscreen and back window.

Carefully parking with the petrol cap side of the car next to the pump she got out, making her automatic silent plea, 'Please make me do it right' while in her imagination she saw the petrol spurting to run down the side of the car or, worse, onto her shoe. But on this occasion it wasn't going to spurt anywhere, for she couldn't get the cap off the petrol tank. She gritted her teeth as if that would give more force but it didn't shift; she took her handkerchief and wrapped it around the cap to give her a better grip but still it wouldn't budge. With her head high and looking to neither right nor left she opened the car door to get back in. She probably had best part of a gallon still, so she'd find a pair of pliers once she got home and get it off that way.

'Don't give up,' a voice said so close behind her that it made her jump and added to her embarrassment.

'No, it's quite all right. I don't need to get any. I haven't time to stop now.'

'Humour me, let me try it for you.' The stranger's smile was disarming, and had he been what she would consider elderly, perhaps even fat or balding, she might have been able to accept his offer with some semblance of grace. But she saw him as neither elderly nor unattractive, a man perhaps her own age with an air of confidence that added to her own confusion.

'I think it's on a crossed thread. Don't worry about it. When I get home I'll do it with pliers.' She just wanted to get away.

Just as she had, he took a handkerchief from his pocket so that he didn't touch the cap, but she could see that in his case he did it to protect his hands. Some of her own embarrassment vanished with her respect for him. He looked so manly, yet his hands clearly never did a day's work. Perhaps they didn't, but they had the necessary strength and soon he was filling her tank for her.

'Really you mustn't bother, I can fill up quite

easily.' But 'Sir Galahad' was apparently deaf, for his only reply was a smile as if they shared a secret. She wasn't used to feeling so uncomfortable. The job done he gave her another smile and a slight and rather foreign-looking nod of his head, making her half expect him to click his heels together, then turned back to his own car.

Back at Newton House it had been much as she'd imagined, her departure hardly registering in the excitement of Peter's homecoming.

'When did you find out you could get away?' Zina asked him as they sat around the supper table. Early supper was the normal meal for the Marchands because when Peter was home he liked them to sit together as a family and when he was away Zina preferred to get the meal over and have a free evening for her music. So supper as they called it was no late evening snack, it was a cooked meal but early enough for Fiona and Tommy to eat with them. They were eating the pork casserole she had made for her mother to reheat, whilst she and Peter were meant to be celebrating at the French Horn.

'Ages ago,' he replied, 'but I wanted to turn up and surprise you all. Much more fun, eh kids? Not just one night in a miserable hotel, oh no, you have me underfoot for a week . . . a fortnight . . . I've no idea. They will let me know when my presence is required. Today the crew are moving to the Suffolk coast to film on location, parts of the storyline where I have no place. So, my love, I've come home so that you three can spoil me thoroughly.'

To the three at the table it sounded like magic, for a two-week uninterrupted stay was a rare event when he was working on a film. Zina even forgave him for not realizing how she had felt when he'd phoned her at the last minute. For all four of them nothing could mar the wonder of that early evening suppertime. No one could have foreseen the storm clouds rising just above the horizon.

Much later Zina was slipping towards sleep, utterly content, all her misgivings laid to rest. She had looked forward to the night away with Peter knowing it would be wonderful, but the last half hour had been more than that. Sometimes his love-making was wildly, almost greedily, passionate; but not tonight. She felt that their coming together had more than simply satisfied their physical needs; it had been a meeting of all that they were. As she drifted towards sleep, she smiled.

So often, when he turned away and settled for the night she would be wide awake, but it seemed this time was different.

'I meant to tell you' – his conversational tone surprising her – 'I met someone called Celia Turnbull, a writer. Have you ever heard of her?'

At his words Zina was wide awake. 'I think I've read everything she's written. I love her books. How did you meet her?'

'I went out for a meal the other night with Herbert' – Herbert St Clare was a director and a friend of them both – 'and this woman was at the same restaurant, eating alone. Apparently one of her books is being turned into a film. Herbert is an old friend so she joined us. You'd like her. Or more to the point you *will* like her. She has bought a place quite near – across the river towards Picton Heath. She's having a lot done to it just like we did here. It appears that last time she was down to see the progress her car packed up on her and she had to leave it behind for repair. So I gave her a lift down. Yes, I think you two will get along well. If you like what she writes you're halfway to liking her already.'

'How exciting. Is she here to stay now, or just seeing how the work is going?'

'Just a week or two – roughing it, she called it, while she checks that everything will be in order. I don't imagine she would be above being surrounded by chaos. She's quite a character. But I won't influence you, you must see for yourself. Give it a day or two and I'll drive over and ask her across for a drink.'

'Lovely.' That's when she decided this was the opportunity to tell him about the letter. 'Peter, now that we're chatting like this, I want to talk to you about a letter I've had. It's from Derek Masters, the pianist.'

'Don't know the name, but you know what a philistine I am when it comes to your sort of music. Is he someone famous or one of your old buddies?'

That remark was the first prick to her bubble of happiness.

'He's sufficiently good that if he were a concert soloist his name would be famous enough for even a philistine to have heard of him,' she retorted, then before she could stop herself she added, 'as famous as a jobbing actor turned film idol. But he is part of the Meinholt Piano Quintet; in fact it was he who founded it. Now I suppose you're going to say you've never heard of *them* either.'

'True,' he agreed affably enough, not a bit put down by her comment.

'You remember I told you I was playing in Exeter last week at a charity concert.' A grunt from Peter. 'Don't go to sleep, please listen, this is important. I haven't even told Mum, I intended to talk to you at lunch today.'

Peter was awake. 'Sorry, interrupting you just a minute. Lunch. I did stop off at the French Horn, you know. We even raised a glass to my bride. Celia thoroughly enjoyed it all. Go on, what about this pianist chap?'

'It sounds big-headed and I don't mean it to, but he made a point of coming to talk to me after the concert and we chatted for a long while. So good having Mum willing to stay the night here. Anyway, he was very complimentary about my playing, and apart from the fact that I thought what a nice chap he was I put the whole thing out of my head. Then yesterday morning I had this letter from him. There are two violinists in the quintet, a viola and a cello – and Derek himself on the piano. One of the two violinists has warned them that she will be leaving in a few months as she's pregnant.'

'Why tell *you*? He hardly knows you.' But from his changed tone of voice she could tell he had guessed exactly why Derek Masters had told her.

15

'He has suggested I replace her.' She had read the letter a dozen times, but actually hearing herself speaking the words was something quite different . . . actually being part of the wonderful Meinholt Piano Quintet! She wanted to say it all again just to hear it spoken.

'But that's ridiculous! Clearly he doesn't know you have a husband and children. You must answer him quickly, it wouldn't be fair to mess him about. He'll have to get someone else.'

'Why?' There was no tone of enquiry in the single word; it was an ice-cold sound dropped into the silence.

'You ask *why*? You can't be serious. Have you no conception of what it would mean to the family and to me to have you concentrating on your fiddle when you ought to be giving your time to the home and the children. You can't expect Mother-in-law always to be at your beck and call. I've never heard a more crazy idea. Didn't you tell this chap you're married with a family?'

There was a long silence; neither knew how to break it. They were rushing towards a precipice and what could stop them going over the edge? After what seemed like eternity but was probably no more than a minute, time enough for Peter to become confident that she had digested his words and seen the wisdom of them, it was Zina who spoke.

'Since I was six years old, I have loved playing,' she said, speaking clearly and quietly, something in her tone telling him her mind was already made up. 'All my childhood and youth it came first in my life, up until I met you. Even then, while you were with the rep you were happy for me to give recitals. But that lasted no time because I was pregnant so soon. I'm still that same person, Peter. I love you as I always have – always will – but I have a life of my own. Next term the twins will be away at St Mary's, the school of *your* choice – a good one, too, as it's co-ed. I agreed with you that it would be much better for them than having to travel each day all the way to Exeter and go to separate schools. If I joined the quintet before the start of term in September I know Mum would be here for them.' Her voice was becoming more strident, a warning that her calm might break. 'Am I supposed to spend my life alone here waiting for phone calls from you when you have nothing more exciting to do, looking for letters from the children, reading, killing time . . .?'

'In a house like this I should have thought there was plenty to amuse any woman. You know you're never kept tied to the house, nor are you ever short of money to spend.'

'I don't want amusement and I'm not thinking of money, I want the joy of making music, combining the sound of my playing with other people's. It's not fame I want, Peter, nor independence. Can't you understand how I feel to be stripped of what was the most important thing in my life? The house won't be neglected, and I know without even asking her that I can rely on Mum.'

'It's the most ridiculous thing I've ever heard. It's almost ten years since you have played except at some local do or other. All right, you trained

17

and you were supposed to be quite promising but, God alive, in those ten years imagine the number of students who have left with as good a record and been playing ever since. Do you honestly think you could keep up with professionals? I don't want to see you humiliated. You practise a bit before you play at some local do, and I expect they all think you're wonderful, but to put yourself on a par with professionals is asking for humiliation. Just play the damned thing for amusement. One pro in the family is enough.'

She wished she hadn't mentioned it. Ten minutes ago they had known the wonder of complete union, nothing else had mattered for either of them. Now she felt she hardly knew him at all. And he? What was he feeling about her?

'You're wrong,' she said quietly, reaching to take his hand in hers, 'except when you're home there isn't a day when I don't play, really play, extending myself I mean and not just playing familiar stuff, for two or three hours. I know I'm better now than I was ten years ago and I just yearn to be part of it. Can't you try and understand, Peter?'

'If you want the truth, no I can't. If you were a writer like Celia Turnbull I'd have no objection, you could combine that with being at home for the family. But what you talk of is sheer selfishness.'

'I'm going to sleep. I shall answer the letter in the morning.'

And so they turned away from each other, lying silently and feigning sleep.

The next day she wrote to Derek Masters

18

agreeing to his suggestion to meet him when the quintet was in Deremouth the following month.

'See what I've written, Peter,' she said, passing him the single sheet of paper. 'It commits me to nothing – neither me nor him – but I *have* to follow it up. Perhaps you're right and I'm not good enough. But I just have to grasp an opportunity like this. I bet when I tell Mum she'll say the same.'

'You're not married to your mother, of course she will. I've given you a good home here, you want for nothing except you crave praise and adulation – or do such words cheapen the classical music profession? I can't understand what's happened to you.'

'Don't, Peter. If you don't understand, I can't explain. I don't want adulation or praise, all I want is to be part of the making of music.'

'For pretty well ten years you've never even mentioned your wretched violin. Is it because the children are going to school in a few months? Do you want to keep them here until they are thirteen and can go straight into the senior school? Are you frightened of being too much on your own here? I can understand that. What you really need is another baby—'

'I most certainly do *not*!'

'How about if we get a flat in London, would you be happier there and just come back here when we're all free?'

'London? How often are you in London? What in the world would I want with that?'

'God give me strength!' With his hands in the air he looked upwards as if for help.

'Shut up, Peter, stop play acting.'

19

In silence they looked at each other, both reading fear in the other's eyes, dread of something they were too scared to face. Then, without either of them consciously being the first to move, they covered the space that separated them and clung to each other like drowning men being thrown a lifeline.

'Perhaps nothing will come of it,' she whispered. Nuzzling against his shoulder, she continued, 'But it's nothing to do with my wanting to escape from all this, it's just something that's missing in my life. I have to try, please understand darling, I *have* to.'

Whether or not he was any nearer to understanding she couldn't tell but when he said, 'Post your letter, the sooner you find out the truth the better' his voice was gentle.

'I love you, Mr Marchand – I hate it when we quarrel.'

'And I love you, Mrs Marchand. I guess that's why it is we have the power to hurt each other.'

The letter posted, they both avoided any mention of Derek Masters' suggestion and Zina didn't touch her fiddle until the Saturday of that first week when Peter took Fiona and Tommy to Bristol Zoo. Even though it was never mentioned, it cast a cloud on what should have been a perfect interlude. Not that the twins noticed anything odd in the atmosphere because Peter and Zina disguised the shadow that hung over them by being exaggeratedly cheerful.

'I wish Dad didn't have to go away. Other people's dads don't,' Tommy whispered to Fiona when he crept along to her bedroom after they'd gone to bed that night. It was a nightly ritual, something they wrongly believed was secret from their parents. They both thought of it as their special time. If they'd had enough money to go to the sweet shop after school there would be a bar of chocolate to share, but with or without confectionery, there was something very special about their whispered exchanges after the light was turned off.

'Other people's fathers are nothing special. Ours is important, everybody all over the country—' to stress the point Fiona corrected herself – 'all over the world I expect, see films with him being the most important person in them. I bet it's great being in films like that. When I get old enough, that's what I'm going to do. Sometimes I'll come home to see you and Mum, like Dad does, and I'll be like *him*, special not ordinary.'

'Better to have him always at home so we were like other families. And you too, much better for us all to be together,' Tommy replied. Then, his mind going to the children in their class at school, he added, 'But we're lucky really, we do have a dad, not like Morna or Vera . . .'

Fiona pondered the point before she replied. 'They must both have had fathers in the beginning. I expect their parents quarrelled and got divorced, some people do. So we're lucky, even if he's away being famous, he and Mum never fight.'

'Crumbs, no. If they did it would be awful; gives you a funny tight feeling in your tummy just to think about it, doesn't it.'

21

But Fiona's mind had jumped ahead to more important things.

'Hey, Tommy, in the morning if it's warm like it was today, let's ask Dad to take us to Deremouth. They'll say—' and here she put on what she called a grown-up, bossy voice – "It's not summer yet, you can only paddle." But, tell you what we'll do, when we get dressed in the morning we'll put our cossies on under our clothes. I bet you Dad'll say we can go in once he knows we're kitted out.'

Giggling in anticipation and imagining the sea as it had been at the end of the previous summer rather than after the storms of winter, they said their whispered goodnight with their thoughts already on the morning. Then Tommy crept back to his own room. At that point even he hadn't considered that Zina might be included in the plan for the trip to Deremouth. It had become routine that when Peter was able to be at home, he spent time alone with the twins, as if that way they would all make up for his periods of absence.

Next morning the sun promised a good day ahead and Peter willingly fell in with the plan.

'Let's go to the café on the pier, can we do that, Dad? Their ice cream is just *scrumptious.*' In Fiona's mind they were already there, attacking a bowl of ice cream topped with delicious chocolate sauce.

'Play your cards right, kids, and we might do just that and have fish and chips for lunch. How would you like that, Zina?'

'Me? I thought this was an outing for you and the twins.' There was no resentment in Zina's tone. 'I have lots to do here. Just you three go. But if I know you're not coming home for the usual Sunday lunchtime feast, I'll cook for early evening instead.'

For a brief instant their glances locked. Eager to get on their way, Fiona gave it no thought. But for some reason there was an uncomfortable feeling in the pit of Tommy's stomach.

'We'd like you to come too, Mum. All of us together would be fun, wouldn't it?' He looked to Fiona to back up his words, but he looked in vain. She was busy working out how to get towels packed in the car without arousing suspicion.

'No, just the three of you go. I'll have dinner ready for six o'clock. OK?' Zina spoke in an over-bright tone that fooled no one except Fiona. Letting her glance meet Peter's again, Zina felt torn. If only he'd hold out his hand to her, just say that the day would be incomplete without her . . . but that was stupid, she told herself. She was there for the twins at any time, like a cooked breakfast before she drove them to school or smooth sheets in their well-made beds, a new tube of toothpaste always ready when the old one had been squeezed flat. That's what mothers were for, she thought bitterly. Well, it wasn't going to be like that, *she* had a life too. Peter wasn't the only one with a career that mattered.

'Come on, then, kids. Bring your anoraks in case it blows up. Spades, buckets, bat and ball; we'll go adventuring. That'll give you a quiet house, Zina.'

Tommy still felt uneasy. Why would Mum want a quiet house? A child so like his father in

23

appearance, one day he would be a heartbreaker if looks were anything to go on. But he hadn't Peter's outgoing, fun-loving personality. He looked uncertainly from one to the other. Understanding him so well, Zina gave him a quick smile and a cheerful, 'Off you go and make sure you've got all your things.' Reassured, he followed Fiona and turned his attention to hiding their towels under the front seats of the car before their mother spied them. They both had a natural instinct for getting what they wanted from Peter, but with Zina they very seldom came out on top.

Leaving them to get settled with their seatbelts on, Zina walked down the drive so that she could open and close the gates and save Peter getting out. His wave of thanks was all she asked, that and the way he pursed his lips in a mock kiss of farewell. Walking on air she went back to the house and straight up the stairs to what was grandly known as the music room. In fact it was no such thing, the only hint of anything musical was a baby grand piano on which Peter would pound out familiar tunes after they had the occasional slightly drunken dinner party for some of his professional friends. With voices well lubricated, everyone would sing lustily. To him, that was what was meant by the word 'music'.

Opening a large built-in cupboard of no interest to anyone but herself, she took out her violin case and the music. With the instrument tucked under her chin she was conscious already of a feeling of contentment. The sound as she plucked the strings, tightening the pegs to make sure the tuning was perfect, was like the caress of a life-long lover; she was at peace with the world.

But it didn't last. Even as she drew the first note she heard the sound of footsteps on the gravel drive. Moving nearer the window she stood just to one side trying to keep out of sight as she looked down at the caller. No one lived near and yet there was no sign of a car. It was a stranger, a woman clearly with no care for her appearance. Her trousers both too baggy and too long, a shapeless three-quarter length coat, all topped with a battered panama hat. What sort of a person would go out looking such a sight?

'Bugger!' Not a usual expression of Zina's but at that moment nothing less would have done and the sight of such an unkempt visitor put extra feeling into the single word. If she pretended no one was at home, the stranger would go away. But even as she withdrew further into the room to be sure of staying out of sight, a shower of tiny pebbles from the drive hit the window.

'Yoo-hoo!' a voice called, a voice very out-of-keeping with her appearance. 'I met Peter, he said that room was where I'd find you.'

There was nothing for it but for Zina to fling open the window and lean out.

'You just met Peter?'

'Yes, he pulled over when he recognized me. He said for me to come and interrupt you, is that OK? I'm Celia Turnbull. I ate your share of your anniversary lunch when he drove me down. May I inflict myself on you or are you frightfully busy? Honestly I'll understand if you're practising; I

25

know how I'd feel if some stranger came barging in when I'm working.'

Had she not given Zina a chance to get a word in or was it the other way round, had Zina been so surprised by her visitor's identity that she was left speechless?

'Peter was right,' she called in reply, 'he knew I hoped we'd meet. I'll come down and let you in.'

'Can't we sit in the sunshine for ten minutes? I'm too muddy to walk indoors.'

So that's what they did, Zina taking her to the wooden garden seat.

'Where did you park? You surely haven't walked all the way to cross the river on the bridge?'

'I'm still carless. It died on me last time I was down and is still at the menders. I came across by boat, no less. When I took the house over, there was an almighty lot of junk in it, a few really good pieces of furniture too. And upside-down at the bottom of the garden, almost hidden in the weeds, was a boat – oh and in the shed three or four fishing rods and a pair of oars. Fishing must have been what the old chap used the boat for, I suppose. It's a great way to get about, peace and quiet all around you. I saw two herons upstream yesterday.'

Zina was already forgetting her pique at being disturbed. This woman was 'real', she wasn't given to polite chit-chat about nothing.

'Let's have a drink,' she suggested, 'what would you like? Coffee or something stronger? Or is that a bit depraved so early in the day?'

'Probably, but don't let's be put off by that. Tell you what I would really like, a beer. Have you got any?'

'Lager from the fridge or room temperature ale? Peter is very fussy about his beer.'

'Ordinary English room temp ale will be perfect. He's a nice man, your husband. All the glitz of his profession hasn't got to him. I really enjoyed our drive the other day. I came here this morning feeling I knew you already. You're a lucky woman, Zina Marchand.'

Zina nodded, her mouth turned into a smile even though her eyes didn't get the message.

'I'll get the drinks, shan't be a second.'

In no time she was back carrying a tray, which she dumped between them on the seat.

'Nothing very exciting, only cashews. If I'd known you were coming—'

'You'd have baked a cake. Sorry, it was rotten of me to arrive like I did. He said you'd be up in the music room and I ought to have known better. I hope it hasn't got us off on the wrong foot.'

Celia was surprised when her remark was taken seriously.

'I thought it had,' Zina answered with more honesty than tact, 'but that was before we talked. Yes, I intended to have a couple of hours practising – it's quite important to me at the moment. But I'm really glad to have you here. I've read every one of your books and loved them all. When Peter told me you were living across the river I was thrilled and wanted to get to know you. But you're not a bit what I expected.'

27

'Now how's a girl supposed to take a remark like that?' Celia said with a deep-toned laugh. 'Do you expect an artist to look like his paintings?'

'I've never met an artist so I don't know. But I have met a few composers – ages ago when I was at college – and I always felt their personalities fitted the music they wrote, light and gentle or bold, full of passion.'

'Ah! Well, I fear you get what you see with me. Anything that comes out between the pages probably owes itself to the dreams of a repressed youth.'

'That I do not believe. I love your books for the very reason that you have such understanding. You must have or you couldn't write as you do.'

'The longer we live, the more we are able to see and understand. But never mind me; tell me about you. Peter says you are itching to get back to your music. Of course you are, you didn't work as hard as you must have done to give it all up and not look back with regret. Now you're thinking of going back to it seriously. He's quite upset about it, isn't he?'

'But he didn't know anything about it when he drove you down. And even now, we aren't talking to each other about it. It's a sort of danger zone; neither of us know where talking about it would lead. When did he tell you? Not this morning?'

'No. I met him the other day. He was on his own walking in the meadow your side of the river; I was on the rowing boat. So I persuaded him aboard.'

'He didn't tell me . . .' Zina looked at her guest

more closely. Surely she couldn't be jealous of a scruffy creature like this? Of all the people she knew, Peter was the most particular about personal appearance.

'He told me about the chance you have. And I shouldn't be surprised if he was more open with me about his own feelings than he had been with you. I imagine he's like all men, all bluff and bluster when it comes to their feelings, frightened to show their hurt.'

Zina frowned. She ought to be angry that a mere stranger could talk to her about something that was simply between herself and Peter. But she couldn't. Any anger she felt was aimed at him that he could discuss their affairs with an outsider.

'I haven't even told my mother about the suggestion. He had no right to discuss my affairs.'

'I dare say you're right, but it did him good to talk. He probably wouldn't have mentioned it had he not told me previously about your giving up your career soon after you were married. He is so proud of you—'

'Rubbish. He's frightened I'll have a life of my own instead of standing at ease ready to jump to attention when he can spare time to be home – and after the beginning of next term it will be the same even though Fiona and Tommy will have gone away to school. He'd like it for me to be here, keeping everything neat and tidy for when he finds time to slot me in for the odd couple of days in his busy life.'

Celia laughed, the laugh that was so right with the deep tone of her voice.

'I dare say there's something of that in it. But mostly I think he is frightened for you. He told me what hopes there had been for you when you left college and how you'd given everything up when you were pregnant. But that's ten years ago and he says although you say you've played by yourself in the house, you have never been tested and tried.'

'I've had almost ten years of practising since I gave up my career and I *know* I play better now than I did then. He says he doesn't want me to be hurt if I get turned down – but the truth is that I am much more hurt that he can't trust me, that he tries to put me down.'

Celia didn't answer straight away and in the silence Zina wished she could withdraw her words. What was between Peter and her was nothing to do with anyone else and yet she had bared her soul to a stranger.

'Be gentle with his male ego, Zina. He needs to feel that you depend on him. Men find it so hard to accept that they aren't the breadwinners. And I don't just mean from the amount of money they put in the pot.'

'Are you married?' For, if she wasn't, what gave her the right to come here preaching?

'Yes and no,' Celia replied, clearly having no suspicion of what was behind the question. 'I've been with Jacques for nineteen years, since I was twenty. He's twenty-two years older than me; my family were horrified, disgusted. They saw me as some sort of a minx coming between a married man and his wife. Of course that was nonsense. Helga Brandt was a bitch of the first order, she had – and I dare say still has – only one interest: herself. At twenty I'd had the odd boyfriend, but until I met Jacques I had no idea about genuine love. He left his wife and we set up home together. She refused to divorce him and anyway she is a staunch Roman Catholic. It didn't matter a damn to me whether we were married or not. We made vows to each other, vows that will last as long as we live. So, you could say I am married.'

As a character Celia became more interesting by the minute.

'Were you writing when you met him? Is he a writer?'

'I was only just out of university. I got a job on a local newspaper, if you can call that writing. But Jacques was an artist, a portrait painter. Now you might ask, what would a portrait painter want with a face like mine? Somehow, that never came into it. We met at a party and left together. I was living in a bedsit in Oxford and he came home with me. Thinking back I marvel that I invited him, folk would say I was asking for trouble. But such a thought didn't enter my head. We made strong coffee and we talked, we talked and talked . . . everything from politics to growing cabbages. There is nothing in this life so insignificant that it can't be discussed. That's what I learnt in those early weeks after meeting Jacques.'

'And you've lived together ever since? That's nearly twice as long as Peter and me. Does he still paint portraits? I'm sure I ought to know, but I'm pretty ignorant about the big outside world.'

'Believe me, being part of the rush and bustle

does little to educate one. I'm thankful to have escaped. Oh, not from Jacques. He's joining me as soon as the place is finished and the floors aren't cluttered with everything in the least expected places waiting to catch him out. You see, he has lost his sight. All he sees is a grey mist to show the difference between day and night. I can think of nothing worse. He has a male carer living with him while I get the house ready.'

'He must be so wretched,' Zina said, by now her thoughts no longer on her own problems. 'Just awful. Dreadful for any of us, but for an artist even worse.'

Celia nodded, tipping her battered hat to the back of her head and holding her face towards the sun.

'He's an incredible man. If I hadn't fallen in love with him so thoroughly all those years ago, I would still have been filled with admiration for him now. In all our years he has never been boring or been bored by life – not even now. Except for his sight he is so fit, so *alive.* He accepts and makes up his mind that life is still for living. For me, caring for him is *humbling.* As the years go he will get older and, I dare say, be more dependent.'

Zina nodded, her mind on herself and Peter. How would they cope with that sort of tragedy? Would he have the courage still to make something of his blighted life? Would she take pride in caring for him? Yes, of course that's how it would be, she told herself, but at the same time she sent up a fervent prayer that they would never be tested.

32

'Jacques and me, we may have problems to contend with, but they are shared problems. When you hear of couples whose relationship goes sour it makes you realize that a shared physical problem will never be insurmountable. Hark at me! I've finished my drink and eaten most of your nuts, now I'll leave you in peace. Forgive me for disturbing you. Look, I always carry a bit of paper and a biro just to jot down any flash of inspiration, so I'll scribble my telephone number and when you feel in need of company please do give me a call so that we can fix something. It'll be another couple of weeks before I have the place straight enough for Jacques to get acquainted with.'

Despite the interruption to her practice time Zina was sorry when her visitor stood up to leave.

'Better than phoning,' she said, 'come and eat with us this evening – unless you work in the evening of course. I promised when they went off to the beach that I would get a meal ready for six o'clock. Is that too early for you?'

'On the contrary, I'll make do with bread and cheese for lunch and come starving hungry.'

'Just one thing, Celia. I wonder why Peter didn't tell me that he'd met you on your boat.'

Celia looked concerned for a moment before she answered, clearly giving thought to what she said. 'I wondered that too. But looking back to our talk by the river, I'd guess he wanted to forget the whole incident, look on it like a confessional. He talked because he needed to get it off his chest. He's puzzled, he's hurt and, well, I suppose the main thing is that he's a *man* and, scratch the surface, you'll find they are all the same, they all want to feel we depend on them. When Jacques was fighting his battle to accept that he could no longer paint, we went through a difficult time. He never tried to stop me writing, he knew he had to learn to accept. Not that either you or I would ever bring in the money of a film idol, but it's not so much the cash as you'd take away from him the knowledge that you depend on him. That's what hurts. Be gentle with Peter.' With the palms of both hands on the crown of her battered straw hat she pushed it more firmly down on her head. 'Now I'm off. I'll be here at six on the dot and I look forward to it.'

Two

As the days of Peter's unscheduled holiday passed, Celia became a frequent visitor. Zina hadn't known such an easy relationship with a friend since her schooldays, and clearly Peter enjoyed her company.

He had guessed he might be home for about two weeks, but two became three and, although he talked often to Herbert, his friend and the film's director, it seemed there were hold-ups and they would be in East Anglia considerably longer than they had expected. So the days drifted by. Zina had a letter from Derek Masters inviting her to come to the rehearsal in Deremouth on the first Wednesday of July.

'Peter, you know I've never practised when you're at home, but now I must. You might even still be here at the beginning of next month when I get put to the test, so I must practise two or three hours a day.'

He looked at her without answering, his expression hard to fathom. Remembering what Celia had said about his being hurt, she held out her hand to take his, then when he made no movement she grabbed it anyway. They couldn't go on like this; their daily cool politeness was driving a wedge between them.

'I wish you'd just make some effort to understand,' she pleaded. 'I'm going to have a try-out at their rehearsal in Deremouth on the fourth of July.' If she'd left it at that, perhaps he might have tried to accept. Instead she went on, with a change in her tone that seemed to shut him out. 'Just imagine it. I shall be sitting in that small group, part of the glorious sound. It's feels like a dream.'

'It isn't where I imagined your dreams had always been. And supposing you don't come up to scratch?'

'Please Peter, please. I'm ready to be turned down. I'll only be away for that *one* day, not much more than a morning, and it isn't like applying for some job where I'll have to start immediately. I'll be here for the children until September. And even if I'm good enough to be accepted I shall mostly be at home. There'll be rehearsals before engagements or recordings, but it's not like a full-time job.' Then, with a change of subject, which she hoped would take that expression from his face, she added, 'And somehow we ought both to take the children when the day comes for them to go to St Mary's.' Surely that last sentence would show him that holding the four of them as a tight-knit family was as important to her as it always had been.

'I will if I can, you know that. They're very young to be thrown out of the nest.'

'When I was a child I longed to go to boarding school, but it was beyond Dad's budget. But you boarded when you were even younger than they are, and you've never doubted how lucky you were with the chances your schooling gave you. It's one of the advantages of their having such a high earner for a father.'

36

Just for a moment they had broken through the barrier that held them apart.

'How about we drive down to Deremouth this morning and rent a boat for the day, or at least until we pick them up at four o'clock,' he suggested with the smile she had never been able to resist. This time his magic had lost its power; she was hurt and angry that he had cared so little that he ignored that she'd told him she must practise two or three hours a day. 'We could do with some sea air. Get your anorak and we could be on the water before eleven o'clock.'

'I can't, Peter. Don't you listen to *anything* I tell you? I can't waste my time on the water, even though it would be lovely on a day like this. I told you, I *must* work at it. All right, I may not be the standard Derek Masters needs, but I'm not going to make a complete fool of myself.'

He shrugged his shoulders and turned away.

'As you like,' he said, his tone icy.

She watched him, disappointed and hurt. 'I'm sorry,' she said. Then as an afterthought, she added, 'Why don't you ring Celia? Jacques will be here soon and after that she'll not be free to take a day out. I'll tell you what, while you're talking to her I'll find some food to throw into the hamper and a bottle of something. How would that be?'

'Sounds pretty good. I'll give her a call.' And from the eager way he picked up the phone and started to dial, she knew his good humour had been restored. She ought to have been pleased; after all, to know he could enjoy a day out gave her the freedom she needed. But as she set about preparing the hamper she felt let down. A quarter of an hour later as she closed the gate after him she glanced towards the house and felt a drop in her spirits. Imagine being on the sea, the purr of the engine as they were taken far from the shore, then cutting it and letting the boat drift, riding the gentle waves . . . just Peter and her.

They had done that one summer day just before the twins had started school and had been 'borrowed' for a few days by her parents. For Peter and her there had been no one in all the world but themselves. Far out to sea, beyond the sight of even anyone with binoculars, naked they had dived overboard. The water had been bitingly cold but they had played likc water babies enjoying the freedom for a few short moments. He had been the first to clamber back aboard, then turned to help her. Dripping and shivering, despite the heatwave, they had dried themselves vigorously, grateful for the warmth of the sun. Suddenly they hadn't been cold any longer. Instead, instinct had made them glance around at the sea, such an empty sea, not even a gull to be interested in them . . .

Standing outside the front of the house Zina let her thoughts carry her back to that perfect day. There had been no other way for them but to make love. The glorious warmth of the high midday sun had been a backdrop like no other, the gentle rise and fall of the boat was a natural movement they had to obey, the very hardness of the wooden deck added to their fast-rising passion. Normally, lying on a soft bed they instinctively held back as long as possible from coming to a climax, but on that early summer day there had been no holding back for either of them as together they'd followed where nature led.

Caught up in remembering that moment, she found herself standing alone in front of the house, her eyes closed, her mouth slightly open, her arms folded in front of her and, without being conscious of what she was doing, firmly holding on to her breasts. Opening her eyes she was aware of what the memory was doing to her.

'Peter,' she whispered, 'oh Peter, what's happening to us? I ought to have gone with you. It would have been like last time, better than last because we know, surely we know, there is nothing more important than what we are to each other.'

But she hadn't gone and as she went upstairs to the music room there was no lightness in her step. But Zina was never one to give way to mood swings, as anyone watching her would have known from the way she crossed the floor and took up her fiddle. The haunting memory of yesteryear was pushed from her mind and soon she thought of nothing but the music she was making.

More than two hours later she went downstairs to get herself some lunch and that's when, as the coffee hissed its way down the funnel of the percolator, Jenny arrived.

'Mum! Nice treat. You can join me in my miserable bread and cheese. Coffee's just ready.'

'I didn't come before, I knew you would be practising. So I waited all the morning until I decided it was time you had a break.'

'How did you know?'

'That you'd be playing? It didn't take much guessing,' Jenny answered, taking the cups and saucers from the dresser. 'Peter saw me in the village as he was on his way to Deremouth to hire a boat. He was just coming out of Osborn's with a punnet of none-too-ripe looking strawberries. He said you'd opted out of a day on the water as you had things to do. And I knew there was only one thing that would have kept you at home. Is he all right about it? No, don't tell me. It's not my business. If he's accepted like the sensible man I hope he is, then there's nothing to worry about. If he hasn't, then it's just between the two of you and better kept that way. What are your chances, do you think?'

'I'm probably so far removed from the professional world that I can't judge. I'm smugly pleased, but then after one lesson that's how one feels with a scale played in tune. Was Peter all right? Had Celia gone with him?'

'Yes, she was in the car. Any other woman and I might have looked askance at their going off for the day together.' Then with a laugh which, despite her words, held no malice, she added, 'But no man's going to get tempted off the straight and narrow by Celia Turnbull. You never saw anything so unsuitable for a day on a boat. I bet she wears her husband's clothes. But she's delightful – and take off the scarecrow outfit and smarten her up, my guess would be that she's an attractive woman. Why do folk do it, and so often the ones nature has treated kindly?'

Zina smiled, imagining her friend. 'The first

time I met her that was how I felt, but honestly, Mum, I don't even think about it now, any more than it has occurred to me what she could look like if she had a good haircut and some decent clothes. She can't be hard up.'

'If she were, you may be sure she'd conform the same as we lesser mortals. Lovely coffee, dear. It always is in this house. That bread smells too good to refuse, so I'll take up your invitation. Then I'll get out of your hair, I know you want to make the most of your time. I'll pick the children up from school, if you like.'

Between mother and daughter there was always an easy relationship and yet it didn't even enter Zina's head to talk about Peter's 'pig-headed attitude'. When the makeshift snack was done and Zina had stacked the crockery in the dishwasher, her mother stood up to go. She viewed herself in the mirror, an unlikely addition in most kitchens but not in that of the Marchands. Turning her head first one way and then the other, lightly retouching her mouth with lipstick and generally making sure she was ready for her weekly appointment with the hairdresser, or more likely simply out of habit, she said in a voice that was carefully casual, 'I know you want to get back to your music, so I'm off now. You'll have had a good many hours today. If I were you, I'd see to it that I'd fall in with any plans of Peter's for tomorrow. I won't stop when I bring the children home. This evening is Camera Club.' Her smile was bright, over-bright perhaps to cover up the sudden mockery of her innermost thoughts: 'Photography! Since when have you cared about photography?' With the smile firmly on her face she pecked Zina's cheek and went out through the back door.

Going back up the stairs Zina recalled her mother's advice. Yes, she was right, of course. Today she would have had many hours alone to practise; tomorrow she would give to Peter.

But when tomorrow came, Peter had already made other plans.

'Any ideas for today?' she asked him in a bright voice when she came back from driving Fiona and Tommy to school. 'Shall we go somewhere or potter in the garden? Tim Briggs doesn't come in today so we would have it to ourselves.'

'Actually I'm tied up. I'm picking Celia up at ten and driving her to collect Jacques. The decorator worked late the evening before last to get it done, and yesterday evening she was having a final check that there were no stumbling blocks to trip him. Poor devil, I can think of nothing worse. He's keen to get settled down here.'

'That's kind of you.' She made sure she sounded as if she meant it.

'Kind to whom? Them or myself? I dare say it's better for her to be able to concentrate on him on the drive home rather than peer at the road ahead, and for me it's certainly better to have company than be cast aside for a violin. I didn't realize when I suggested it that you were going to make yourself available. However, she jumped at the offer. Imagine what it must be like for the poor chap. If she isn't driving she will be better company for him. I've been looking forward to meeting him.'

'Yes, of course. So have I.' So why couldn't she let herself suggest that she went too?

For her it turned into another long day with her music.

And so July pushed June into history and the day came when she drove to Deremouth with her fiddle case on the back seat of the car. It took more willpower than she'd known she possessed to walk firmly up the steps of the town hall where rehearsal was to take place for the evening concert.

In her mind she had imagined that if she were successful she would be replacing someone young, someone much as she had been when her own short career had come to an end. Emily Cornhill was very different from the girl Zina had expected. Perhaps she was younger than she looked, but first impression was of a woman well in her forties and disgruntled with life. Having introduced them, Derek Masters left them to get acquainted. It was immediately clear that Emily looked on whoever took her place as an interloper.

'You haven't played professionally, I believe,' she said as Derek left them. 'Well, you'll find it very different from entertaining a few friends at home.'

Zina wanted to reply in the same vein, but she reminded herself how she would feel if she were in this woman's position. Perhaps Emily had a grown-up family and this 'afterthought' had caught her when she imagined she was safely beyond childbearing.

Despite the lack of welcome Zina made herself

smile as she answered, 'I know. Perhaps there are other violinists to be heard before Mr Masters makes a decision.'

'Oh no. His mind is already made up.' Then with a change of tone and dropping something of her hostile manner, she said, 'When he came back from hearing you play at some charity concert he was full of praise for you. Well, it stands to reason he was, that he could have written to you suggesting you should come here today to sit in my seat.'

'Put like that it sounds as if I'm trying to usurp your place. Perhaps he only wants someone until you feel ready to return?'

'With a baby? You have children, he told us so. But I suppose with a husband who is the hearthrob of the silver screen you have a nursemaid.'

Zina's friendly manner was clearly wasted on Emily Cornhill. She surprised herself that instead of feeling annoyed at it, she was sorry for the woman.

'I have twins, a boy and a girl. But they are off to boarding school in September and I have a mother close by. Anyway, Mr Masters can't have made his mind up. I've not played in a piano quintet since I left college.'

'Oh, he's made his mind up all right. Very taken with you, he was. Well, I'd better introduce you to the rest of us – not *us* for much longer, I am leaving after the recital in Bristol on the seventh of September.'

Derek Masters watched from the sidelines as they became acquainted. Gradually Zina's

44

nervousness subsided. It was clear that the only one to show her anything but a warm welcome was Emily whose hostile attitude extended to all of them. At precisely eleven o'clock Derek moved to take his seat at the piano and, carrying their instruments and leaving grim-faced Emily, Zina and the other three followed. Zina's heart was pounding, silently she pleaded that she would acquit herself well – and then the music started and she forgot everything else. Her mouth softened into a hint of a smile of its own accord as she followed the music, beating time silently, and feeling herself transported by the glory of being part of the sound. She forgot Peter, she forgot the twins and her mother; there was nothing but *this*. She didn't even question to herself whether her playing was up to the standard of the others, for her anything outside the perfect timing and the purity of sound had no meaning.

By half past twelve it was over and she was putting her fiddle back in its case.

'I knew you wouldn't fail,' she heard Derek's voice close behind her.

'I'll do?'

'You'll more than do,' he answered. 'Let's sit down over here while we discuss what's involved. You will have time at home, we only give a recital every week or so, then of course there is rehearsal time. We like to think of ourselves as a West Country quintet and although we occasionally do play further afield, you'll find that most of our recitals are within travelling distance of your home. Then, not very frequently, there are recording sessions. Our first recital after

Emily leaves will be the seventeenth of September. From what I saw this morning you need no more rehearsal time than anyone else, but as it will be your first performance with us let's say we meet in our rehearsal room on the fifteenth at eleven o'clock. We rehearse at my apartment just outside Bristol. I'll give you a card with my address. Now, it's time to discuss remuneration.'

By one o'clock she was driving home, her two lives overlapping as she covered the miles. If only Peter could be happy for her, perhaps even get involved when he had a chance. But at the thought a smile tugged at the corners of her mouth. Just imagine him becoming enthusiastic and knowledgeable about chamber music!

To her surprise he was in the garden, looking for weeds to pull up when she arrived.

'Glad you're home,' he greeted her, opening the car door and holding out his hand to help her out. 'Was it rough, love? I've been worrying about you all the morning.'

She had a flash of conscience as she realized that once the music started she had given no thought at all to home or family.

'I was nervous when I got there, but not once we started playing. It was like stepping right outside myself, playing and hearing not just the sound of my own violin but the whole perfect . . . perfect harmony . . .' Lost for words she looked at him helplessly, trying to will him to understand even though she sensed his with-drawal. 'It must be like that for you too, when you play a part with other people you must become the character. Is that so different?'

46

There was no answering warmth in his expression as he shrugged his shoulders and answered, 'It doesn't take me over as your morning seems to have done to you. I wonder you could have given up so easily when the twins were coming.'

'I didn't give up easily, but I had to prioritize and you and our marriage came above everything. It always will.'

Instead of answering he raised one eyebrow in that unique way she had seen in the characters he played on the screen. Was his reaction genuine or was he overplaying his role? Half an hour ago she had been riding on a cloud of happiness, but he had the power to pull her down to earth with a painful crash.

'So am I to assume you intend to be part of this band of travelling musicians? What is it you want that I can't give you, Zina? What more can I do?'

'Just remember that you married a violinist, not a housekeeper.'

'Don't be ridiculous. Of course I was happy for you to give recitals in our early days, it brought us in money that we needed and I was proud that you could do it.'

'Proud of what? That I could supplement the housekeeping bill or that I could make music?' She held his gaze waiting for a truthful answer.

'You know I don't go for your kind of music, I'd be a hypocrite if I pretended I did. I was proud that people paid good money to come and listen to you.' With a smile that took away all her anger, he added, 'More money than they paid to see my rep company at work. But Zee,' he said, shortening her name as no one else ever did, 'we don't need money. We're doing fine. And what if one of the children gets sent home from school for some reason, or if there are events at St Mary's for parents to attend?'

All this time they had been standing by the car, the driver's door still open. Now she turned to slam it shut.

'Do you think I haven't considered the children? Of course I have. But they are very wise for their years and they understand that you have to be away a lot – far more than I shall be. And I don't think they are stupid enough to imagine that playing in a quintet is less important than standing around all day on a film set, or repeating a few lines time and time again like you have to.'

Seeing his sudden change of expression and his look of a sulky child who can't get his own way, she couldn't suppress her chuckle.

'Oh come on, you old grouch, look on the bright side,' she urged. 'I wasn't as bad as you kept telling me I would be and – and – Peter, I wish I could make you understand, it was pure magic.'

Of course, she shouldn't have said it; she realized that as soon as she'd spoken, but it was too late to bring back her words.

'I'm sorry you have to look elsewhere to find magic,' he said, his voice cold and expressionless.

It was too much for Zina. She started to laugh, putting her arms around his neck and raising her head so that her lips teased his.

'There's magic and there's magic,' she whispered. 'Our variety is quite different.'

And she was held tightly against him, so tightly she felt she could scarcely breathe.

'Don't change, don't ever change,' he whispered. 'Don't let it spoil what we have.'

'Nothing could spoil what we have, darling, pig-headed, precious Peter.'

That evening he had a phone call telling him the crew were returning to the studio in two days' time. During those two days they neither of them spoke of the future; like skaters venturing on ice, fearful that the thaw had started, they hid their fear of what they didn't want to face.

When, two mornings later, still in her dressing gown in the early light of dawn she watched his car turn out of the drive, the excitement she felt for her own future was forgotten in a premonition that they had lost something precious. Nothing would ever be the same again, not for them and, so soon, not for the children either. Involuntarily she shivered.

When the children broke up for their long summer holiday they felt hard done by that their father had gone. It would have been so much more fun if he'd been at home, but he'd told them it would be some weeks before he'd get back except for just a few hours at a time. They would get days at the beach with their mother but that wasn't the same as a proper holiday with all of them together. Neither of them liked to actually say that a day on the beach with Zina wasn't nearly as much fun as it would have been with him.

On their bicycles Fiona and Tommy went for cycle rides round the country lanes never far from home but with a thrill of freedom and independence. The thought that they were old enough to go away to school added to their feeling of near-adulthood.

'A job for you two,' Zina told them at breakfast about a week before the end of the holiday. 'I want you to cycle over to Bicton Lodge for me.' They seemed to sit a little taller at the idea of being entrusted with the mission. 'Today, your gran's birthday, she's coming to tea so let's make it a bit special and ask Celia and Jacques to come as well. Their phone doesn't seem to be working so I've written a note. Promise you'll be very careful on the road if you cycle with it. You've only got that one bit of proper road, where you have to cross the river bridge, then on to the lane to their house.'

'Yes, we know the way, Mum,' Fiona assured her. 'And of course we're careful, we always are, aren't we, Tommy? Only stupid people aren't careful. "Yer need to 'ave yer wits about you, m'duckie, such fools some of 'em are on the roads. Don't use the wit the good lord gived 'em."' Fiona was rewarded with a giggle of appreciation from Tommy and a quick 'sshh' from Zina as she saw Mrs Cripps, their daily helper, push her bicycle past the window to prop it up against the wall of the one-time stable block. Hard-working, rough and ready, with great affection for the family, she had been with them as long as they had lived in Newton House and it irritated Zina to suspect Fiona was mocking her.

Pleased to be trusted with an important errand, they set off.

'We'll wait for an answer, Mum, and tell them their phone is up the creek,' Tommy shouted, meaning to put himself in charge of the expedition. But before they reached the end of the drive Zina could see from the way Fiona was pointing and talking that she had taken over. As Fiona's bossiness did so often, it annoyed her. Tommy was every bit as capable, but he never fought his corner. However, she had other things to think about and first and foremost was to drive into Deremouth and see whether she could find a cake worthy of the occasion; if she couldn't, it would mean going to Exeter – not for a moment did it enter her head that she could have made one and iced it appropriately, for Zina was no domestic goddess and today was important.

The invitation was accepted and arriving home the twins were excited at the thought of a birthday party. They had packed their own presents, and they worked hard getting the garden table and chairs carried so that by afternoon they would be in the shade of the horse chestnut tree. Then it was Fiona's idea that they – or at any rate *she*, for after all no one bothered about what boys looked like – would wear her party frock. All went well and when teatime came the children's behaviour was perfect. They hadn't grown to nine years old to be seen and not heard, but listening to them and watching them at the tea table Zina wished Peter could have been there; he would have been proud.

The chatter was general but Zina let her attention wander to Tommy and Jacques.

51

'Would you like another cup of tea, Mr Brandt,' Tommy was asking. 'May I pass your cup to Mum?' He even avoided the trap that usually tripped him and remembered 'may' and not 'can'. Zina felt a smile tug at the corners of her mouth.

'That's jolly kind of you, Tommy. Tea in the garden like this is a real treat, isn't it.'

'Yes, rather. Usually we sit on the ground, but today is special because of it being Gran's birthday. And, of course, because you are here.'

'A special occasion, not like a picnic, eh? Ah, that's my tea, is it, thank you, son. Now you tell me all about this school you and your sister are off to. Are you looking forward to it – quite an adventure.'

'Yes. Rather! I expect it will be great.' He tried to make his answer sound natural and not to let anyone guess that he was frightened to imagine how dreadful it might be, so far away from home and Mum and things he loved.

But he didn't fool Zina who had been listening with one ear while she made herself join in the conversation with Celia and Jenny. Oh, my poor little Tommy. Can the others hear the bravado in your voice too? Watching Jacques, Zina was sure at least he heard beneath the cheerful tone. Had the loss of his sight made him more sensitive to atmosphere, she wondered. Whether it had or not, concentrating on Tommy, he talked about his own days at boarding school, Zina was sure making it sound much more of an adventure than he had found it at the time. Listening, Tommy seemed to swell with pride that a proper grown-up man – one who was quite old from the viewpoint of his own nine years – should enjoy talking to him as if going to boarding school would elevate him to the same level.

It was as they moved away from the table to sit in the sunshine that everything changed.

'You two can go and play now,' Zina told the twins. She almost added a reminder that Fiona mustn't get her dress dirty but changed her mind. Even as a little girl she had never thrown herself into games with no regard for what she was doing to her appearance and, now, as she left the table it was obvious that her party frock was at the front of her mind. Tommy was making towards the side lawn, which was home to a climbing frame, swing, see-saw and a sandpit, nowadays used as a landing ground for practising long jumps.

And then it happened! Just as the adults started to move towards the terrace came a thud and an involuntary cry!

'Oh God!' Celia shrieked as she ran back to the table. 'Don't try and move, darling. Let me shift the chair out of the way then I'll help you.'

'Don't fuss,' Jacques panted from where he was sprawled on the grass where Tommy's chair had thrown him.

'It was your bloody fault, Tommy, leaving your chair stuck out like that,' Celia shouted, her thoughts just on Jacques.

'Tommy, come here at once,' Zina called out even though Tommy was already on his way. 'How could you have been so stupid? Just because we had tea out-of-doors doesn't mean you leave your manners behind. Come and apologize to Mr Brandt.'

53

Worried on account of the man who only minutes ago had made him feel he was a friend and had spoken to him just as if he were a grown-up, humiliated that he had been so unthinking, hating knowing everyone was looking at him, Tommy kept his eyes fixed on Jacques who was struggling to get to his feet. The chair had been moved right out of the way and although Jacques wanted to put the incident behind him, Tommy could see how his hands were shaking and how he was panting even though he wanted everyone to think his fall hadn't upset him.

'Are you alright?' Now Celia's voice was gentle. 'I'll pull your chair back and you sit quietly for a few minutes. I'll stay with you.'

'Don't fuss. I can manage.' Once on his feet he felt for the table, pressing the palms of his hands on it as if that way no one would notice how they shook.

'Mr Brandt, it was all my fault, I'm sorry, ever so sorry,' Tommy said timidly, reaching to lay his hand on top of Jacques's and speaking just to him. But it was the feeling of that trembling hand under his that was his undoing. Until then he'd fought not to let tears get the upper hand, but now his battle was lost. He sobbed loudly, helplessly. Probably he didn't even realize himself that he was crying about far more than what he had done to his friend, his tears were a safety valve for much that he'd kept hidden as these weeks of the school holiday had melted away so quickly.

He wanted to creep away, somewhere no one could find him, to be anywhere but where he was. He knew they were all looking at him. He'd been stupid, he'd shown them that he wasn't growing up at all; and it had been so good only a few minutes ago when Mr Brandt had been telling him tales of the time when he'd been a boy at boarding school. Now, choked by sobs, he felt sick, from shame, sympathy or simply because he imagined just what poor Mr Brandt must be feeling knowing that everyone was looking at him and he could see nothing. 'It had been such a nice teatime, too.'

It was his last few words that helped Jacques more than all the women fussing around him. 'So it had, lad. Then I had to do a damn-fool thing like that. Not your fault, Tommy, just my own. I usually feel around me with my stick to make sure I can step ahead but—' he leant towards Tommy, feeling to rest his hand on the quivering shoulder, then he spoke quietly in a manner that went a long way towards the teatime spirit that had been lost – 'between ourselves, today I was showing off and purposely left the stick in the car. Now then, to show we're still friends, how about you show me your own bit of the garden, eh? We'll both dry our tears and you give me a guided tour, describe it all to me.' He held out his hand for Tommy to take.

'I'm so sorry,' Zina said softly to Celia as they watched the two of them go, the way Tommy pointed things out and their progress halted while he described what he saw, showing clearly that the guided tour was in progress. It seemed that Tommy's spirits were reviving as he painted his word picture of the landscaping of the garden to Jacques. 'Jacques is a remarkable man.'

'It's not fair, Zina. What has he done to deserve it? It tears me to pieces to watch him – and yet from somewhere he finds the strength to accept. I'm sorry I shouted at Tommy like I did, I didn't mean to upset him. It's just that I can't bear it when things go wrong for Jacques.'

Jenny stacked the tray, Zina carried it into the house and loaded the dishwasher and by the time the guided tour came to an end, the three women were sitting talking on the terrace, the incident happily behind them.

It was towards the end of August, and Tommy was paying his nightly visit to Fiona's room.

'I like it, don't you, when Mum plays at night? Makes it sort of snug up here with us just listening and whispering.'

'Um . . .' Fiona's agreement was half-hearted. 'I'd rather listen to records like Dad puts on. Just hark at it! It wouldn't be so bad if she played a piano, then there might be a tune. I expect she's quite good, though.' This was said in what could only be called a condescending tone. 'Dare say she must be for those people to want her to be in their group or band or whatever they call themselves.' Then, with a complete change in her voice as she assumed the character of the faithful Mrs Cripps: 'More like someone's trodden on the cat's tail, if you ask me, m'ducky. Gi'e me sommit with a bit o' go in it, summit wot makes you wanna tap yer feet!' She said it with a giggle that took away any malice. Then, pleased with her effort she added for good measure, 'Not my cuppa tea m'dear,' ending with Mrs Cripps' customary sniff of emphasis. At that they both fell about laughing.

'Do you reckon that when we get to school they will put us in dorms near each other so I can creep in when the teachers go away?' Tommy was determined no one, not even she from whom he'd never had secrets, would suspect the ache in the pit of his stomach when they talked about it. He just hoped that without their putting it into words she would understand and feel the same. But he was disappointed.

'Don't know. Doubt it,' she answered and clearly Fiona the Brave was ready for anything. 'Be a lot of fun though, about twelve of us in the dormitory, I expect. Don't you go and blub or anything sissy. Promise.'

'Course I won't blub,' Tom answered. 'I'm not stupid.'

'No, I know that, silly. But if there are a lot of new boys in your dorm and someone else starts because he doesn't want to be there, don't you let it make you join in. I know what you are; you're brave enough if you get hurt, cut yourself or fall off your bike, but get in an awful tizz about such silly things. Look at the fuss you made when Mr Brandt fell over your chair the other day. If anyone ought to have cried it was him for falling over.'

'Shut up about it,' Tom growled. He didn't want to remember. Imagine not being able to see, not even to know what you tripped over, just being hurtled down and having nothing to save you. It had haunted him. To understand the real horror, when he'd been on his own he had shut his eyes and made himself tumble; it had been much worse than falling with his eyes open. Even thinking about Mr Brandt's fall was awful. He had tried not to cry but it had been no use. Surely Fiona could understand and not keep on about it. 'Anyway,' he said, a note of defiance in his voice, 'you don't know, it might be you who gets upset if you don't like the way things are at school.'

'Stupid,' Fiona said with a laugh and again bringing Mrs Cripps among them, 'we'll soon knock 'em inte' shape and no mistake.' Then, changing the subject, she added, 'We mustn't forget to take the money Dad left us. Got to keep it hidden, mind. Don't tell any of the others we've got it.'

'Course not. It's just for emergencies; that's what Dad said. Rich, aren't we!'

Their nightly conversations were always in whispers, even though Zina would never have heard them, concentrating as she was on her playing.

Peter came home to see them off to school on the twelfth of September.

Just about to slam the front door and join them for the start of their journey, Zina saw her family waiting out on the forecourt. Even though in a few days' time she was to join the Meinholt Quintet for rehearsals, at that moment her family were her whole world. They were standing by the cars, the children in their brand-new uniform, grey with red braid and trimmings, their ties red and grey stripes, Fiona's skinny legs made to look even thinner by her grey stockings. The two cars were packed for the journey. About to follow them out, Zina stopped to look at them as they stood deep in conversation, or rather Peter was talking while they listened intently and nodded. She wanted to impress the memory on her mind; nothing would ever be quite the same again for any of them. These were the three people who meant the world to her; she felt a great surge of love for them.

Then she slammed the front door and ran down the steps to join them for the start of the journey into their new life. With the roof of his red sports car open, Peter took Fiona. It hadn't been easy to get her portmanteau into the space behind the driver's seat, which looked like a seat but would have been useless for anyone with adult legs. For the child off on this new adventure, as she saw it, the sports car was so much more thrilling than having to go with her mother in the family Volvo. She hoped there would be some of her future associates there to see her arrive in such style and with a father who was no ordinary man but someone who would be recognized as special.

Tommy willingly opted to ride with Zina. He did wish Fiona wouldn't always want to attract attention; it was so embarrassing.

'Mum, will you be scared about playing? I don't mean just playing at home or in the village where you know the people, I mean with a huge hall full of strangers listening.' He asked it in a serious voice as they drove.

'No, not scared, just thrilled and grateful that I have the opportunity.' She heard it as a serious question and gave him a truthful answer. 'You see, Tommy, whether or not there is an audience makes no difference once the music starts; it's being part of the *sound* that matters.' Zina realized, as she had so often, how easy it was to talk to him, forgetting how young he still was.

He took in her words and gave them thought before he answered. Then, just as Zina had decided the conversation was to go no further, he said, 'I think that's how I would feel, Mum.' There was a pause, but this time Zina sensed there was more to follow. 'Mum, I think you are the luckiest person, honestly I do.' He stressed his words to make sure she realized he wasn't just making conversation for the sake of something to say. This was important. 'I read the brochure for school, Mum, and it said that there could be private music lessons. Do you think I could learn to play like you do? Please. Honestly, it's not just because it's what you do, honestly it's not that, but Mum, if there is someone to teach me the violin could I please have lessons? In the hols you could hear me practise and one day when I get good enough we could play together. They wouldn't say I was too young, would they? Everything always seems to be for people who are older, unless it's dancing and stuff like that.'

'You're certainly not too young. I was six and some are even younger than that. If you want to do it properly you would have to be prepared to give up a lot of playtime to practising, you'd have that as well as your prep.'

'I know, and I would, truly I would.'

'I'll tell you what we'll do, Tommy. When we get to St Mary's we'll find out if violin lessons are possible. If they are I will bring you my half-size fiddle. I had that when I was about your age and I've always kept it. You'll soon grow into needing a full-size one, but it's better to start on one that's just right. I must have kept it all these years hoping that one of you would want to play. It's in the cupboard at home and I bet it'll be glad to be making music again.'

She had sensed Tommy's unacknowledged nervousness about going to school, just as now she felt he was more relaxed. Perhaps the thought of learning to make music gave him a connection with home.

That special day Peter's visit was brief, he'd come simply to see the children into school and, after that, wouldn't be going back to the house as he had to be on the set early the next morning. With two the same age it was rare for either parent to be able to concentrate just on one of them and on that drive to St Mary's he heard Fiona's plans for the future.

'When we get there, Dad, I expect there will be other new people arriving like us. I bet you there won't be anyone else with a dad everybody will recognize. Do you mind when strangers know who you are?' Then, with a chuckle, she said, 'I bet you like it really; I know I would.' And before he had time to consider her question and answer it, she went on, 'Do you know what I want to do – well, I really mean what I'm *going* to do, because nothing is going to stop me? I'm

61

going to be famous like you. I'm going to be a really top-line actress. I'll be in films because that way you get more people to see you and hear you than if you are just in the theatre.'

For her this journey alone with him was a wonderful opportunity to confide her dreams knowing he would give her his uninterrupted attention and sure that he would understand.

'It's not all fun and glamour, you know,' he warned her, speaking as he might to an adult and adding to her feeling of importance, just as he intended. In fact he expected that before the time came for her to consider her future seriously she would have changed her mind many times; she was far too young to know what opportunities might tempt her in a direction different from that which he had followed, but he never talked down to either of the twins. 'Tomorrow morning while you are still cosily cuddled up in bed, I shall be up at five o'clock so that I can be ready for a long day's work starting about six o'clock in the make-up department. To be honest, life was a good deal easier when I was in the rep company. Not much money in my pocket and, often, not very comfortable digs, but by the beginning of each tour we'd learnt our roles and rehearsed the six plays we were putting on for that season and that was that. Just one show a night, each play was performed for a week and at the end of the six-week stint on we went to our next town. Film work is tiring because it is so repetitive. We can spend a whole day getting a short scene right and it can be the very devil to make each retake sound fresh and genuine.'

'Yes, Dad, but it's worth it. It must make you feel tall as a giant when you think that everybody, *everybody,* knows who you are. It's going to be like that for me. "Set yer mind on summut m'duckie, and work at it, then sure as eggs is eggs you'll get where you wanna be."'

At her impersonation of Mrs Cripps, Peter laughed. Even so, he was impressed and gave her a quick look of appreciation. If she grew up as lovely as she promised, and with the ability he was sure she possessed, she might indeed be a star of the future.

'For a moment I thought we'd brought Mrs C with us. You've told her all about it, then?'

'I talk to her a lot. I like to listen to her. It gives me a chance to copy her voice. The trouble is that everyone else I know all speak the same, but listening to her you can almost seem to see the – the sort of homeliness of her – sort of warm and giving.'

He reached his hand and took hers for a moment. What a remarkable child she was. With her sort of perception, and if she didn't change her mind in the meantime, the acting profession would find a treasure in her.

'Will you be able to get home for our half term, Dad? Please, *please* try.'

'I imagine I'll be there. We're almost at the end of shooting, then I shall be what the profession likes to call "resting". I hope it lasts for a few weeks, although with your mother fiddling her way around the country I shall wish I'd never been persuaded to send you two off to school.' He knew it was far from the truth and it had been he who had wanted them to start at boarding school just as he had himself, but in that moment the most important thing to him was to tighten the bond that had always existed between him and each of the children.

'You mustn't be sad about us, Dad,' Fiona assured him in what he'd always thought of as her 'maiden aunt' voice. 'I'll look after Tommy if he gets homesick, honestly I will. And I'll be all right. I'm actually looking forward to it.'

And when he raised his left hand in her direction she clasped it in both hers and planted a kiss on it.

The twins both managed to bid their parents farewell with no outward sign of what they may have been feeling. Fiona, as always, was keen to take the next step towards maturity and Tommy, not quite man enough to look either parent in the eye, managed to follow her example as they were led away by one of the prefects on duty to see the new intake of pupils safely installed.

As they disappeared from view Peter turned to Zina.

'The end of an era. Well, my professional wife, I should say good luck to you and tell you I hope you'll be as happy playing that confounded instrument as you expect. And of course I want you to be happy. But I want to be the one to make you happy, not some merry band of music makers. I love you, Mrs Marchand. Don't forget me in this new life you are intent on making.' There was nothing loving in his tone.

'Please Peter, don't say it like that. It will make

no difference to us. I'll probably always be at home when you come back. Mostly the concerts are in the west region so I shan't stay away overnight.'

He raised his eyebrow in that exaggerated way she never felt was completely genuine.

'Be home by bedtime, will you my dear, to make sure I'm not deprived?' If only he could have said it with a note of teasing humour in his voice, but his tone was cold.

'Don't, Peter. Not here, not now.'

He leant forward and lightly kissed her brow, then turned and climbed into that racy car the children so loved. Without another glance he started the engine and drove away while she turned back into the building to find where she had to make arrangements for Tommy's violin lessons.

That done, there was no sign of the children. It seemed they had already been spirited into their new and strange life. She went out to the waiting Volvo and, with one look back to the building in case either of them was watching from a window, she got in and switched on the engine. She needed to drive, to concentrate on the road, anything to take her mind from things she was frightened to face. Her comfort came from the knowledge that she had arranged violin lessons for Tommy.

But what about Peter? As she drove, perhaps she wasn't even aware how much she clung to resentment against him as a shield to protect her from misery over parting with the twins.

As Peter travelled further and further from her he wanted more than anything to turn back. The four of them had always been a close family unit. Now the house, which had given them such pride when first he had been able to buy it, would more often than not be empty. If in his heart he knew he was exaggerating and in truth Zina would be there far more than she was away, he preferred to see it from his own angle. Where had they gone wrong, or was the honest truth that she had never been fulfilled in her marriage? Had he failed her? No, damn it, of course he hadn't. He'd never understood what she saw in 'her sort of music'. Just imagine a couple of violins, a viola and a cello, with a piano tinkling in the background! And she wanted to be part of that 'glorious sound', as she called it, said it was magic. Certainly not how he thought of it. 'There's magic and there's magic' he could almost hear her saying it. Oh damn it, Zee, I thought it was all so good. How long have you been craving after this other world of yours while I believed I was the centre of your universe? That's what hurts. I thought I had all of you and now I find there is part that I can never possess, can never even share. He felt the sting of tears, not the sort of tears he could produce when he threw himself into the emotion of a scene, but tears that ached in the back of his throat and made him bite the corners of his mouth as his vision blurred.

I love you, Mrs Marchand, he had said, as he had through the years and always she had answered 'and I love you, Mr Marchand'. But not today. Back in that empty house would she think of him? Would she long to have him there with her? Would she, hell! She'd be up there in that music room practising some bloody quintet as if the world depended on it.

But, in that, he was wrong. When Zina arrived home dreading the emptiness she would find waiting for her, she saw Jenny and Jacques on the garden seat and Celia sitting cross-legged on the grass looking as much at ease in the position as a child would have been. Yet Peter was still at the front of her mind. By now he would be halfway back to the set. I love you, Mrs Marchand, he had said. Why hadn't she given him the answer he expected? Why had she let angry misery stand in the way? Looking at the three people waiting for her she was ashamed.

Three

With the suppleness of a child, and quite out of keeping with her general appearance, Celia was on her feet and coming to meet Zina.

'Tell us if you'd rather be on your own,' she said as she came close. 'How were they when you left them?'

'Fine.'

She heard the brittle note in Zina's voice. Were they being insensitive or helpful in wanting to give her support when perhaps she would rather be by herself to face emotions she probably hadn't been prepared for? With no children of her own Celia tried to put herself in Zina's place, at the same time cursing the claim the film studio had on Peter when surely this would be an evening he and Zina should have been able to share. 'Peter had said that he wouldn't have a chance to come home with you,' she explained even though she was only repeating what they all knew, 'and we didn't like to think of your being by yourself.'

'Even when they were at the baby school more often than not I rattled around by myself in an empty house.' Even if Celia took her words at face value Zina was uncomfortably aware of her lack of gratitude for their care and tried to make amends. So she went back to the question of the twins and answered with honesty. 'I don't think we need worry too much about them,' she said as they joined the other two waiting in the shade. 'Fiona will have them all dancing to her tune in no time and Tommy will come in for a bit of reflected glory on her account. I'm going back tomorrow to take Tommy my half-size fiddle. You remember it, Mum? It seems I haven't kept it all these years for nothing; Tommy wants to have lessons. He talked a lot about it on the way.'

'Funny boy,' Jenny laughed, 'Fancy waiting until then to tell you. Or did you suggest it to him?'

'No. I would never do that to either of them.' Then with a laugh that was more genuine, she added, 'It would be a waste of time on Fiona, that's for sure.'

So often Jacques listened, seeming to take comfort from the sound of their chatter, but now it was he who spoke. 'If Tommy had taken the fiddle with him you wouldn't have had to bring it afterwards. Knowing that you would be coming back would have made it less of a wrench for him to say goodbye.' He spoke quietly, a slight smile tugging at his mouth as his sightless eyes were directed toward the sound of their voices.

'Then I'm afraid he'll be disappointed. I'm told it has to be delivered during class hours and I shan't be able to see them.'

Celia moved towards Jacques and rested her hand on his shoulder. Looking at them Zina felt a sharp stab of envy, followed almost immediately by shame. How could she envy them? Yet theirs seemed to cast most relationships into the shade. She pulled her mind back to the moment.

'Lovely to find you all here,' she said, her voice taking on a note so bright that it must have fooled them all. 'If you really want to do me a favour, then stay and eat with me. I overstocked on this week's order, somehow it seemed wrong to cut down while the twins were still at home. So the freezer is bulging and the cupboards too. Will you stay and help me eat some of it?' The truth was that when she had phoned the orders she had hoped that Peter would have come back with her after taking the children to school. Just the two of them in the house, something they hadn't known since their early days. In her weaker moments as she'd drifted towards sleep, she had imagined them together walking on the downs or working in the garden, finding the old easy companionship. Only in love-making did they come close and, even then, how much was simply the need to satisfy their sexual loneliness? But for the moment she was thankful to have a reason to prepare a meal and later in the evening glad to have to make herself play a part in the general conversation. In truth her straying thoughts were far more on Peter than on the children. Was that natural? Perhaps it was the closeness between the twins that gave her some sort of assurance that as long as they were together she had no need to worry. When the conversation turned back to them she really believed the truth of her answer.

'Fiona was prepared to find everything to her liking, and if it wasn't she was determined to sort it out. As long as she is there Tommy will cope.' That had been their view right from when it was first decided (when *Peter* had first decided) that they were ready for boarding school.

Celia's glance was probing, but Zina set the smile firmly on her face. And so the first hours of living alone passed. In her head, though, she couldn't help agonising over what Peter was doing and all that they'd said earlier that day. *He should have arrived back by now. Perhaps he'll phone tonight. Perhaps he was only making himself spiteful to me because he felt so wretched about saying goodbye to the children. I love you, Mr Marchand. But I couldn't say it. Why couldn't I?*

They were sitting over their coffee when she let her alert expression slip. Why didn't he phone? He must expect that she'd be here on her own . . . probably he was out surrounded by friends, letting the world see the entertaining, sociable Peter Marchand beloved of all, friends and fans alike.

'. . . timed so well.'

She pulled her mind back under control, realizing her mother was speaking to her.

'Sorry Mum, I didn't hear what you said.'

'I said that you'll hardly have time to miss the others being about the place. A few more days and you'll be a part of the quintet. It's really all timed remarkably well.'

'Yes, perfectly.' Don't let any of them guess at the shadow Peter was determined to cast on all her excitement. Because he was paid so highly (overpaid, nearer the truth, was her silent and uncharitable thought) he saw it as a personal slight that she wasn't willing to sit and twiddle her thumbs waiting to rush at him with open arms when he found time to look her way.

'Zina my dear,' started Jacques and from his voice she knew he was the one who had been aware of the charade she'd been playing even though he probably assumed it was a mother's natural unease for the twins, 'it's time we left you.' He let his fingers lightly rest on the face of the special watch he wore. 'Had you girls realized that it's gone ten o'clock. By now those two young folk will have been sound asleep for an hour or more.'

Ten minutes later both cars had gone and both dishwashers were loaded. The small supper party might never have happened. There would be no phone call now. Climbing the stairs Zina wanted just to put the day behind her. But it hadn't finished with her yet.

Sitting in bed trying to force herself to concentrate on a book, which surely couldn't have been as dull as she was finding it, she was unprepared for the shrill bell of the telephone. He must be finding it as hard as she was to end the day!

'Peter,' she blurted his name even before she'd got the bedside receiver to her ear.

'It's me, Mum.' A voice so quiet she could hardly hear.

'Tommy, I thought you'd be asleep. Is everything all right? Speak up, I can hardly hear you.'

'Shh, got to whisper, Mum, I've crept down to the payphone. Lights have been out ages. I've been waiting until they were all asleep. Dad gave us some coins, you see. For emergencies, that's what he said.'

Emergencies! What had happened! They shouldn't be there, miles away in a strange place when they could have been happily asleep in their own beds.

'What's happened?' How hard it was not to let him guess her misery. 'Are you OK both of you?'

'Boys and girls all together for supper, Mum. I sat with Fiona. So I expect I'm luckier than most of the new ones. Most didn't have anyone they even knew.'

'You and Fiona always have each other.'

'I wanted to speak to you, Mum. Sure you're not lonely, Mum?'

She heard the misery he tried to hide by pretending that she was the reason he couldn't settle for sleep.

'I'm missing you both, but I was very proud of the way you and Fiona marched off, Tommy. Having children growing up so fast takes some getting used to.' She made sure there was a smile in her voice, for she knew him well enough to recognize how lonely and frightened he was. 'Cuddle down in bed and go to sleep, love. Give my love to Fiona in the morning.'

For a second or two the line was quiet, then he said, 'No, you see I can't do that, Mum. It's best I don't tell her I spoke to you. If she knew and I got copped out, like I said, she'd be in for trouble too.'

Poor little love. They shouldn't be there. It was Peter's fault, all his rubbish about boarding school teaching them to stand on their own feet, making a man of Tommy.

'I'll want to hear about everything at the weekend, Tommy.'

'You'll be playing in the quintet. Mum, Mum enjoy it, won't you. We'd better phone you on Sunday in case we get the time wrong. Your first recital, Mum. I'll be thinking of you and waiting for Sunday to hear all about it.'

Her love for the little boy was a physical ache. He always understood.

'And I'm thinking about you all the time and being so proud of you both. Tomorrow I'll bring the fiddle for you.'

'Good-o. I'll see you.'

'No, I have to stick to the rules too. I have to bring it during class time. But you know it comes with lots of love and I'll be imagining you having your first lessons.'

'Better go back to bed. Someone said they come round to check we're all asleep. Goodnight, Mum. 'Spect it's nice there. Have you been playing your fiddle? I've been imagining it. Got eight of us in this dorm. Hope they don't wake up being miserable.'

'If they do, Tommy, you're just the man to cheer them up. Night night, love, God bless. Off you go to dreamland.'

Then there was only the dialling tone.

Time works its own pattern and during the coming weeks her life was almost as changed as the children's. Only Peter's carried on as usual; or, nearer the truth, Zina believed it did and if she could have looked in on the film set where he was working she would have seen nothing to

74

alter her opinion. An actor to his fingertips, no one with him questioned his unchanging cheerfulness. Before his fleeting visits home he always enquired whether there was any point in his coming, would Zina be free? Only *she* wasn't treated to a display of cheerfulness. He made no secret of his feelings when he phoned her one evening during the week preceding the half-term break.

'I take it you'll make yourself available to fetch the children?' There was no smile in his tone.

'I know it would be no use asking you to be responsible,' she answered him in the same vein. She had never been so filled with such a need to hurt him – to hurt him just as he did her.

And yet when the Friday evening came the house was filled with excited chatter. Like all children the twins were aware of atmosphere and she was determined nothing must cloud their few days at home. Supper was held back until Peter arrived, and even though the curtains were closed against the dark night, she and the children heard his car as it turned off the road at the end of the drive and approached the house much too fast, stopping with a loud squeal of brakes and throwing gravel in all directions. Peter was home.

'He's here . . . Dad's come . . .' and forgetting the conjuring trick Fiona had been performing, the two of them rushed to open the front door and hurl themselves at him as he got out of the car. Zina stayed behind, concentrating on checking the oven and making sure the table was ready. *It's got to be good, all of it, every moment. For the children's sake he's got to stop carping and being so mean-minded, expecting me always to be waiting for him with open arms – and I don't just mean in bed, even if he likes to think I do. It needn't be like this. It could all be so good.*

'Where are you, Mum?' she heard Tommy shout as they dragged Peter in, each pulling one hand.

'I'm in here, getting the table ready,' she called from the dining room. 'Just coming.'

Still with the children pulling him, he was led to where she was laying the dining table. To add to the festivity she had even put the candelabra out, just as she did on the rare occasions they had dinner parties. The twins exchanged a glance, each seeming to grow an extra inch. Zina longed to be able to throw herself into Peter's arms and, had they been alone, perhaps that's what she would have done, but he made no attempt to free himself from the hold the twins had on him. So instead, and still clutching a handful of forks, she came towards him and raised her head to give him a light kiss on his cheek. Perhaps she did it for the children's sake for certainly it was on their account that she made sure her voice was bright when she spoke.

'You made good time. Not too much traffic?'

'Enough. How long before supper? I wouldn't mind a quick shower if the kids aren't starving.' By now he'd got his arms back to himself again and as he spoke he moved to the sideboard to pour a drink. 'I'll take this up with me. One for you?'

'Not at the moment thanks, not while I'm sorting out the meal.' Now why did she say that?

Perhaps because it had always been his habit when he arrived home to pour out a drink to put the drive behind him; in the past he had always automatically poured one for her too.

'Be quick, Dad,' Fiona called as he turned to go upstairs carrying his glass, 'we've got masses to tell you, all about everything.'

'I'll be so quick you won't have time to miss me.'

He was as good as his word and ten minutes later they were sitting at the table while he carved a joint.

'This looks scrumptious, Mum. Do we get pudding too?' Tommy asked hopefully, for in the days when they'd been at the village school, the twins' supper was always something warm but seldom with a dessert; if Peter had been arriving late, the children would have eaten alone and been dispatched to bed and only 'the growns', as they talked of their parents, would have had a full-blown meal later. Going to boarding school seemed to have raised their importance in the household.

They sat some time at the meal table while the twins regaled them with word pictures of their new life. Actually most of the word pictures were Fiona's with just the occasional 'that's right, isn't it, Tom' or 'Tom missed that, didn't you, Tom, because of having to practise. Pity, because it was good fun.' Then, with her eyes fixed on Peter, she said, 'Dad, I waited until you were home to say about it, but we're doing a play at Christmas. Not the usual Nativity one like we used to do in the baby school. It's all about a beggar child at

Christmas and how she gets taken into a rich man's house out of the cold and gets to play with his children. It's sort of showing how there is no difference in the children whether they have lots of nice things and good food or whether they have nothing. Deep down they are all the same. She has parents and they are beggars too. You'd think they wouldn't have let her be taken off by the rich man, wouldn't you? I suppose if they hadn't, there wouldn't have been a story. Anyway they did. Then they come to fetch her and the rich children share some of their things with her and the man gives her parents some money and food. It's a sort of lesson for us all to help other people and understand that we're all the same. Anyway, all that isn't the important bit. The *important* thing is that *I* have been chosen for the part of the beggar girl. It's the biggest part in the whole play and I have lots of words to learn. I expect they gave it to me because they know about you, Dad. But, you just wait, you'll see: I'm going to make it something people will always remember. It's not just for the school you see, it's for parents and so forth to come.'

'I'm sure you'll make it something we shall all remember,' Peter said, his expression of pride seeming to set the two of them apart. 'If I have to move heaven and earth, be sure I shall be there in the audience.' Then, as if he remembered that he also had a son, he added, 'And you Tommy? Are you in the play?'

'Sort of. I'm just a kid in the crowd. And they don't call me that – Tommy, I mean. I suppose it's for little kids. At school I'm just Tom.' Then, turning to Zina, he said, 'But, Mum, Mr Messer said to tell you that he is pleased with how I'm doing with my music. And, Mum, he said – not meaning to look for pupils, but he just told me it – he said that it's a help to learn to play the piano too, not just one sort of instrument.'

'And he's right. I started both at the same time, but always loved the violin most.' Did she imagine that slight raise of Peter's eyebrows as he watched her? 'We'll see if they can fit you in for the second half of the term if you have time for two lots of practising. Do you think you could manage?'

'Perhaps he doesn't want to,' Peter suggested.

'Oh, but I do, Dad. If you let me it would be super. I really want to do it. I don't mind if I have to miss out on something else instead. Rugger, that's what the older ones play, but I'd rather have extra time for practising.'

Fiona's chuckle took the sting out of her remark as she said, 'Well, at least on a piano you won't make that awful scroopy noise like you do on the fiddle.'

'I *don't*.'

'If you don't, you're more clever than I was when I first started,' Zina laughed. 'It's hard in the beginning not to press your bow too hard on the strings. But it's something that you get over as you practise.' She was so aware of each one of them at the table, a new pride and confidence in Tommy's (she must try and remember that he was Tom now) expression as he took in what she said, while Peter and Fiona seemed to share a secret that cut them off from the others.

But perhaps it was all in her imagination. Here they were, the four of them together, a whole weekend ahead of them. She hated to admit even to herself that she was relieved she had no commitment with the quintet until the following Thursday; so until she drove the children back to school on Tuesday afternoon she could almost believe everything was as it used to be. Why was it she couldn't tell Peter that she had offered accommodation for the players to stay at Newton House with her after their recital in Exeter the following week? Any other friend and she would have told him, sure of his pleasure. But this time she knew she must say nothing and, with cunning alien to her nature, she hadn't even told her mother.

If only they had had more than just those few short days and nights, or if they had been away somewhere new to them all, a family on holiday for two or three weeks, then their future might have been very different. She tried to make believe that everything was as it had been, determined that for the weekend of their half-term break that was how it would be. She wanted to speak about it to Peter, but how could she? To acknowledge that she couldn't feel the same atmosphere of love in the house that she had always taken for granted could destroy any hope of finding it again. But perhaps Peter had always been so wrapped up in his 'other life' that for him there was no undercurrent. Was the difference in herself? In him? She was frightened to look for the answer.

For that half-term weekend she and Peter both

made sure no one rocked the boat. Fiona seemed to have settled happily enough at school (or, Zina suspected, more likely she was moulding things to suit herself where possible and, faced with rules that must be obeyed, she was taking the comfortable way out and accepting). Tommy told them less but Fiona assured them he was settling and he never seemed to be in trouble with his work. He would never become a ring-leader; rather he'd grow into being a private person, giving of himself just so much and no more. The one thing that was clear was that he loved his music lessons.

'I hope he isn't going to give too much of his time to learning music,' Peter said as the weekend drew towards its close. It was Sunday night; by morning he'd be gone. In his maroon silk pyjamas he would have turned many an infatuated fan's head as he stood in front of the mirror peering at his reflection, a silver backed brush in each hand as he made sure he was ready for bed. His tone was perfectly normal, he might have been making polite conversation to a stranger, yet Zina heard it as a criticism.

'No more than Fiona will to her play-acting. If he really enjoys it and gives his mind to it, it will be with him all his life. Most things we learn at school may stay tucked away at the back of our minds, but this will be a faithful friend to him come what may – always suppose he sticks at it. And I have a feeling he will.'

'No bad thing for a lad to excel at any subject, but I don't want him to miss out on sports, team-work, being part of a like-minded bunch of lads, accepting discipline and learning to take responsibility.'

'Oh, come on, Peter. He's only nine years old.' She felt they were skating towards thin ice, but wasn't prepared to hear any criticism of Tommy.

'He could have learnt to play music at home with you.'

His tone hadn't changed and yet, for her, what he said seemed to wipe away some of the cloud that hung over them. At least he was acknowledging that music had always been part of her life.

'Not the same, and anyway he's not here for me to teach him,' she answered as she snuggled down in bed, moving close to him as he lay down. Before the family stirred tomorrow he'd be gone. Surely now they would find each other, nothing else must matter but *that*. 'It's all gone so fast, Peter,' she said, moving her hand across his chest as he lay on his back. 'Monday tomorrow. Have you set the clock?'

'Unfortunately. Five thirty I must be on the road.'

She wriggled even closer. 'Good thing we've come to bed early.'

'Oh, hell, Zee, why can't it be like it was? Is it just that the kids are growing up?'

'It is the same, Peter, please, please, it has to be.' She felt the warmth of his body against hers as she undid the buttons of those maroon pyjamas, excitement and joy mounting in her as she knew they were in him. His warm hand was moving on her, telling her that his need was as great as her own. 'Nothing else matters, only us, only this,' she heard herself whisper and, in those moments, for both of them she spoke the truth. She felt that the barrier that had held them apart was gone. She could feel the pounding of her heart. Tonight was different, tonight she believed it was as if they acknowledged they had sailed through troubled water and reached a safe shore.

They were close again, there were no shadows or doubts. Both so aware of it, they wanted these moments to last forever and yet they had no power to slow the need that drove them. As he raised himself over her she knew from his quickened breathing and her own soft moan that it was beyond their power to slow where nature, and surely love, was driving them. Tonight their climb to the heights would be quick, there was no other way. Their movements were wild, with hands, mouths, tongues, with everything that they were, they raced to a climax that brought alive every nerve in them.

'Peter,' she gasped with hardly enough breath to speak at all, 'Peter. Wonderful . . . always must be . . .'

And he, rolling off her with hardly more life than a rag doll, replied, 'Always . . . never change,' words that were barely audible as he gasped his way towards recovery.

They said no more. In those magic moments she believed misunderstandings were behind them, there was nothing they couldn't overcome. She reached to the cord to switch off the light. Peter was already asleep. Downstairs the grandfather clock in the hall chimed and struck midnight. It was a mere five hours until the alarm would put an end to their night. Lying on her back she hugged herself. Tonight had been like a miracle, time that had seemed to lift her right out of the world and banish the misunderstandings and bitterness she had felt between them. How could he sleep after that? It was as if they had been fighting to recover something they had lost. And had they? They had made love each night of the weekend, of course they had, he'd not been here for nearly a month; and always it was good for both of them . . . but not like tonight. Tonight had banished all the shadows. Zina now felt cleansed of the anger and bitterness. Perhaps this was how one felt coming away from Confession. Always it was like climbing a mountain, feeling exalted when he brought her to the peak. But tonight it was no ordinary mountain; tonight was Everest. *I wish I was tired, but I'm wide awake, I want to remember every second.*

She'd thought herself to be wide awake, yet within two or three minutes she was sleeping as soundly as he was himself. At five o'clock the shrill bell of the alarm clock woke both of them. Monday morning and for Peter the half-term holiday was already over.

By late Tuesday afternoon she was driving home, the twins delivered back to school and arrangements made for Tommy to start piano lessons as soon as they could be slotted into the timetable.

The Christmas play was everything that Fiona had confidently expected. As in any school

84

production there were those in the cast who showed about as much life as a wooden statue, just as there were one or two who, despite all the training on voice production, couldn't be heard clearly from the back of the hall. But Fiona fitted into neither of those groups. Perhaps it was a talent inherited from her famous father, certainly the drama teacher believed that was the case and intended to choose their future productions with an eye to her being given a leading role. And perhaps from Peter she also inherited her personality: never did she become self-important, always she was happy to praise others, always she was good-natured and eager to give of her best. And 'her best' was quite brilliant. She would learn her words willingly and well (often to the neglect of maths, Latin, geography and so much more which had no bearing on the goal she had set herself) and, once word-perfect, imagine herself into the role living every emotion with complete disregard of drama teacher or audience.

As the months went by Peter watched her with ever-growing pride. Yet as, during this same time, Tommy (or Tom as he had become used to being known) gave hours of each day to practice and brought a glowing report from his music master for both violin and piano, his father's interest was little more than polite praise, given with a rider that 'I hope you're not neglecting the other opportunities the school gives you'.

On the surface he and Zina had a stable marriage but, scratch that surface, and they were two unhappy people moving on parallel lines held apart by what he saw as her selfish indulgence in a life in which he and the children had no part. Whenever he was free he came home, first enquiring whether she would be there or was she off somewhere with her merry band of music makers. Any weekend when the quintet was playing away from the district, or even locally enough for her to get home after the recital, he decided to stay where he was. Yet when he did spend time at home, he and Zina didn't quarrel; between them there was a superficially friendly courtesy that unfailingly led them to end the day with love-making. Still he led her to climb the mountain, although Everest remained but a distant dream.

The only way to hide from what was happening to them was to fill their lives and make sure the image they presented was of a happily married couple sharing pride in their two children. With her mother, Zina always made sure she was cheerful, that her voice had a ring of friendliness if she spoke about Peter after one of his brief visits. But Jenny was no fool and not one to be hoodwinked by a cheerful voice. Hadn't she always known what a selfish creature he was? He'd always assumed that his career was of major importance to the family and yet not once had he ever expressed his pride in what Zina was doing. Jenny saw very little of him but she knew Zina well enough to see behind the smiling facade she presented. She believed the trouble stemmed from their sending the children away to school; she never had agreed with it, believing that a parent's greatest duty was the guidance and upbringing of a family. However, she had always been careful not to put her oar into their pond, so she kept a watching brief.

The twins had been away at school more than three years on a morning when Jenny was feeling more depressed than she was prepared to admit. A click of the letterbox told her, just as it did each morning, that the paper had arrived.

There were times when she longed to do something wildly different and she was never more aware of it than when she stooped to pick up the newspaper. What have I let myself turn into? Friday morning and the daily monotony is broken because there is not just the daily but the weekly rag as well. 'Jolly hockey sticks!' She said it aloud, the sneer in her tone plain to hear, then back in the kitchen threw both newspapers onto the table and turned to pour her breakfast coffee. What should she do this morning? Mrs Morris would be in at half past nine . . . 'Friday, bedrooms today,' she would say as she stepped inside the house, 'with only the one been used I'll have time to give the windows a shine too.' Bedrooms, landings and stairs, drawing room, dining room, Alice Morris took pride in her work and kept to a strict routine. This morning Jenny knew she was being a coward, but she decided to escape. It was too early yet, but later she would drive over and see Zina. Friday and the quintet were playing at Dricombe this evening, only an hour's drive away so she wouldn't leave until well into the afternoon. Of course, his lordship wouldn't grace the house with his presence this weekend (Jenny didn't consider that he might not even be free; in today's dispirited mood she preferred to think the worst of him). Pouring her coffee she took it to the kitchen table, but still her thoughts ran away with her. 'It's not fair on her,' she muttered, then took a gulp of too-hot coffee and put the cup back on her saucer with a clatter. 'Not that Zina tells me, but I'm not blind. He doesn't like it if she can't give him all her attention. Suppose he hadn't been "discovered" or whatever they call it, suppose he'd still been in that rep company, he would have been glad enough for her to work then. Why are some men so arrogant? Not you, Richard, you never were. For more than five years you've been gone. Shall I ever get used to being by myself? It's not just missing *you*, the way we always talked about everything we read in the papers, the way we laughed at the same jokes, listened to the same music, yes of course I miss you for all that and for everything that you were – that *we* were, because now that you're not here I know I'm not the person I used to be, I spend my life dashing around filling the hours, trying to pretend any of it matters; but it's the pointlessness of everything now that you're gone. Alice Morris will come in here this morning full of vim and vigour, looking forward to making the bedrooms shine. I ought to be ashamed. She's been a widow for years and she still has a purpose. She'll work her butt off this morning, and for what? Just for me to shut the door on the clean rooms for another week. There's no point in any of it. That's what I can't get used to. I go to town and make myself try on clothes, buy something pretty as if it matters like it used to when we were together. But what's the point? I go to local meetings, and what a charade it all is.'

Picking up her fast-cooling coffee she drank it down like a thirsty man in a four-ale bar, then with new determination washed the cup under the running tap. She was ashamed. How could she sit there grizzling when it was such a beautiful morning? She'd mow the grass, then she'd have an hour pulling up weeds. By then it would be nearly lunchtime and she'd drive over and drop in on Zina. With the morning planned she was able to greet Alice Morris with her usual smile and then set about getting prepared to spend her morning outside.

If there was one thing geared to raise her spirits it was working out of doors. There had been rain in the night (enough rain that reason told her she ought to leave the grass and concentrate on the weeds while the ground was soft, but she was in no mood to listen to reason). The morning sky was a clear blue with not even a wisp of cloud. As soon as she pulled the starter of the motor mower and took her first steps up the large rectangular lawn she was lifted from that cloud of depression. She walked the length of the lawn, then back, then up again, back, up, with each step getting more satisfaction out of what she did. It was nearly an hour later when she heard the garden gate. She didn't stop, expecting it would be Zina and imagining that she would take the shears and trim the edges. But when there was no familiar 'Hi Mum' she assumed it must have been someone putting a leaflet through her front door. So on she went, keeping a steady pace, up the lawn, back again, then turning to continue, concentrating on keeping the lines straight and imagining the tennis court that used to be marked out here each summer in what seemed like another life. It was as she turned to start another row that she heard a step on the path and cast a quick glance over her shoulder.

The man coming up the path by the side of the house was a stranger. And yet, was he? For a moment she couldn't think why he was familiar, and then it dawned on her.

'Why surely it's Mr Masters? Is something wrong?'

'I regret you have the advantage. Would you be Zina's mother? She has mentioned to me that you have sometimes come to recitals, but we have never met.' His manner was very formal, made with a courteous bow of the head, the action teasing the back of her mind with something she couldn't bring to the fore. Then in a completely different tone, as if his words were spoken spontaneously before he had a chance to hold them back, he said, 'Until this minute I'd never connected you with the lady with a stubborn petrol cap – but that was so long ago that you will have forgotten.'

Switching off the motor on the mower she came towards him, her laugh completely natural. 'That's it! When I turned and saw you I recognized you from the recitals, and even while I've been watching you play I'd always had a niggling feeling I'd seen you somewhere before.' Then with a chuckle, she said, 'Sir Galahad of the petrol cap – an incident I'd tried to brush out of my memory.' She held out her hand to him, thinking how different he looked in corduroys and an anorak rather than the evening suit he wore for recitals. 'Were you hoping to find Zina here? How did you know where I live?'

'Yes to the first question, but the second wasn't as simple. I knew you were somewhere in the village here, she had mentioned it, but I didn't know your name. However, in a village nothing is secret. I asked the butcher if he could tell me where I would find Zina Marchand's mother.'

'I'm sorry but she isn't here. You've been to Newton House?'

'No reply there – and her phone seems out of order. I reported it to the telephone people before I left home. You've not heard the regional news this morning I take it?'

'No, is there something special? News is seldom the kind to lift the spirit so I wait until six o'clock. Why do you ask?'

'A big fire last night in Dricombe. The Victoria Hall where we were booked to give a recital this evening was gutted. I heard it at seven this morning and I've got messages to the others, but couldn't get through to Zina so I thought I'd better come and give her the news myself.'

'Was anyone hurt do you know?'

'I imagine not, I'm sure if there had been injuries they would have reported it. Apparently the alarm was raised in the early hours but the fire had a hold on the property by that time.'

'Sad. A local hall like that can be the hub of the village. I know here the village hall is where every

91

local event is centred.' Then pulling her thoughts back to the reason of his call, she added, 'I don't expect Zina's far afield. I had intended to drive over to see her later in the morning when I'd dealt with the grass. It's the mother instinct, you know,' she added with a laugh patently aimed at herself, 'I thought if I turned up about lunch time she would be bound to eat something before she set off. It's such a temptation not to bother preparing food just for yourself. I imagine she must be planning to get on the road in good time for you to be able to run through the music together before you all get dolled up for the evening.'

He'd thought of the 'petrol cap lady' so often since that day when he had found her at the garage. It made no sense, but he felt it was like meeting an old friend.

'Somehow I must stop her making a fruitless journey. Would you have any idea where she may be? The hairdresser perhaps? There was a chap working in the garden but he said he hadn't seen her today.'

'I doubt he would have. They leave him to organize himself. Neither Zina nor Peter are gardeners – although when I heard the gate this morning and thought it was probably her, I had the idea I might get her to do the edges with the shears.' Immediately she wished she could withdraw her words. Would he think she was waiting for him to offer? Clearly she could remember how he had protected his hands when he undid her petrol cap.

She needn't have been embarrassed; he made no such offer.

'Go indoors and help yourself to the telephone,' she suggested. 'Through the kitchen into the hall, then it's the first door on the right. If you reported her phone was out of order at the start of day, you never know, by some miracle it might be working again. Sometimes it can be a fault that doesn't need a home visit. Mine was like that a couple of weeks ago and they sorted it out almost immediately. Now I've started I want to get this cut, but the edging can wait until tomorrow.'

But it worked out quite differently. Zina arrived while he was indoors hoping for better luck with a second call. Suddenly the mood of the morning changed for all three of them. Derek Masters had left his apartment feeling less than pleased that while the other members of the quintet had been contacted by telephone, he was faced with a thirty-mile journey to find Zina. Then reaching her home only to find she wasn't there had done nothing for his good humour. So he'd made his way to Myddlesham, remembering that that was where she had mentioned her mother lived. That he had been so out of humour by the time he drew up at her gate was completely unsuspected by Jenny, just as was her earlier fit of the blues unsuspected by him. How could he be disgruntled when his morning had brought him face-to-face with the petrol cap lady? That alone would have raised his spirits, but the sight of her in well-worn and patched slacks with a check shirt many sizes too large (presumably her late-husband's), sleeves rolled up, for if they hadn't been, all hint of her having hands would have been lost, was enough to drive every other thought from his mind. His greeting had been formal and courteous, giving no sign of what was going on in his mind. But before more than the first sentences had been spoken he was as relaxed as Jenny was herself.

'Still no reply,' he called as he came back from the house, hardly expecting to be heard above the noise of the mower as Jenny marched up the last strip to be cut. Then he saw Zina emerge from a shed bearing a pair of shears. She came towards him smiling a welcome. 'Thanks Derek, Mum tells me you reported my phone. So we have a day off. I just suggested to Mum that you both come back to the house with me when I've trimmed these edges, then I'll rustle up some lunch.'

He felt he was being swept along on a current too strong to be resisted, even if he'd wanted to. The day was young, the recital cancelled and the sun shining. Perhaps the petrol cap lady had other arrangements, although – and a smile tugged at the corners of his mouth – she was hardly dressed for socializing.

'There!' Jenny switched off the motor regarding her efforts with satisfaction. 'Now then, Zina, did I mishear you or were you inviting us to lunch? What do you say, Mr Masters? Can you spare the time? You've come a long way, you deserve a break before you set off again. Give me ten minutes to get the garden off me.'

'As Zina says, this is an unexpected day of freedom. May I suggest that you allow me to take you both out somewhere.'

'What a lovely idea,' Zina replied and beamed with pleasure, 'isn't it, Mum?'

'You know what?' Jenny told them, 'this morning I got up with a fit of the miseries; really had a black dog on my back. Now you've chased it right away. An unexpected treat – what could be better? Are you sure you want to add even more miles to your day, Mr Masters?'

'Indeed I am,' he asserted in his formal way and not for the first time it struck Jenny there was something in his manner not quite English. 'But there is one thing on which I insist: my friends use my Christian name, Derek, and I should be honoured if you would consider me to be your friend.' Then bestowing a smile on Jenny (a smile Zina privately saw as uncharacteristically flirtatious), he added, 'And would it not be in order for me to address you as something other than "Zina's mother"?'

'I'm so sorry,' Jenny laughed, 'I knew your name, I forgot you didn't know mine. 'I'm Jennifer Beckham – just Jenny.'

He held his hand out to her and, enjoying herself enormously, she grasped it.

'How do you do, my friend Jenny.'

It is ridiculous, she told herself, as she hurried away to get tidy for the outing. Here I am, nearer sixty than fifty, but I feel as excited as a sixteen-year-old being asked for her first dance. Ridiculous or not, I'm going to squeeze every bit of joy out of the unexpected turn of the day. In future, if the recitals weren't too far away, she would go to hear the music just as she had previously, but she was unlikely to talk with him on those occasions any more than she did with Zina. She always bought her ticket beforehand, went straight to her seat and left as the audience crowded out as soon as it was over.

Today was something quite different, she wanted every hour to impress itself on her so that she could relive it afterwards. Perhaps she was extra buoyed up by the contrast between now and how she had felt earlier. Little more than ten minutes later she rejoined the others who had given up on trimming the edges and were coming away from the shed having put mower and shears away. In well-fitting trousers and a short-sleeved checked shirt, with her face washed and made-up enough to make her look groomed but natural, she made a delightful picture.

'Where to, my friend Jenny, coast or country?'

'There's a pub on Exmoor where the food is reliably good and the views enough to take your breath away. It's always been a special place. Would that be too far?'

'Today is holiday, we shall not be watching the hands of the clock. First we will follow Zina home so that she can leave her car, then we will all travel together.'

Perhaps she would look back and remember it afterwards as more than just a bright patch in a dull grey life.

Four

If Zina imagined that Jenny needed her to bridge the gap between herself and Derek Masters, she very soon realized her mistake. At rehearsals, Derek was always pleasant, good to work with, consistently keeping a friendly distance between himself and the other members of the quintet. Away from the environment of music, she had never thought about him, so she was surprised by the sound of the easy chatter in the front of the car – surprised by him and by her mother too. With the windows half open there was too much wind and tyre noise for her to join in their conversation or even to keep up with what they found to talk about, but she was aware just how long it was since she had heard her mother's tone so animated.

'Not much further and we take the lane to the right. We're almost there,' Jenny was saying to Derek, turning her head towards the back of the car so that Zina felt herself included, and sounding as excited as a child catching the first glimpse of the sea after a long journey.

'Be it on your head if the only thing they can provide on a Friday is bread and cheese,' Derek answered, his voice suggesting that his pleasure was as great as hers.

Watching them and half hearing what was said made Zina wish she hadn't accepted Derek's invitation, certain by now that she had only been included because he could hardly have done less. When they drew into the car park of the ancient inn on the moor, she had her excuses ready. Outside was a blackboard on which the day's menu had been chalked.

'We're really too early to eat,' she said. 'Mum, why don't you and Derek choose what you want and give yourselves time for a walk? It's only just gone twelve and food won't be ready until nearer one.'

'Oh but you'll walk too,' Jenny said, her tone wavering between a statement and a question.

'In these shoes? Not likely. I ought to have thought and changed them when I dropped the car off. But tell me what you want ordered and I'll go in and chat to our old friend while I have a drink and tell him you'll be back – when? Shall I say one o'clock?'

Was she imagining it or did she read relief in Jenny's expression? Certainly neither of them tried to make her change her mind and watching them set off she was conscious of an unfamiliar feeling of anger? Or was it disbelief? Whatever it was, even before she'd got inside the familiar inn it had been replaced by shame and irritation on Jenny's account. How could a woman of her age, a widow after a long and happy marriage, be so stupid? She was behaving like a teenager setting out on her first date. Even when she was younger, Zina thought, I never remember seeing her look at Dad like she was looking at Derek. If he'd been the sort of man who chased after women and played them at their own game, it

98

wouldn't be so bad, but his work was his whole life. He must be laughing at her. That he'd suggested the trip at all was surprising, but if Mum is as desperate as all that for a male friend she'll find she's wasting her time on him. (And of course she *wasn't* desperate; why, her days were more full than most people's, always dashing around doing things in the village.) It was humiliating to watch her.

Once inside the lounge bar of the inn, her spirit took an upward turn. It meant nothing to Bert Saunders, the landlord, that she was the wife of a screen idol; he hadn't visited a cinema for thirty years and remembered her as the little girl who had come walking with her parents and been too young to be allowed inside the bar.

'On your own today, Zina? Nothing the matter with your mother, I hope?'

'Not a thing, she's fine. She and a friend are walking up an appetite but I wasn't prepared; high heels weren't designed for the moor. I'll order for the three of us, they said they'd be back here by about one o'clock. We'll all have the same: Mrs Saunders' steak and kidney pie.'

'Let me pour you your drink first, then I'll nip out the back and tell Kitty your order. Then we'll have time for a bit of a chat. I'll be wanting to hear how those two chil'un of yours are getting on. Must be into their teens I'd be guessing. Fair puts the wind up you the way the time runs away.'

So with the order given and a gin and tonic passed to Zina and 'something for yourself' in a half pint glass waiting on the bar, he came back prepared for his 'bit of a chat'. He had always been one of Zina's special people. Rich, poor, beautiful or plain, Bert Saunders wasn't taken in by appearance and, perhaps because of that, he drew out the best in everyone.

'And how about you?' He asked, taking a good draught of his ale and settling with his elbows on the bar. 'Still off playing that fiddle are you? Your mother drives over sometimes on her own, you know, and she tells me all about you. Remember when you used to be a nipper and your dad used to buy you a glass of ginger beer and a packet of your favourite cheesy biscuits to have out there in the car. Nice man he always was.'

'He was very special,' Zina agreed, the way the conversation had turned resurrecting her anger for the way Jenny was behaving.

'You know what I always think – mind, I wouldn't say this to her face – but I reckon when your ma drives out here it's looking for memories. I watch her sometimes walking off to the moor; not like it used to be with the two of them, aye, three of you when you were around. Rotten luck to be left on her own at her age.'

'Even more rotten for him to die so young.'

'Ah. A good marriage, I reckon that's the best thing anyone can wish for in this life. No one's is all beer and skittles, but given a good partner then there's nothing that'll beat a person. Your husband still acting is he? Don't think I've ever met him, no, not had the pleasure. Not a walker maybe?'

'A good stomp on the moor takes more time than he usually has. One of these days when he is home for more than a brief day or so we'll come over and he'll get acquainted with Mrs Saunders' pies. It's not just the moor folk come out here for. This place has always been a bit special for as long as I can remember.'

'Bless your heart, m'dear.'

The atmosphere of the old inn was working its magic on her, and by the time Jenny and Derek arrived she knew the meal would be the crowning success of the trip. The table talk flowed easily and she forgot to be angry with her mother.

It was half past five when Zina watched Derek's car disappearing down the drive. The weekend loomed ahead, long and empty. But before any such sentiment had a chance to take root she let herself into the house, thinking that between half past five and six o'clock was the time the children in the twins' year at St Mary's were allowed to have phone calls. But it seemed every other parent had the same idea for it took her a quarter of an hour of dialling and redialling before the ringing tone told her she'd got through between calls. A young voice answered and said she (or perhaps he with a voice not yet broken) would find either Fiona or Tom.

'Hello, it's Tom here.'

'Hi, Tom.'

'Oh Mum, it's you. That's nice, I thought you were off somewhere playing this evening. Are you all right? Is anything wrong?'

He listened to the explanation about the fire and then about the trip to the moor.

'And now you're by yourself? Pity you didn't

101

have the recital, Mum. What are you going to do? I suppose Dad's not coming if he thought you wouldn't be there.'

'I'll be OK. I'll probably see Celia tomorrow. Now tell me about you.'

'Not long now before the exams – music ones, I mean. Mr Messer has definitely put me down to take two grades, four and five in both, he says I'm ready. It's exciting, isn't it, and a bit scary too. Were you excited when you were learning?'

She laughed. 'Yes Tom, I was, but like you say a bit scared too. I'd forgotten just how excited until you started up the ladder and that brings it all back. You've done remarkably well, you know. If you pass them all that'll be wonderful, but two at a time is a huge challenge so you mustn't be disappointed with yourself if it's too big a step to take. To be on grade five after three and a half years is tremendous. Everything else going well? And what about Fiona?'

Tom chuckled. 'She's on cloud nine, getting ready for the end of term play. I sneaked in and watched the rehearsal the other day and, Mum, she really is *good*. Not just that she knows her words but she's so good that she makes it all seem real. You wait till Dad sees her this time; he'll be chuffed as anything.'

'If he allows himself to spare the time.' Her words were spoken before she could hold them back. Then, as if to wipe them out, she laughed and added, 'Only joking. He's so busy lately that he hardly even gets home. But I'm sure he'll manage the play.'

'It isn't that he hasn't much chance to get home

that made you sound cross, Mum. It's because he doesn't get excited like *we* do about *my* music exams. But, Mum, he isn't meaning to be nasty, he just doesn't understand. But acting, well that's different. I expect you and me don't really feel as thrilled as Dad and Fiona do about how well *she's* doing. It isn't anybody's fault, don't you see? It's just that they don't sort of get the feel of it like we do. I'm quite glad really; it's something special just for us. Does that sound mushy? I don't mean it to.'

'Oh Tommy, I wish you were here and I could hug you. Yes, it makes it special for *us* and I expect prancing around in front of an audience is just as special for *them*.'

'Better not let *them* hear you call it prancing about,' he said with a giggle. 'I'd better go, Mum. Telephone time ends in ten minutes and there are people waiting for calls from home. Just as long as you're OK.'

'Good night, love. God bless.'

'And you.'

She rang off, realizing how talking to Tom always lifted her spirits. She made some coffee and raided the biscuit tin, so much easier than thinking about cooking food. Then she moved her car into the garage, from where she had left it in front of the house when she'd changed to Derek's for the trip to the moor, before going back into the empty house and turning on the television with more hope than expectation. When the late evening news finished she decided it wasn't too early to go to bed, putting an end to the day.

103

It was during the night that something woke her. She didn't know what it was she'd heard, she was just aware that there had been something, but by the time she was really awake and listening everything was silent. Yet she knew she hadn't been dreaming. Could it have been an animal, a fox perhaps walking on the gravel? She listened, aware of the thumping of her heart. She always told herself she wasn't nervous living alone. So why, now, was she gripped by cold fear? There it was again . . . someone was trying to tread quietly. She had set the burglar alarm, and now she reached to the bedside table as if she needed to reassure herself that the telephone was to hand, then getting out of bed, she put on her dressing gown and tied it tightly around her slim waist. As soon as she heard the shrill alarm bell she would ring the police – and anyway at the sound of it surely any would-be thief would make an escape. Hark! Another scuff of the gravel. She remembered how when they had bought the house Peter had had the existing tarmac driveway covered with thick gravel as a deterrent to burglars. There was no reason for her to creep, but instinct prompted her to move silently to the window. She could see no one, and there was no sign of a vehicle, but there was the sound again! Whoever it was must be keeping very close to the building, out of view from the bedroom. Moving without a sound, and in the dark, she groped to find a chair and carried it to the door where she propped it so that it would crash to the ground if anyone tried to get in. Reason ought to have told her that a burglar was unlikely to make for her bedroom when there were richer pickings downstairs. But perhaps she was letting her imagination run away with her, perhaps it was no more than a fox – or the puma that people claimed to have had sightings of recently. No, hark, there was a different sound! A downstairs door being closed carefully, quietly! Someone had got in and the burglar alarm hadn't worked. All these nights when she'd set it so confidently had it not been working? She felt sick with fear as she tried to imagine where, in the dark room, she could put her hand on something with which she could attack the intruder. The best she could think of was the silver-backed hand mirror on her dressing table, so she groped across the room to have it ready. She didn't want to damage it. It used to belong to her father's mother, a grandmother she had been close to, and her great-grandmother before that; even though it was out of keeping with the modern decor of the room, it was something she treasured. But, she told herself as she clutched the silver handle in her clammy and shaking hand, Gran wouldn't have stood any nonsense from the sod, she'd be right with me. If she brought it down on his head it might not do him any serious harm, but hopefully it would be enough to stop him in his tracks. Beyond that she was frightened to let herself imagine.

She must keep calm, she must think rationally. Yes, of course, it was no use waiting until he was trying to get into the room. Now was the time to phone the police. Perhaps there might be a motor vehicle cruising on its round not too far away. For a second she let herself believe they might get here in time to catch him red-handed. But as she took the first step towards the phone, fear stopped her in her tracks. Footsteps as stealthy as her own were coming up the stairs. Her mouth was as dry as sawdust; she felt every nerve alive with terror and knew she was a trembling wreck. It was hard to keep a firm grip on her meagre implement of defence as, with no time for telephoning, she got into position with her arm raised ready to attack if the falling chair didn't frighten the intruder away. She remembered she had heard on the news of an elderly woman being raped by a night-time intruder. She told herself that she was strong, she would fight . . . but how could she fight when it was as much as she could do to breathe?

In the dark she stood trembling with one hand on the doorknob so that she would be ready the minute the chair was knocked aside. Yes, she felt the knob move, oh God, help me, help me! I mustn't miss. Whoever he is, if I don't hit him hard enough he'll have the advantage. But he's on strange ground; I'm not. It took no more than a second for the thoughts to fill her mind as the doorknob turned. Then everything happened at once. The chair was thrown from where she had propped it, expecting to hit the intruder's head she misjudged and brought the hand mirror down on his shoulder in the same second as the room was flooded with light and she found herself face to face with Peter.

'In God's name, what the hell do you think you're doing?'

Anger, shock and relief vied for place, but all she was capable of was dropping to sit on the side of the bed, her whole body shaking. Relief destroyed every bit of her self-control.

'I thought . . . I didn't know . . .' Her voice rose hysterically. 'You with your stupid bloody surprises . . . why didn't you tell me you were going to turn up in the middle of the night? I thought . . .'

'Why didn't I tell you? Because I didn't expect you to drive home after an evening recital in – wherever it was. Who do you imagine but me would have turned the alarm off before it had time to go into action? A burglar would hardly have known the code to clock in even if he'd found it in the dark.'

A minute ago she had been sweating with fear; now she couldn't stop shivering. Her nightdress felt clammy and when she took off her dressing gown she pulled it from her shoulders, let it slip to the floor and kicked it out of the way. He was looking at her in that way which so often annoyed her, one eyebrow raised. Without a word she took another nightdress from her draw and slipped it on.

'There was no recital. The hall was burnt down last night.'

This time when he looked at her she recognized laughter in his eyes. 'Did someone feel *that* strongly?' he said with a teasing chuckle, yet without the malice she so often detected.

She was recovering. She replaced the chair to its usual place and the hand mirror to the dressing table before she climbed into bed.

'What made you decide to come as late as this? I wish you'd come earlier so that we could have had the evening. Evenings are the hardest part here by myself.' Back in bed again, her fright behind her, she watched him pulling off his clothes and throwing them unceremoniously onto the chair which a minute or two ago had been barricading the door. 'I've just thought – when I heard footsteps outside I looked out but there wasn't a car. How did you get here?'

'I drove straight to the garage. When I saw yours parked there I knew you were home.' Then with that mischievous smile, he added, 'That's why I crept – never thinking you'd be preparing a knockout blow.' He'd been living the last few hours on a reserve of energy which seemed suddenly to have given out. 'At last, bed. Did you know it's nearly four o'clock. Tonight, Mrs Marchand, I'm coming to bed unshaven.'

What a weak fool she was, she told herself. All he had to do was speak to her in that tone of voice and all her misgivings were laid to rest. She turned towards him, nuzzling her face against his neck.

'Nearly four o'clock,' she mused, 'it must have been way after midnight when you set out. What made you decide?' Even as she asked it, she imagined him ending his evening and wanting to be with her, close to her like this. Why else would he have come so far in the middle of the night? For her, sleep was far away – but then, unlike him, she'd already had more than five hours in bed. A contented smile teased the corners of her mouth as she wriggled closer.

'I hadn't meant to come. But, Zina, there's a lot we have to talk about. This is an unnatural way of living, for both of us. The future is going to be different. It has to be. We'll talk about it tomorrow, that's why I came home. God, but I'm shattered. Do you realize I've been up nearly twenty-four hours.'

How could he settle for sleep after what he'd said?

'Peter,' she whispered, sitting up and bending over him. But she knew from his breathing that he was beyond talking any more. 'Peter, wake up. How will it all be different? What have we got to discuss?' She tried to shake him, but it was no use. Twenty-three hours of wakefulness ending with a long drive had defeated him.

Peter usually slept quietly, but in his exhausted state the only reply she had was a cross between a snort and a snore. She lay on her back gazing at the dark ceiling. Such a little while ago she had been a trembling mass of fear. So she was still, but this was fear of another sort. Gazing up into the darkness she was too full of despair to marshal coherent thought at all. Up until now, she had believed that he derived pleasure in hurting her because he was jealous of the hold her love of music had on her, but over these last years had the truth been that he'd been drifting away from her, caught up in a life in which she had no part? Had he fallen in love with someone else? Who could blame him, mixing as he did with women of both beauty and talent? She felt herself to be plain and dull. Things to discuss . . . an unnatural way of living . . . it couldn't go on . . . a future that was different. No matter how exhausted he was, how could he say those things and then fall straight into sleep? Into her mind came the image of Celia and Jacques, the union between them strong and unchanging.

Trying to sleep was impossible for Zina. She turned her pillow, she couldn't relax no matter how much she tried to hold her thoughts away from what he had said – or, even worse, half said. Having come to bed early her best sleep was over before she had been woken and finally she gave up the battle. Carrying her dressing gown and slippers she crept downstairs. But upstairs or down made no difference, there was no escaping from his veiled hints. She needed no light, every step was familiar to her. In the dining room she sat at the table, feeling the smooth shining wood under her fingers. She thought of how their lives used to be and what they had become. When the children were small, at the baby school and here with her every day, she would never have believed it possible that between herself and Peter anything could ever change. When had they gone wrong? They were a *family,* each one dependent on the others. Even now, although he was too pig-headed to acknowledge it, she was at home far more than she was away. Perhaps he was bored with her.

When she joined the quintet and he made such a martyr of himself was that just because he was frightened to face the fact he was bored with her, bored with the odd weekends at home with the children, missing his jolly lot of actors and the like, all living in their world of glitz and make-believe? She knew she was making herself think that way, building her defences against whatever she had to face when he put flesh on the skeleton he had given her in the night.

If there's someone else, surely I would have known. Love-making is when we always come close, not just with our bodies but with our spirits too, that's what I've always felt. But for him had it just been physical sex?

She realized how long she must have been sitting, her elbows on the table and her head in her hands. Already it was almost light. Making an effort she went into the kitchen and switched the kettle on. Tea or instant coffee? She disliked the thought of either but with determination reached for the packet of tea bags.

So a new day started and, while Peter still slept, she showered, dressed, put on her make-up and told herself she was steeled and ready for anything he threw at her. It was not much after nine o'clock when the telephone rang. She answered it on the extension in the dining room.

'Not too early for you, Zina?' came Jenny's greeting, a note of repressed excitement in her tone, something Zina chose to ignore.

'Early? I've been up ages. Everything all right? It was a nice trip yesterday, wasn't it? Bert Saunders never changes – and neither does the cooking.' There was nothing in the way she said it to hint how she had felt watching Jenny's behaviour.

'Really good. That's why I'm calling you so early. I thought with Peter being away you might

111

have come over and I wouldn't want you to get here and find me out.'

'Actually, Mum, Peter is here,' she said, still keeping a tight rein on any hint of expression. 'Where are you gadding off to, then?'

'I don't know about gadding off,' she replied, clearly on her guard. 'Derek and I are having a day in Bath. He's getting tickets for us to go to a Beethoven concert this evening.'

'Mum, I don't like to think of you driving all that way on your own at night. Can't I book you into a hotel? I'll look in the *Yellow Pages* and do it for you, shall I?'

Some of Jenny's carefree anticipation for the day faded. How could Zina know just what yesterday had done to her? Mum, Gran, she was proud to be both those things, but most of all she was *herself.*

'Sweet of you, dear, but there's no need. I've got it sorted, a private hotel with parking, and they sounded nice people.' No need to say that Derek had made the booking for her.

'That's good. You'll enjoy the concert, I'm sure. But Mum . . .' And here she hesitated. 'Listen Mum, don't take this the wrong way – oh damn, I don't know how to say it – I only want what's best for you, but don't give yourself a chance to get fond of Derek, or read too much into his attention. You'll only get hurt. The quintet is his life. He's like any other man, I expect, at any rate any man without a wife, and once in a while perhaps likes a bit of light relief with a lady. But he's got to his age without getting ensnared, so you may be sure he's never wanted anything

112

serious, so he won't let it happen at his time of life.'

'Zina, I—' But Zina didn't give her a chance. 'I don't want to sound horrible, and I know you must want a man to go about with sometimes – but yesterday I could see how excited you were to have that trip out, and if *I* could, then so could he. He must have felt flattered. Just let him see that you aren't looking for anything more than he is himself. I mean, don't imagine that a few invitations give you—'

'Stop it! Stop it, can't you,' Jenny rasped. 'It's no business of yours or anyone else's what I do. If I make a fool of myself, as you say, then it's my own affair.' Her voice croaked and then broke, her wildly shouted words hardly intelligible as she sobbed. 'Just because Richard isn't here you think all I want is to be a *good woman*, rushing around helping others with a sweet smile on my face. Well, sometimes I just think *bugger the lot of it*. There's only one person who would understand and that's him, Richard. You want me to be here living on memories – you think I'm *old*—' when Zina tried to interrupt, she carried on – 'because I'm a widow and never looked outside the life he and I had together, you think I can live on that for all the years that are left to me?'

'That's not true, Mum, you do more with your days than most women. If Dad knows and watches he must be so proud of the way you have built a worthwhile life.' There, that must have got through. The noisy crying had given way to no more than an occasional snort. 'It's because we love you, Mum, me and Dad too, that we don't want you to make a fool of yourself. Try playing hard to get, then you'll see if Derek really enjoys taking you about or whether he'll lose interest.'

There was a moment's silence and then in a cool and distant voice, with no more than the interruption of a sniff in the aftermath of her stormy outburst, Jenny said, 'You've never needed to tell me how much Peter resented your going back to your fiddle, I knew it without being told – he's the sort of man who would. But I have a better idea for you, one he might even approve: why don't you become an Agony Aunt?' Then with a snort that wouldn't be repressed, she added, 'Except that you've never known the agony – and please God you never will.'

'Oh Mum, let's forget it all. I just don't want you to make a fool of yourself. Truly I'm sorry, I didn't mean to upset you. I shouldn't have said anything.'

'No, you shouldn't. You should have minded your own business and let me make mistakes in my own way. Anyway, I'm out today and staying in Bath tonight. I'm glad Peter is home.' Then suddenly there was nothing but the dialling tone.

Zina replaced the receiver. She would give so much to have the last ten minutes again, to play it differently. Always she and her mother had been so close, or so she had thought. And yet through these last years while she'd honestly believed Jenny had been fulfilled with all the village good works and the local societies she had spent her time with, had it been no more that a facade to hide behind? Maybe, as she said, she wasn't old, but she was certainly old enough and had years enough of a truly good marriage that surely she could build something without needing another man. All very fine for her to say Dad would understand how she felt, perhaps he would, but he would expect the man she wanted to be *him*.

If the telephone call had spoilt the day for her mother then Zina was sorry, but at least it might make her think twice before she behaved like some stupid teenager with her first boyfriend.

'Was that one of the kids on the phone?' Peter's voice behind her startled her.

'No, it was Mum. She thought I would have been on my own and might drive over, so she was warning me that she'd be out for the day. I didn't expect you to be up yet.'

'I'm a five o'clock man, remember. You can't change nature's clock just because of a late night.' Then with a boyish grin, he added, 'Anyway how can a poor man sleep when he's got a bruised shoulder? I wish we'd had a camera set, it was quite a scene, wasn't it.'

She had the grace to laugh; indeed she needed to laugh, surely that way she would clear her troubled mind.

'Next time if I hear someone creeping about I shall take it to be you – and perhaps end up murdered or worse in my own bed and all our valuables taken.'

'There won't be a next time. That's what I want us to talk about. Last night something I had been toying with in my mind was finally settled, and even though it was a late night I wanted to come straight home. If you'd told me you were going to be here I might have hurried things along and got here a bit sooner. But I saw no rush to get back to an empty house—'

'I know the feeling,' she cut in, not prepared to listen to his martyr act.

'Listen Zina, things have got to change. This is nothing of a life for either of us and hasn't been for a long time.'

She leant forward pressing the palms of her hand hard on the dining table. Now he's going to tell me . . . breath properly, hold your head up, stand straighter. In those seconds she saw them in a divorce court, all their possessions being divided, the house sold, herself in a flat somewhere with just enough room for the children to spend half their holidays with her, then like rootless people going on to spend the other half with him. Thank God she could earn her own living. Yes, thank God for that other part of her life that he so despised.

'Are you OK, Zee? You look shaky.' Zee, the old nickname, and spoken in a tone of real concern.

'Feel a bit shaky. Just had a row with Mum. Nothing important. Go on with what you were saying, about things being different.'

'Here, sit down.' He pulled a dining chair for her and then one for himself.

'Looks as if we're at a board meeting.' She made a pathetic attempt to lighten the situation. 'Go on. You're chairman.'

'I expect I told you the great Hermann Zeiglar was over here from Hollywood. I've seen quite a lot of him over the last weeks, visited him and his wife a few times at their hotel in Maidenhead – times when it's not been worth my while driving down here to an empty house. I suspected he was interested in signing me up, but he'd not put his cards on the table. Then, last night it came to a head. His wife is a real charmer, but I suspect a pretty hard-nosed businesswoman, probably the power behind the throne. He invited me for dinner at his hotel and I could tell it was something important when he had the meal sent up to their suite so that we wouldn't be disturbed.'

'He's from Hollywood? So he's here to make a film in England and wants to sign you up for it? You're not lined up for anything once this shooting finishes are you, so the timing is just right surely? Not much to discuss about that, surely you're not hesitating whether to agree, are you, if this Hermann whatever-you-called-him is so important?' She wanted to laugh, to shout, to cheer, to dance, and yet she sat as still as a statue waiting for his answer. He always talked to her about any contract he signed, told her what he was doing. But it was obvious he saw this offer as significant. And for this she had lain awake!

'It seems that he came to England with me in mind. Just imagine what it means! It'll be a huge change for all of us – you, me, the youngsters. It's not a run-of-the-mill picture, it'll be the biggest epic film to come out of Hollywood since – I suppose since *Gone With the Wind* all those years ago. Imagine what it will do to my career.' Then, with a laugh he couldn't have repressed even if he'd wanted, he added, 'Can't you just

117

see Fiona's face when she hears she's to live in Hollywood. Beverley Hills, that's where we'll be.'

Wherever her imagination had carried her, it had certainly not been to California. How long would it take to make the film? It would be an experience for the children, but after perhaps as much as a year away, how would they settle back? Would Tom have fallen behind with his music and would he still be able to get into a music school as Mr Messer hoped?

But Peter's excitement was infectious. It was so long since they had looked at each other with such certain hope.

'They break up in not much more than a fort-night,' she reminded him. 'By then you'll have finished on the set – be officially "resting",' she added with a teasing laugh, thinking how far from the truth it would be. While he seemed to look ahead as if all they had to do was pack their bags and be off, her feet were dragged to the ground more quickly. There were bookings for the quintet for many months ahead and she couldn't walk out until a suitable replacement violinist was found. Then, what about her mother? And the house? Close a house for perhaps a year, especially one as old as Newton House, and it would be a sorry sight to come back to even if the garden was still looked after.

'You must have been imagining something like this for all the weeks you've been getting to know this Hermann man, but for me it's come right out of the blue. We've never even considered living abroad and certainly not in America. But Peter, how long have you signed a contract for? Is it just for one film? And what happens after that?'

'Where's your faith in me, woman?' Nothing was going to burst his bubble.

'You sound very cock-a-hoop. And of course so am I, and proud as can be. But you didn't answer – is it just one film?'

He reached forward and took both her hands in his. 'At the moment that's what I've signed,' he told her, this time making sure he sounded suitably solemn. 'But I talked to him about the future and there's no doubt this isn't just a one-off. A wonderful opportunity, Zina. Not just for my career and a better life for both of us, but think of the kids. What chances it opens for them! All that sunshine. We'll sell up here and have a house high on a hill, a garden with a huge pool. Can't you just see it! Say something, darling. Tell me you're as excited as I am. Just imagine, to be sought after by the great Hermann Zeiglar! Tell me what you really feel.'

'Just at this moment mostly what I feel is relief. Peter, I've been worried, frightened, everything seems to have changed and I was too frightened to look for the reason. Or was it just in my mind? You don't come home nearly as often as you used to in our first years here. Remember, when the children were tiny – and then at the baby school. Here alone in the evenings, I've even imagined you'd fallen for someone beautiful, someone who—'

'And you were right.' With his hand under her chin he seemed to force her to meet his gaze. 'It must have happened about fifteen years ago and

119

I've been in love with her ever since.' His voice was full of gently teasing affection, but from his slightly hesitant expression she could tell that he knew he was pushing the boundaries when he added, 'The trouble is she has another lover, not one made from flesh and blood.'

She let the remark go unanswered as he pulled her to her feet and they stood close in each other's arms, rocking gently as she nestled her face against his neck.

'And what about you?' he whispered, his face rubbing the top of her head. 'Will you come with me to this Brave New World, or do I still have to take second place to that damned instrument?'

This time she knew what her answer had to be. She gave herself no time for second thoughts. 'If that's where your life will be, then so will mine. So will the children's.' She had such a confusion of sensations: relief, thankfulness (surely above all others, thankfulness), excitement, joy, panic and a sense of defeat. Was this what he had always wanted? Perhaps the Hollywood contract hadn't necessarily been part of the equation, but he was to get his own way and she must leave the quintet. For more than three years she had stood her ground, never allowed to forget that in his opinion she was failing the family by chasing her own rainbow, and yet unfailingly being lifted right out of herself into that other world of music. But they had come to a junction and she had no hesitation in acknowledging that, come what may, they must travel the same road.

'But Peter we have to be sensible. We can't

just pack a suitcase and walk away. We have commitments.'

'I feel wildly irresponsible and joyful at the moment, in no mood for digging for commitments. Nothing seems quite real. Filming should be finished in a couple of weeks by which time the kids will be almost at the end of term. Come what may I'm not breaking my promise to Fiona, I mean to see her play, we can't disappoint her and pull her out of school before that.'

'There's more to the evening than the end of term play,' she reminded him. 'There are other items, dancing, a choir, the school orchestra and three solos, one of which will be Tommy's.'

'Yes, I know. It's going to be a long evening, no doubt some good and some pretty hopeless. I hope Tom won't let nerves get the better of him.'

'He has no reason to be nervous; he has a remarkable talent. Have you forgotten that Mr Messer has been talking to him about getting in at one of the foremost music schools, either Manchester or London.' She held her bottom lip between her teeth remembering how the music master had talked to her when she had driven the children back at the end of their last half-term break. Was it fair to uproot him at this stage? Of course plenty of first-rate musicians trained in the States, but Tom was so sure of the way he planned his future here in England.

'If he wants to find somewhere for lessons once we get settled there's no reason why he shouldn't. I expect the schools teach as well there as here. But I wouldn't mind betting that being dropped

121

down somewhere so different, our young Tom will suddenly blossom and find lots of new interests.' He picked up the conversation where he'd put it down. 'We'll have to get the house on the market. You could go and see the estate agent on Monday. Tell the Meinholt lot that you're leaving the country, give the keys to the agent and power of attorney to the solicitor and off we go. Simple.' Then kissing the end of her nose just as she used to see him do to Fiona when a tantrum threatened because she wasn't allowed her own way, he added, 'We'll be on that plane in less than a month.'

His excitement was infectious but she still couldn't escape an underlying feeling of irritation. Perhaps it was because he had brushed Tom's prospects to one side so easily or perhaps because he was being impractical.

'You're a dreamer not a realist. We can't just walk away without tidying up all the odd ends.' Then, her voice softening as she moved her head away from him and looked around her. 'Remember when you first made enough money that we could buy this house? Remember, Peter? Think how thrilled we were when it was filled with workmen making it just as we wanted.'

'I remember it all.' And she knew from his soft voice that, like her, he was journeying back down the years. They were silent, still holding each other but now far enough apart that they were looking around, each conjuring up memories. 'It's full of the spirit of our years.' He was the first to speak. 'The twins taking their first tottering steps, can't you just see them, Fiona staggering ahead and Tommy following trying to catch her – and think of the stories the fireside rug in the sitting room could tell of so many evenings, just us when they were in their cots and asleep. The only light from the log fire; just the two of us. Once you start to think back the memories come tumbling at you. Christmas trees that reached to the ceiling . . . filled stockings to be carried up and exchanged for empty ones . . . Easter egg hunts in the garden . . .' They were silent, following their own paths through the years. When he spoke again she knew he had put the images behind him. 'If another family comes here our spirit will be gone and they'll start with a clean sheet.'

'I hate to imagine another family here. I want it to stay just as it is.' She shared all Peter's enthusiasm, yet something seemed to be holding her back. What had happened to the people they used to be that they could plan to shut the door for the last time on the home that had given them such pride, had been for them a symbol of Peter's success and everything that was good in their marriage.

'Stay just as it is? Is that what you've thought when night after night you've been here alone?' Peter replied.

'Anyway,' she carried on, all her determination now back in place, 'we'll put those same spirits into somewhere new. As long as we are all of us together and the children won't suffer for such a big move at their ages, then it will be fine. When did you promise you could go?'

'I told Hermann I'd fly out during the second

week of August, about six weeks away. Not long, darling. Can't you just picture the kids climbing up those steps into the plane, the world at their feet. Theirs and ours too.'

'I'll tell Derek on Monday. But Peter I can't imagine he'll find a replacement as quickly as you seem to think.'

'Well, dammit, he'll just have to. Or play with one short.' The all-too-familiar pout was back in his voice.

'Don't be ridiculous' was on the tip of her tongue, but somehow she stopped herself saying it. Instead, in a matter-of-fact voice, she replied, 'Well, fingers crossed that he knows of someone, perhaps he's heard someone play – like he did with me, remember? But most players worth their salt are tied up already and, just like I shall, they'll have to give a reasonable notice that they mean to leave.'

'Well, use all your feminine guile. Tell him I'm playing up rough – or better, tell him that I am committed to go and worry about leaving you to face all these odd ends you say we have to tie up.'

No wonder she laughed. Even if he were still to be at home, there was no doubt in her mind who would be the practical one when it came to tying up odd ends.

That morning they talked of very little other than their plans and it was while they were sitting in the garden about to start lunch that Peter's mind came round to Jenny.

'Why did you have a row with Mother-in-law? She doesn't usually interfere in your life,' he said,

124

his concentration seemingly on uncorking a bottle of wine.

'She never interferes. It was the other way round – and I'm not proud of the way I behaved.' He didn't probe, but she found herself telling him anyway.

'Derek Masters, you say? I didn't know she even knew him.'

'She didn't until yesterday, that's what makes it so stupid. Peter, I thought she was making a good life for herself without Dad. But when I warned her off Derek and said he was a confirmed bachelor and probably wanted a bit of temporary fun – it was awful. She was hysterical, saying Dad was the only one who would understand.'

For a moment Peter didn't say anything, concentrating on pouring their wine, then digging into the salad bowl for his favourite snippets, at the same time avoiding lettuce except for one token leaf.

'You know what I think?'

'Something profound,' she teased, 'if your expression is anything to go on. Tell me.'

'It occurs to me that Mother-in-law is due for a bit of pleasure—'

'You think I shouldn't have spoken about it to her? But Peter, don't you see I had to for her own sake. Of course she was having a good time; except for Dad I don't expect a man had paid her the sort of attention that Derek did since before she was married. When she thinks back and remembers what I said she'll make sure she doesn't act like it again. And she's out with him again today – and probably tomorrow if she's found herself a hotel for the night.'

'What Mother-in-law needs is some fun in her life. What about if we take her for an adventure in the great US of A?'

'Yes, of course I hope she'll visit; it would be a lovely break for her. But she is so involved with things in the village and it's not the sort of journey we could ask her to make for less than, say, a month. I'm sure it would make saying goodbye – especially to the children – easier for her if she knew that once we were settled she would be coming to see us. We must talk about it to her, that'll make it less of a wrench for her when we go.'

'I wasn't thinking of a holiday. What about if the whole lot of us pull up sticks and go together. We'll get a place big enough that she can have her own quarters. It would be a new life for her; she'd make new friends. Some of those American women carry their years well, I bet they don't sit at home with their knitting – and she's a very good-looking attractive woman.' Then he added with a teasing twinkle in his eyes, 'Even though you do think she's old enough to know better.'

Did Peter have any idea how often Jenny had been irritated by his flippancy and lack of responsibility, seeing him as behaving like a stupid teenager instead of a grown man? Zina felt her eyes swim with burning tears. 'Hey, hey, it's not such a bad idea as that is it?' he asked.

'It's a wonderful idea. Peter, you really are a very nice man.'

He was enjoying himself. He had never referred

126

to Jenny's unspoken criticism of him, but Zina was sure it hadn't passed unnoticed.

So on that sunny Saturday he and Zina planned for a future, confident that their lives would be as cloudless as that June blue sky. If for her there was sadness that her cherished career, which had started so late, was to be cut short, she made sure she gave no sign of it. Peter was a wonderful success, she told herself, and she was grateful that no matter how he became richer in both fame and wealth nothing would change him. Not usually a man to show his emotions (except on the screen) but what he'd said to her that morning came back to her time and again: '. . . about fifteen years ago I fell in love with her and I've been in love with her ever since.' And she knew that whatever she had to sacrifice she would follow him to the ends of the earth.

The more they discussed their arrangements the clearer it became, even to him, that he would have to go on ahead, for it would be impossible for all those 'odd ends' to be tied up by the second week of August.

On Sunday evening, just as he had so many times over the years, he prepared to set out for the familiar drive back to the country hotel where he lived when he was working. He'd been there for so long that the elderly couple who ran it were used to referring to Room No. Three as 'Peter's room'. Each working morning they would hear him drive away before six o'clock. Neither of them were filmgoers and even though they knew they had an actor under their roof it made him of no more importance than if he'd been a bank clerk or a school master. He was always pleasant, never gave them any trouble nor much work either, for he was out of the place too early for breakfast and more often than not didn't come in until late when he'd order a whisky in the small bar and take it to his room.

Jenny listened to all Zina had to tell her, both of them determinedly avoiding any reference to their last conversation.

'This man came to England with the intention of casting him, you say? My word, that's an accolade. How long will he be in America?'

'I was coming to all that, Mum. And I want you to hear it not just from our point of view but yours too. He wants us all to go, to pull up roots, the children and me, and you too. An adventure, Mum. He says we'll get a house big enough that you have your own space. When he said "and Mother-in-law too" it seemed like providence. It's what you need Mum, a fresh start, new friends.' Then with a chuckle, and coming the nearest either of them had to their stormy telephone conversation, she added, 'No more committee meetings and do-gooding.'

She'd assumed her mother would agree with no hesitation, that she would be glad to put behind her the hold the local community had on her time. But Jenny's expression told her nothing as she said, 'It's kind of him, kinder than I deserve.'

'He didn't look on it as kindness, Mum. He wants us to go as a family.'

'Truly, I'm grateful. I shall write and tell him so. And the thought of being without you all

– the children altering all the time and me not seeing – makes it very tempting to accept. But I am what I am because this is where I belong. My future isn't in a foreign land. I got in a state when we talked on Saturday, Zina, but even so I meant a lot of the things I said. Yes, I resent the call the village has on me, but I'm not proud to admit it. When Richard died I know it was out of kindness I was asked to do things locally – everyone needs to feel they have a purpose, that they are still necessary. That's something that you may not understand now but you will do if ever you are left on your own, which please God you won't be. I suppose that's where one would say my do-gooding has come in. But things are going to be different. It's been in my subconscious for some time, but I know now that you don't have to serve to be necessary. There are people even in this village who never raise a finger for anyone else, but they are necessary because they radiate happiness.' She looked very directly at Zina as she chose her next words. 'I was frightened to look ahead, just filled every day so that I didn't have to think of the future. But now the future is . . . is . . . well, it's changed. Don't say anything; please don't say anything. It's as if a fog has lifted. Zina, can you honestly see me living amongst the glamour of Hollywood. I'd love, yes really love, to be with you, but Devon is where I belong.'

Zina wanted to know how much Derek had to do with this sudden vision for the future, but she couldn't mention his name for fear of stirring the embers of their telephone argument.

'Think about it, Mum. It's come to you from out of the blue, so sleep on it for a while. I have to go to the agent in Exeter and then I shall drive on to see Derek. It's only fair to tell him straight away.'

'He did mention that he was going to be out all day today, though.' She said it pleasantly just as if Derek Masters were an old family friend. 'That was such a kind thought of Peter's, I shall write to that hotel he stays at straight away. And now that I've made a decision to do less of the local stuff – all these silly societies which to be frank hold no interest for me – as soon as you get settled I'll come a-visiting.'

And so they laid the ghost of that telephone conversation and, at least superficially, parted on their usual note of affection. Yet before Zina got a mile out of the village she passed Derek driving in the opposite direction.

Five

At the prospect of the move there was no holding Fiona's excitement. She read the film magazines even more avidly than she had before, imagining herself as part of a world of glamour far in excess of anything she was likely to encounter even if they found the hilltop home her parents talked about. The truth was that none of them had more than a fanciful idea of life in Beverly Hills. All four of them created images of what they expected to find, each one viewing the future from a different angle. In Fiona's mind were pictures of long, powerful, open-topped cars, glamorous women and handsome men, sunshine, visits to their home by the famous, people who up until that time had seemed to her to occupy a planet removed from mere mortals. Tom said very little. He dreaded looking towards a future where he saw the end of the dreams which for months had filled his mind. The one person who understood his unspoken fears was Zina and, if she were honest and dropped her new-found determination that she would sacrifice anything out of thankfulness that she and Peter had found their way back to each other, her own thoughts weren't so very different from Tom's. Peter took it for granted that they all shared his opinion: they were on the brink of sharing a new adventure. The flippancy, which was so often a part of Peter's conversation and annoyed Jenny, gave no hint of his deep love for his profession or his intense determination which, together with natural talent, had brought him to the present stage of his career. For him, Hollywood represented a new and taller ladder to climb and he approached it with a will to succeed.

The house was on the market, but although the agent had brought one couple of would-be buyers, a look of hope on his face when he considered how much he would make from this sort of sale, it remained unsold. The couple had moved on and finally decided on a four-bedroom house with a small garden in Myddlesham for a quarter of the price. Ernest Harding, the agent, suspected they had probably only shown an interest in Newton House because they'd heard it belonged to Peter Marchand. The truth was that a property like that was unlikely to attract a local purchaser. He would have to advertise it further afield, put a picture of it in the national property magazines, but it was easier to sell half a dozen smaller run-of-the-mill houses than an old Georgian mansion in all that ground and sitting in the middle of nowhere. It had stood empty for longer than he cared to remember before the Marchands took it and had so much work done. Before that it had struck him as cold as a tomb, and although it was much more comfortable now, it must cost a mint to run. In his opinion it needed another film star, or someone who'd won the football pools, someone with 'new money' like the Marchands must have had when they bought it.

By the time the children were collected for their

long summer holiday, work had already started on sorting out anything they wouldn't take with them to California. Peter had rarely been seen to work with such enthusiasm in the house; nor Fiona either. Each day they filled either the boot of the Volvo or the back seat of his sports car and went to deliver their contribution to one of the various forthcoming summer fêtes where there would be appropriate stalls. At this season of the year it was in Deremouth they found the best outlet for outgrown clothes, toys, children's books and general bric-a-brac and were received with open arms by the RNLI in their never-ending challenge to finance the lifeboat service, something for which holidaymakers gladly opened their purses. Nearer to home though, they didn't forget the weekly stall working to pay for repairs to the church clock in Myddlesham. When they'd unloaded their one-time treasures and been thanked, Fiona couldn't stop herself telling any voluntary helpers she hadn't seen on earlier trips about why they were sorting out their things and how soon they would be moving to live in America. It was a thrill just to hear herself saying it.

By that time there was no escaping the fact that Peter would be travelling alone.

'I don't see why we can't all go, Mum, it'd be horrid for him to set off all by himself,' Fiona said as she and Zina were going through the bookshelf in what was known as the den. 'And he won't have nearly such a good time looking for a house if we aren't there with him. If you wait for someone to come and buy this one, we

133

might be here for ages, perhaps even by Christmas we won't be gone. I wanted to get there and get into school and all that.'

'Well, it's no good grizzling to me about it,' said Zina, not even attempting to hide her impatience. 'Anyway, you might try and think of Tom. If we all rushed away as if we just turned our backs on everything, what about the grades he's been working so hard for?'

'Once he gets out there I bet he'll do other things. And anyway he plays the piano jolly well now and I expect the fiddle too. I don't mean to sound nasty to you, Mum, but the fiddle won't be that much fun for him later. It's always good to find someone who can play the piano at parties and things. Anyway, it'll be different out there, you can see it will from the movies. He may learn to ride a horse or to sail or something. He's quite brave.'

'If he'd wanted to do those sort of things he could have done them here. Fiona, he loves music and you love acting.' She remembered Tom's giggle when she'd talked of them 'prancing about on the stage'. 'So how would you feel if I'd been given some wonderful chance to play in Russia or Italy or somewhere and we all had to pack up sticks and go. He might have found what he wanted amongst the people who loved that kind of music, but for you it would have been very different.' Then, taking herself firmly in hand, she continued, 'It's fine to rush headlong at something that's not going to last, but this is a big move. You've lived in this house as long as you can remember. When we go we shall all be sad to leave it. It may be that, although we shall come back on holiday, we shall never live in England again. We can't just turn our backs and walk away.'

'Well, anyway—' Fiona meant to have the last word – 'it's still rotten for Dad to go on his own.'

Neither of them had noticed Peter standing outside the open doorway of the room where Fiona's words added support to an idea that had been prodding at the back if his mind. But in un-Peter-like fashion he said nothing, sensing the moment wasn't right.

'That's enough for this load, I'm taking the Volvo into Exeter. How about leaving the kids to make a start on their own stuff out in the sheds while you and I go, Zee?' The way he said it and the use of the 'Zee' which was almost an endearment tipped the scales just as he meant them to. This was important. In only a few days he would be gone and the more he imagined putting his plan into action, the more eager he was to talk to her out of hearing of the twins.

They'd hardly turned out of the gate when he could wait no longer.

'What do you think of this for a good plan? Don't say anything, just hear me out before you jump in. There's sound common sense in it. At the kids' age we want as little upheaval for them as we can manage and it seems to me that we ought to aim to get them into their new school at the beginning of a term rather than have them arrive when everyone else is settled into an annual syllabus.'

'Of course I agree with you. Ideally that's what

we could have done, but as things stand there's nothing for it but to send them back to St Mary's until I can bring them over.'

Peter threw a brief glance in her direction, but not so brief that she couldn't recognize his suppressed excitement.

'That's no good for them. They aren't babies; they are old enough to want to be involved in a move as important as this, not pushed around like items of luggage. *I* think – and I'm sure you will too if you look on it from their point of view – yes I *honestly* think that when I fly out next week they ought to come with me.'

Her first reaction was disbelief that he could have suggested anything so ridiculous. How could he take two children to a strange country and expect to leave them alone while his own days would be full? It was probably as well Jenny hadn't been a fly on the windscreen listening to the conversation! Hadn't she always known he had no sense of responsibility?

'Whenever did you have that brainstorm? As if you could arrive out there, book into a hotel and then leave them to their own devices while you familiarize yourself with your work!'

'It wouldn't be like that. Honestly Zina, there is logic in it. It was Heila who suggested it – Heila Zeiglar. I had a call from Hermann just a while before we came out, that's why I suggested you should come with me into town so that we could talk about it. Not like us, the Zeiglars were late-starters and their two youngsters are about the same age as Fiona and Tom. She says why don't the three of us move in with them while

136

you see to all these odd ends you say we have to sort out.'

'The most important thing we have to do, forgetting who travels when,' she said in a voice that told him she didn't think the suggestion deserved consideration, 'is to make sure we get to the solicitor to sign that power of attorney so that my signature alone will always be sufficient. You haven't even called them back to find out about the appointment.'

'OK, OK, we'll look in while we're in town. Leave it to me, I'll persuade the girl on reception to slip us in between appointments,' he said, briefly turning to look at her with that laughing twinkle in his eyes that seldom failed him. Then more seriously, he added, 'But about the kids, don't you see that if they stay with Hermann's two they'll have ready-made companions. They can start school with them when the time comes.'

She could picture it all so clearly, just as she could picture herself watching while the agent brought people to look around the house, opening cupboards, standing by the windows deciding if they liked the far views from the back of the building, whispering to each other, making her feel an outsider in her own home. And then driving away to be heard of no more, while she was left to wait for the next batch to be brought and the next after that, each looking at beloved Newton House with a critical eye, trying to find faults that would give leverage on the price if, indeed, they were interested enough to go that far.

'Talk about treating them like luggage!' she

137

snapped, trying to disguise her own feeling of emptiness. All of them would be gone, only she would be there to watch the breaking up of their home, see the furniture carried away, furniture they had chosen with pride and loved for all the years they'd been there. She wouldn't let herself consider that in any case the children would be back at St Mary's long before that was likely to happen so inevitably she would be on her own. But they would be there on the other end of the telephone. They would be only a few miles away and not far beyond all the miles of a great ocean and continent.

She imagined her final days of being at Newton House. She could almost hear the heavy tread of the removal men as they carried each item out to be taken to the salerooms. Was this progress? Was this the fulfilment of Peter's ambition? She thought of their long-ago excitement as they'd attended house sales, buying the pieces that had fitted so well into Newton House. For them it had been the beginning of the realization of their dreams. The only new furniture they had bought had been for the twins when they had been given separate rooms; down the stairs those two identical suites would be carried, out of the house and out of their lives. Then would come everything from their own bedroom, surely the backdrop for the very core of their union. The beautiful genuine Georgian furniture would be carried from the dining room, and from the kitchen the board where she used to pin the artistic offerings from the baby school. All of it would be loaded in the waiting vans. Her expression gave nothing away, she mustn't allow anyone, least of all Peter, to guess how she dreaded the coming weeks or more likely months. Once the house was empty, her footsteps would echo as she walked from room to room for the last time, she alone would go through the heavy front door and close it on all their years.

'They'd be much better coming with me.' Peter was speaking seriously. 'Imagine what it would be like for them back at school here, not knowing how long before they got uprooted. Zina, if there's a good alternative we ought to take it. They may think themselves almost grown up but the truth is they are only children and more than anything what they need is security. Coming with me would lift them right out of the sale of the house, the disruption of everything they've known. Don't you think we owe it to them to accept Heila's offer? Boarding school is no place for them while their home is being torn apart.' She knew what she ought to say, but the idea was too new to her. 'Say something, Zee. This is the beginning of the rest of our lives; we've got to do it as smoothly as we can, not add more heartache than there is bound to be anyway. Imagine when their summer holiday ends, think how they'd feel being driven away knowing things would never be the same. If they come with me they won't have a chance to be miserable, they'll be starting out on the adventure.'

'Bully for you!' she growled.

Taking his hand off the steering wheel he reached to take hold of hers.

'Truly, truly I'm sorry darling that you're not

coming right from the beginning. How about I phone you every day? Will that help? But about the kids, don't you see the logic?'

'Yes I do. I do because I know what the upheaval will be whether it's when they're at home or when they're at school. I can see it's much kinder for them to have a quick move from one life to the other.' Then after a brief pause and using all the courage she could muster, she finally said, 'All right, I agree for them to fly with you. But on one condition: we don't just give it to them, cut and dried. You can talk to them; you know the Zeiglars, I don't. Then, Peter, it has to be for them to make their own decision. I don't want them to feel forced out of the nest before the nest gets thrown out of the tree.'

'Good girl. Oh hell, Zina, why couldn't it have worked out so that we could have all set off together. I wish things would get moving. I can't imagine anyone not wanting our house.' His hand was still holding hers, and now she raised it to hold it against her lips.

It was nearly two hours later, the solicitor been seen and the forms signed just as Peter had anticipated, the boxes of toys and piles of clothes handed in to a shop in aid of Dr Barnardo's Home, when with his usual squeal of brakes Peter drew to a halt at the front door of Newton House.

The music room window was open and they could hear the sound of the piano. It might be said that Tom was doing his practice, but that was only half of it. Tom had been playing for most of the time they had been out, not because

140

it was his daily time for practice but because it was a pleasure. In fact he would have been surprised to learn how long he'd been up there and it was lucky that Fiona had been happily reading aloud from a book of plays she'd found on a shelf, casting herself in the lead role but changing her voice to suit each character. For her too the time had slipped by unnoticed.

'It sounds as though there's a visitor,' Peter said, glancing towards the window of the music room.

'If you took a little more interest you would know without having to be told. That's Tom playing.' They both stood still, listening. 'Now perhaps you can understand why Maurice Messer has been hopeful of Tom being accepted into the music school. He works hard, and loves every moment of it. That's a rare thing for children, the average have to be chased off to do their practice each day, but not Tom. It's study and recreation rolled into one. He started late by professional standards and have we the right now to take him away from something that is so important to him?'

'The United States has plenty of fine orchestras, and I promise you if it means so much to the kid we'll find him a teacher even if he can't learn at school. But from where I stand I wouldn't mind betting if he never has another lesson he's learnt enough to play and enjoy it.' Then he added with a teasing half wink, 'If you like that kind of music.'

Looking up at the open window and listening to her beloved Tom, Zina found nothing to smile about in the remark.

141

It was after a quick and cold lunch that she told the twins. 'Your father has a proposition to put to you. But before he does, I want you both to understand that neither of us is going to persuade you one way or the other. You must be free to make the choice.' Quite naturally she said 'choice' not 'choices', sure that whatever they decided nothing would separate them. 'You don't have to give an answer straight away, you can go off and talk about it together first.'

So Peter put the suggestion to them exactly as earlier on he had to Zina, confident of what their answer would be. Tom's expression told him nothing, and Fiona's everything.

'Think about it,' Zina started, 'go and talk by yourselves if you want to. If you decide you like th—'

'But of course we do, Mum,' Fiona interrupted. 'Gosh, just think, we shan't have to waste our time going back to school here, instead it won't be just you, Dad, who has the excitement. Except for poor old Mum, we shall all be on our way. And fancy us actually going to live in a house belonging to *Hermann Zeiglar*.' Then, with an excited giggle that refused to be held back, she said, 'I wish we'd known before we broke up. Would have been lovely to have told everyone. Still, never mind. We shan't see any of that lot any more. Gosh, Tom, can you believe it?'

Peter was watching her with an indulgent smile. But Zina was watching Tom, who sat silently and avoided looking directly at any of them.

'Well, that's one travelling companion for you, Peter. And how about you, Tom?' Zina

142

prompted him. 'I expect you want time to think about it.'

At that, Fiona looked at her in genuine surprise. 'Of course we'll go together.' Her tone telling them that she was amazed her mother could be questioning it. 'I expect they want to hear you say it, Tom. Tell them and keep them happy,' she ended with a giggle which was no more than an expression of her excitement.

'I'll wait till Mum comes.' His words weren't as clear as he meant them to be, but it's hard to talk when you have to bite hard on the corners of your mouth to keep it from wobbling.

'Don't be daft.' Fiona was used to taking the lead and she knew Tom well enough to realize he would find it hard to let his head rule his heart. 'That might not be for ages. Gran says that even when that agent finds a family who want to buy the house it still takes ever so long. Not like buying a bag of sugar, that's what she said.'

It was unusual for Tom to glare at his twin as he did now, but anger was easier to cope with than the misery that threatened to overwhelm him.

'I'm not going to clear off and leave Mum.' Then misery getting the upper hand, as he added, 'I don't see what we have to go at all for. We were all right here. We liked it, didn't we? All of us?' He closed his eyes as if that way he could hold back the tears. He was thirteen years old; he mustn't let them know how hard it was not to cry.

'Every day of it, old chap,' Peter answered, his perception surprising Zina. 'But we blokes sometimes don't have much choice once we have a career and a family to be responsible for. A few more years and you'll find that out for yourself. But if you stay back and come out with your mother that will take a weight off my mind.'

Zina's expression told him more than any words.

'But Dad, that's stupid.' Even if they hadn't been able to see the scowl on Fiona's face they would have heard it in her voice. 'He won't even be *here*, he'll be back at St Mary's only a few weeks after you and I go.' Then to Tom: 'What help do you think it will be to Mum once you go back to school?'

But the argument had put mettle back into Tom and his voice was as clear and strong as hers as he answered, 'I shall be in the same country, we can talk on the phone because it will be the same time of day for both of us. You'll be hours and hours behind, so many hours that it . . . it . . . sort of puts you out of reach.'

Between the twins the argument went on as they went outside to start sorting their things in the shed. And that's where they were when the phone rang.

'Call him in, Peter. Let's tell him.'

'It's not like you, my love, to rush headlong without thought.' And in that Peter was right. Usually it was she who lived with one foot hovering over the brake.

'This is different. Peter, this is the chance he has dreamed of, a chance I would have dreamed of at his age so I understand just how he feels.

144

Didn't you see at lunch just how upset he was? He clung to the thought that he wants to stay behind on my account, but that's only because he must have been frightened to tempt fate by letting himself imagine anything as wonderful as *this*. When Mr Messer took him for an interview, he said – Maurice Messer said, I mean – how well everything had gone and how well he had played. I knew he was hopeful but then there must be dozens of young hopefuls out there, some will be accepted and some won't. I could hardly get a word out of Tommy about it and would have thought it had been a flop if Maurice Messer hadn't said how well he had played.'

'Should we be glad or sorry, though? Staying behind to travel with you is one thing, this is quite another. I'd worry less if it were Fiona, although God perish the thought. But Tom – well, can you imagine him? Surrounded by strangers, all of us thousands of miles away. Damn it, Zee, wouldn't it be kinder to refuse the place?'

'It would be unforgivable.'

And so together they went out to the shed, where the twins were sorting the long forgotten treasures of their early childhood.

'Mind you don't break that, you great lump,' they heard Tom say as they came within earshot, 'some little kid will like it.' They saw that he was sorting out old shrimping nets which ought to have been thrown away years ago, while Fiona was on a wooden rocking horse they'd shared in their early years.

'Take care of your hands, Tommy,' Zina called

as their shadow fell across the two inside, 'they belong to a great musician of the future.'

He looked up from what he was doing, his mouth felt suddenly dry. Was she just pulling his leg or was she telling him that they'd heard he had a place? He seemed to have lost the ability to speak.

'Mr Messer phoned.' Peter put him out of his misery. 'It seems you impressed them very favourably at the college so they are offering you a place.'

Fiona was looking from one to the other, suddenly frightened. Before they had known anything about going to California she had accepted that if Tom were offered a place at the music school it would mean his leaving St Mary's. But this was something quite different; he wouldn't even be coming with them to their new Hollywood home. Not for the first time she hated the hold his music had on him. All the time they'd been at St Mary's it had always come before anything else, but she had been sure that once they were away from wretched Mr Messer, as she thought of Tom's champion, he would be hers just like he used to be.

'But that's no good now, Tom.' Stripped of any chance of hiding her fear, Fiona stood up from the horse and tried to will Tom to meet her gaze. All her life she had been able to bend his will to her own and never had it been more important than this. 'We're not going to be living in England any longer, so you'll have to turn it down.'

All Tom seemed capable of saying was 'Gosh . . . gosh . . .'

'This must be your own decision, Tom,' Peter said in a man-to-man voice. 'As Fiona says, it will mean you are left behind when it's time for your mother to join us in California. No chance to get home for half-term breaks or occasional weekends. There must be other students from overseas, so I assume someone would see you through the airport when you came for holidays.'

Listening to Peter, the reality hit Zina. If only this idea of all moving to America hadn't happened! It wasn't the first time she had thought it; it was an unacknowledged background to her mind much of each day. Packing up their old items to distribute amongst the fundraisers of one sort or another brought back so many memories. Yet to look ahead, what was there? She pulled her mind back to Tom and went into the shed where he seemed incapable of saying anything other than his original 'gosh . . . gosh'. Hugging him she spoke softly, just to him, and remembering what he'd said about music being something the two of them shared.

'You're doing so well, Tom. So proud of you.'

Her words helped him marshal his wits.

'Dad, you won't mind if I don't come with you? It's not that I didn't see it as a great chance and all that, but, gosh, I've been frightened even to let myself start to imagine I'd actually get a place.'

'Your mother will tell you that what you two get up to isn't my scene. But, Tom, I'm proud, yes, I'm extremely proud. You've worked hard and you deserve your place.'

For Tom that was too much. Praise from his mother he could take just as he could from Mr Messer, they were knowledgeably assessing his progress, but he'd never expected to hear it from his father. He took from his pocket a handkerchief that was evidence he had been taking the dirt off an old bicycle, then turned away from them on the pretext of blowing his nose while he managed to rub his eyes at the same time, hoping no one noticed.

'I bet there are places just the same in America,' Fiona said. 'If there aren't, how do you think they train people?'

No one answered her directly, but after a pause Peter held his hand in her direction as he said, 'Well, young lady, it seems that you and I have to do the honours for the Marchand family in the New World. Think we can manage?'

'You bet we can, Dad. They'll wonder what's hit them. And we have to find a house too. It'll be up to us to choose it.' Fiona was ready to move on.

'I'll go and phone Gran, shall I? She'll be chuffed as anything.' Tom's effort at clearing out the shed was short-lived. 'And I bet she'll be glad one of us won't be going to America. She's never said but she must be awfully sad that we're shifting off. With us gone from here she'll be all by herself. I could go to her if I get weekends or short times off, couldn't I? She'd like that.' But when he dialled her number, even though he let the phone ring for ages in case she was in the garden, there was no reply.

Later in the afternoon, when he considered

she'd had time to get home even if she'd been as far as Exeter, he decided to cycle to Myddlesham to tell his news in person.

'She may be somewhere for the whole day,' Zina warned him, trying not to imagine where that day might be spent.

'Don't worry. If she hasn't got home I'll put a note through the door. You know me, Mum, always a man for belt and braces, just in case. So I've got a piece of paper and a biro in my pocket.'

The miles between the two houses were soon covered, spurred on as he was by the message he was taking. But some of his anticipation ebbed when he saw a car in the drive of her house. He hadn't considered there might be a visitor. When she didn't answer the front door he walked down the side path to find her in the garden.

But surely he knew that man, or at any rate he knew him by sight. He was the one who played the piano in Mum's quintet, he'd seen him once when he'd gone with Gran to a recital. But why would he come here?

'Hello, Gran,' he called. 'I cycled over to tell you something.' And from the way he said it she guessed the news he'd brought. Until he had interrupted, she and the man had been sitting at the garden table, the remains of what must have been tea in front of them. But on hearing what Tom said, she jumped up, whispered something to her visitor whose instant reaction was as spontaneous as hers, then they both came towards him, their expressions making him feel ten foot tall.

'You've been accepted?' she called, unable to contain her excitement until she reached him.

If he'd passed an academic exam, no matter what, even though she would have spoken the same words of praise, they all knew this was different. This was music; his young success and his outlook for the future seemed to carry her back down the years to the heady days when Zina left college with such great hopes for her future. But Tom wouldn't throw everything up and get married. When he married he would be even more inspired to climb to the heights in his career.

'Pop indoors and get yourself a cup and saucer – and a plate,' Jenny told him, delighted to see him with a chance to get to know Derek Masters. 'There are cakes to be eaten up. We'll talk some more all about it. If the others are in America you know you can always come to me for breaks too short to go over there. Oh, what fun it's all going to be!' Tom loved to hear her talk in that excited way; he had been sure that would be her reaction. He hurried off to collect his crockery, eager to join them, feeling himself to be well on the way to belonging to the world of established musicians. It really had the atmosphere of a party and how good it was that her visitor was Mr Masters.

'We were having a sort of lunch cum tea picnic,' Jenny told him when he came back with his crockery. 'You can fetch another garden chair or you can sit on the grass, it's quite dry.'

'I'll fetch a chair, Gran. If I'm down there on the grass I can't see what there is to eat and those cream doughnuts look good.'

'Sorry we've eaten all the ham salad, you'll have to make up on cakes.'

Derek Masters was watching him, his quick smile in Jenny's direction telling her that he liked what he saw. That this was the grandson she had talked of with such pride fitted into the picture he had formed in his imagination. Of course he knew Zina, but only as a member of the quintet, never really on a personal basis. There was something reserved about her that told him she wouldn't welcome the relationship that had developed between himself and Jenny over these summer weeks. A man who'd been a loner for more than thirty years, he had the strangest feeling that today destiny had brought the three of them together for a purpose.

Once the last of the cakes had disappeared and the teapot run dry, Jenny stacked the tray, Tom carried it to the kitchen and Derek went through the open French doors to the drawing room. It did strike Tom as an odd thing for a casual acquaintance to do, but when he heard the first chords from the piano he forgot to be puzzled.

'You go and join Derek,' Jenny told him, 'he's calling you to the piano. A pity you haven't your fiddle here.'

But before she had the crockery washed up and the kitchen clear she could hear they were playing a duet. How proud she felt. Always darling Tommy had been the shadow following Fiona, but even in this one day, now that he knew his future was settled, she could see a difference in him. And what a tale to tell them when he got home and said that he had played with Derek

151

Masters. What a tale indeed, she added silently and with a worried frown as she thought of the things Zina had said. Well, let her think what she liked. It was a long time since she had felt so free, so much herself, as she had over these summer weeks. Was he such a confirmed bachelor that he didn't even suspect the longing that being with him stirred in her? As if in self-protection she took her handbag from where she'd dropped it on the hall table when they'd come in and retouched her make-up. Then with one last quick glance in the mirror she went to join the others, going into the room quietly and sitting down believing she hadn't been noticed.

'Will you play something, sir? Please?' Tom asked as the duet ended, speaking as he might to Mr Messer at school, the 'sir' coming quite naturally.

'And then you must go, Tom,' Jenny reminded him, 'you've a long ride ahead of you and they'll think something is wrong if you're not home before dark.'

But the evening had about it a touch of magic, at least Tom knew that it did for him, and time slipped by until it was Derek who said he had some rope in the boot of the car and if they tied the bike on he could still get Tom home before the last of the daylight faded.

And so ended an evening which Tom felt he would never forget – in all probability an evening he *did* never forget, the end of a day which had lifted him from childhood to adolescence and in Derek Masters given him a role model to emulate. Derek refused his invitation to come into the house, saying it was time he was on his way, so at the end of the drive of Newton House they untied the rope and lifted the bicycle to the ground.

'Thank you for bringing me, and thank you for . . . for . . . the music and letting me play with you.'

'Give it all that you are, Tom, and in a few years it will be me who will be thanking you.'

Jenny was watching from the window. He hadn't actually said that he would come back once he'd taken Tom home, but neither had he said goodbye or made arrangements for when they would see each other again. Please make him come. It has been such a specially wonderful day, this morning listening to an organ recital in the cathedral then, on the way back, stopping at that old inn and sitting outside in the sunshine, simply idling the time away with comfortable conversation. Make him come back; please make him want to be here as much as I want him. Yes, yes, that's his car, but he's coming from the wrong direction. Why would he have gone into the village at this time of evening when the shops are closed? He'll see I've left the double gate open. She cared nothing for prying neighbours, although in fact there was no one about to see him turn in at the gate, or Jenny as she came out to meet him. When he got out of the car she saw the reason for his trip to the village. In his hand he had a bottle of champagne. Her heart seemed to miss a beat.

'I thought that delightful grandson of yours needed us to drink a toast to his future,' was his explanation as he followed her back into the house and through to the drawing room where the French doors were still open even though by now dusk was turning to darkness. 'He tells me he didn't start lessons until he went to that boarding school. It's remarkable what he's done in the time – and seemingly on two instruments. Yes, I see his as a future to be watched, especially now that he's to get first-class training.'

She tried not to let him guess what her first reaction had been when she saw the champagne.

'I don't know how he'll feel when the others go and he's left behind. He's not quite the man he feels himself to be today.'

'He'll have you, dear Jenny.'

'A grandmother. He and Fiona have always been so close. He needs youth.'

'Youth is relative.' Derek was looking at her in a way that defied her turning away. 'What would the young think if they knew what knowing you has done to me? Probably laugh at me, at both of us. Do you know what I'm saying?'

She reached towards him and raised her hands to rest on his shoulders.

'I know what I hope you're saying.'

'For more than thirty-five years I've not let myself even think about sharing my life with anyone. I'm human. I've wanted, yearned, for someone to love. Sometimes I've despaired at the hopelessness.'

'I don't understand. You say you've never thought of sharing your life and yet you've yearned for someone to love.'

'Jenny, you and I could make a full and happy life together. I'm right, aren't I? These last weeks since we've been so much together I've known a sort of inner happiness I hadn't believed possible.'

She moved closer to him, raising her face. Her heart was pounding, her legs and arms left weak as she pulled his head nearer, her mouth slightly open as it sought his.

Whatever his good intentions had been, they were lost as, with the pent-up emotion of years, he kissed her.

'No! No. I can't. Oh God, Jenny, why have I let it happen?' He pulled himself back from her yet he hadn't the strength of will to move right away. 'More than anything in this world I want you for my wife—'

'Yes, oh yes,' she breathed.

'I can't marry you. All these years I've known I can't marry. Jenny, I ought not to have let this happen. I have a wife.'

She felt stunned. Whatever she had expected him to tell her, it wasn't that he was married. 'But . . . but . . . are you separated?' It didn't occur to her that he might have a wife at home and all these weeks had been philandering with her.

'Not in the way you mean. I'll tell you the whole story. I'm not proud that I let this happen, God knows the last thing I want is that you are hurt. You are dearer to me than anything in this life.'

'Then nothing else matters. Whatever you are going to tell me can make no difference. If you

155

love your wife, then go home to her. But if it isn't as marriage should be, a true bonding of two spirits, then nothing you tell me can come between us.'

He drew her to the sofa so that they sat side by side.

'Eva and I met just as I was leaving college. It was at a party; mostly my fellow students but someone brought her as a guest. There was a lot of music – and she sang in the purest soprano I had ever heard.' He was talking with his eyes shut and Jenny knew memory was carrying him back. 'A glorious voice. At twenty-one I fell in love. She haunted my every thought. Emotionally it was the same for both of us. My parents were against our marrying. The usual reasons: too young, I'd only just trained for a career, had no hope of keeping a wife etc. Her father wasn't happy with the idea either, but he didn't oppose it as mine did; she had no mother. She was already twenty-one and we got married despite all the objections. I expect they were right and we were too inexperienced, but the first few months we were in seventh heaven. Then she was pregnant and everything changed. Physically she wasn't ill, but she changed. It was as if she was full of fear; not just about the coming baby but fear of life, fear she couldn't control. She couldn't sleep and the doctor gave her some sort of tablets. One day I came into the room to find she had the whole bottle of them tipped into her hand and one by one she was taking them. I was terrified. I didn't know how many she'd taken. I doubt if she knew either. She had just one goal, to finish her life. I got the rest of them away from her and forced my finger down her throat. She struggled, screamed, sobbed, fought, all the time retching as I moved my finger to the back of her throat. At last, thank God, she was dreadfully sick. It was a nightmare that haunts me until this day. That night she lost the baby. At the time that seemed like a tragedy, but I know now it was a mercy. I was earning a meagre living from recitals and supplementing it by teaching, often having to leave her on her own, but always she was on my mind. I knew she shouldn't have been left by herself. Then about a month or so after the sleeping pill incident I came home to find her unconscious, a knife by her side and her wrist slashed. There was blood everywhere. She was deathly white but I knew she still lived, for the deep gash on her wrist was still bleeding. That was the end, Jenny. We were given no choice. The ambulance carried her away but there could be no bringing her back. After the incident with the sleeping pills and losing the child, she had seemed to recover, sometimes even to be her normal self. But this time was different. In the hospital she had to be restrained, all she wanted was to escape from a life that terrified her. She was transferred to a psychiatric hospital. To this day that's where she is. In the first year or so when I visited her I liked to think she knew me, I even tried to make myself believe that she would recover and come home. But that was thirty-five years ago. She knows no one, not even the nurses who attend her every day, feed her, bathe her, care for her like a young baby. Hope died a long time ago. In these circumstances I know I could have divorced her but such a thing never entered my head. My career became my whole life. Jenny.'

Derek's eyes were open now as he turned towards her and gripped both her hands. 'Can you understand why it is I can't do it? She wouldn't even know. But I can't.' Jenny saw his eyes redden as they filled with the burning tears he blinked away. 'I think of us as we were, so full of hope and confidence – and I can't do it to her. She had no control over what her life was to become, hers and so mine too. Only later I heard that her mother went the same way, and her aunt. So perhaps I should thank God there was no child. But if I'd been told when I first fell in love with her, it would have made no difference. I would never have believed it could happen to Eva.'

'Life can be so cruel,' Jenny whispered, imagining the agony Eva must have endured in those early months of marriage when she had suspected the first signs of what was happening to her and been terrified of what was ahead. Moving her fingers gently against Derek's, Jenny suddenly remembered the day he'd come to her rescue at the petrol pump, how she had silently scorned him for the care he'd taken of his hands. Then he had been a stranger. Who would have believed how over these summer months he could have come to fill her life?

'Poor, poor, Eva,' she said softly, 'and you too, Derek. Of course you can't do it to her. It makes no difference that she wouldn't realize – *you* would and *I* would and it would cast a cloud.' She sat a little straighter as if that would add emphasis to what she was going to say as she turned to look directly at him. It even surprised her that she could take the step she proposed and have no sense of wrongdoing. She was nearing sixty years old, her code of morals rooted deeply in her since childhood. And yet she felt no wrong. 'Derek, Eva will be your wife as long as she lives. The young husband you were all those years ago will always belong to the Eva you married and surely somewhere, deep in her soul, that young girl still belongs to you and always will. And, for me, nothing will ever take away anything I felt for Richard, felt and feel still and always will. But our lives should be more than "yesterday", there's today and tomorrow. You and I can't be man and wife with a certificate to prove it; but nothing we share in the future, nothing we feel for each other, can cast a cloud on the love you and Eva shared. Neither can it touch the love I had, and shall always have, for Richard. But what of the rest of our lives? Do you really care if people see us as immoral?' Then with a chuckle that took years from her, she added, 'For myself, I don't give a jot.' She tried not to think of Zina as she said it.

'What are you saying? Jenny, I want us to be together for the rest of our lives, not just a few hours of each day, but everything, all that we are. Are you saying that even though we can't marry, our lives can still be bound? Are you willing to flout convention and live with a man who isn't your lawful husband?'

Jenny felt utterly carefree as she nodded and said, with the chuckle he found so endearing, 'My grandad used to say—' and she took on what she considered a manly voice – '"the law's an arse" and as for local gossips, well, who cares? If I were young enough to give you children I might change my name to yours for their sake, but we have no one but ourselves to consider. What we bring to each other is very different from that first experience. Perhaps it's richer, deeper, based on a foundation of experience.'

'No young swain ever felt more desire than I do for you, Jenny. For so long I've tried to deny every natural urge or need, but . . .' He drew her close against him, as he said, 'You haunt me. Never in my life have I craved love, whole and complete love, as I do from you.'

Her answer was to move her mouth against his and, knowing exactly what she did and why she did it, let the tip of her tongue gently explore.

Pulling her head back a little, she whispered, 'Stay with me. Tonight. We have the rest of our lives, but first don't leave me tonight.' Then, suddenly fearful of losing the wonder of loving, of letting it be swamped by all he'd told her, she added with a laugh hiding behind her words, 'We've no need to wait three weeks for the banns to be called.'

A reliable and unchanging mother and grand-mother, that may have been as the family thought of her, but she had had a happy and full marriage. When Richard had died, with her heart and mind she had missed the companionship, the sharing of jokes, of music, of their home and garden, while with her heart and body she craved the love that no amount of filling her days with good works or outside interests had lessened. In the loneliness of night her body ached for love. And tonight she and Derek would find that miracle together.

Suddenly she stood up and walked to the open French doors looking up at the night sky. Then she turned and held her hand for him to join her. Together they walked out into the summer night.

'This is where we make our vows, under God's starry sky. And I do, solemnly and with all my heart I swear before God that I will be as a wife to you and love you all the days of my life.'

He was almost afraid to trust his voice. He spoke softly, his gaze on that summer night sky as he made his vows. 'I vow before God that I will love you faithfully and with all that I am until my life's end – and then, please God, beyond.'

There was no passion in the kiss they exchanged, rather a reverence as if they were surrounded by a mystique beyond worldly understanding. Then, without a word they went back inside, and while she closed the French doors he uncorked the champagne.

The next day she would have to tell Zina, but on that night she was ready to leave tomorrow to take care of itself.

Six

At Newton House Peter had decided that this morning they would attack the attic rooms where it had been all too easy to accumulate things which might just as well have been dispensed with right from the start. In such a large house, and especially after the first year or so of marriage when Peter and Zina had had to learn the lesson of thrift, they had often fallen for the temptation of dumping anything 'that might come in handy one day' at the top of the house.

'Come on, kids, there's work to be done,' he said as he stood up from the breakfast table. 'I've got a whole lot of bin liners.'

'I'll come up and say goodbye before I head off to Derek's, but first I'll just give Mum a call,' Zina told them, but the twins were already halfway up the stairs, sure that there must be interesting treasures to be discovered. Zina smiled as she watched Peter follow after them, a roll of bin liners in his hand; this sorting out bug seemed to have bitten him. And yet she knew without a doubt that he had always loved the house as much as she had herself. However, today she wouldn't think about the house or the move, for the quintet had arranged to meet at midday in Derek Masters' apartment near Bristol to discuss programmes for forthcoming recitals.

Hardly had the excited chatter of the others

faded, as they shut themselves behind the door at the top of the attic stairs, when the telephone rang.

'Zina? It's me,' came Jenny's familiar greeting, but there was something in her tone that alerted Zina. Something must be wrong.

'What's up, Mum?'

'Nothing. Everything is fine. But Zina I need to talk to you. Not on the phone. Will you have time to slip in here for a few minutes on your way to Derek's?'

'Of course. Are you sure you're all right? Your voice sounds different. It must be the line. The others are sorting the attic rooms and I'm not getting involved. So I can be with you in about twenty minutes. Get some coffee on. You're quite sure everything's OK?'

'Of course. I just wanted to make certain you would have time to drop in for a second before going on.'

Whatever Zina imagined her mother wanted to talk about, came nowhere near what she heard as Jenny poured their coffee.

'This morning you will see Derek at rehearsal, that's why I wanted to be sure to talk to you first.'

'Why, what's wrong, Mum? Have you seen the folly of your ways?' She said it teasingly, somehow trying to steer them back into the easy relationship which until these summer months had always existed between them.

'Quite the reverse. Zina, I dare say you look on me as over the hill, beyond all the love business. I know that's how I would have viewed my

163

own mother when she was the age I am. But the more years you live the more you come to understand.'

'But . . . but what's this got to do with anything?'

'It has everything to do with what I want you to understand. You know Derek was here yesterday because he drove Tommy home. And what wonderful news the boy had brought! Bless him, I've never seen him so confident. You'll leave him here? You won't make him throw his chances away and go with you? This can be his home whenever he is free and you should have seen him yesterday playing a duet with Derek. He looked ready to burst with pride.'

'Of course he'll take his place at music school, Mum. And thanks, I knew he could look on this as a base. As for Derek Masters – how can you want to encourage him here?'

'Why do you dislike him so much? Just tell me one thing you find wrong with him.'

'Just one?' Zina said with as laugh, then taking a sip of coffee, 'Nice coffee, Mum. Until he started hanging around you, although I'd worked with him for nearly three years, I neither liked nor disliked him. I didn't know him, and neither does anyone else in the quintet. He treats us all the same, instruments to bring life to the music. And that's the way I'm happy to leave it. How can you spend so much time with him, Mum? The man's a bore, a bore who brings magic out of a piano.'

It was hard to read Jenny's expression, indeed neither face nor manner gave anything away as she said, speaking very calmly, 'Your opinion only shows how little you know. Yes, he brings magic from a piano, and he has brought magic back into my life, and I truly believe that I have to his. That's what I wanted to tell you. Derek and I will be together for the rest of our lives.'

'But you can't do that! I know you must have been lonely, lonely for Dad. If you were telling me that you had decided to marry again to someone else, perhaps someone you have known here in the village for years, someone who has been your friend, *that* I could understand. But you've known Derek Masters no time at all. Three months? Probably not even that. I can see he would have found you attractive, you're still nice looking and I think mixing so much with us, with the children, has kept you young for your age. Oh, for goodness' sake, Mum, didn't I warn you right from the first that you were letting him see you were over the moon having a man talking to you and listening to what you say.' She looked at Jenny, but there was no sign that her words had got home. 'Tell you what, Mum,' she said, trying to move the subject away from dangerous ground, 'you just think again about coming to America with us. You mustn't feel tied here because of Tom; there will be plenty of overseas students at the music school so there must be arrangements for those who have nowhere to go for short breaks. Tom will be fine. I always thought you were contented enough here, perhaps I ought to have seen below the surface better.'

'Of course I shall miss all of you, but even before I knew Derek felt the same way as I do,

I couldn't pull up my roots and go to America.' Then with a chuckle that came to her unexpectedly, she added, 'A bit like suggesting that an old woman from the wild and woolly west or even the glitz of Hollywood could make a new life in dear peaceful Myddlesham. Perhaps I imagine it all quite wrongly, but I don't think I could ever fit into a world so bright and shiny, so blatantly modern and artificial.'

'Perhaps it won't be, perhaps that's just the rubbish they dig up to sound sensational,' Zina answered, not letting herself acknowledge that her own instinct was much the same as her mother's. 'Anyway,' she added with a note of defiance in her voice, 'one doesn't have to be influenced by it. I certainly don't intend to be, and over the years nothing has ever changed Peter, so I don't think Hollywood is going to. Stability comes from your home and the love of the family around you.'

'Indeed it does. And so I shall stay here, but not alone. You must watch the time, don't get late for rehearsal.'

'You don't need to kick me out for a bit. Mum, isn't there *anything* I can say to make you see? All right, I don't understand what you can possibly find to fall in love with in Derek Masters except the music he makes. Perhaps I might learn to know him better if I were still to be around, but I shall soon be following Peter, so that isn't going to happen. But for you to talk of marrying a man you've only known for a few summer weeks is – well, it's asking for trouble, for both of you.'

The next thing was the stumbling block Jenny had been dreading.

'I wasn't talking of marriage. There can be no marriage. He has a wife.' For once Zina was lost for an answer and so Jenny went on to tell her the whole story.

'If he is honestly serious about you, Mum, if his wife is certified insane he has grounds for divorce and he must know it, even if he pretends he doesn't. Why don't you tell him you'll marry him once he is free; that would give you time to be sure of what you were doing.'

'No!' Jenny almost shouted the one word.

'But why? There would be no problem. Or does he hang on to being married so that he can escape the noose?'

'Oh Zina, did we bring you up to have so little heart, so little understanding or care for other people? Would you have that poor woman stripped of the only dignity she has left to her? There was a time when she was Derek's whole world. He has had to build a life without her, but to divorce her for something done to her by nature would leave a stain. Surely you can see? We can't do that to her even though she lives in a world of her own and would never know.'

'I may not have the understanding to see *that,* but I can understand only too well what it will do to you to be seen as living with a man who isn't your husband. Why it's almost an insult to marriage, to Dad.'

'Never!' Then glancing at her watch, she added, 'You ought to be on the road. I'm glad I've told you. Just one thing I ask, I *beg,* Zina. If you talk

167

about it to Derek, be kind. Don't hurt him. To hurt him is to hurt me. Can't you wish us well, even if you think we are heading for disaster?'

Zina stood up to leave, then hugged her mother. 'I do wish you well, of course I do. I've hated to think that I shall go away and you'll be alone and lonely. But I can't see that a life with a dry stick like Derek Masters is the answer. Think of Dad, remember the fun everything was if he was there. Don't rush, Mum.'

'I do think of him, I always will. The *me* that was his will always be his. But do you think he would want me to be miserable for the rest of my life? If you do, you belittle him. Anyway it's too late for words of advice. Derek was with me last night and after your meeting today he will come back here. This is his home now.'

'Think, think, Mum. Are you ready for the gossip, the slights you will endure from some of the narrow-minded variety – and every village has them? One night is different from a lifetime.'

'Off you go,' Jenny said, managing to instil affection into her tone. 'Drive carefully and keep your mind on the road.'

It was as she heard the car move away that she let her thoughts go back to Zina's parting shot. One night, she had said, as if it had been a few hours isolated from the rest of their lives. But then Zina hadn't been witness to their solemn and holy vows spoken under the stars.

In front of the twins Zina said nothing of what she believed to be her mother's mistaken way of

168

running away from loneliness. It wasn't until she and Peter were in bed that she told him.

'You've worked with him for some time, what have you got against him?'

'Working with him is one thing; he is a brilliant pianist.' She had expected Peter's support and he could hear the pout in her voice. 'But he's dull. The rest of us in the quintet are all friends, mates, but he never joins in, he never relaxes.'

'So? He clearly does with your mother. Nobody can choose the right partner for someone else – and thank God for it, because if they could I should never have got beyond Mother-in-law's front door.'

'Stupid. Of course she is fond of you.'

'After all this time she knows I'm here to stay, and she's learnt to make the best of it,' he said, with a laugh only just below the surface. 'Her opinion was never important to us any more than yours will be to her about her choice of a hus— of a life partner. Go with the flow, Zina, my love, if you don't, you may find yourself to be the loser.' Then with a chuckle she could tell held affection, 'I bet when I asked your parents for your hand in matrimony that will have been pretty much the advice your father gave to her. There are only two people who really know whether the magic is there for them, and that's the couple themselves. Wriggle closer, I need a cuddle.'

Willingly she wriggled. But much later she lay awake remembering what he had said, even though she still couldn't see what her kindly, pretty, fun-loving mother could find in dreary Derek Masters. She would have been surprised

– and, from the viewpoint of a daughter, probably shocked or even disgusted – if she could have looked in on the couple. While Derek shaved, Jenny was lying in a bath of scented bubbly delight, moving further towards the taps, the end she was facing, so that when he shed the remainder of his clothes he climbed in behind and drew her to lean back against him.

When Peter was at home the days always seemed to melt, but never as quickly as this time when the date of his departure loomed ever closer. It was two days before he and Fiona were to leave when, saying nothing to Zina, he disappeared in his car. He didn't analyse his motives as he drove, but he knew that he wanted the parting between himself and Jenny to be without shadows. And subconsciously there was the thought that if he went away and left any bad feeling because of her relationship with Derek, then it would only make Zina's life harder.

Arriving he saw that Derek's car was in the drive so he left his in the lane and walked round to the back of the house.

'Morning Mother-in-law, may I come in?' he called as he opened the back door about two inches.

'Of course you may.' Her voice came from the open window of the upstairs landing. 'I'm just coming down. You'll find Derek in the drawing room.' Almost as she finished speaking she started down the stairs. Perhaps she was frightened Peter might have come in less than friendship. 'Are you on your own?'

'Yes. I'm keeping Zina busy making sure every-thing is packed. Fiona is much too excited to concentrate on anything as mundane. I wanted to see you and Derek, if I may dispense with formalities, and my time is running short now. I came early in case you were off out.' Then going into the drawing room, he held his hand towards Derek, liking what he saw. From the firm grip of the handshake and the direct way this lover of Jenny's held his gaze, he decided she had made a good decision.

'I couldn't disappear to the States without meeting you.' Then with a quick smile that had won hearts both sides of the Atlantic, he added, 'I had to know that Mother-in-law was in good hands. We wanted her to come with us, you know.' Then, turning the smile on Jenny, he said, 'Now I can understand why you weren't to be persuaded.'

The atmosphere relaxed and Peter was actually sorry that he would probably never have the opportunity to get to know Derek well. But, he had come with half an idea in his head, and now he followed it through.

'Are you two free this evening? Tomorrow is my last day and I don't want to have to do anything except be at home with Zina and the kids, but if you can manage this evening I'd like to book us a table somewhere in Deremouth – a sort of celebration with all of us together. It'll be on the early side because of the youngsters. What do you say?'

'Does Zina know?' Jenny sounded almost timid, something quite out of character.

'Not yet, Mother-in-law. But she will as soon as I get home and she will be delighted, that I can promise you.' He held her gaze as he said it and they both read each other's thoughts. Yes, she could trust him to persuade Zina. There was so little time before they would all be gone, and as things were between Zina and her at the moment she could see no way of their being as close as they used to be. The memory of their last encounter was constantly at the back of her mind. In that moment she forgot how often Peter annoyed her and felt genuine warm gratitude.

'Thank you, Peter. We'd love to come.'

'We'll pick you up at, say, just before seven? We can squeeze Fiona into the front with us, she doesn't take up much room and the back seats three quite comfortably. More fun if we all travel together.' And that last sentence set the scene.

Despite Zina being less than keen on the idea of including Derek Masters in their last evening out together, Peter's power of persuasion worked wonders. She managed a welcoming smile she was far from feeling as they settled into the car, but how could they have what Peter described as an evening of fun when Derek Masters didn't know the meaning of the word? She had always found him easy to work with and she never let herself forget that it was through him she had joined the quintet, but she had no idea what went on in his mind. He never joined in the general conversation between the others; they never really expected him to. He was a different generation from the rest of them. So it was a sobering thought to have him part of their last family outing. How different it would have been if her father had been with them still. And look at Mum, she scoffed silently, as starry eyed as a sixteen-year-old instead of a grandmother.

That was as they took their seats at the reserved table in Deremouth's Imperial Hotel. As the evening progressed she saw another side to Derek's character. He could never be an excitable, animated man, but his conversation was interesting. And what came nearer than anything to endearing him to her was his obvious interest in Tom. He gave the boy his full attention and drew him to talk, sharing views with him in a man-to-man way. If anything could take away the worry she had tried to hide about leaving Tom when she followed the others to their new life, it was watching Derek with him.

Peter ordered champagne, not one bottle but two (quite oblivious of Jenny's irritation that 'he always has to go over the top, one would have been more than enough with wine for the meal, but he's like an excited child'). And perhaps she wasn't so far from the truth, for tonight he looked with pride on them all, his precious Zina, their children, both acquitting themselves so well, Mother-in-law looking prettier than many a woman half her age and Derek Masters, a man so different from the picture he had built in his mind of the originator of that quintet which took so much of Zina's time and interest. Tonight looking around the table he felt a moment of regret that this would be the only time they would all be together before their lives changed. When the first bottle of champagne was uncorked and poured he proposed a toast to Jenny and Derek, welcoming him into the family. Fiona took a gulp rather than a sip and the bubbles got up her nose and made her sneeze just when she was fancying herself as entering a world of sophistication.

Then it was Derek's turn. 'And may I ask Jenny and Tom to join me in a toast to this wonderful new step in your career, Peter, and happiness for all of you in your new surroundings.' As he finished speaking he held his glass to clink it against Tom's, his action seeming perfectly natural and giving no hint that he understood exactly how forlorn the boy suddenly felt.

'And now it's my turn,' Zina said as they put their glasses back on the table, 'this time I want us to drink to Tom, setting out on the first important stage of what I'm sure will be a career to bring him success and, even more important, fulfilment.'

This time Tom had to keep a tight grip on the corners of his mouth as he mumbled, 'Thanks Mum.'

They were all affected by the emotion of the last minutes and it took Jenny to set the mood back on course for the remainder of the evening.

'And here was I thinking one bottle of bubbly was more than enough. There's one bottle gone and our glasses are empty already.'

It was a rare thing, indeed, for her to catch Peter's glance and share with him a moment of affectionate understanding. And so passed an evening they knew would stay with them long after it was over and their lives had changed.

*

The solitary drive back from Heathrow was something Zina had dreaded. Newton House waited, nothing in it changed from when it had been home to all four of them, and yet when she opened the front door the familiar sight held no welcome. It was a house, nothing more. This is stupid, she told herself, think how often Peter has been away – more than he was here, really. Hundreds of times I've come back to an empty house, but always I have felt its welcome. It's all in my stupid imagination. I must pull myself together and just make sure I'm soon on a plane myself and he'll be at the other end to meet me. But we shall be without Tom. From today that warm, complete feeling of all four of us living together is gone. How shall I feel when I'm the one on the plane, leaving England, leaving my darling Tom?

Letting her mind jump first in one direction and then another, she sat on the second stair gazing ahead at a future that held no reality. What did *she* want with Hollywood and the trappings of glamour? Nothing. If she'd given it any thought at all it was Tinsel Town with its stories of broken marriages, fame the goal to be reached by whatever means. But she would go to the ends of the earth as long as Peter was there for her. Then without her realizing it, she smiled. Peter was the one certainty. Fame had to be his goal, in his profession how else could success be measured? But that was fame for the work he loved, it had no bearing on the man he was. If only they could have gone on as they were, this house a place untouched by his other life,

175

somewhere he escaped to at every conceivable opportunity.

It was no use sitting here daydreaming, it was time she started counting her so many blessings, she told herself. Life has a way of working things out, just think of how her opinion of Derek had changed, and how he had come up with that idea of Tom going with Jenny and him yesterday to a concert in Cheltenham and staying the night in a hotel afterwards. Didn't that show him to be sensitive enough to want to spare the boy being there to see the moment when Peter and Fiona left Newton House knowing it was for the last time. Surely for Tom to be collected yesterday by someone of Derek's standing in the world of music must have helped him through his good-byes to Fiona and his father. With her eyes closed she let herself relive those moments.

'Have fun, sis,' Tom had said, his voice suddenly croaking and Fiona not even trying to hold back her tears as she hugged him.

'Wish you were coming.'

Then while he'd still managed to hang on to his control, he'd turned to Peter and said, 'Bye Dad, see you in sunny California when I get a proper holiday.' Trying to be a man already, he had held out his hand but Peter had pulled him tightly, almost fiercely, into his arms, kissing the top of his head and rumpling his hair.

'Bye Tommy—' the childish name had slipped out – 'take care of your mum. See you soon.' Probably only Zina had known how hard it had been to keep a hold on his own emotions. Watching them, such misery had possessed her.

Soon it would be her turn to say goodbye to Tom, to go far away where she wouldn't feel herself a part of his progress, wouldn't be able to share with him the joy she knew he would find as he developed from a talented boy to a master musician. That had been the moment when she had been conscious of how thankful she was that her mother had refused their suggestion that she should come with them. Her only solace in leaving Tom behind was her certainty that his relationship with Jenny and increasingly with Derek Masters would always be there for him.

Finally, with one arm lightly round Tom's shoulder, ready to usher him out to the car, Derek had held out his hand to Peter. They must both have been as aware as she of the struggle the boy was having to hold back his tears as Fiona had openly sobbed. Remembering, she seemed to hear Derek's voice clearly as his hand was taken in Peter's in farewell: 'Get yourselves somewhere to live with room for guests and when Zina flies out how would it be if we all came?' His voice had been full of hope, seeming to defy the misery of partings. 'We'd have to make sure it was holiday time for Tom and as long as I have enough notice I can work around engagements – or even travel separately if I wasn't free to come with the others. I know Jenny won't be happy till she has seen where you live. Does that strike you as a feasible suggestion?' It did and even helped Tom through his bad moment.

Now it was all behind them. Soon Tom would be starting his new life at the music school and she would be left to pretend she wanted the agent

177

to bring someone as keen to buy Newton House as she and Peter had been. But it was only pretence. This wasn't just bricks and mortar, their very souls were in these rooms. Hardly thinking what she was doing she climbed the stairs right to the one-time dumping ground in the attic which now stood empty. Then down again, into each room, everywhere the spirit of their years tightening its hold on her.

'Mum! I'm home, Mum. Were they all right? Fiona didn't cry any more did she? Was she miserable? I've been thinking about them all morning.'

'Where are the others?' she asked making sure her voice was bright as she hurried back down the stairs. 'Didn't they come in?'

'No, they lobbed me off at the gate.'

'Was it a good concert?' She was pleased with herself that she could sound so cheerful.

'Yes, I'll tell you about it – the music and the posh hotel – I'll tell you later. But first what about the others? Did Fiona cry? Was she miserable?' It was only then that she consciously realized just how cheerfully Fiona had said goodbye.

'No, not a tear. I think she had cried all her tears when she said goodbye to you yesterday. But, Tom, time goes so fast. Before you know it, it'll be your turn to pack your bag and be off to your new life. When you get your Christmas break perhaps we'll be ready to join them, all of us together like Derek suggested.'

'Yes, in no time at all, Mum.' He was determined to make himself the man of the house, someone she could rely on. 'But are you sure you'll be all right on your own here? Dad said for me to take care of you, but I won't even be here.'

She gave him a quick hug, which at that moment they both needed. 'Between us, Tom my love, we have four big feet. And we're going to show them just how capable we are of standing on them.'

Her reward for the effort of her brave words was the sound of his giggle.

That afternoon a phone call from the agent told her that he had a couple who'd driven from Bournemouth and wanted to view. Of course he had a key but was calling her out of courtesy (and, no doubt, to give her a chance to make sure everything looked temptingly attractive).

She always felt that a house was more likely to sell if the owner took the would-be purchasers on their tour of inspection, but this time she was introduced to Mr and Mrs Warburton from Bournemouth then left the agent to take them round the house and garden.

'They seemed quite nice, Mum,' Tommy whispered, but she was sure his feelings were very much like her own and he just wanted them off the premises. Once the house was sold he would have no home of his own in England. His roots would be pulled up and not replanted. Their glances met and what they read was yet another tie that bound them.

'I don't know much about money, I mean what Dad earns and all that, but Mum, does he have to sell this house so that he can buy one in that Beverly Hills place Fiona keeps on about?'

179

'Probably not. But, Tom, if for the rest of his career he stays out there, this is an extremely expensive place to keep. And there's nothing sadder than a house left empty and unloved.'

'It would never be unloved, we'd always love it even if we were the other side of the world.' He sounded quite aggressive. 'I hate not going to be with you and Fiona and Dad,' he started, and then, honesty refusing to be silenced, continued, 'but I'm awfully glad I haven't got to go and live out there. Do you really want to, Mum?'

Dear Tom, he was like no one else. He deserved a truthful answer.

'From what I imagine – and I may be quite wrong – but from how I've always thought of it, it's not my scene at all. I would love us all to have stayed here, for everything to be as it was before Peter got this chance. But this is a good career move and so of course he had to accept. And he has as good as been assured they want him to sign a longer contract. But me? There is only one reason I want to go, and that is Peter. I want us to be together. Selfishly I wish you were coming too, even though I envy you every-thing that is ahead of you.' Then she gave him a friendly and unsentimental squeeze to put them back on safe ground before they got swamped by the sort of emotion she knew Tom would have found embarrassing. 'Before many years are over you'll find yourself on the concert platform, you'll travel and soon realize the world is a small place.'

'I've got a lot to learn before that, Mum. But

even if that ever happens I've always seen *this* as the place at the sort of centre of it all – the place to come home to.'

'I know, Tom. It's always been our safe haven.'

'Couldn't you tell Dad you want to keep it – if he could afford to, I mean? We could always have holidays here.'

To tell him that what he suggested had been a dream at the back of her mind too seemed disloyal to Peter. So all she said was, 'Life moves on for everybody. I wonder whether Mr and Mrs Warburtons' will be moving this way?'

'Humph! Hope not!' Tom growled. From his tone he was already mentally sticking pins into their effigy.

But two days later the agent phoned saying the Warburtons found Newton House ideal for their requirements and hoped for a very quick move. Apparently she was a mental nurse and, subject to the surveyor's extensive report, they had approval by the bank for an eye-wateringly large loan. They intended to turn Newton House into a nursing home for the mentally disabled. They would need work to be done: large bedrooms divided into two or, in the case of Zina and Peter's, three; extra bathrooms would be built and metal bars fitted to all the windows. But if all went well they hoped to be able to open during the first half of the following year.

But in the event their hopes for a quick move were dashed by the tardiness of the surveyor. By the time he made his visit, spending most of the day examining every smallest detail, Tom had already started at the school of music; by the time his report was passed to the bank it was almost Christmas. What Zina didn't know was that the Warburtons' dream of a quick move to Devon had been partly built around the sale of their own house in Bournemouth near the hospital where Adele Warburton worked. It was in a chain of property sales, and when one link broke it meant delays for everyone.

Derek knew that Zina would be leaving the quintet before long, but decided to do nothing about replacing her until the date of completion was known. It seemed that everything was in limbo as the weeks went by. Had she been more enthusiastic about the sale she might have started disposing of any furniture that was no longer being used. But some inner sense of protection warned her that nothing was settled until the point of no turning back was reached and contracts were exchanged. Nearer the truth, she was still lacking the courage to break up the home.

From California came letters from Fiona, letters full of the wonders of her new life and peppering the pages with names of the famous. Although Peter had taken an apartment nearer the studio, she had willingly stayed on with the Zeiglar family. They were people who loved entertaining and she found herself in wonderland. Briefly she mentioned the school she had started attending, but her sights weren't on classwork. And from Peter too came letters, but his were quite different. He told her little about his work, but left her in no doubt that although he had been shown friend-liness, he was as lonely for her as she was for him. When he heard that the Warburtons hoped for a quick sale his response was immediate. She should leave everything to the solicitor and fly out to join him. But something stopped her doing as he said. Not exactly a premonition, but some nameless feeling that the time hadn't arrived for her to walk away. Perhaps it was that she wanted to wait until Tom had been home for the first time so that she was reassured that he was man enough to be left behind.

When Tom came home for the Christmas holiday it was obvious he had come into his own in his new life.

'Mum! Where are you, Mum?' she heard him shout as he rushed into the house after a bike ride.

'I'm in the drawing room trying to make this wretched fire burn. Did you have a good ride?'

'I went to see Gran and Granderek – that's what we decided he should be called. It seemed silly to call him Grandad when he isn't, but I couldn't say Derek or Mr Masters. So we decided on Granderek. I like it, don't you? I must write and tell Fiona. But Mum, that's not what I rushed home to tell you. It was this: they suggested that instead of decorating and pretending Christmas here was just like it always has been, what we should do is pack a bag and go and stay there. What do you think? I don't mean for all the time I'm home on holiday, but for Christmas.'

She sat back on her heels as she knelt in front of the fire that showed very little promise.

'Go away for Christmas?'

'Don't you think it's better, Mum?' He seemed to be choosing his words carefully. 'It's always been sort of magic, Dad home, decorating the tree in here, everything. But it seems silly – and wrong somehow to do all that when the others aren't here. Gran seemed ever so excited. Don't you think it would be the best thing, Mum? If Fiona and Dad phone and we're here with no holly and all that – or even if we decorated like we always have – it would sort of seem sad for them as well as us. Don't you think they'd have a better time too if they thought we were with the others?'

She mustn't let him guess how she was battling against tears that stung her eyes and threatened to spill down her cheeks as she knelt with her back to the room. If she'd still been alone as she had all the morning, misery wouldn't have hit her so suddenly. It was Tom's words, his child-like longing for the magic of Christmas and her awareness that it wasn't in her power to find it for him. She blew her nose and muttered something he didn't quite catch but he believed she directed her words at the unpromising coals as she poked more slithers of wood between them hoping to bring a flame. Then, having had a chance to overcome her bad moment she said in a voice that hinted Peter wasn't the only actor in the family, 'I think that's a rather splendid idea, Tom. I'll ring them this afternoon, Yes—' and by now she was right back in control – 'it'll be quite different. Not so much fun maybe, but lots more music. This year we need it to be different, and so it will be for Fiona and your dad.' She stood up, casting one last glance at the sulky coals. 'Well, I've done my best with that; it can please

184

itself whether it burns. Let's go and find some lunch.'

'Sounds good. I'm pretty hungry, aren't you?'

She knew that he was playing a game as much as she was herself and would have given much to make his holiday everything it ought to be. Perhaps their salvation was to spend Christmas with her mother and Derek.

'Gotta keep everything up to the mark,' the loyal Mrs C said sagely one wild and wet morning towards the end of January. Zina suspected the remark stemmed from the fact that she realized the scarcely lived-in rooms didn't merit a daily cleaner and was frightened her hours would be cut. But that was something Zina would never do, Mrs Cripps had been part of the household right from when they first moved in. 'You never know when you'll get a knock on your door and there will be someone else to snoop about. Nothing like a good shine to show the place is in good order.' She'd said it so often as she worked that Zina could have joined in the chorus, but on that January morning it seemed Mrs Cripps was 'set for a good chinwag', as she liked to call it. 'And I'll tell you something – mind, it's not a thing I would talk about outside but, truth to tell, the fact is that as the days go on I dread the time coming when you shut the door on this place. Last night, true as I stand here, I slept hardly a wink for thinking about it. It's come to be like home to me, that it has. Oh I dare say when the evil day comes I'll find myself some-where else – well, truth to tell I won't 'ave no

185

choice, my Bert he brings in no more than enough to pay the rent and feed the cat, bless him.' Then, with a laugh that was a rare thing with Mrs Cripps, she continued, 'My Bert, I mean, not that darned cat. Rubs round my legs he does, making believe he loves me—'

'Bert or the cat?' The words were out before Zina could hold them back, somehow bringing the two such different women close.

'Oh Mrs M, m'dear, what a one you are. Yes, not coming here is going to really upset me. I've known those two dear chillun almost since the day they were born, yes and now the cards are on the table I don't mind admitting I've loved them like family. Bert, he'd tell you how I carried on when they went off to that school, worried all night I did. Ah and you and Mr M must have done too. But there was no need, when they came home for their holiday, I mind how full of it all they were. Bless them.' She sniffed and made a pretence of wiping her nose. 'And here's me carrying on as if it's me matters, not you. You must be wanting to get it all done and be on your way to Mr M and little Fiona – not so little these days, I reckon she thinks she's proper grown up. Can't help wishing Tommy wasn't going to be left out of the adventure, but there you are, if everything was perfect in this world what would heaven be for? That's what my old gran used to say when I pestered for something I couldn't have. There now, I reckon those forks and spoons shine fit for a king. Now I'll go and give them a good wash and have them put away. Then what about tatties? Shall I get them peeled for you?'

'No, don't worry. I don't need potatoes today.'

'Now then, Mrs M, m'dear, it may not be my place to tell you what you should or shouldn't do, but start cutting down on enjoying your food and you're on a slippery slope. It's plain to see that you've lost weight these last months – and I wouldn't mind betting that Mr M is picturing you just the way he left you. What's he going to think when you turn up out there amongst all those big bosomed, red lipped, toothy women, like a skeleton dressed in her best?'

It was too much for Zina. Quite spontaneously she hugged the daily who through the years had woven herself into their lives. 'Oh Mrs Cripps, you've no idea how much I'm going to miss you.'

'Get along with you!' And out came the handkerchief again for another nose polish and a sniff. 'Just you bear in mind what I say. Let him find you as he left you.' But what chance was there of that when it was she on her own, poor girl, who had to bear the breaking up of their home?

Leaving her, Zina retreated to the music room. There was no recital that week but she needed the comfort that never failed her. Like a caress she ran her hand over the beautiful shining wood of the back of her fiddle, then tucked it under her chin and started to adjust the tuning. Already the dark, grey day seemed lighter. The next hour passed quickly and she was surprised when, with a light tap on the door, Mrs Cripps appeared.

'Just to say I'm off now. I did you a few tatties, want them or not. They're all cooked and mashed so they'll be nice and tasty if you just give them a fry with whatever you're having. Oh, hark now, there's that dratted phone. You run on down and take it. See you tomorrow.'

But instead of running on down, Zina went into the bedroom and lifted the receiver.

'Hold the line, I have a call from the United States.'

She seemed to freeze. Something must be wrong. When Peter rang, because of the time difference, it was always late, often after she was in bed. But in California it wouldn't even be daylight yet. Every conceivable disaster crowded her imagination and then she heard Peter's voice.

'Zina, all night I've been thinking.'

'What's happened? What's wrong?' In her hurry she had left the bedroom door open and she saw Mrs Cripps was waiting, her face a picture of worried curiosity.

'Shooting finished yesterday except for maybe a few retakes and I've been offered a five-year contract. Reason tells me I ought to take it.'

'Reason tells you?' Why was her heart thumping so hard? 'You mean you're hesitating?'

'For your sake and the kids' I ought to snatch at it, they are offering me more than I ever let myself hope for. But oh dammit, Zee, we don't belong out here. Everyone has been hospitable, welcoming – but this isn't the life for us. I want you to be honest, tell me the truth. Would you be disappointed if I turned it down? That's why I'm ringing. You're having to hang around so long and if all this time you've been looking forward to moving out here, then of course I'll sign. Even if it's not our sort of lifestyle, we'll be together, we'll make a home. Perhaps I'm a fool even to hesitate . . .'

'Disappointed? Peter, if you knew how I've been dreading saying goodbye to all this. I wanted to come, because I wanted to be with you. Wherever you go that's what I want, you know that. But each morning I dread picking up the post in case I find that everything is going ahead with the sale and they want me to sign the contract.'

'Don't sign it. Oh, that's wonderful.' She could hear the relief in his voice. 'This is going to upset Fiona, she has been thrown in the air and come down right side up, you've never seen anyone so thrilled with each day. In her mind she's on her way to stardom already. But she's a child, she'll adapt.'

Mrs Cripps had crept nearer the open door by that time and was trying to attract Zina's attention with a stage whisper. 'Everything awright, Mrs M, dear?'

Her hand over the mouthpiece, Zina nodded, her smile saying it all. 'Wonderful. Peter's coming home. I'll explain tomorrow.'

So, satisfied, in fact more than satisfied and with new hope in her heart, Zina's faithful protector stomped back down the stairs and out to collect her bicycle. It took more than a rainy day to deter Phyllis Cripps, especially with Zina's words echoing in her mind. Peter coming home. What did it mean? That he was coming to take his share in clearing the house? And so he should, it wasn't right for an able-bodied man to go swanning off, leaving everything. In her opinion a man should be head of the house, just like her Bert was, and that shouldn't mean leaving all the donkey work to his wife. But supposing he was really coming home, shaking the stardust of that Hollywood place off his boots and coming back where he belonged? No wonder she pushed her bike out of the shed hardly noticing either wind or rain. Then tying her waterproof hood more securely under her chin, off she pedalled.

Back in the bedroom, by that time Zina had replaced the receiver. Like everyone's life, hers had seen highs and lows, but never had she experienced anything to equal this. She for whom lunch had held no interest was suddenly hungry.

By mid afternoon she had told the estate agent they were withdrawing Newton House from the market, she had phoned their solicitor with the same message and, getting no reply from her mother, she had driven over to Myddlesham and put a note through the letterbox. Tom's days were very full, a school syllabus had to be covered as well as the hours of music, so she could never talk to him until after eight in the evening. The hours seemed endless as she waited impatiently. When at last she was able to tell him the news he was silent so long she thought the line must have died.

'Tom? Are you still there, Tom?'

'Yes, it's just . . . gosh . . . oh gosh, Mum . . . are you sure? We'll still be there, at home, all of us? Gosh . . .' Miles away though he was, she seemed to see him so clearly.

'We'll sleep soundly tonight, Tom.'

'I'll say! And Dad turned the contract down,

he wants to be back at home too.' Then, with a undeniable hesitation, he added, 'What does Fiona say? Awful, Mum, we're over the moon – and Dad wants to come back too – I hope she's not too cheesed off about it. Did he say if she was all right?'

'He hadn't told her until he'd spoken to me. But you can be sure he'll see she's OK. They understand each other.'

By the next morning the rain had stopped, driven away by a gale that made the boughs on the trees dance wildly. The garden was a glistening wonderland, or so it seemed to Zina in her relief that it had been given back to her. As promised she told Mrs Cripps of the change of plans, and administered the necessary hug when a few tears of joy escaped.

'I'm that pleased, I could cry. Been so miserable I have, thinking you'd all be gone and I'd never know whether it was all bright and good for you. You're not too cut up about not getting your trip?'

Zina laughed. 'Do I look cut up? We all love it here. It takes something like what happened to make you realize how lucky you are with the things you already have. Peter turned down a wonderful opportunity, and he was right. This is where we belong – over there what would I have done without you to keep me in order?'

'Get along with you! Bless the girl. And what about young Fiona?'

'You know what I think? If when she comes home we all show how excited we are that they have decided they'd rather be here, then I think she'll slip into the role. On the other hand, if we ask her how much she minds, we are likely to have a tragedy queen on our hands.'

'Bless 'er heart, 'tis to be hoped you're right, but she was mighty puffed up with pride when she went off. Now then, Mrs M m'dear, what would you like me to be getting on with? No point in wasting more polish on the furniture for a week or so now we know no one's going to be poking about. What about I give Fiona's room a real good doing, get the curtains washed and make everything nice and welcoming for the child?'

Leaving her to her labour of love, Zina decided to drive to Deremouth. Knowing Peter and Fiona would be coming home as soon as the final retakes were done, she felt she couldn't settle in the house. But before making for the coast she couldn't resist breaking her self-made rule not to disturb Celia and Jacques before she knew they would be ready for callers. Exactly how much help Celia gave Jacques as he prepared himself for the day she had never been told but she was sure he would hate to be found before he felt ready. On that morning though she seemed incapable of thinking of anything beyond her own relief and joy.

Still at breakfast in the dining room, Celia saw her car draw up.

'A car,' Jacques held up his head, listening. 'It sounds like Zina's Volvo.'

'Ten out of ten,' Celia laughed. 'I hope nothing's wrong; it's not the usual time for a social call. I'll go and let her in.' Then as she opened the door and ushered her in, she said to Zina, 'Go and say hello to Jacques in the dining room, I'll just get another cup and saucer. We were lingering over breakfast. Nothing wrong is there?' But just to look at Zina told her whatever she had come to tell them couldn't be bad news.

'Never mind the cup. I want to tell both of you. I ought not to barge in so early, but I just couldn't wait to tell you. I did try phoning you a couple of times yesterday.'

'We were in Exeter all day. Come on then, don't keep us in suspense.'

And so she told them, even admitting to them for the first time how much she had dreaded leaving Newton House and how some inner voice had told her it was a mistake for them to pull up their roots and live abroad. Only now that she was certain Peter felt exactly the same did she feel free to be honest.

She knew their delight was as real as her own. Despite it not being quite ten o'clock in the morning Jacques moved four precise steps to the drinks cabinet and took out a bottle of Madeira.

'It may not be our usual tipple but . . .' He ran both hands over the bottle as if to reassure himself. 'Yes, I think this is the one, Madeira fits the bill quite well. We can't hear news like this without raising a glass. A little thanksgiving. We are not going to lose our friends, Celia my love. I'll leave you to pour it out.' Then turning in Zina's direction, he stated with a teasing smile, 'I'm in disgrace,' and reached his hand out to touch Celia. 'I didn't aim straight getting us our nightcap. And I've been caught out before by these long-stemmed glasses.'

So they drank their first sip to 'a long future of friendship', their second to 'Peter and his wish to be back in the British film industry' and drained their glasses to 'all our tomorrows'.

Zina continued on her way to Deremouth, not because she needed to shop but because doing nothing was impossible. Although with dawn the heavy rain had gone, the gale showed no sign of decreasing. It suited her mood perfectly. She drove the car up the track towards the cliff-top walk where, battling against the wind, she locked it and left it, buttoning the keys into her anorak pocket. From here on she would walk the path, invigorated by the wind, which was almost fierce enough to lift her off her feet and blow her on her way. It would be too far to go all the way to Chalcombe, the nearest village, or more truthfully it would be too far to battle her way back from Chalcombe against the headwind, but she meant to stride out for a mile or so before retracing her steps. After so many dreary days there were other walkers making the most of the sunshine, a couple ahead of her on the cliff path and one or two walking their dogs on the shore below. Lost in thoughts that twenty-four hours ago she would have been frightened to let herself so much as imagine, she felt herself to be projected forward by the wind. Wonderful!

Then she heard something. It sounded like a child whimpering – or could it be an animal? Going to the edge of the cliff she leant over and saw a small, black and white terrier puppy. He

194

must have been blown over the edge and his fall been broken by a clump of bushy undergrowth. For him to get back up was impossible and with one false movement he would be hurled to the beach.

'All right, boy, I can reach you. Steady boy, don't move, I'll get you.'

The dog tried to wave his overlong tail, which did nothing for his security. But how could she tell him to stay still when the sound of a human voice was met with his natural reaction? He was near the top, in fact the top of his bushy protection was level with the top of the cliff. She knelt down and leant over, feeling his grateful lick on her hand. But she still couldn't get a grip on him, so she moved a little further towards the edge and tried again. She had him! Clutching him by the scruff of the neck and gritting her teeth, she raised him until she could grab him with her other hand too, and then he was on terra firma. For a moment he stood quite still as if he was sizing up the situation and then forgetting all about his rescuer he shook himself vigorously, sneezed twice, then raced after the couple of walkers, presumably his owners, who by then were a long way ahead along the cliff top. For him the adventure was over and they were unlikely to hear about it as the puppy had no means of telling them.

From half-hanging over the edge of the cliff, Zina wriggled back and got to her knees preparing to stand. It was as she was half-kneeling and half-standing that an extra ferocious gust of wind almost made her lose her balance. She heard the noise, it sounded like thunder but thunder didn't make the ground move like this. A yard further from the edge she would have been safe, but reason seemed to have left her as she felt the ground under her crumble and she was thrown. The bush that had broken the little terrier's fall slid away, the grassy cliff-top crumbled to follow, taking her with it. The walkers on the beach below heard the great roar of broken red sandstone that only minutes before had been the cliff face. One or two screamed, a child cried; but Zina, her long fall bringing both her and the one-time cliff face to the beach, was still and silent.

Seven

'Oh Lawks, now what can they be wanting?' Mrs Cripps muttered to herself, climbing from the steps where she was taking down the curtains in Fiona's bedroom. One thing she was sure, a police car didn't come calling at a house unless it brought trouble. Oh Lawks, surely not something gone amiss with young Tommy, away like he is. Or the missus? No it couldn't be anything wrong with her, she was right as nine pence when she went out.

She heard the slam of the car door and hurried down the stairs, for some reason feeling she was protecting herself from bad news if she could get the front door open before the policeman knocked. But hurry though she did, he got there first.

'I believe this is the home of Mr and Mrs Marchand.' The uniformed officer greeted her.

'And so it is, but the missus is out. There's only me here. Anything I can help you with?'

'Just tell me where I can contact Mr Marchand.'

She didn't like his manner. For two pins she'd like to knock him off his perch. Some of these chaps thought that get them in a uniform and they were a cut above everyone else. She sniffed, a sign of her displeasure. But what could the law be wanting here? Not trouble, please not trouble.

'That I can't do,' she answered, hoping her tone told him she was in control of the situation.

'There's only me at home. He's out there in Hollywood.'

'Ah, Peter Marchand. I knew he was local. I hadn't made the connection. Perhaps you can tell me where a relative might be found.'

'There's Mrs Marchand's mother, Mrs Beckham she is, she lives just as you get almost into Myddlesham village. I know the house right enough, but I can't think what she calls it. Drive on the road to Myddlesham and just before you get there there's a pair of semis on the right side of the lane, then on a bit and one house standing all by itself on the left. That's hers. Why don't you step inside and speak to her on the phone? That would save you the journey if she's out. There's no one else. Or if you give me the message I could see it gets to them.'

'I'll call on Mrs Marchand's mother. Thank you for your trouble.'

She shut the door on him almost as he turned away, then leant back against it as if her spring had suddenly broken. The police, oh dear, oh Lordie, it must be something bad or he wouldn't have made such a secret of it. Then she straightened up and hurried to the telephone. The bobby couldn't be there for a few minutes; she'd have a word first.

'This is Phyllis Cripps, Mrs Beckham. I'm just giving you the tip that the police just called here wanting to speak to someone in the family. Closed up like a clam, wouldn't give an inkling of what he'd come about. So now he's on his way to you. And there's the missus out in that motor car, well it stands to reason I'm sick with worry.'

'Of course you are. I expect they have their rules.' Jenny forced her voice to sound calm and not hint at the panic that gripped her. 'Perhaps it's something with one of them in America and the message got sent through to the local police. Please God it isn't trouble, real trouble. Don't worry, Mrs Cripps. I'll call you back when they've gone.'

'Thanks ever so much. I knew you'd understand that I can't go home worried that one of them is hurt. But it may not be that at all, it may be – I don't know what, but something that doesn't concern me. Surely not trouble though, today of all days just when the missus was so bubbling over with happiness that they aren't packing up and going off to that movie star place. I reckon we'll all say a big thank you that he's come to his senses. We've all got our allotted place in this world, that's what I always say, and if we think we make our own rules and do as we like, then we're asking for trouble. That's why I was so cut up when I thought I was going to have to say goodbye to this place and all of them. Feel they're like my own after all these years.'

Jenny tried to focus her mind on what Mrs Cripps was saying and keep a smile in the tone of her automatic replies, but it wasn't easy when in her imagination she saw Zina in a car crash, perhaps firemen cutting her from the car . . . Zina, our little Zina, Richard. Richard, help me to be strong. It must be a road accident, what else could it be? Surely any trouble in America would have been phoned to the house, and so it would if something was wrong with Tommy. Zina had always been a sensible driver – but the same can't be said of some of them on the road.

Jenny understood why it was that Phyllis Cripps needed to talk, but for her it was almost a relief when the police car drew up outside and with a promise to call her back she rang off. In the first instance the policeman was as unforthcoming to her as they had been to Mrs Cripps, although more courteous.

'I wouldn't know his number in California,' she told him. 'Why should I? But if you like to come in and wait a moment I'll call the house and ask for it.'

'I explained, madam, I've already called there before coming to you. There's no one there except the cleaning woman.'

'That'll be Mrs Cripps. Come in and I'll ring her.'

And just as she expected, the receiver was picked up immediately bringing to mind an image of Phyllis Cripps hovering with her hand ready on the receiver.

'No news yet, my dear. The police have come to me for Peter's phone number in California but of course there's no reason why I would have it. Be a dear and look it up, I know Zina will have put it in the book.' She took an almost childish pleasure (or as near to pleasure as she was capable of feeling) in thinking she had scored a point against the too-officious-by-half policeman who had taken a high-handed attitude to the faithful Mrs Cripps. Then, as she scribbled the number on the message pad, she said, 'Thanks a lot. I'll give you a ring when they've got through to

Peter.' Then to the policeman: 'There's the number. You can use this phone.'

'Thank you.'

She moved outside the door to allow him to make the call in privacy. But a minute later he called her back in and told her, 'Mr Marchand wasn't available but I left a message on his line. However, madam, since you are the nearest relative here—'

'Yes? What's happened?' She held her hands clasped tightly together, it was the only way to stop them shaking.

'Mrs Marchand fell from the top of the cliff in Deremouth and has been taken unconscious to the hospital there. I'm sorry; it must be a great shock for you. That's the only information I have; I'm sorry I can't tell you more.'

'Thank you.' She sounded calm and dignified, determined not to let him see how her whole body ached as her imagination pulled her from one direction to another.

'We'll be happy to drive you to the hospital.' Did she detect a note of uncertainty, perhaps as if, his duty done, he was able to understand something of what she was feeling?

'Thank you, but there's no need. I shall drive myself,' she answered, with a consciously gracious nod of her head. 'I'll see you out.'

The door closed on them, and she was alone. Zina . . . from the cliff to the shore . . . but surely she couldn't have . . .? No, only yesterday she had been so full of relief and joy that Peter felt just as she did, as soon as he was free he was coming home. How could anyone fall off that cliff and live? But even as the thought pushed into her mind she pulled away from it, frightened even to contemplate the possibility.

True to her word she phoned Newton House where again the receiver was picked up at the first ring. The news temporarily seemed to strip Mrs Cripps of all power of speech, but when she found her voice it was evident she was crying.

'Oh, the poor dear girl! Tell you what, it's this blasted wind must have swept her off her feet. When she left here not two hours ago she was full of excitement that Mr M was coming home. Where's the justice? I tell you, Mrs Beckham, I swear to God I'd give my right arm for this not to have happened to her. And him, poor dear man, it's going to knock the stuffing out of him.'

'I'm going over to the hospital now but they won't let me stay long I don't expect so I'll slip in and see you on the way home.'

'That's real kind of you, Mrs Beckham. If they let you sit with her a bit, I'll just hang on here.'

Before Jenny set out for Deremouth she put a call through to Derek's flat. He had gone to Bristol to collect music he had ordered for the quintet but had told her that on the way he would call to collect the last of his personal things from his apartment before the agent showed it to prospective tenants. She dialled the number and listened to the ringing as she counted. Then a voice told her there was no one available to answer her call but she could leave a message after the tone. She left her message, the sound of her voice speaking the stark words adding to her misery. She had to pull herself together and think of the family. With a determination she was far from feeling, she went upstairs for her coat and handbag, then collected her car keys.

At Deremouth Hospital she was directed to the Intensive Care Unit, the sight of two parked ambulances adding to her sense of unreality that this could be happening.

'My daughter has been brought in after a fall from the cliff,' she said, waylaying a rosy-faced nurse who looked young enough still to be in the schoolroom.

'If you wait a moment I'll find Sister and see if she can tell you anything. Here, you sit down.' She took Jenny's arm and turned her to the bench seat. 'I'll see what I can find out.' With that she scurried off, making a silent plea that Sister would come and talk to the poor, frightened-looking woman herself.

It was no more than three or four minutes that Jenny was kept waiting, but to her it seemed interminable as fear battled with hope, and hope with despair.

'I'm sorry to keep you,' a bright voice brought her mind back from where it had strayed. 'Your daughter isn't out of theatre yet. I understand there is a head wound and damage to her shoulder and various bones broken. She is having surgery.'

'Oh, thank God. You mean there's nothing worse than broken bones and flesh wounds?' But how could the Sister know when she hadn't even seen Zina?

'I understand there was a cliff-fall and she was hurtled down with the rubble. That must have broken her fall. I can't tell you yet the extent of the breakages to her bones or how bad the injury to her head – naturally there will be bruising and lacerations.'

In her relief Jenny tried to make her mind work rationally.

'She must have parked her car on the cliff. I wonder if the key is in it or in her pocket. I must get it taken home.' Her imagination was jumping from one thing to the next, settling nowhere. 'When can I see her?'

'It won't be possible today, I'm afraid. It'll be some hours before she regains consciousness. But after today as long as she's kept in Intensive Care, visiting for next of kin is at anytime. Has she a husband?'

'He's in America, so I am her next of kin.' She felt a moment's shame at the satisfaction she found in saying it and, as if to ease her conscience, promised herself that as soon as she was home she would speak to Peter.

'She was wearing no identification,' the Sister was saying, 'All we know about her is that she was brought here from the foot of the cliff. Does she live locally?'

So Jenny gave her the details she wanted, noticing the sudden look of interest at the mention of Peter's name.

'I'll send the nurse out with the car key if it's in her anorak pocket and if you like to phone this evening we can tell you how she is. Perhaps you can give me your phone number in case of any emergency.'

'Can't I wait until she comes out of theatre?'

But she had to accept that there would be no chance of seeing Zina that day. So, promising to phone later, Jenny left. Driving towards Newton House she told herself she ought to be grateful, they had sounded positive, almost as if accidents of the sort were a daily occurrence. And that's what she stressed to Phyllis Cripps whose reddened eyelids told their own story.

True to her word Jenny put a call through to the service apartment where Peter was living. She knew the police had received no reply, but that seemed to her to be hours ago. It was only when her call wasn't answered that she realized that in California it must be the middle of the night. What sort of a life was he living out there that he wasn't home and in bed? Her resentment (resentment or jealousy?) was never far below the surface and the unanswered ringing was all the justification it needed.

Until Derek had come into her life Jenny had lived alone since Richard's death, but even then the house hadn't seemed as empty and lifeless as it did as she turned away from the telephone. She took off her coat and started towards the stairs to hang it away, but instead dropped to sit on the bottom tread staring blankly at nothing and feeling the hot sting of tears.

Richard, she cried silently, I don't know what to do. What will have happened to her? Broken bones . . . unconscious . . . a head wound . . . and how must she have felt as she lost her footing and was thrown? Remember how she used to follow you around like a shadow when she was a toddler? Remember how you used to help her with her maths homework and the way she used to yawn? Remember when she brought Peter

Marchand home, her eyes like stars and such pride in telling us he was the junior lead in the Marley Players with a season in Deremouth. Did you really like him, right from the first, or was it that you couldn't bring yourself to hurt her? I saw him as a playboy, not just a player. And now where is he? Partying the night away! But when he came to you asking your permission for him to propose to her, you didn't hesitate. Am I wrong to think the worst of him? Later when I've phoned the hospital I shall try again to talk to him. I must remember how good he was in the way he came here to welcome Derek into the family when Zina was angry and wouldn't try to understand about us. And now there's this . . . Zina, our darling Zina. Richard, when we pray it's not just words we speak, surely we pray with our souls, and nothing can have destroyed your soul. With all your soul, pray like I am that Zina will be well. Please God don't take her away, don't let her be hurt for the rest of her life, help her, please, I beg.

Sitting at the bottom of the stairs she made no attempt to stem her tears. That's how it was she didn't hear the key in the front door. The first she knew was Derek's shadow falling across her and then she was in his arms.

'I phoned to tell you . . . you weren't there,' She said, making a valiant attempt to gain control.

'I heard the message as soon as I arrived. So I came back.'

She was no longer alone, even some of the fear gave way to hope.

*

Peter was spending the evening with Hermann and Heila, something he often did. But on that particular night there was a difference in the atmosphere. Previously they had been content and relaxed in each other's company, an easy companionship just as there was between Fiona and their children; now though they were all conscious that Peter, having declined the contract, would soon be gone. Of course they would meet again over the years but he would never be part of the Hollywood scene. Then there was Fiona, a child of talent and beauty with the offer of a small role in her first film. Surely he couldn't insist she should return home and again become the child she had been before her eyes had been opened.

'Let her have her chance,' Heila tried to persuade him, her accent a combination of her mid-European roots and the New World. 'I give you my word I would be as a mother to her.'

'If you take her away, my friend,' Hermann explained as he weighed into the argument, 'she will remember it for the rest of her life. Even if she finds other opportunities, this will always weigh heavily against you. Put yourself in her place and you will see we are right.'

'She is one of twins,' Peter answered, imagining Zina and their home. 'What would it do to Tommy to lose her? And to Zina?'

'And to you, my dear friend, except that you will lose her even more surely if you impose your will and take away the chance she dreams of. Let her make this one film. I am confident she will use it as – to speak the expression of your people – a springboard. Undoubtedly she has talent, talent and that magic something for which I do not know the word. She will make her mark and then that will be the time to let her make her second film in England if that is what you desire for her future.' Hermann had the sense not to stress that for the golden future of Fiona's dreams Hollywood was where she should be.

Peter could see the wisdom of their advice. Fiona's screen test had proved to be everything she had hoped and had lead to the offer of a juvenile role in a film which at present was being cast. Obviously, due to her age, the decision for her to accept had to be his. What would Zina's reaction have been if she had been here with them? Imagining himself in Fiona's place he knew exactly what his choice would be. He must talk about it to Zina before he signed. Then his mind went off at a tangent as he recalled the excitement and relief in her voice when she heard that they were coming home. Without talking to her first he couldn't bring himself to agree to return on his own. So he steered the topic onto safer ground and, not for the first time after an evening visit there, he accepted their invitation that he should stay the night. That's how it was that before six in the morning he was driving towards the set and decided that on the way he would stop at his apartment to change into casual clothes.

Automatically he checked the phone to see if there were any messages and found one from Deremouth Police asking him to call their number.

For the local police to phone him must mean – mean what? Trouble – an accident? A fire at the house? But why should the police phone, why not Zina? His heart seemed to be beating right into his dry throat as he waited for the connection.

'Deremouth Police Station,' came the voice, cool and unemotional.

The actor in him came to the fore as he answered, 'My name is Marchand. I'm calling from California. I believe you tried to contact me.'

And perhaps the actor in him helped him to reply calmly as he heard what they had to tell him, just as it helped him to phone for a taxi to take him to the airport. His mind would go no further than that. He collected his passport but it didn't even enter his head that he was still in his dinner suit; nothing mattered except to get home to Zina. He gave no thought to Fiona nor to any retakes at the studio. Only when he was waiting to board the plane did he get in touch with Hermann.

With future engagements already booked for the Meinholt Quintet, very early the next morning Derek set off to Bristol, this time with an extra and even more pressing mission than collecting music. With Zina so suddenly out of the quintet she must be replaced immediately as by evening they were starting on a three-day programme on the south coast. He had contacts in Bristol and it was imperative he found an immediate stand-in.

209

Jenny made herself wait anxiously until nine o'clock before she set off for the hospital. After a sleepless night she felt frightened to let herself imagine Zina propped up in bed and smiling at the sight of her, and even more frightened of the alternative she wouldn't let herself consider. When the nurse indicated the small room (hardly more than a cubicle) where she would find Zina, her relief was physical, seeming to make the blood tingle in her veins.

'How is she?' She made herself ask it in preparation for what she would find.

'We're keeping watch on her, she's not regained consciousness yet. Sister can explain to you. If you like to go and sit by the bed, I'll ask her to come and see you.'

Jenny was unprepared for what she found, for there was very little of Zina visible. Although her head was bandaged, her swollen face was free of dressings but the cuts and grazes were painted with some sort of yellow balm beneath which the skin was greenish/grey with bruising. On one side blood was being injected into her from a drip and, on the other, a clear fluid which Jenny didn't recognize.

'Zina,' she whispered, knowing there was no hope of Zina being aware, 'you're going to be all right. You just lie quietly until you're ready to wake.' Then, silently, she added, 'Please God, make her well. She looks so dreadful. Why? Why did it happen?' She was still standing gazing at the unrecognizable figure when Sister came in. 'She looks dreadful. I don't know what I expected . . .'

'It's not twenty-four hours yet,' the Sister said, her voice bright and purposeful. 'We are keeping a careful watch on her. I understand her husband is abroad, so I imagine you will be visiting. You may come at any time while she's in Intensive Care. I expect you worried all night,' she added kindly, 'but now you've seen her and you know she is being taken care of, you really ought to try and get some rest. Once she regains consciousness she'll be glad to have you here.'

Grateful for Sister's purposeful manner and seeing the wisdom of her advice, Jenny nodded.

'Yes. I'm sure you're right. I'll come back later and perhaps she will have woken.'

'You may visit at any time, but I suggest you give her until this evening. If she wakes we'll tell her you've been in and will come later. But it might be a good idea to phone first.'

Jenny felt lonely, helpless and disconsolate as she walked back down the stairs of the hospital. Evening seemed a long time away. Once home the day dragged, every few minutes she checked the time. As soon as the grandfather clock in the hall struck half past five she dialled the hospital and was put through to Intensive Care.

'This is Zina Marchand's mother. I'm coming to see her this evening but Sister told me to telephone first. Can you tell me how she is? Is she awake?'

'I'm so sorry but there can only be one visitor at a time in Intensive Care and her husband—'

'Her husband is in America. She only has me.'

'Oh, but her husband is here. He arrived about an hour ago.'

211

The answer was so unexpected that for a second Jenny could think of nothing to say. Into her mind sprang the things she had thought about him when there had been no answer to her calls – and all the time he must have been on his way. She was ashamed of her thoughts and yet resentment fought for the upper hand. One visitor only – and he would always take precedence over her.

Forty-eight hours after the accident, in the small side-room there was no change in Zina. Her head was bandaged, her right shoulder had been broken, three ribs, her right arm, wrist and middle finger, her right tibia and her left femur. Her breathing was shallow, but at least she lived.

By her side on an unrelentingly unkind wooden chair dinner-jacketed Peter kept vigil, just as he had for over thirty hours, hardly taking his eyes off her as he fought the battle to stay awake. In the circumstances it would hardly be true to say luck had been on his side, but at least, arriving at the airport, he had been able to check in to a flight due to leave within the hour. A taxi from Heathrow to Newton House where, without even going inside, he had collected his own sports car and driven straight to the hospital.

Every few minutes a nurse would look in on the unchanging scene, stand over Zina with a worried expression, sometimes feeling her pulse and then disappear. And at intervals one of those same nurses would ply him with cups of tea or offers to send down to the hospital shop for sandwiches – something he declined, because the thought of eating made him feel sick. Perhaps he didn't realize just how hungry he was, for his conscious thoughts went no further than this small room and the haunting sight of his beloved Zee.

Leaning down so that his head was next to hers on the pillow he whispered into the space as near her ear as the bandage allowed. 'Darling, darling Zee, hear me, *please* hear me. Come back to me, Zina, don't leave me. Wake up, Zee, please, please. Oh God *please*.' His voice was hardly a whisper at all. He had never before felt so helpless and alone or so frightened. So the minutes had turned to hours, night to day and into another night.

It was about five in the morning, he ached in every limb, his eyes were bloodshot with tiredness. Suddenly he was wide-awake. Did he imagine it or did she move her eyelids? In a second he was on his feet bending over her, his face only inches from hers. 'Wake up,' he breathed, his hand gripping hers, 'look at me, oh darling, yes . . .' For a moment her eyes were open, she gazed blankly, then they closed again. He was at his lowest ebb. 'Come back, wake up, bring her back, *please* God. Zee, don't leave me, I can't live without you.' Seconds passed as he silently pleaded and she lay quite still. Then there was a change. Again her eyes opened and this time there was a difference, they weren't staring blankly into the middle distance they were looking at him. He believed she tried to smile, had it been possible with a face so swollen.

'You hav . . . ven't . . . shaved. Can't . . . to bed . . . like that.' Words that were barely audible, but words for all that. It was as if she had no

213

idea of anything that had happened or even where she was, except that she was with him.

Almost beside himself with anxiety, fatigue and thankfulness, his control slipped beyond being held back as a sob broke in his throat. 'Thank God, oh thank God.' He hardly knew what he said or what he did as in relief he wept. One of the young nurses was there instantly. 'She spoke. She knew me,' he told her, keeping his back to her and holding his jaw stiff as he tried to hide his display of uncontrollable emotion.

The nurse held Zina's wrist and nodded to him encouragingly. 'Her pulse is stronger. It's what we've been waiting for. I must go and report to Sister.'

While she was gone Peter had a chance to get his face in order. He heard the soft footsteps coming quickly along the corridor and a second later Sister was confirming what the young nurse had already said.

'She's moved into a natural sleep. Now you must go home and rest. She will sleep for some hours, perhaps all day and well into the night. And so should you.'

Zina was starting on the road to recovery.

Outside in the early morning of winter, daylight barely a hint of light in the eastern sky and it must have been an indication of the state of his mind that he decided to call and give Jenny the news on the way home. He had been told that she had been phoning the hospital, but his thoughts had gone no further than Zina. Jenny's ever-ready resentment of him had turned to anger that he should have taken precedence over *her* and with only one visitor allowed, made sure that each day *he* was that visitor. Why couldn't he have considered *her* and realized that she, too, had a right to keep watch? She supposed he considered he was the only one who mattered and she didn't count. That was her immediate reaction, one that became more firmly entrenched as the hours went by. Derek and the quintet were away and originally she had planned to accompany him. He had no choice other than to go, and with Zina in hospital Jenny naturally had stayed at home feeling confident that with Peter in America she would spend time each day at the hospital. Often enough she had been irritated by what she considered Peter's flippancy and immature need for fun, but nothing could compare with the angry jealousy that gripped her as the hours passed and she heard nothing from him. A more fair-minded side of her nature nudged her with the thought that he must have dropped everything to rush home so quickly.

It was just after six in the morning, still dark and cold, when she turned over in bed snuggling into the warmth, glad it wasn't time to get up. Then she seemed to freeze! She knew the sound of that wretched engine, the vintage sports car so dear to Peter! What could he be calling here for at this hour? Had he been sent for to go to the hospital in the night? But at this hour that could only mean . . . no, she hadn't the courage to let herself imagine. Instead she pushed back the covers and got out of bed, pulling on her dressing gown as she hurried to the window. Probably too frightened to think clearly she expected to be able to see him, but there was nothing but the dark shape of someone coming through the gate. Please, please, she begged silently, too frightened to put words to her plea.

Still pushing her feet into her slippers she hurried to the stairs and ran down to open the door before he reached it. In the bright light from the hall she was shocked at the sight of him. Pulling him inside, she closed the door.

'They sent for you at the hospital?' But even as she asked it she knew the question made no sense. If he'd been called from his bed he couldn't look like this: unshaven not just for hours but for days, still wearing a dinner suit, sore-eyed, pale and exhausted he was scarcely recognizable as the screen hero beloved of so many.

He who made a practice of hiding his emotions, joking so irritatingly rather than expose the depth of his feeling, was too tired and too thankful to think of anything but what filled his heart.

'She woke,' he said, his face working so that he could hardly speak, 'she knew me. Haven't shaved, she said.'

'And then? Tell me, Peter!' She heard her shrill voice; she heard the fear in it.

He made a supreme effort, taking a deep breath as if that would give him back his control as he said, 'They said she would sleep for hours now, a natural sleep. She's going to get better.'

In the next seconds neither of them consciously moved and yet he was held in her arms and she felt his last hold on control snap as he sobbed.

'Have you been there all night?' Even as she

asked she realized it was a stupid question in view of his appearance, but she sensed that when he gained control he would want to forget the last few moments.

'Came on the first plane when I heard. Been there ever since.'

What a moment for her thankfulness to be over-taken by guilt at how often she had thought badly of him.

'Oh, my dear boy. Have they fed you? I'll get us something and make some coffee.'

Getting out his handkerchief he wiped his face and shook his head. 'Thanks, but no. I could keep awake while I was watching her, waiting for a sign. But now Mother-in-law, all I want is to sleep. So thankful, you don't know how thankful.'

'Oh but I do know. She's my daughter.' Could some of the animosity of years be rearing its head again? 'You're not in a fit state to drive. Leave your car and I'll take you. Derek took the Volvo back to the house so you can use that until he gets home tomorrow, then we'll both drive over, he'll drive yours and I'll bring him back.'

'I can manage and when I get there I'll just roll into bed.' At that stage he wanted just to get home and Jenny wasn't even dressed.

'I'm not going to have you drive into a tree. Zina will have trouble enough to overcome without that. It's not even light yet, no one's going to see me.' And then with an impish smile that somehow helped both of them to find normality, she added, 'And if they do and think I've been on the tiles all night, that'll give the

217

chattering masses something to get their teeth into.'

As Zina started on the road back, she felt frustrated by her reliance on someone else for her every need. In hospital she managed to brush her own teeth using her left hand, but that was about all. Of course she was stiff, and apart from broken limbs her body ached and was bruised and sore, but she was determined not to think of herself as an invalid. To her way of thinking an invalid was a person with an illness; she had broken bones but was disease free. So her natural optimism returned.

It was five days after the accident and she had been told she was to be moved into the ward the next day. Halfway through the morning Peter arrived.

'Having a good day?' he asked, bending to kiss her in greeting.

'You sound remarkably perky. My day? Oh thrilling,' she answered, her voice heavy with sarcasm for such a stupid question. Then, more honestly, she said, 'Peter, I'm not *ill*, I feel I want to be doing things for myself, that's the hard bit. But I think my face is beginning to feel as if it belongs to me again.'

'How about if tomorrow you come home?' To her ears he sounded insensitive. She was in no mood for finding humour.

'That's not funny,' she replied with a pout in her voice.

'Tomorrow let's get you home to your own bed.' A good job Jenny couldn't hear him!

'Stop fooling, Peter.' And this time he realized how near the surface tears were for all the attempt she made to sound unscathed.

'Over this I would never tease, Zina, you know I wouldn't. I couldn't mention it yesterday when I came because nothing was settled. I had an appointment to see Mr Clifford, the surgeon who put you back together again, and he has agreed that tomorrow, instead of being moved to the ward, you can come home as long as we install a couple of fully trained nurses for the first weeks. Nice chap, he even helped me engage two he thought would be right. You must have made a good impression on him for him to be so willing.' It honestly didn't occur to him that having a famous name might have tipped the scales. 'So tomorrow morning, m'lady, you are to be brought back home. Our Mrs Cripps is beside herself with excitement. I reckon she thinks we could do without the nurses, she's so keen to play a sort of motherly role. So? What do you think?'

With her left hand – one of the only bits of her not hampered by plaster or bandage – she took his right one and held it to her sore and still swollen face.

'Silly to cry,' she whispered, her mouth moving on the back of his hand. 'So pleased. Peter . . .'

'Happy tears, my darling.'

'Happy, thankful, grateful. Have you got a hanky?' she sniffed, 'Wipe my face, please.' With remarkable gentleness he wiped it, first her cheeks and then her nose. 'I love you, Mr Marchand,' she told him, seeming to set the scene for the next stage in their lives.

219

'And I love you, Mrs Marchand, despite the scare you gave me.'

The next day the ambulance took her home and, from the moment the stretcher was carried up the stairs, those days in hospital began to take on the feeling of a bad dream. This was where she belonged and where she was determined she would soon become the person she used to be.

But it wasn't as easy as she expected. The large bedroom had belonged to Peter and her; now there was a single bed in it as well as the double, and her nightly companion was a nurse while Peter was in the room across the corridor. But, she told herself, that was just one more reason why she had to make every effort to see she progressed even more quickly than they anticipated. Perhaps had she suffered a sickness of the body her own willpower might have helped, but setting bones can't be hurried. Her first step towards normality came when the bandage was finally removed from her head, or so she anticipated with excitement. As she sat in bed the nurse removed it and the doctor examined the healed wound and, with thankfulness, she heard him say that it could be left uncovered. When they'd gone downstairs she waited eagerly for Peter to come back from seeing the doctor out so that he could carry her to sit in front of the dressing table. Previously, when her head had been re-dressed she hadn't seen herself in the mirror, but there was nothing normal about her appearance for the hair had been shaved on the right-hand side from the front to almost level with the back of her ear.

Now all that was visible was an ugly scar from a jagged wound stretching to an inch or so below the natural hairline on her forehead. In the triple mirror she could see that her left profile was the woman she'd been; the right profile a stranger and, to her mind, a hideous reminder of something she wanted to forget. Seeing her expression Peter stood behind her, his hands on her shoulders.

'Peter, I can't go about like that,' she croaked, frightened to trust her voice to say more.

'Wear your wound with pride. Isn't that what we used to say to the kids when they came to be bandaged after tumbling?'

'What pride can I have in being a sight like that?' she gripped her trembling lips tightly together, holding the corners of her mouth between her teeth. She knew she was being childish; she knew she ought to be grateful that she was healing well; but shock at the sight of her reflection stripped her of everything except misery coupled with shame that she couldn't find the grace to be thankful. 'Don't let anyone see me.' Then, glaring at him in the mirror as if the whole thing were his fault, she added, 'And don't give me a lot of rubbish about it'll soon start to grow; it'll take months, you know it will.'

She knew she was behaving badly: she knew and had neither the will nor the desire to put on a show of bravery. Right from the time of regaining consciousness she had been looking forward to having the bandages and plasters removed, somehow expecting that she would automatically be restored to how she had been before the fall. In those first moments of facing

221

what had happened, she knew that there would never be any going back. Even when her hair grew, she could see a future with the plasters removed and perhaps she would be left with a limp or with one shoulder higher than the other. Every possible disaster crowded her mind, each one taking hope of regaining her former self further away. Small wonder she lost the battle and cried. Tears were a relief; it was as if she had been holding them in check until at last the floodgate had burst open. She turned on the stool burying her face against Peter as he drew her close, caressing the back of her neck.

'I'm sorry,' she managed to gasp. 'I'm stupid not to have expected to look a mess.' It was hard for her to talk as she sobbed and hard for him to understand her words. But even without words he understood just what she was suffering. He had watched her, each day marvelling that she could appear so untouched, assuming a cheerfulness that surely had to break before real healing of her mind could begin. Gently he moved his fingers on the back of her neck as he held her to him, silently begging that he would find a way of helping her.

'Cry, my precious, Zee. Let the tears wash away your disappointment. Don't be frightened to cry. If you knew the tears I shed while you were lying unconscious. Just helplessly looking at you and begging that you wouldn't be taken from me.' He dropped to his knees, holding her close so that now he felt her wet face against his neck. 'Now all I can do is thank God you are here. Turn round, look in the mirror, we'll both look

222

and make friends with your shaved head, we'll be grateful together that we are where we are. It might have been so different. Does a few months waiting while your hair grows really matter so much?'

'. . . sorry Peter,' she mumbled as she tried to stem her tears, '. . . behaving badly. I am grateful, thankful, of course I am.' Another gulp. 'Stupid of me not to have expected to look like it. And, yes, I know it'll grow. But that's only one bit of me. What about when the beastly plasters come off? Will nothing be like it used to be? Thought I was going to be back to normal.'

'Darling, when your plasters come off for a little while your skin will look a bit withered. But that will last no time at all.'

She said nothing, just sat looking dejected and sniffing.

'Listen,' he said, raising his head, 'that's Mrs Cripps' step on the stairs, I'll call her in. Don't move.' And before Zina had a chance to stop him he shouted, 'Mrs Cripps, can you come in here a second.'

The door opened and there she stood, vacuum cleaner in one hand, doorknob in the other.

'Why, fancy that then, Mrs M, m'duckie, you've got rid of that wretched bandage and got the air to your head. There's nothing like a bit of God's fresh air for healing a wound. Now then let's have a look at what they did to you. Looks a real good neat mend,' she said as she came to the dressing table and peered at the wound. 'Clean as a whistle.' But there was no pretending she didn't see Zina's tear-ravaged face. 'Now then,

223

m'dear, there's only one person going to give it more than a passing glance and that person is you, yourself. If it really worries you while the hair is growing back you can always alter your parting and comb it over this way. What do you think about that for a good idea? Mrs Beckham did tell me once that her hairdresser had been to the house – remember a year or two back when she sprained her ankle. Bet you a pound to a penny she'd come over and set you up real pretty again.'

Peter had stood back from them, watching and listening. He saw in the mirror how Zina's miserable expression subtly changed; and did he imagine a gleam of hope in her bloodshot eyes? No wonder he looked with affection at the faithful Mrs Cripps; he'd known she wouldn't fail.

'You called me in. Was there summit you were wanting? I got sidetracked seeing the bandaging gone.'

'No, that's what we wanted to show you,' Peter answered.

Taking up her vacuum cleaner Phyllis Cripps went on her way, warmed by the knowledge that they had wanted her to share those first moments towards the missus getting back to being herself. Poor dear, plain as a pikestaff it was that she'd been crying. Disappointed at what a difference it made to how she looked, no doubt about that. Then inspiration struck, and dumping the vacuum in the corridor she went back and knocked on the bedroom door.

'It's only me again,' she said as Peter called for her to come in. 'I just had a thought. That

224

hair of yours Mrs M, it came to me that I've heard it said that the top man from Sebastian's in Deremouth, that'll be Sebastian himself – what a mouthful of a name for a chap to have, but I've heard it said that it's not his name at all, he's really plain Sam – but any road, he's what they call a top-notch stylist, still has a successful place in London right in the posh part and only came to Deremouth because of his wife's health. So I was just mulling it over in my mind and I thought, why don't you have a word with him and see what he thinks he could best do to it while it gets growing. Then, I was thinking, once it's an inch or two, he could cut all of it, shape it real nice so that it all grows together. By the time the days start to warm up you'll be glad to have short hair. You got a real nice face, good-looking girl you always have been, short hair might look just the ticket. Just something to mull over in your mind. But it could be a wise move to speak to Sebastian rather than going straight to the local shop in Myddlesham – not that Mrs Beckham's hair doesn't always look nice, 'cos it does. But she's got pretty hair and never changes the way it's done. The local shop may not have the know-how of a top-notcher straight from London. You just think about it.'

'I've started thinking already. Mrs Cripps, you are a honey.'

'I second that,' Peter said with a laugh as he held the door open and Mrs Cripps went to join the waiting vacuum cleaner.

That same day Peter drove to Deremouth and talked to Sam Slade, better known as Sebastian.

Being the local celebrity might have left him unspoilt and even on that visit to the ex-London stylist it didn't enter his head that it could be because he was who he was that the hairdresser agreed to fit in a visit to Newton House that evening after the salon closed. So came another step towards Zina feeling like a human being again.

Progress was as fast as the circumstances allowed and she was helped enormously by Peter's never failing little surprises. Of course, with both legs in plaster she was confined to bed or, at best with a heavy shawl around her shoulders, carried to the window where she was lowered to sit on a chair by the side of the radiator, for despite the sunshine it was bitterly cold outside. There was a day soon after the hairdresser had performed a clever restyling of her cruelly cropped hair when she heard a lot of movement on the stairs. Despite asking Peter, the nurse and Mrs Cripps what was happening, they all told the same story: early spring cleaning, or to use Phyllis Cripps's opinion, 'Vacuuming's all very well, but once in a while everywhere needs a proper clean, a good hard brushing, then a wash down of the woodwork. You'd be surprised at what can be got out of stairways you think are kept neat and clean day by day.' By that evening all three of them were proved to have been telling her less than the truth.

'I get fed up eating by myself,' Peter told her. 'Time you came down and kept me company.'

'*You* get fed up! You think I don't?'

'Time we did something about it,' he said with

that smile of a naughty child pushing his luck as far as he could. And perhaps there was more of Jenny in her daughter than anyone had realized for Zina threw an impatient look in his direction.

'Time you went down,' she said in what he teasingly called her schoolmarm voice.

'OK,' he agreed cheerfully, at the same time throwing back the bed covers and starting to lift her.

'Stop it, Peter, you idiot,' she shouted as, carrying her, he reached one hand just far enough to twist the handle of the bedroom door then kicked it open with his foot. 'Peter, stop fooling about. Don't you dare try and carry me down those stairs, we'll end up both falling. Please Peter!' If only the nurse would come back upstairs, he might realize how stupid he was being. She buried her head against his shoulder as if that would ward off what must be going to happen.

He could hear she was genuinely frightened and held her a little tighter, but that 'silly smile' was still on his face. They were on the landing, then he was lowering her.

'I *told* you! I said I was too heavy!' She moved her head back a little so that she could look at him – and still he was smiling, such a cocky, pleased-with-himself smile as she found herself deposited, not on the ground but onto the seat of a chairlift where he fastened the clasp of the strap that held her in. In a flash she realized what the noises she had heard had been – and he'd even had the special strap fitted because she couldn't bend her arms sufficiently to hold on. He pushed a switch and taking her hand in his walked by her side as she was carried safely down the stairs where there was a brand-new electric wheelchair waiting. No wonder he bore the expression of a conjuror who had just successfully pulled a rabbit out of his hat.

'Oh Peter, what am I going to do with you and your secrets?' Her anger and fear had given way to shame that she hadn't trusted him, followed immediately by a rush of love.

'Well now, let me think,' he answered, his smile teasing her, 'you could say, "thank you dear Peter, I'm going to have fun on that" – and I bet the kids will too. Pity we didn't have it ages ago, they're really too old now to make the most of it. I tried it out first and made Nurse Ward have a go too,' he chuckled as he might have done as a ten-year-old. 'Now then, I'll just show you how the chair works. You can drive yourself; it's dead simple. By tomorrow you'll be a go-anywhere kid.'

They both knew that was an exaggeration for, plastered as she was, even getting into clothes was out of the question. But once she was downstairs and safely in the electric chair she could move about without help, and she could sit in it at the dining table. In her excitement she overlooked that she couldn't bend her arms enough to use a knife and fork and would still have to be fed. But independence was brought a huge step nearer.

Since her accident the housekeeping had been taken over by Edith Hume who previously had come to cook for their not-very-frequent dinner parties, or often during school holiday times so that days out never ended with Zina having a meal to prepare. Peter had called at her house the day before Zina was allowed home from hospital and she had agreed to work full time for the present. She'd always enjoyed coming to Newton House and had been pleased to be able to tell her friends how well she got on with Peter Marchand and his family. Her husband worked at a neighbouring farm where they lived in one of the cottages and she was glad to earn the extra money. Mentally she gave herself a pat on the back that she had pleased them well enough that Peter had turned to her in this emergency.

To Peter's surprise, Zina raised no objections when he told her that Fiona had been offered a small role in a film and, since she would be waiting out there until he returned for any final retakes, he thought it would be unkind not to agree to her accepting. Remembering the child's excitement at the prospect of their moving to America, and imagining what her own reaction would be to the suggestion of a protégée performance for Tommy, she backed Peter's opinion and he wrote giving his consent.

At Newton House a new pattern evolved. When Peter could no longer put off his return to the States where there were one or two scenes to be re-shot, he was able to leave knowing that the routine was working well.

It was a warmer than normal late May day when the taxi brought him home and across the front grass, using both feet but still with the support of crutches to take her weight, Zina came to meet him. One look at him and she knew how pleased he was with her progress, making her even more eager to tell him that the nurses were no longer in residence. She stood straight and threw down her crutches, her thin legs taking her weight as she held her arms towards him. Held in his close embrace she felt she had her life back again. The driver unloaded Peter's bags and with a shrug of his shoulders climbed back behind the wheel and drove off feeling himself to be invisible to both his fare and the woman too. Good job he'd been paid up front before they left the airport – paid and generously tipped too.

'Stand back and let me look at you.' Peter pulled back a few inches the better to see her. 'God, Zee, but you look good. Two arms, two legs—'

'All complete. A bit scraggy.' As if to demonstrate just how scraggy, she held out her arms for inspection.

'What's the old saying about the nearer the bone the sweeter the meat? Zina, Zee, I've missed you so much. You always said you were fine, but I know what you are and I was worried.'

Suddenly she moved away from him and turned to where the taxi had been.

'Peter, what sort of a mother am I for heaven's sake? I saw you and that's all I thought about. Fiona must have gone straight indoors. I feel awful.'

'Ah!' He hadn't looked forward to this

moment. 'I let her stay on out there for a bit longer. There wasn't time to talk about it to you. I'd intended to collect her on the way to the airport and there was an accident – oh, not with the cab I was in—' when he saw her expression, 'but it held us up and I knew I'd just have to collect her with no time to spare. When I got to the house she was full of excitement. She's been offered another film, not a cameo part but the juvenile lead. Hermann was wild with praises and the kid just begged and pleaded I wouldn't make her come home. When the shooting is done she'll come back, but it's a few months that might give her an opportunity she'll never find again. I tell you, Zee, that kid has a rare talent; we can't, we *mustn't*, let her down.'

'She's only fourteen, she ought to be at school still. Do you want her to grow up thinking the world begins and ends with some sort of make-believe, her face plastered with grease paint?'

His eyes teased her as he said, 'A good thing I have a hide like a rhinoceros. Hermann has promised to make arrangements for private tuition for her; it happens all the time for kids who work on films. I honestly do agree, she is far too young to abandon her lessons and she needs the discipline of learning. We handed her over to a boarding school here without querying their methods, so let's trust him.'

'You're a softie, Peter Marchand. I can't think why I love you like I do.'

'Must be my natural charm,' he replied, drawing her closer, 'you haven't a chance against it.'

231

'That's good,' she replied, 'life would be so dull if you lost your fatal fascination.'

He went to pick up her crutches. 'Do you need these or can you trust yourself just to me.'

'You or a couple of wooden props? There's no contest.' So with one arm round her and the crutches tucked under his other, they walked back to the house where neither of them were surprised to find Mrs Cripps had had 'one or two last minute jobs' she'd wanted to see to rather than go home on time.

'It's that nice to see you come home,' she greeted Peter, 'now we'll all be in good step again, eh Mrs M? Where's our little Fiona, has she gone straight up to her room without saying hello?' When they explained, she shook her head in disbelief. 'Bless my soul, that little mite she was not so long ago and now – well, beggars belief, that it does. Gets her talent from her dad, I suppose. Was looking forward to seeing her. Al'ays she would come and chat with me, used to sit wherever I was, happy as a sandboy while we chatted.' Hearing her, into Peter's mind sprang the image of Fiona sitting in the car with him as he drove her for the first time to boarding school. That had been the day he had felt certain of the career she had ahead of her.

'She'll soon be home, Mrs Cripps.' Zina made herself sound positive. But she knew you could never turn back time and find things as they used to be. Every experience leaves its mark and for Fiona this one would leave a mark both deep and indelible.

That evening they were in the drawing room

232

when they heard the telephone. Peter went to answer it and she couldn't hear his words, nor even his tone, so it wasn't until he came back into the room that she was sure from his expression that something was wrong.

Eight

'That was Tom.' And she sensed from his voice that he was angry.

'Is he OK? You had a long talk. Had he reversed the charge?' Zina asked with an affectionate laugh.

Not answering her directly, Peter went to the cabinet and started to pour their drinks. 'The usual, I take it?' Then passing her a glass, he answered, 'No, he'd been saving his money ready for a long call. You ask if he is OK. Yes, it's plain he's in his element there. In fact it wasn't either of us he wanted to speak with; he called expecting to talk to Fiona.'

'Poor Tom. Do all twins have their sort of bond, I wonder? We ought to give him more loose money for his calls so that he can speak to her sometimes.' Peter didn't reply and she could see his thoughts weren't on what she had said. 'Are you sure nothing was wrong? If there is something, please Peter I want to know.'

'Young Fiona needs her bottom smacked, that's what's wrong. She's so over the moon with her own affairs – and I can understand that, of course she is – but she ought to think of someone else besides herself occasionally, especially she ought to think of Tom. The kid was upset. I suspect he was fighting tears. He phoned wanting a long talk with her and then found she wasn't here; so

234

that was a let down. And I expect that's what brought him low enough to tell me the rest. Do you know, in all these months she'd been out there she has only written to him once and that was in the first week or so. Poor chap, he gets no replies to his letters to her. He asked me to confirm her address because he thought he must be sending them to the wrong place.'

'And . . .?'

'Oh, he sends to the right place, she's just so wrapped up in herself . . . Honestly Zina, she's got to behave better or we must insist she comes home. He begged me not to mention it to her, that's what really upset me. He knows, and we both know too, she's tough and she's always been able to turn things to her own advantage. Unfortunately from his point of view, Tom isn't as hard as she is. He knows it and I suspect if he thought we got on to her about it and said she was to write, it would take all the joy out of hearing from her. How often did she write to you while I've been back in the States this last time? Does she answer your letters?'

'When I think about it, she hasn't written at all. But I knew she was all right because you always told me.'

She could tell that Peter was angry by the way he put his glass on the occasional table in front of them and drummed his fingers against his knee.

'I'm going to phone her,' he said, getting up and going towards the door as he spoke.

'No, Peter, please don't. Tom would be mortified.'

'*He* would indeed, but *you* are made of sterner

235

stuff. I shall tell her what I think of her for not writing to you and then, casually, say I suppose she sends regularly to Tom but she also has a duty to write home. Trust me, I won't drop Tom into it. She's got to understand that affection is a two-way thing, she can't expect folk to give it to her if she is too lazy and selfish to care about them.'

This time he was gone even longer than the first. Somehow a cloud had been cast on the evening. Zina knew that his anger was based on his own feeling of hurt that Fiona, who had always had such a special relationship with him, could have behaved like it. By the time he came back it was his turn to look miserable.

'I guess I laid into her more heavily than I needed to, but Zee, we have to teach her, don't we? She said to tell you she thinks about you all the time—'

'Never mind about me, I think perhaps the female of the species is tougher than the male over some things. What did she say about Tommy?'

'She cried. I made her cry. I feel such a heel.'

'No darling, not a heel. A good parent – and it's not easy at this distance.'

After a moment Peter's mouth twitched into what was almost a smile. 'She threw the phone onto the desk, I heard it, and I heard how she stamped off, it sounded as though she banged her feet on the stairs and then a door slammed. The exit of a drama queen. Hermann could hear there was trouble and, ever a peacemaker, he came on the line. I told him what it was all about

236

and he said—' and at this Peter took on the voice of the German-born American citizen – '"Gee man, what do we guys do with these women? Don't you worry, the fair Fiona is in kind hands. I will give her ten minutes to come to terms with the error of her ways and if she's not down the stairs by then with a smile on her face, Heila will go and have a nice quiet talk with her. She's a great kid. OK man, a bit full of her own importance at the moment, of course she is, but there's not a selfish streak in her true character. You and your good lady put it right out of your heads and I give you my word in half an hour she will be a happy bunny again and before she goes to bed tonight there will be two letters in the mail box."'

Peter tipped back the remains of his drink and put his glass down. 'An early night for us tonight, Zina?' he suggested in a voice she found hard to resist. 'Back in my own bed.' Then holding both her hands in his, he asked, 'Have you missed me as much as I've missed you?'

'Your bed?' she answered with a soft laugh, '*our* bed. And yes, I've missed you every night and every day. We have so much time to make up. But Peter, let's wait a bit before we go up. Pour us another drink and put some music on for a while.'

He raised his eyebrows. 'That doesn't sound like the lady I've been dreaming of.'

'Tonight is so special. Do you know how long it is since we were together?'

'Together in bed? I know exactly how long. I went to the States in the middle of August leaving you with two good arms and legs, and here we are with another summer on us. Isn't that long enough for us to have to wait?' There was a teasing note in his voice even though he did as she suggested and the room was filled with the sound of a Viennese waltz. His idea of music was very different from hers, but the soft background of the lilting waltz was a bridge between the two.

'I don't want our night to be spoilt with worries about the children. Tonight belongs to us, just *us*.' She tried to explain why she wanted to move on from the children before the start of their own time.

He sat down by her side on the settee and took her hand in his. 'You're a nice lady, Mrs Marchand, I expect that's why I married you.'

'Rubbish! You married me because I decided I wanted you for my husband and once I had you in my sights you hadn't a chance,' she said with a laugh. 'But, about tonight, nothing must spoil what we've waited so long for. Me in working order again and you home, no one in our world except *us*. Nothing must spoil it; not worrying about Tom being hurt or about you grumbling at Fiona. They have to sort themselves out, darling, that's a lesson life teaches everyone.' She rested against him and felt his arm go round her.

'You make it sound easy,' he whispered, turning her head so that she was looking at him, her face only inches from his. 'Perhaps women are harder than men, like you say. Zee, if I ever lost you I'd have no courage, no hope, no will to live.'

'And no choice either. One day either you or I will have to face it, darling Peter. Please God

238

not for many, many years, not till we have a brood of great-grandchildren.' Her mood seemed to change, he could sense it in the way she drew her head away from his. Then she leant forward so that she moved her parted lips on his as she murmured, 'Please sir, I've changed my mind. I want you to take me to bed, I want us to make glorious love, we have nine months of frustrated loneliness to make up for.'

'If it were winter with a fire in the hearth, I wouldn't wait to take you upstairs . . .' He sounded as though he spoke with clenched teeth. 'I'd like to tear off your clothes this very minute and have you on the rug. Come, woman. Bedtime.'

Still she moved her mouth on his. 'We can make our own warmth.' She was unbuttoning his shirt, then she was kneeling in front of him moving her face against his bare chest. Outside, dusk was deepening as she reached to turn off the table lamp, her excitement mounting. Both of them were stripping off their clothes; only free of them would they find complete abandonment to the need that drove them.

The Viennese waltz was replaced by a tango. Which one led the way they didn't question but in seconds she was in his arms, her naked body close against his as he took her weight and they rocked gently in time to the music. This wasn't so much dancing as it was a preamble to where they were heading; and with the certainty of what was within their grasp, their passion mounted with the rhythm. He heard that familiar soft half moan in her throat telling him more than any words, a sound that had haunted him in the isolation of his hotel bedroom, and from his quickened breathing and his nakedness pressing hard against her, she knew their moment had come.

'Now, now Peter.' She drew back from him far enough to move his hand to her breast as together they sank to the ground on the soft furry rug. The night was their own, the music changed again, this time to a rumba, but to them it was no more than a background to what filled their hearts and minds. Peter was home.

Films had brought him fame beyond the expectations of his early years, and since he'd left the repertory company soon after they'd married he had never been back on the stage. But, apart from his realization that a future in Hollywood wasn't for him and certainly it wasn't for Zina, one of the things that had decided him against signing that five-year contract was a meeting with Carl Weinberg, an Austrian by birth who was visiting friends in Hollywood. England was his adopted country and, as a most successful producer on the scene of London theatre, his name was familiar to Peter. Immediately they'd met they had felt themselves to be on the same wavelength and talking to him had reawakened Peter's original stage ambitions. More than that, when Carl returned to London he would be casting for a production of Shakespeare's *King Lear* and he'd talked to Peter about Lear being a challenging role, finally offering it to him, pointing out that it would be a good career move. The last time Peter had acted in a Shakespeare play had been when he'd been in the sixth form at school and had played the lead role in *Richard the Second*. The opportunity to play King Lear had triggered something that had lain dormant over the years and it had seemed providential that the proposition had been made when his career needed the excitement and challenge a return to the stage would bring.

That first night at home, when they were gloriously satisfied and content and finally lay down in bed, he talked to Zina of what he had in mind.

'It'll be a most important career move,' he said. 'It *has* to be a success, or it'll leave a stain that will be hard to get over. But Zee, it's what I need. Think of it, Lear tugs your heart strings, one of Shakespeare's greatest characters.'

'You know what, my precious Peter? You're maturing really well. You're moving into serious theatre, the sort that isn't touched by the faint-hearted. You'll get right under the skin of Lear, I know you will.'

In the dark she felt him nod. 'I must. I want to. It sounds silly perhaps, but reading the play I've wept for him and with him. Can I do it? I've never wanted a part as much as I do this one. You think I can make it, Zee?'

'I know you can. It's funny about Shakespeare, isn't it? We all study his works when we're at school and far too young to appreciate what we read. Is that so that we get the feeling of the beauty of the words, do you suppose? Honestly, at fourteen I believed I was put off for life.'

'I'll make Lear live and breathe for you. I must.'

She had never known him to talk like it about

any role in the past. In fact, he seldom mentioned the characters he played. But this was different. This would mean he had hours of work ahead of him learning lines, lines that must be word perfect. And as if his thoughts had followed her own, he said, 'I've been given a glorious responsibility, to bring flesh and blood to a character that is part of drama that has been our heritage for centuries. And I will, I swear I will. It's years since I've learnt lines, and never ones that mattered so much that not a syllable must be wrong.' Then with a laugh that left her in no doubt how thrilled he was to have been handed this life-changing role, he added, 'It's like the day I was made head boy at school, a combination of being lifted right out of myself, being a bit frightened by the responsibility and yet proud, so proud.'

'I'm proud too. And Carl what's-his-name must be a very wise man to have recognized you're not like so many of them – all front and no back, to use one of Mrs Cripps's favourite expressions. You'll be a great success. Promise you won't let it change you, I love you just as you are.'

'Change me? If anything it might make me humble.'

'After tonight's performance humility would be out of character.' Lying in the dark she wriggled closer to him, moving her hand down his naked body, secretly exploring to see if his recovery had been as quick as her own. Finding her goal, her hand moved on him. She believed King Lear must be on her side; thoughts of him had driven sleep away. 'The night's ours, I'm

242

wide awake and if you tell me you're ready for sleep you'll be fibbing.' She spoke softly, tenderly but he detected laughter just under the surface. Downstairs they had been driven by a physical need that couldn't be denied. Now was very different.

'The woman's a temptress,' he teased softly. 'Is there no satisfying her?'

'Try her and find out,' she answered. With her mouth on his she moved her tongue lightly, almost teasingly on his lips. Downstairs their love-making had been driven by love and by a physical need that could be satisfied no other way; laughter had played no part. But this was different. She reached to put the bedside light on and they looked at each other, not with sultry, driving passion, but with laughter in their eyes, laughter that was as much an expression of their love as their earlier sensual desire had been. And so he brought her again to the mountain that together they climbed, not Everest this time, but sunny slopes where wild flowers grew, and after they reached the summit they looked at each other as they had before the climb started and laughed, not because there was anything funny, but from pure joy.

Through the time Peter had been away, Jenny had often driven over to Newton House, sometimes on her own but, as Zina recovered, more often with Derek. In the past it had never been her habit to drop in casually when Peter was home, something that had annoyed Zina as she'd seen it as a slight on him. Then Derek Masters had come into the picture and things had changed. The two men were very comfortable together, perhaps drawn by the fact that neither had ever followed a profession where he left home in the morning and returned in the evening. A musician and an actor, both had known good and bad lodgings in their early years, which had been one of the reasons why, when Derek had formed the Meinholt Quintet, he had arranged their recitals in the West Country and, as far as possible, looked for members of the quintet from that region. That way, their nights away from home were limited.

It was an evening late in the summer when Jenny and Derek were having dinner at Newton House. Although it wasn't yet officially autumn, the temperature had dropped and there was a log fire burning in the open grate of the drawing room where the four of them went after the meal.

'What about some music?' Jenny suggested, ashamed of her smug feeling of pleasure that 'their sort of music' would shut Peter out. 'Are you up to playing, Zina, if Derek accompanies you?' There, Peter my lad, we're not all philistines where music is concerned. You see, Zina will never be completely yours; she's one of *us*.

But he played the perfect host – or perhaps it was the perfect actor – as he went up to the music room and turned on the electric fire.

'Is Zina getting the coffee?' he asked when he came back. 'We'll have that before we go upstairs. I've put the fire on but it'll be a while before it gets as warm as it is in this room. If you find it cold, Mother-in-law, Zina can lend you a wrap.' He gave no hint that he realized she had suggested

244

music expecting it would make him feel outside their magic orbit.

A quarter of an hour later Zina picked up her fiddle, running her hand over the smooth beauty of the wood in something of a caress. For so long she had been unable to play and, even when all the plaster had been removed, she had yet to hold her fiddle for more than two or three minutes at a time, as if drawing the bow over the strings was a necessary part of life. But tonight she would test herself; she would make music. No wonder her heart thumped, whether from apprehension or excitement. Turning the pegs to tighten the strings as she tuned up and Derek took his place at the piano, she felt whole again, the misery of the past months was surely behind her. Although she'd been free of plaster for some weeks the physiotherapist had been treating her regularly and had told her not to do anything to strain her arms or shoulders. She remembered the warning as she tucked her fiddle under her chin, but surely strain meant heavy lifting or carrying; her violin had been part of her life for so long that it could never come into that category. And yet, until that evening, a silent voice had warned her not to play.

Derek had looked through the music and passed her the violin score of a Brahms Sonata. For nearly half an hour they played while Jenny listened, feeling thoroughly satisfied with where life had brought them all, and Peter kept an anxious eye on Zina. Jenny was enjoying the music but, perhaps even more, she was enjoying seeing an expression she construed as impatience on Peter's face. How could Zina have married a man with no appreciation of something so much part of her life?

As the last notes died away she said, 'That was a joy! What else will you play?' delighting in believing she could read Peter's thoughts.

'I think you should stop, Zina. You haven't touched that fiddle for months until now.'

'It's probably good exercise for me,' she answered, at which Jenny nodded, feeling the point was hers. Zina remembered the warnings against straining the muscles, but playing a fiddle was hardly heavy work. So she tried to ignore the pain and prove what she said to be correct: exercise must be doing her good. All she knew for certain was that making music was like a drug to her and she had been deprived of it for far too long. 'The Caesar Franck is in that pile, Derek, I'd love to play that again.'

So they started again and Jenny relaxed in her chair with a smile of satisfaction while Peter gave the impression of sitting on the edge of his chair waiting for it to be over. He wasn't aware of what they played (not that he was really listening anyway), all his concentration was on Zina. He knew how desperately she wanted to rejoin the quintet, he even gave a passing moment's sympathy to her temporary replacement who would soon find herself looking for a new slot to fit into, but at the front of his mind was concern for Zina. When she had joined 'that merry band of travelling musicians' he had been full of resentment that they could mean so much to her. But now his one hope was that she would be deemed fit to follow where her heart led, for he had come to understand that it was only in his own mind that her love for music could ever come between them. When he had seen the physiotherapist out after a recent visit, he had spoken to her about Zina's prospects. The outcome of the conversation had been a visit from the doctor who, when asked, had been very evasive. 'Once you commit yourself there can be no lessening of the pressure, no turning back,' he had hedged, and, 'Rest is what it needs, my dear. Not only were bones broken, but muscles were torn. The last thing you want is to force yourself to do more than nature wants. A recital is a very different thing from playing at home where you can stop when you feel you've had enough.' So it was little wonder that Peter watched her so carefully. They had been playing for about three quarters of an hour and were halfway through the second movement of the Franck when from where he sat on the edge of his chair he seemed ready to spring into action any second, certain he saw a change in her and yet not sure what. Still she played the notes but he felt she had lost her original abandon into the sound and played mechanically.

Neither Jenny nor Derek suspected that anything was wrong until her right arm flopped and her bow fell to the ground. Her eyes were closed and although her left hand still held the neck of the instrument, with each second her grip was going. Like a Jack-in-the-Box Peter was out of his chair and across the space that divided them, taking her weight as he supported her. She seemed unaware that Derek, too, had jumped to his feet and taken the violin from her before picking up the bow. Although she was conscious, she was quite limp, leaning helplessly against Peter. Pain filled her whole mind.

'Perhaps she should have sat down to play,' Jenny suggested, 'like she will when she starts back with the quintet. I expect it's been too long for her to stand, poor child.'

No one answered her and Derek closed the lid of the piano.

'My fault,' he said, 'I should have said I'd had enough after the Brahms.'

'Silly,' Jenny answered him affectionately, 'as if she would have believed you.'

Peter wanted them gone; Zina seemed unaware of their presence. With her arms hanging limply to her sides, she leant against Peter and perhaps she didn't even realize that she was hiding from a truth she couldn't face; she was aware of nothing except the pain in her neck and shoulders. If she knew that her mother and Derek were leaving she gave no indication of it. She seemed to have no more strength than a rag doll.

'I think we should leave you to get her to bed,' Derek suggested.

'Oh, but I can get her undressed and into bed,' Jenny said and perhaps her words did filter into Zina's mind for Peter felt her press closer against him.

'We can manage,' he told them. 'I'm sorry the evening has ended this way, and so will Zina be when she realizes. If you can see yourselves out I'll take her straight across to the bedroom. I don't think there's any need to fetch the doctor out, we know exactly what the trouble is. She'll be fine by the morning.'

'That seems to treat it very casually.' The mother hen in Jenny had the upper hand. 'The poor girl is barely conscious. Look at her, she's not really with us at all.' Her eyes met Peter's and she made no attempt to hide her natural dislike of him, his cavalier way of dismissing Zina's near collapse reigniting the embers.

But it was Derek the peacemaker who had the last word.

'She had had her arms raised putting a strain on her shoulder muscles for far too long, muscles she hasn't used for months. We should have had more consideration than let her do it. As you say, Peter, by morning she'll be herself again. We'll give you a ring around breakfast time so that you can set Jenny's mind at rest – and don't forget we're always available if you need us.'

All this time Zina had kept her face away from them, only Peter knew from the dampness on his neck and her short, almost silent, jerky breaths that she was crying. Still they stood in the same position as the sound of the footsteps on the stairs grew faint and then there was the slam of the front door. Only then did she lose her hold on control and he heard a great gasp for air as she sobbed.

'Is it still so painful?' he asked her anxiously, having assumed that once she had let her body sag the pain in her muscles would ease.

She shook her head. 'It's not that,' she answered, having as little control over her voice as she had had over her arms a few minutes before. 'I can't do it, Peter. The physiotherapist warned me – when she was massaging me and you were out of the room, she told me that I shall always have to be careful. Do a little at a time, that's what she said. But that's no good,' she gulped, 'you can't play a fiddle a little at a time.'

'Do as she says, Zee, and little by little you might find yourself able to increase how long you play. Tonight wasn't a fair test, you were straight in at the deep end.'

'Was magic,' she sniffed, 'the first five minutes. Then it started. I made myself think I could work through it, I didn't think it would be like that.'

'Play every day, just until it starts to hurt, but no longer. Perhaps two or three times a day, perhaps more, but always stop as soon as the pain comes. You might find that your muscles will get stronger and gradually without your realizing it you will be playing for longer before you feel the strain.'

She nodded, but the look of hopelessness was still there.

As the weeks passed she did as Peter had said, playing many times in each day, always stopping when the pain started. It made no difference. After not many minutes the pain was there coming between her and the music. She talked to the doctor, she wrestled with herself, finding the courage to do what had to be done and finally she told Derek he must find a permanent replacement for her in the quintet.

Meantime Peter had found a one-bedroom flat in Central London and moved there when the play went into rehearsal, always driving home at every opportunity of a free day. About every fortnight a 'Dear Dad and Mum, Everything is really exciting here' letter arrived from Fiona and, from talking on the phone to Tom, Zina knew his were much the same. Peter's rare laying down of the rules must have been taken to heart.

'Come back to town with me for a few days,' Peter suggested to Zina one Sunday afternoon. 'Go out and spoil yourself with some new clothes. Daytime I'm tied up but we'd have evenings—' then with a light kiss on the end of her nose – 'and nights.'

So a new regime was born. When opening night came for *King Lear* she watched his every move and heard his every syllable, felt the sting of tears, whether of love and pride in him or for the poor king, she didn't ask as she felt herself falling in love with him all over again. Only she knew of his own fear, only she knew of how desperately he needed his stage debut to be a success. Sitting in the front row of the stalls she felt her own heart racing as he entered the stage and she prayed with all her heart that the audience would be carried with him.

It was she who crept out before he was awake the next morning to bring home the newspapers.

'Peter! You can't lie there sleeping! Open your eyes – and ears – and listen to what the critics have written. I've checked them all, and you just hear what they say about you. "Peter Marchand, in a bold move from screen to stage, brought King Lear to life carrying the audience with him."

251

And just listen to this one: "I have seen King Lear well acted many times, but Peter Marchand's performance lifted the sad and demented king to a higher plane. A night no member of the audience will easily forget."'

'Thank God,' Peter whispered. 'Not just for me, but for the play; it deserves nothing less.'

When Tom came on holiday, to start with Peter stayed in the flat by himself coming home for weekends but after about three weeks when he returned to London, Tom went with him. In a one-bedroom flat there wasn't room for all three of them so Zina stayed at home. As they said their farewells her mind turned to Fiona, always so dear to Peter. Of course it was good to see 'the boys' together but she knew as she watched the car disappear out of the drive that Peter's thoughts must have strayed the same way as hers. How much are any of us masters of our own destiny?

Fiona, little more that a child in years if not in experience and happily settled with Hermann's family, had been offered a contract for five more films, probably films that would carry her almost through her teen years. Zina's reaction had been that 'the child can't be out there on her own, she must come home'. Peter's personal feeling had been more complicated: he hated his darling Fiona to be so far away, always he had been her guiding star and now that had been taken from him. He knew her well enough to be sure that they were missing her far more than she was missing them and all that home had meant to her. And, more than Zina, he realized that an

252

opportunity like this was unlikely to come again and knowing how excited she was at the prospect of five more films, he signed the contract giving his consent. Also he was honest enough to know that if they insisted that she held to the bargain that she had been left behind so that she could make just the one film, it would put an insurmountable barrier between her and her family.

Tom spent the week in London with Peter, going twice to watch *King Lear* and feeling it brought him closer to his father than he had ever been. When they came home the following Saturday night – or more accurately Sunday morning by the time the evening performance was over and they'd driven from London – they found Zina still up and waiting for them. Usually when she'd been at the flat during the week she would bring the car to the theatre to collect Peter and they would drive back together, having a supper of sandwiches and coffee as they came. She always got extra pleasure out of this routine journey when first she would drive while he ate and then, somewhere near Andover, always in the same lay-by, they changed places and Peter took over for the rest of the journey and she ate her share of the sandwiches. She enjoyed it especially because it seemed to symbolize just how unchanged he was with the years. By the time they reached home the night was usually half over, just as it was on the Saturday night/Sunday morning when she waited for him to drive back with Tom.

'The lights are on downstairs, Dad. I wonder

if Mum got us anything to eat before she went to bed.'

'Better than that, she's opening the door for us.'

'Nearly half past three and she's waited up for us. Gosh!' Just for a moment Tom's surprise and pleasure made Peter ashamed that he could take it for granted she would always be there waiting. But as she ran down the front steps to open the car door, shame was forgotten. Not for the first time Zina was glad they had no near neighbours to be woken by their excited voices and slamming of car doors before they went inside. Always when Peter had been working away, the highlight of her week, the moment she looked toward, had been his arrival home. And that night, with Tom there too, there was a feeling of celebration. That it was the middle of the night did nothing to detract from it.

Tom's week had been crammed. Two evenings with King Lear, one listening to a chamber music recital in a church, two with full orchestras in concert halls and, doing much for his fast-growing confidence, wherever he'd been he'd travelled on the underground and never once got on a train going the wrong way. He was ready for anything.

'What about you, Mum? How's the fiddle arm?'

'I can play for ten minutes before it starts to hurt and fifteen before it really gives me gip. But I've been working at the piano. Except for accompanying you or playing carols at Christmas, that sort of thing, I hadn't played for years. Like you, I'd given my heart to the violin and let the piano drop. So I've been getting to grips with it again.

254

I know it will always be second best to me, but I'm so thankful I had the early training. It's like riding a bike – you never forget.'

'That's good, Mum. We'll still be a team, we can still play together.'

Peter envied them their easy camaraderie.

'Any letters from Fiona?' he asked.

'One for us and one for you, Tom. I put yours in your bedroom, Tom.' There had been no news in the letter and she didn't doubt that his would be pretty well the same. 'Nothing momentous in ours, in fact at first glance I thought she was wasting her time out there. The word "party" keep jumping up at me out of the page. But I'd misjudged her. Page two was about filming and what she's doing – but I don't think she sees it as work, rather as having a good time.'

'I wish she was filming here in England,' Tom said, 'but isn't it great that she's doing something she really enjoys. Can't you just see her; she sort of bubbles with pleasure, doesn't she?'

Both his parents were watching him, Peter with a new understanding nourished by the shared week in London, Zina with pure love.

Through the next few years Peter and Zina moved forward in a rut, a comfortable rut taking no note of the passing of time. The only reminder was the development of the one-time children, both of them so set on where they meant their lives to take them.

Fiona had been in the States for almost a year and a half the first time Zina flew to California to see her. It wasn't possible for Peter to come as he was still on the London stage in the guise of King Lear, but they agreed that she should go alone this time and when the run of the play ended he would do the same thing, that way Fiona would have two visits rather than a joint one to look forward to. Except for seeing Fiona and setting her mind at rest that she was happy and settled, the holiday did nothing for Zina more than confirm what in her heart she had always known – living as she did at Newton House in an isolated spot in South Devon was where she belonged. There was no doubting Fiona's pleasure and pride in showing off her new surroundings, for her they fell little short of paradise. As a child she had been enchantingly pretty, but the girl who waited for her mother at the airport was no longer that same child. Less than two years older but Hollywood had put its stamp on her, a stamp she wore with pride. She might have been any age from fourteen to nineteen, discretely made-up, casually dressed in denim trousers and a plain white shirt, it was no wonder heads turned to look at her as she spied Zina in the crowd emerging from the arrivals gate. She waved and waited while the mass of people jostled for place as they hurried along.

Putting down her heavy suitcase Zina took her in a bear-like hug.

'Oh but it's good to see you. But where's the child who went off with her father?' she said with a laugh.

'I guess I've come a long way since then, Mum. You look just the same; that's the nice thing about mums. I'll take the case. I've got a cab waiting outside.' Picking up the case she raised her eyebrows. 'Gosh, whatever have you got in here? It weighs a ton.' But, ton or not, before she'd walked half a dozen paces while Zina felt her first twinge of irritation knowing her actress daughter was making the most of the not-terribly heavy load, a middle-aged man appeared, his smile including them both.

'That's looks to be mighty heavy. May I be of assistance?'

Both answering at once, Zina said, 'That's very kind, but we have a cab just outside so we can manage.'

But overriding her, Fiona put the case down and gave her most radiant smile to the stranger as she answered, 'That'll be a real life-saver. My mother doesn't know how to travel light.'

Reaching the cab Zina knew she sounded buttoned-up and prim as she watched the stranger hand the bag over to the driver and held out her hand to him. 'That was most kind of you.'

'Surely my pleasure,' he answered with his remark directed not at her but at Fiona.

'My pleasure too,' she chuckled. 'I was more than glad to hand it over. Thanks a load.'

Was it natural for a mother to resent being passed over for her daughter, Zina asked herself, not feeling proud of her behaviour? It was the first time she had ever felt herself to be anything but young. Thirty-six years old and pushed into the sidelines by a daughter who had forgotten that at just fifteen she was surely still a child. Had they been right in letting her take her golden opportunity? Or, if they'd brought her home where she belonged would she still have rushed to find the confidence of adulthood before her time? If only Peter had been with them there would have been no cloud on the scene.

For Fiona the meeting had been all she had hoped. Her mother would understand that she was no longer just some kid, she knew about the world.

The not-as-heavy-as-Fiona-liked-to-pretend suitcase contained more new clothes than Zina had bought for years and during the fortnight she was there she wore them all; and never had she felt so out of step with the people who now made up Fiona's world. She was invited to dinner with famous Edwin Cummings and his wife, (Edwin was co-starring with Fiona, playing her father) and proudly dressed in her new dinner gown, a closely-fitting creation with sleeves and high neck, for she had always been led to believe that bare arms and low-cut bodices were not correct for dinner. But here, apparently, there were no such rules. The female guests seemed bent on outdoing each other in how much body they could expose: open side seams showing legs as high as legs go, low-cut bodices that left nothing to the imagination, some had low backs, all had bare arms. Zina had no wish to dress like it, but being in a group of people so different from herself made her feel ancient. She told herself that was ridiculous, she was only thirty-six and many of these people were far more, and yet she felt dowdy in her expensive and demure creation. If only Peter were here. The only ones she was at ease with were Hermann and Heila, but as

Fiona had persuaded them that she wanted to rent an apartment for the fortnight of her mother's stay (and Heila had made the necessary arrangements so that it was rented in her name because of Fiona's age) she didn't see as much of them as she had hoped.

'How's it going? It's great to think of you two girls together,' Peter said when he phoned at four in the afternoon California time.

'I don't think we need to worry about her; she's fine. Full of confidence, and loving everything American. She's at the studio most days, all day – and feeling very cock-a-hoop with herself.'

He laughed tolerantly. 'And you? How do you feel in the environment of glamour? Are you going to tell me you regret the choice we made?' And she could tell from his tone that he knew what her answer would be.

'You know my idea of heaven? But I can stand all the razzmatazz for a short time just to know she is in her element. I wish, wish so much, she hadn't got this burning desire to be part of the scene here. Not for the first time it makes me think of Mrs C's expression – you know, the one that something is all front and no back. Is that what you felt, Peter? It must have been.'

'It certainly wouldn't have suited us. But I'm glad the kid's enjoying it all. Don't worry, Zee. At her age excitement is an essential part of life. I just hope we have given her firm enough roots that she'll not get too swept away. Does she look well?'

'More than well, she looks radiant. And that's not mother love; it's fact. You should see the looks that are cast in her direction as soon as she puts her nose out of doors. And this is the home of beautiful women. I feel a complete "has been".'

She heard the affection in his laugh and assumed it was for Fiona until he said, 'Has been, is now and will be forever more, that's what you are my beloved Zee. If you were here this minute . . .'

'At four o'clock in the afternoon?' she laughed, feeling herself more desirable by the second.

'Midnight rainy London town, but whatever time, night or day, you know what you do to me. This is the longest fortnight since I took the flat. I expect you wish you were staying with the kid for longer but I'm just waiting for the moment you walk through that arrivals gate.'

'Me too. Oh Peter, I do miss you. It must be all in the mind. After all, more often than not you've been away and I've never felt cut off from you like I do here. I should land at a quarter to ten on Sunday morning, your time, so what shall we do? Go to the flat? Or go home just for what's left of the weekend?'

'If you aren't too shattered for the drive, let's go home. Back where we belong. There won't be much weekend left so maybe you could come back with me for next week.'

'Bliss. If I were a cat I'd be purring just thinking about it. Any news of Tom?'

'No, the difficulty is that when he's free I'm not. We'll call him on Sunday. I did ring Mother-in-law this morning though and I was glad I had. She'd expected Derek home but he'd just phoned to say he'd had to put the car in, it had played up on the outbound trip to Penzance and when

260

he went to collect it, it wasn't ready, so he won't be back until this evening. I think she was glad to chat – even to me.'

'You are a good chap.'

'I know I am. Aren't you just a lucky girl!' If Jenny had heard him, her more kindly than usual sentiments would have vanished.

In the early hours of Sunday morning the cab took Fiona back to Hermann's where she was dropped off before it carried on to the airport with Zina.

'It's been great showing you everything, Mum,' Fiona said as they started the short drive. 'I bet you have second thoughts now you've seen how great everything is out here and poor old you has to go home to dull, sleepy Devon. Maybe I could drop a hint that Dad might be prepared to have another think.'

'He refused on his own account, not just on mine. We belong in dull, sleepy Devon, as you call it. And it's waiting to welcome you back when you have a holiday.' Somehow even as she said it she was sure that if Fiona had time to kill she would choose somewhere other than where she had been a child. 'Don't grow up too quickly, will you. Stay young and carefree as long as you can.'

'Oh Mum, you make me laugh. I know lots of grown ups, am friendly with them and they treat me like an ordinary person not some half-witted kid, but none of them are full of care, even though some have been through horrid times – unhappy marriages, all that sort of thing. But they've got over it and found plenty of fun still in life. Give

261

my love to Dad and tell him I'm looking forward to him killing off that wretched old King Lear so that he can come over.'

'And Tommy?'

Fiona chuckled. 'You called him Tommy, just like when we were little kids. Yes, give Tom my love and tell him there's a lot more to life than that fiddle of his. I meant to ask you, Mum – are you playing back in the quintet again? You haven't talked about it.'

The question took Zina by surprise, for she knew she had told Fiona in letters about having to give up playing.

'No point in talking about it, there's nothing I can do about it. I can't play any more. I had to give up.'

'You mean Granderek didn't wait for you? That was mean.'

'He waited ages with a temporary replacement, but I had to face up to not being able to play any more and he took her on permanently.'

'Why don't you try to get taken on by someone else now that you're better?' Not for the first time Zina felt disappointed in her daughter. Did she never read what was written to her, or listen, *really listen*, to anything unless it concerned herself? She wished she'd not even been asked about her fiddle, especially when in a few minutes they would have said goodbye.

But Fiona had already moved on to the next thing, pleased that she'd remembered to ask about the fiddle and not realizing she hadn't listened properly to Zina's reply.

'Tell Dad I hope *King Lear* soon gets put to

262

bed. It'll be great when he comes out. I'll get Heila to rent the apartment again. Can't you just imagine it, it'll be a blast, me and Dad together. We're almost there. I've got my key out ready. Have a good flight, Mum. It's been great, hasn't it?' Then with a giggle she couldn't suppress, she added, 'Back home, think how you'll be able to boast about all the famous people you've met. He's slowing down; we're nearly there. I'll give you a hug in the cab and then get out quietly so I won't wake them at this ungodly hour. Give my love to Tom and Dad and tell them I've got lots to show them when they come.' Then a hug and she was out on the pavement – or the side-walk as she would have called it.

So Zina went home thankfully to England and to Peter, as sure as he had been that as long as Fiona was with Heila they had no cause to worry about her. A few more months and the curtain fell for the last time on *King Lear*. True to his word Peter flew out. Perhaps for him the visit was easier, he was at home in the world that seemed to have turned Fiona's head and to have a fortnight sharing an apartment with her was a new and rewarding experience. Perhaps he was able to see beyond her enthusiasm for celebrity and all people famous; or perhaps she didn't feel the need to impress him by dropping well-known names into the conversation at every opportunity as she had with her mother. He had set out on the trip uncertain what her rise to stardom would have done to their old relationship; but half an hour with her and he knew that nothing had changed for them. They both loved the intimacy of cooking their own breakfast, of having deep and serious conversations about the way she hoped her career would go. Her one disappointment was when she tried to persuade him to rethink his decision about coming to Hollywood she found that he was not to be moved.

As time went on, Peter went for a brief spell whenever he was 'resting' and once each year Zina spent two weeks in California, usually planning the visit to fit into Tom's programme as his own career developed, not in the blaze of glory that had accompanied Fiona's but with engagements as a soloist in programmes of minor orchestras. The lives of the twins had moved in different directions and as they approached adulthood they lost the closeness that had held them apart from the rest of the world in childhood.

Nine

'They make a handsome – beautiful – couple,' Zina spoke softly to Peter, although in the loud buzz of voices it was unlikely anyone would have noticed what she said even if she had shouted.

'Good looking, yes. But I think you're jumping the gun, handsome young men are pretty commonplace out here. I don't know what sort of life partner I would expect for her but I've never considered looks would be near the top of her priorities.' As he answered he was looking to the far corner of the large room where Fiona and Ivor Huntley were talking together. The godlike young man, with his fair hair and bronzed good looks had been her co-star in *Out of the Shadows*, which had had its premier that evening, culminating in this party. With Peter, Zina had attended many parties in England following premiers of his films, but none had had the aura of glamour (and to her mind artificiality) that surrounded her here in Hollywood. Always she had felt herself to be among friends even if she had been meeting many of them for the first time; here she felt no more than Peter's appendage, plain and dowdy despite having spent the afternoon having her hair 'tarted up' as she thought of it and wearing an evening dress that had cost what she considered quite immoral. For Peter it was different; he was recognized and respected in his own right not simply as Fiona's parent.

What were they doing? Fiona and Ivor had stepped up onto a dais at the end of the room, standing hand-in-hand until he literally yelled to make himself heard above the clamour. 'Quiet, everyone. I have an important announcement to make.'

'Christ, no!' Peter whispered. 'No, it can't be *that.*' Zina took his hand in hers but he didn't seem to notice. Fortunately the eyes of the other partygoers were on the couple on the dais so only *she* saw the anguish in his expression.

'Tonight you have watched Fiona and me on the screen and seen just how well we slot together,' he said, 'and now I'm inviting you to come one stage further with us.' Then, down on one knee while Fiona held her left hand to be taken in his, he said, 'Fiona Marchand will you be my wife?'

'I will,' Fiona answered, with all the solemnity of a marriage service, at which he produced a ring from the inside pocket of his dinner jacket and slipped it onto her finger and the press cameras flashed. Then, with a complete change of mood and a hint of the Fiona of old, she stated, 'But when I make up my mind what I want, I want it *now.* I want to be married while my parents are visiting from England – Peter Marchand, did you all know he was my father? They go back to England at the weekend.'

'Tonight is too soon to fix it, but I'll see about it first thing in the morning,' Ivor answered with all the charm that was sending him to the top of the popularity charts.

Looking at Peter, Zina tightened her grip on his hand. The tic in his cheek was working overtime and, before he tightly closed his eyes, she saw the tears well up.

'Darling,' she whispered, again quite unnecessarily for everyone else in the room seemed to have sprung to life and pushed to get close to the happy couple with their congratulations, 'we mustn't judge him, we don't even know him yet. She's not stupid; she must love him.'

Her words must have broken through his misery for she felt his answering grip of her hand as he answered, 'Pray God you're right. Your father must have said much the same to Mother-in-law,' he added, trying to force a note of hope into his voice. 'But she's a child still, an excited child thrilled with where life has brought her.'

'She is no child. How can she be after the years she's been out here. We ought to go and meet our future son-in-law. Try and put on a brave face, for her sake, Peter. Good or bad, we are always there for her. And just because we don't know him, it doesn't mean that he isn't worth knowing. Let's push to the front and give her the blessing she deserves.'

They did their best. Recognizing Peter and knowing Fiona was his daughter, the well-wishers made way for them and he proved his acting skills as he congratulated Ivor and held his beloved Fiona in a bear-like hug.

The wedding was arranged for the following

267

Friday and everything went off according to plan, press photographers having a field day. When Zina and Peter returned to England the following day the young couple went with them. They didn't come to Devon but took a cab from Heathrow to London, promising to visit before they returned to the States.

'You'd think the first thing she would have done would have been to go to hear Tom play, or at any rate to *see* him if she didn't want to go to the concert,' Peter said as he switched on the engine and started to drive out of the long stay car park. 'He's playing in Manchester on Tuesday but she says they have things to do in London. What can be more important than seeing Tom? He'll be dreadfully hurt.'

'Maybe all brides can think only of themselves. And to be fair, this is their honeymoon. How many couples spend their honeymoons visiting relatives, no matter how dear? A week ago none of us would have anticipated any of this.' Zina was as unhappy about the marriage as Peter, and yet she couldn't really say why. Ivor seemed pleasant enough, albeit conceited. But then probably most young men in his position would have been the same. There weren't many Peters in the profession.

'Please God she's done right. Is there any substance to the fellow?' he muttered more to himself than to her.

'And that's history repeating itself if ever I heard it. And see how wrong my parents were. They didn't know *you* any more than we know *Ivor.* It's hard for parents to trust their children's judgement but, Peter, Fiona has always calculated what is right for her; she's nobody's fool.'

His answer was a grunt.

Back in Devon, Zina went to see her mother, prepared for her attitude to be much the same as Peter's – and her own too if she were honest. But Jenny surprised her.

'Sometimes the young ones understand each other better than the next generation can. You say she's happy?'

Zina thought before she answered. 'Almost too happy. I think that's what worries me; I feel there is something not quite right. She's not content, she – she's – I can't think how to explain.'

'Could it be that she's just being Fiona? Contentment isn't part of her make-up, always she's been wanting to be off to the next thing. Marriage may be the making of her.'

Zina laughed. 'Never let her hear you say that, Mum, "be the making of her", I mean. Wife and mother would be bottom of her list of priorities. I suppose that's what worries me. When I married Peter and found so soon that I was pregnant, for me marriage came first, there was no contest. And yet, until then, music had always been my guiding star. When, or should I say if ever, she finds she's pregnant I believe she would be devastated.'

'That may not be for years; she's young. Just wait until the time comes, my dear. Nature sorts all these things out – something to do with these hormones people talk such a lot about these days. We never used even to hear the word, but now it seems an excuse for everything.'

After a week in London the newly-weds came to Newton House and Tom joined them for three days. It should have been wonderful. Peter wasn't due to start rehearsing *Macbeth* for another fortnight so, surely these few days were something they had dreamed of for years. Except that Ivor never passed a mirror without glancing at his reflection there was nothing to dislike in him and he was obviously under Fiona's spell. So why did Zina have such a feeling that all wasn't well? It might have stemmed from something in Fiona's manner. She seemed to be on edge; her smile too bright and her laugh too loud. They were due to go back to California on the last Sunday in June, just the time when Peter had planned to return to the flat in London ready for rehearsals. So Zina decided to go to the flat with him, then together on the way they could see the young ones off at Heathrow. Late afternoon of the day before they were due to leave Fiona went to find Zina in the garden where she was scratching around on the rose bed looking for any weed daring to rear its head.

'Mum, I've got to talk to you. There's something I have to tell you.'

Fear gripped Zina, but fear of what she didn't know.

'We're in an awful mess, Mum. I can't go back to work like I am. I'm pregnant.' There! She'd said it and immediately some of the fog of misery lifted.

'But you can't know yet, not for certain. Maybe if you're late it's because—' she said the first thing that came into her head while she was gripped with a sick feeling of fear. It couldn't be true, not in these days of the pill. Fiona was too wise.

'Oh Mum, don't be so pathetically naive. I'm not stupid,' the girl snapped. 'I thought you would have guessed when I wanted us to be married so quickly and come over to England.'

'It never entered my head. You said the wedding was because we were out there with you. How late are you?' But what a stupid question; for clearly Fiona was late enough to have no doubts. 'You can't be very late, you don't show at all.'

'I'm pretty well up to missing for the third time. And I hate it,' she croaked, on the verge of tears. 'I don't want it. I hate it, Mum. Everything was so perfect and now this has happened and it will all be ruined. I'll get fat and ugly.'

Ignoring her outburst Zina asked, 'How does Ivor feel about it? Can't he make you see that having a baby is – yes, it's life-changing – but Fiona, it's wonderful.'

'That's rot! It's a bloody disaster. It'll mean I can't work for months and months, not till I've had the brat and got my body in shape again – if I ever do. It's my own fault. I hadn't wanted marriage, we were having a wonderful time. But it's my own fault. We went away for two or three days and I guess I had more to drink than I realized and I forgot all about taking the pill. Just one night without it and this happens. If I'd thought about it the next day perhaps I could have taken something, done something, heaven knows what, but I couldn't even remember going to bed and it wasn't until I got late that I realized that was when it must have happened.'

'What does Ivor say? How does he feel about it?'

'He wanted us to get married anyway. But until this happened I'd said no, we had the best of all worlds as we were. With the pill I had no worries and the thing that mattered most to me was a career.' A sob caught in her throat, but she fought it. 'Now see what's happened to me. It's not fair. My boobs feel hard and gross and look disgusting, got veins showing on them – already without my clothes on I look beastly.' Then she gave a loud and out of character sniff and wiped the back of her hand over eyes and nose. 'That's why we went to London instead of coming straight here. I had an appointment to see a top-of-the-tree gynaecologist. I'd read that some people could get abortions in England – and anyway no one knew me here, I couldn't possibly have tried in the States, the papers would have got hold of the story and that might have been the end of me. So we went to London and I was sure that he would get me right. But he refused. Talked a lot of bilge. Examined me, asked me loads of questions about my health. He didn't know who I was, I said I was Fiona Cripps—' and here she surprised Zina by giving what was almost a chuckle when she thought of the cleverness of her name – 'and that I had been using the pill ever since my husband and I had been together, but one night I forgot and I begged him that surely one slip ought not to ruin my life. Don't know how he had the cheek to charge for the time I wasted with him. He said I was the right age to have my first child – first! First and last! – and gave me a lot of codswallop about how much love a baby brought to a marriage. Stupid git!'

'Fiona love, he spoke a lot of sound sense. Supposing he'd given you an abortion and something had gone wrong. Giving up a career for a baby might seem hard now, but you won't have to give up for ever.'

'You're darned right I won't. You did, but then that was different. There are masses of violinists, whether one person plays or another can't matter. But in films it's different; it's important to keep in the public eye. All I've done in the past will get forgotten. It'll be ages before I can start again. Being in films is what I've wanted as long as I can remember and it was all like a dream come true. Now it's all going to be spoilt.' She lost the battle and her face crumpled as she cried and felt herself taken in her mother's arms. 'I've got to tell Dad and he'll be – he'll be angry at Ivor – and worse than that he'll be disappointed and hurt. Don't want to hurt Dad.' Her words moved Zina more than any angry outburst could.

'Do you want to tell him yourself or would you rather I did? What about if we wait and I tell him when you and Ivor have gone?'

'Gone?' The suggestion had had the effect of stopping her crying. 'But don't you see? I can't go back out there getting to look more like a barrel every day. We've got our plan all sorted out. Ivor will go back tomorrow like we booked and he will say that I am following when I'm better but I have been feeling dreadful, he expects I've got a tummy bug of some sort. Then in a few weeks he can tell them that I'm still groggy and the doctor has confirmed that it's the early part of being pregnant. He'll say that you and Dad are worried about me and for the time being I'm staying on here because I'm having such a bad time I can't face the long flight. He'll make it very plausible, Mum; use all his skills. He has to get back because he is lined up to start filming in a week or so.'

'Well,' Zina said, her cool tone seeming to draw a line under the subject, 'you appear to have it all sorted out.'

'It seems the best thing to do. This is my home. I thought you'd want me here.'

'Of course we want you here, Newton House is our family refuge. And once Peter has had time to digest what we tell him, he will be over the moon.'

'That's what I thought. Can I borrow your hanky? Thanks.' She scrubbed it over her tear-smudged face then passed it back with a smile that appeared more natural than Zina had seen since she arrived. How was it that after crying as she had, she wasn't left with bloodshot eyes? 'Now, I'll tell you what, Mum. We'll be kind to Dad, we'll tell him that I've been feeling groggy, been sick in the mornings, we'll pile it on. Actually a couple of months ago it was the truth, every morning when I got out of bed I had to rush to the loo to be disgustingly sick like some dirty drunkard in the gutter. Revolting. Anyway Dad needn't know any of that, we'll tell him the

274

same story as later Ivor will tell our friends back home.'

'Oh no we won't! Peter is to be told the truth. Not until Ivor has gone. Tomorrow you can stay in bed in the morning and I'll see them off and say I'm staying here with you because you don't feel well. But once Ivor has gone Peter will be told the whole truth. And so will my mother. We can't build a baby's life on a foundation of lies.'

'Don't see why not. Dad won't like it. You won't be doing him any favours.'

'Lying is never a favour.'

That night lying in bed it took all Zina's will-power not to tell Peter the whole story, but she kept silent.

'Are you OK, Zee? I've been watching you, you haven't seemed yourself at all this evening?'

'I suppose it's because the youngsters are going tomorrow.' How she hated saying it. But as soon as she could talk to him properly she would confess tonight's lie as well as the whole miserable tale. The important thing was that there wasn't trouble between Peter and Fiona's husband just as they were parting.

'I know,' he said, drawing her close. 'I hope she's happy. He seems a pretty decent chap and I'm glad we've had this chance to get to know him better before they disappear. Do you think she'll be all right with him? There are so many broken marriages out there; do you think they have the makings of a lifelong bond in that environment? God, darling, I'm so thankful we didn't let ourselves be drawn into it.'

'Um . . .' She snuggled close to him. 'Me too.'

'I don't want her to go, and yet it'll be lovely to be just the two of us again.'

'Remember what we always used to say? I love you, Mr Marchand.'

'Used to say? Yes, I suppose that's true. When did it happen that there was no need to use words any more? I love you, Mrs Marchand,' he said with a gentle laugh, 'perhaps we ought to tell each other more often like we used to.'

'No need. Time does funny things, doesn't it. Two people young and at the start of their time together like Fiona and Ivor, two people like we were all those years ago, I suppose you need to say it. But now, it's different, isn't it. Of course I love you and you love me, but the difference is that we sort of become like two halves of the same whole.' She shivered even though she was warm. 'Quite frightening really.'

He didn't answer except to draw her closer. Would it ever be like this for Fiona and Ivor, she wondered. But she wasn't ready to look for the answer. Instead she nuzzled her face against Peter's neck, so familiar, so much part of life.

'I'm not very tired,' she whispered. 'Are you?'

'Five minutes ago I might have been, but now I'm not. Fancy us with a married daughter. She probably sees us as over the hill.'

Zina's hand moved down his naked body, knowing his mind had kept pace with hers.

'She knows nothing,' she whispered. Then for both of them, Fiona was forgotten.

Next morning the lie continued when, still lying in bed, they heard Fiona's door open, then the family bathroom door shut with force enough to

276

make sure no one could avoid hearing it. Fiona was acting out her part. They heard the flushing of the cistern, then it seemed she was coming out but instead, to be doubly sure she'd been heard, she ran back with another slam of the bathroom door and a minute later another flush of the cistern. Next time she came out, instead of going back to her own room she padded along the corridor to theirs, tapping on the door and opening it at the same time.

'Mum, I feel awful. Been ever so sick. Are you both all right? Could it be something I ate?' She gave a loud belch, her body convulsing, then fled back with another slam of the bathroom door. Zina felt wretched that this Oscar-meriting performance was for Peter's benefit.

'We can't let them fly today,' he said, suddenly wide awake and sitting upright. 'They must change their flight.'

'Ivor has to be back, that's why they chose the flight they did.'

'Are you feeling all right? There's nothing wrong with me. We all ate the same food. Shall I ring for the doctor?' He was more than worried; he was frightened. Even as a child Fiona had never suffered anything more than a mild bout of measles and the occasional cold. The thought of her being thousands of miles away and perhaps being ill was unbearable. 'Well, if *he* has to go back, so be it. But she can't travel like that. You can't drive up with us today, you must stay here to look after her and we'll keep her until she is quite better, then if I'm not home you can drive her to Heathrow.'

It was all going just as Fiona and Ivor had planned. Zina had never felt so wretched. By ten o'clock she had said goodbye to her new son-in-law, received a worried kiss of farewell from Peter and was watching the car disappear down the drive.

'They've gone, Mum,' Fiona called from her viewpoint at the landing window. 'I'll get up now. What shall we do today? It's going to be lovely and sunny, we could go to the beach this morning.'

Barefoot and in her pyjamas Fiona looked very little older than she had when she'd gone off to the States with Peter more than eight years ago. Zina hated herself that she could feel so unsympathetic. If Fiona had no thought for anyone but herself, was that anything new? But this morning her attitude couldn't be ignored.

'For heaven's sake! Sometimes the way you carry on makes me so angry!'

Fiona made a mock frightened face. 'Oh dear, Mum. You haven't caught that bug, have you?' she teased. 'You sound a real old grouch. Come on, cheer up. Let's go to the beach.'

'I may be an old grouch, but if I am then you can blame yourself. I hate deceiving Peter, lying to him. I'll drop you off at the beach, but make sure you take money with you so that you can get a taxi home. I'm going to London.'

'But you told Dad you'd stay here because of me not bei—' One look at Zina's expression and she fell silent.

'I might even get to the flat before Peter does, by the time he's taken Ivor to departures. It's a long drive, there and back in a day, so I'll stay overnight. Anyway, after what I shall have told him I don't want to leave Peter by himself.' She knew she was being spiteful and hated herself that she could behave like it and feel such a need to hurt her own daughter.

'I'm not the first girl to have been taken advantage of,' Fiona said sulkily.

'What? Oh, I wasn't thinking about the baby. It's your whole attitude, Fiona. It's no use talking to you. Perhaps we've been to blame. We've always let you get away with behaving as if no one mattered but yourself. We saw how when you were children you always made Tommy give way to you, so perhaps the whole thing is our own fault.'

'Tom would want to help me. He cares about me.'

Zina ignored the implication behind the remark. 'If you're going to the beach you'd better get your swimming things on under your clothes. But don't be long; I want to get on the road.'

'Shan't go on the beach. When I said it I forgot what I'd look like in a bikini. Leave me here. Perhaps later on I'll go for a walk.' Then more cheerfully, she added, 'Or I could go and see Gran and Granderek. There's a bike in the shed, isn't there?' Already she'd turned cheerfully to the next thing. 'I shan't tell them anything. I'll just say I was very sick in the night and couldn't face a journey but Ivor had to get back – and that you've gone with Dad to London. When she has to be told I'll let you do it. She won't notice, will she?' she added, smoothing her skirt over her still almost flat stomach.

'It's hardly likely. She saw you a couple of days ago. She may ask you to eat there but anyway there's plenty of food in the fridge. I'll be back probably early afternoon tomorrow.'

Peter not only drove Ivor to Heathrow but he decided to wait with him until the sign came up that his flight was checking in. This time with just the two of them together was important. This young man was Fiona's husband, the foremost man in her life, which was something her doting father found hard to accept. But he knew he had no alternative if he were to keep his special relationship with her and so, during their short stay, he had gone out of his way to be friendly to the newcomer to his family. Strangely though, considering how unexpectedly Ivor had been thrust on them, he found nothing to dislike in 'the boy' as he thought of the handsome young god less than half his own age. In the refreshment bar they sat together drinking coffee and talking with remarkable ease.

'You take me back a quarter of a century,' he said, 'in years if not in the state of your career. At your age I was permanently hard up, moving from town to town every six weeks acting in rep. I was pretty well thirty when my first break came in films.'

'I guess a few years in rep, as you call it, gave you a pretty sound base to build on when you went back to the theatre. Did it feel strange?'

'Not actually strange and yet not familiar. I shouldn't wonder you think it's nonsense when

I say one can feel the atmosphere – the vibes – from the audience. But it's true. There will never be the money in stage work that there is in the film world, but there is an indefinable something. You know how it is in films, the sequence of events has little or nothing to do with when the scenes are shot. Wonderful training for an actor; tears today, laughter tomorrow, tears again the day after, all emotions you have to conjure up as necessary. But there is nothing, absolutely nothing in this world like the moment when you step out onto the stage, hearing the very silence in the auditorium and yet drawing the audience to you so that they are moved by the emotion . . . hark at me, don't let me get on my hobby horse.'

'But Fiona said you have a film coming up?'

'A war story. I read the script before I accepted. One great advantage of the passage of time, I accept what I *want* to do. Shooting isn't due to start until the back end of the year. Ah, that's your flight. They're starting to check in. If Fiona isn't better by tomorrow I'll see she has the doctor to look at her.'

Ivor was biting his lip, clearly worrying about something. Then, not quite looking at Peter, he rushed into what he knew he had to say.

'Last check-in won't be for ages. Look, sir, look Peter, I gotta tell you. We fixed it like this so that Fiona could stay behind. She's not sick, not like she wanted you to think. She'll be with you for months. She's pregnant. Zina refused to tell you till I'd gone, maybe in case you kicked me out.' In stunned silence Peter listened as he

281

was told the whole story. 'We arranged I would go and then Zina would break it to you. I guess I may be a heel, but I can't go off without giving you the chance to tell me what you think of me. But I do love her, that's God's truth. For months I'd been begging her to say she'd marry me, but she wanted us just to go on living together like we were. Then this happened.' He made himself meet Peter's gaze. 'I wish, honest to God I wish, it wasn't like this. I wish we had got hitched when I moved in with her and now maybe it wouldn't have been this way. I wish you'd say something, tell me I'm a bastard, because that's how I feel running off back home and leaving her like this. But she won't come back, you see, not while she's altering and getting, well, fat and all that. I wish you'd say something.'

The tic in Peter's cheek was working overtime, he could feel it but had no control over it. This boy had made his beloved Fiona pregnant. But be fair, he told himself, Fiona would never agree to anything she didn't want. If they loved each other and wanted to share their lives surely they should be happy. Zina and he would be grand-parents. His mouth twitched into something that might have been from the working of the nerve in his cheek or it might have been a sign that he was trying to make himself smile.

'If you and Fiona are happy about it, does it matter that the child will be born so soon? All that will get forgotten.'

'Sure it will. But happy about it? She's dead against it. Coming like it has when she's doing so well, you can understand how she feels.'

Silence for a moment while Peter considered what Ivor had said, his mind taking him back to when Zina had first been pregnant. Then, speaking his thoughts aloud, he said, 'Zina was being hailed as a violinist with a great future when she first found she was expecting the twins. She gave up and it was years later that she went back to it, never as a soloist but as a member of quite a leading quintet.'

'Zina plays the violin? Fancy that. Fiona never told me.'

'No, I don't think she was ever very concerned, not like Tom was.' He tried not to admit to the hurt he felt that something so important to Zina could have meant nothing to Fiona. 'She doesn't play now; not since the accident.'

'Accident?'

'She had a very serious accident. She was standing on the edge of the cliff in a gale when it crumbled taking her down with it. She has very limited use of her shoulders.'

'Gee, but that's tough. I never knew. Is that how she got the scar on her face? What rotten luck. You know something? The more you hear of things other folk have had to get over, the less of a tragedy you see in your own troubles.'

'Troubles? Surely a child to a married couple is hardly that.'

'Oh, not troubles for me. I was thinking of poor Fiona. I just wish she could think of the good side. Here we are, hitched for life and what better than a nipper to sort of hold us together. You reckon once she's out of the limelight she'll get used to the idea? Then once the baby is born and she comes home, she can find a real nice pad for us out Beverly Hills way and get a nanny and she'll be right back where she was.'

'You must go, man. There will be a long queue for checking in by this time.'

And so they parted, Ivor happy with the way the last half hour had turned out and Peter, if not happy with what he had heard, at least feeling far closer to the young man who had usurped his place in Fiona's affection.

There was garaging at the flat for only one car so Zina drove to an underground public car park where she could leave the car overnight, then walked the half mile or so, hurrying in the hope of arriving before Peter. She had wanted to make the place welcoming, some quite irrational feeling telling her that that might take some of the hurt out of what she had to tell him. But as she opened the door she knew she was too late.

'Hello? Who's that?' he called from the living room.

Not answering she went straight to join him. For a second they looked at each other in silence, she suddenly groping for words to explain why she had come and he, having heard what Ivor told him, knowing exactly why.

'Peter, I have to talk to you now. I couldn't until Ivor had gone.'

There was something in the way he was looking at her that made her uncomfortably conscious of the charade Fiona had acted out and her own silence.

'Ivor told me himself.' But his tone gave no

hint of how he had received the news. 'How long have you known and not seen fit to tell me?'

'Don't look at me like that, as if it's me who's made such a bloody mess of things.'

'How long? All the time they've been in Devon?'

'Of course not. Since yesterday afternoon. She came to find me in the garden and told me.'

'And you decided it wasn't important to let me into your secret? And this morning when she pretended to be ill, you played along with her, still thinking it wasn't anything to do with me?'

She was tired, driving all the way from Devon had given her a knife in her shoulders. It took all her willpower not to burst into tears, but anger came to her rescue.

'Don't be so beastly childish. I knew if I told you, you would probably have blown your top, maybe even kicked Ivor out, as if whatever happened hadn't been her doing as much as his – probably more. He's her husband now, like it or not.'

'He'd been begging her for months to marry him but she wanted to stay as they were.'

'He had? She didn't tell me that bit.' She began to wonder what else Fiona had seen fit to omit.

'He said he'd wanted them to marry when he moved in to live with her.'

'It seems you know more than I do; she didn't tell me they'd actually been living together, just that they came to London hoping for an abortion. And here I've driven all this way to break it to you gently.' A minute or two ago anger had helped her regain her control, but now, as they looked at each other, both of them feeling helpless in

285

the face of problems they couldn't solve for someone they loved, her face crumpled and she was in his arms. The tears were healing; they washed away much of the anger she had felt towards Fiona's selfish view of life. She, who had come meaning to give support to Peter, found the positions were reversed.

'The usual?' he asked unnecessarily a minute or two later as he went to the drinks trolley.

'A bit early in the day but, yes please, I need it.' She sat down on the settee and closed her eyes, not even looking when he put her glass on the little table by her side. Then he sat down next to her and she felt his hand massaging the top of her back. 'Um,' she purred. 'That's nice.'

It wasn't often he lost his patience with Fiona, but at that moment he did as he recalled his conversation with Ivor where he learnt how Fiona hadn't even considered her mother's lost career or the repercussions of the accident.

'I'll drive you to Exeter in the morning and get the train back. That journey is too long for you to do on your own.'

'I thought you were due to start rehearsals?'

'Not until the afternoon. I'll leave you to drive on from Exeter and phone from there saying I may be a bit later, then when I get back to Paddington I'll get a taxi straight there.' With the sort of smile that Jenny had always found so annoying, accompanied by a half wink, he added, 'They'll just be glad to see me.'

'That's a very un-Peterish remark.'

'This has been a day enough to jog anyone off course.' Then, lifting her hand to his mouth he kissed it and said, 'Take your drink and go and have a hot bath, it'll ease your shoulders after that drive.'

'You've had a long drive too and actually my shoulder is getting easier already.'

He heard the invitation in her voice and, standing up, held out his hands to pull her onto her feet. Then together, carrying their glasses, they went to the bathroom.

'Three o'clock in the afternoon,' she chuckled, 'I feel like a naughty child doing something she shouldn't.'

'Child? I prefer you as a naughty woman spending her Sunday afternoon in just the way we want.'

There was something wonderful about being together in their fourth-floor flat, the world shut away from them. In the last twenty-four hours they had had the foundations of their family life rocked almost off course, but now the truth was out they were happy with where it had brought them. Fiona would be home for probably eight or nine months, for she wouldn't want to go back to California until she saw herself in good enough shape; there was going to be a new member of the family for them to love; they approved of their new son-in-law, although to that Peter added the rider that he would now find it difficult not to be the most important male in her life. So, all in all, they gave themselves to the rest of the day looking no further than the present and each other.

Back at Newton House, as Zina parked the car in the garage she saw Mrs Cripps had come out to speak to her.

'I'm glad to see you back home, Mrs M, I've been that worried about poor little Fiona. Not a bit herself, she isn't. Says it's a tummy bug and that's why she couldn't go back with that handsome young hubby of hers. Poor little soul, what with that and perhaps she's one of those who get a lot of pain when it's their time of the month.'

'No, I'm pretty sure it's not that.'

With a 'just between ourselves' look and lowering her tone, even though there was no one to hear, Mrs Cripps went on: 'Being new to marriage has upset the dates, I expect.' Then in hardly above a whisper, she continued, 'Any road, when I went to give the bathroom its daily clean I found blood drips the poor little soul couldn't have noticed.' Then with volume increased to normal, she added, 'She's still in bed and I told her that was the best place for her till this tummy bug leaves her in peace.'

'I'll go up and see her. Thanks for taking good care of her, Mrs Cripps.'

'Well bless the girl, of course I take care of her. Husband went off all right, I suppose. Nice young man. Must be a relief to you and Mr M to know she has found herself a good man; such goings on you read about amongst some of those film people – oh, not our Mr M, he's different.'

Zina laughed, nodding her head. 'He's special,' she agreed as she turned to hurry indoors and up the stairs to Fiona.

'I'm home,' she announced quite unnecessarily and in an over-cheerful voice. 'Have I missed anything while I've been in London?'

'Not very likely, is it?' came the unpromising reply.

'Mrs Cripps believes you've got either a tummy bug, as you told her, or are having a lot of pain with a heavy period. She said there was blood on the bathroom floor. What's happened?'

'Nothing's bloody happened, but it's not for the want of trying. I cut myself. I didn't go to Gran's yesterday, I was here by myself and I made the most of the chance.' She glared at her mother as she spoke, as if she were to blame for what she thought of as fate working against her. 'What else can I do? I climbed Old Ben, the tree Tom and I used to play on, then swung from a high branch and dropped off. All it did was give me a sore ankle. I skipped till I could hardly breathe, pretty well finished off the bottle of gin – neat – then I threw up, so that was no good.'

'But Fiona, why? The boys have taken it in their stride, in fact I think they got on really well and Peter respected Ivor for telling him the whole thing. And as we said last night when we were talking about it, you'll be staying here as long as you want and when you go back with the baby to the States, Ivor plans that you will have a nanny so that you can work.'

'Shan't need a nanny; it's just a devil come to plague my life and I'll get rid of it, I swear I won't have it. Anyway—' just from her voice Zina knew the sulky expression on her face – 'it's easy for Ivor, he's not the one having the brat. I hate it, Mum, I never knew I could hate anything like I do this *growth*. You talk a lot of twaddle about how it'll be different when I've had it

– after my body has been torn to pieces to get the thing out and probably left me with stretch marks so that I can't wear the sort of things I like—'

'You mean go about half-naked looking more like a street walker than someone's wife?'

'You don't know anything about fashion, proper glamorous fashion. I shouldn't think you ever did. Anyway, in your day things were different. I thought of the shopping I'd done in London; not for clothes, for things to help shift this *thing* that's like a growth inside me. I'd heard about people using a knitting needle or a long crochet hook.' Her eyes were closed and she might have been remembering the horror of her lonely and frightened hours rather than talking to Zina. 'I tried and tried, over and over, pushing them further than any man had gone, but all they did was make me sore. All night I kept trying. Then when it was just starting to get light I went out to the tool shed to see if there was anything better I could try. Was so sore by that time that I didn't care how much I hurt myself. I found what I wanted.' She was probably lost in her memories, for she stopped speaking.

'What was in the tool shed?'

'What? Oh, the tool shed. It was this.' From under her pillow she brought out a long and rusty looking screwdriver.

'For God's sake, you're not telling me you put that thing inside you? Fiona, grow up and stop being such a little fool. Your child is here to stay. Surely if all the dreadful things you've done to shift it have failed, you've got to accept that you

290

are going to have it in a normal way when the time comes. This is where things are and this is what we have to make work.'

'I won't. Don't you listen to anything I tell you? I am *not* going to have this – this – *thing*.'

'What was the blood in the bathroom?'

'I did it with this.' Again she held up the filthy and rusty screwdriver. 'I saw there was blood on my hand and so I pushed harder and harder. But I was frightened. I suddenly thought, at three months would it be a third the size of a baby. How much would it hurt, and how would I get rid of it so that no one knew what I'd done? Would it have arms and legs? Too big to go down the loo, so I'd have to wrap it up and burn it in the garden before you got home. I had it all planned. I sat on the loo and pushed like I've seen people told to do in films, and all that happened was drops of blood from where I'd broken the skin with the screwdriver . . .' By now she was crying, long, hard, dry sobs. 'At first I thought that was the beginning and soon the *thing* would come. Was so frightened, yet sort of excited. Never felt like I did as I just kept stabbing as high as I could push it.'

'You might give yourself blood poisoning with that dreadful thing. Stop that noise, Fiona and listen to me for once. Are the cuts still bleeding?'

'Don't think so. And I thought I'd done it, I thought I was getting rid of it.'

'Instead of thinking just of what's convenient to your own life, stop calling the baby a thing as if it's so much rubbish and start to think of having a new person, perhaps a little girl like you used to be, a person who will soon have dreams of her – or his – own. Maybe it'll be a boy like Ivor. But one thing I bet, it will grow up dreaming of acting like its parents and grandfather. And you want to deprive it of life? Don't do it, Fiona. You came into the world with love all around you. Can't you give that gift to a baby of your own?'

'It was different for you, I expect you were pleased when you knew you were having us. But I'm *not* and there's nothing you can say to change my mind. If I'd never gone to America, if I'd always been stuck here and seen nothing like you seem to like doing, then I might have felt different. I know what I want – and it's not a baby no matter what wishy-washy talk you give me.' She wiped the palms of her hands across her eyes and nose now that at last she had stopped her hysterical crying.

'You're not ill. Get up and pull yourself together. Go and have a long, hot bath and put plenty of disinfectant in the water – and make sure the water goes right inside you, anywhere that disgusting screwdriver might have touched. The next thing is you'll be getting blood poisoning. There are far more dangerous things than having babies.'

'I don't care. If I get this blood poisoning you keep on about perhaps I'll die. Better that than go through having a baby and then being lumbered with it for the rest of my days. I never want any children; Ivor knew I didn't. I just want to be *me*.' She'd got as far as sitting on the edge of the bed and now she looked so miserable that Zina's anger was overtaken by pity. What a child she still was, something that her next words confirmed. 'Everything was so good; me and Ivor living together; lots of friends; always so much fun, even working was like a wonderful dream come true; pressmen following us around. Now I've woken up and it's all gone and there's nothing.' Hardly the sentiment of a bride of less than a month.

'There's plenty to be happy about if you would stop dwelling on what you *don't* want. How do you think Ivor feels having to go back without you simply because you want everything to go the way that suits you? Stop thinking just of yourself for a few minutes and consider others. Are you enjoying knowing what the way you are behaving will do to Peter when he is trying to concentrate on rehearsals? As for Ivor, I just hope when you talk to him on the phone it won't be just about yourself and your self-pity. When I had to give up, do you think it was easy? It's not a bit of good sitting there with a face like a thundercloud.'

Fiona's thundercloud became even more threatening.

'It was different for you. When you gave up you wanted kids. I don't—'

'Yes, we wanted children. If a couple is lucky enough to have a family then it's a blessing. But when I talk about having to give up I meant after the cliff fall—'

Fiona looked at her in genuine surprise. 'But you can't compare that with what's happened to me. You weren't young and with everything before you. You were only messing about to fill up time because Tom and I were away at school and you wouldn't have wanted to hang around here on your own. I expect you quite enjoyed having something to do, but it was hardly a career.'

The remark caught Zina unprepared and she felt the burning sting of tears. She felt hurt and angry, but most of all she wanted to put an end to the conversation before she disgraced herself. Without looking at Fiona she walked to the door.

'Have a bath and get dressed and don't forget to put plenty of disinfectant in the water. I'm going down to talk to Mrs Cripps.'

'Mum! Mum you can't tell her about the – the—'

'That Peter and I are going to be grandparents? Yes, I shall tell her and I shall tell Mother. Mrs Cripps has been with us since you and Tommy shared a twin pram; she cares for you as if you were her own. Lesson number one for you to learn is that loyalty from people who care for you through good times and bad is worth a thousand times more than the glitz and glamour you set such store by.' And with that she went out of the room shutting the door with a positive click. She had no feeling of triumph in the way she had talked to Fiona, in fact she felt defeated. Instead of going down to report to Mrs Cripps she retreated to her bedroom just as the telephone rang. Peter? But it couldn't be, he couldn't have got even to Paddington yet.

'Mum, it's me, Tom. I rang the flat first but there was no reply, so I thought I'd just try you at home but I didn't really expect to find you. I thought you'd sure to have gone on to London to stay with Dad. Did you wait and see them off at Heathrow yesterday? I haven't got much change, but I just wanted to know they had got away OK.'

'Give me the number of the phone where you are and I'll ring you straight back. Nothing to worry about, but a lot to tell you.'

As the weeks dragged by Fiona was physically well, but there was nothing reassuring in her quiet acceptance. In fact she showed no interest in anything as her time of waiting went by. When Ivor had a chance to get back for a short visit she accepted his presence but showed no emotion, or so it seemed to Zina and to Peter who managed to join them from the early hours of Sunday morning until Monday when, just as he had after his previous visit, he drove Ivor to Heathrow on the way back to London.

Summer gave way to autumn. Fiona, who even as a child had cared about her appearance, took no interest in buying maternity clothes and wore those Zina bought for her. As for collecting a layette, when Zina suggested to her that she ought to make a list and they could have a day in Exeter so that everything was ready, all she said was, 'That nurse person left a printout of what she wanted.'

That was on a Sunday evening and Peter was at home. He watched with concern; there was something very wrong, it was as if all the life and hope had been crushed out of her.

'I'm not going back until early Tuesday morning, so what about if the three of us have a day out tomorrow. Bring your list, Fiona, not just what the nurse wants but everything that ought to be ready – clothes, pram or whatever babies use these days.' Then, with that smile that had always told the twins there was fun to be had, he added, 'We'll go adventuring.'

Watching them, Zina felt the scene would be imprinted on her memory: Fiona, her beautifully made-up face as lovely as ever it had been, her swollen body somehow pathetic in that moment. In the brief glance that passed between father and daughter she felt Fiona's armour of defence crack, but it didn't break. Immediately she had herself in control as she shrugged her shoulders and said, 'Mum knows more about what babies wear than I do. Anyway I don't feel like lumbering around in town. You and Mum go. Or we could just phone up and read out the nurse's list and whatever Mum thinks the—' Something in her father's expression stopped her speaking of the unborn child in her usual way. 'Whatever Mum says is needed and it could just be delivered without the bother. I don't really care.'

Did she sense the change in Peter? If so she gave no indication. Certainly Zina did and felt a sudden fear. It was seldom, in truth almost never, that he lost his temper and she hated to see the way his mouth tightened and the change of expression in his eyes. When she reached her hand to touch his he seemed not to notice.

296

'Then it's time you *did* care,' he said, his voice dangerously controlled. 'There are plenty of girls right now who are pregnant like you are, girls with no husband and no family behind them. You have both and to act as though you deserve pity for your situation is not only dishonest play-acting, but it's unfair to your mother and to Ivor too. How much happiness do you imagine you bring to this house with your behaviour? None. You give no thought to your husband, to us nor yet to Tom.'

His outburst seemed to have put the spirit back into Fiona. She stood straighter and raised her chin as she looked coldly at Peter.

'Perhaps I shouldn't have taken it for granted that I was welcome here. I apologize Mother if you find my presence an inconvenience.'

Zina started to speak but before the first word was out Peter cut in.

'For Christ's sake, Fiona, stop playing the tragedy queen. Another month and you will be a mother yourself, a mother and a wife. You're not the first woman to find pregnancy doesn't suit her lifestyle, but you're luckier than most. You have a husband who seems to dote on you and looks forward to taking you back to that place you find so attractive. When you calm down and look the facts in the face without the drama you thrive on, then you'll be a happier person yourself – and more pleasant to be with. At eight months that poor child you are carrying ought to have clothes, a crib and all the paraphernalia waiting ready. Tomorrow we shall go to Exeter and arrange for it all to be delivered.' Then, his tone softening as he looked at the child who had always been so especially dear to him, he said, 'If you get down off your high horse and come too it'll be a fun day out. Think about it.'

'I can think of nothing less like a fun day out,' came the reply, the drama queen clearly not yet laid to rest. 'And I expect, Mother, you think you deserve a day without having me underfoot.'

'If this is the way you usually behave, then she certainly does.'

'I shall leave you in peace and go to bed.' Fiona turned towards the door ready for the grand exit.

'Come with us,' Zina implored as she tried to lighten the atmosphere, not so much for Fiona's sake as for Peter's. 'You ought to be the one to choose. I'll guide you with what a baby needs, but Fiona, once you collect up the tiny things the baby will need, I promise you'll feel different.'

'De-da, de-da, de-da,' Fiona mocked insolently with a scathing look at them both.

'That's enough! If you can't behave, just go to bed.' Peter's voice was hard with anger and in that second two things happened: he seemed to realize that Zina was holding his hand and his grip tightened until she felt her fingers being crushed, and Fiona lost her hold on the drama queen who had helped her through such an unprecedented scene with her father and with a loud howl burst into tears – real not crocodile tears. In a second Peter let go of Zina's hand and was on his feet holding the sobbing girl in his arms.

'I'm sorry, Dad. I'm so miserable. Don't want a beastly baby spoiling everything. I knew it couldn't last. Was so happy. Now there's nothing. Don't want to be a bloody mother, old and ugly. Hate it, hate everything. We've never quarrelled, you and me. Hate quarrelling with you. Say it's all right, Dad.'

Zina stacked their coffee cups on a tray and carried them to the kitchen. The moment belonged to Peter and Fiona. After a while she heard the girl going up the stairs, her light tread carrying the message that all was well. It was safe to go back to the dying embers in the drawing room.

'I've put another log on the fire and poured us a drink,' Peter greeted her. Then holding out his hand to draw her down to his side on the settee, he said, 'Here's to this time next month when it's all over.'

'Amen to that,' she agreed. 'Do you want to waste tomorrow in baby shops? I could go the next day if you'd rather.'

'I think a day out is probably just what we need. And this new scrap of humanity deserves its bits and pieces bought by folk who are ready to give it a loving welcome, wouldn't you say?'

'She'll feel differently when she holds it. I think more than anything she's frightened. A day out . . . we haven't had a day out together for ages.'

He put his arm around her and she nuzzled against his neck. Tomorrow they would leave most things to be delivered, but she decided that they'd bring one or two tiny garments home with them; surely the sight of them would move Fiona's mind forward and, instead of the unborn child being a 'thing', the clothes would help her to see ahead to when the birth was over and her future free of fear.

In the warmth from the burning log, with Peter close, and the atmosphere of anger gone, Zina had a new feeling of hope. Whatever he and Fiona had said to each other she didn't know, neither did she want to know; but in that last hour of the day she found herself looking to the future with hope she hadn't known for months.

'Silly to worry about things,' she murmured, not explaining where her thoughts had taken her. 'Not long and it'll all be over and she'll be her old self again.'

And she believed she spoke the truth.

Ten

'Have a quick bath, then pretty yourself up and come with us.' Zina tried to put enthusiasm into the suggestion when she looked into Fiona's bedroom on her way down to rustle up some breakfast. 'We thought we'd be away as soon as we're all ready. We could get through the shopping quickly and then drive out of town to get a pub lunch in the country.'

'Jolly hockey sticks!' was Fiona's answer, with what sounded like a sneer. 'Little minds are easily pleased. I shall stay in bed till I hear Mrs Cripps go. I can do without her empty-headed prattle.'

Zina turned away, shutting the door sharply, the action speaking as clearly as any words just what she thought of the remark. Fiona glanced round the room, the room that had been hers almost as long as she could remember, then she buried her head in the pillow as if that way she could escape a day she was frightened to contemplate. Just before nine o'clock she heard both doors of Peter's car slam and then the deep throbbing purr of the engine. Sitting up in bed, for the umpteenth time she opened the drawer of her bedside table and checked its contents. Ouch! That hurts! Having gone through her pregnancy suffering with no physical pain, sitting in bed she drew up her knees and bent forward gripping them as if that would drive the pain away.

301

Gradually it eased until she almost believed it hadn't been as violent as she'd imagined. Then she wriggled to lay down. Had something happened? The wretched thing was still. That's when she realized she hadn't had that revolting feeling of it moving inside her since she woke. Perhaps it was dead. But if it had died before it was even born how would they get it out of her? She was frightened to think. But what did it matter? What did any of it matter? Hearing Mrs Cripps plodding up the stairs, she turned on her side and pulled the bedclothes high around her, pretending to be asleep. When she heard her bedroom door open she didn't stir.

'Poor little lass,' the faithful cleaner shook her head sadly, 'nought but a child herself.' There was nothing unusual in her speaking her thoughts aloud, it was the habit of years. 'Best I leave the vacuuming till she's up and about, don't want to wake her with my clatter.'

Nor with your stupid chatter, Fiona thought scornfully, then stamped firmly on the feeling of shame.

Almost silently Mrs Cripps closed the door, then clumped down the stairs taking the vacuum cleaner with her. Peace! Now they'd all gone. Oh no, the pain was coming again. No, oh please *no*, don't let it be the baby starting to come. Wish Mum was home – no I don't, of course I don't. It isn't due until just after Christmas. Ivor ought to be here, I wish Ivor was here – no, of course I don't. I'm glad he isn't. There mustn't be anyone. Yes, it's the pain again. Perhaps it hurts like this because it's got something wrong with it, ooohhh, ough. No. I mustn't call out. She'll come back up with her stupid blabbering . . . She mustn't; no one must come. I feel all wet . . .' Whimpering silently, she put her hand beneath the bedclothes to try and find out what had happened. Yes, the bed was wet. Did that mean the baby was starting to come? Please God help me, don't let me mess it up. This is it! It's *got* to be now, there's no time to mess about. There's no time to even think about it; it's got to be *now*. So frightened. Wish Mum was here. No I don't, no I don't. She'd try and stop me doing it . . . got to be by myself . . . I wish . . . no use wishing . . . too late for that . . . too late for anything . . . don't even think.

The shopping expedition went well and soon after eleven o'clock everything was ordered and paid for.

'She may think she's hard done by, but in fact she's jolly lucky. Pram, baby bath, cot, carry cot and car seat, a better wardrobe than most babies have waiting for them. Mrs Ivor Huntley's baby will lack for nothing,' Zina said as they travelled in the shop's lift down to the ground floor.

'I wish that were true,' Peter answered. 'What she or he will lack is more important than any of those things we've just bought.'

'It'll be different when it comes,' Zina said fervently, 'please God it's got to be different. What's happened to her, Peter, that she can behave like she does? It's as if her personality has changed. She's like a stranger.'

He shook his head, and she wondered what had

gone on between them the previous evening while she bided her time in the kitchen. 'It's not her parents she should be sharing these months with; it's her husband. When does he arrive for Christmas?'

'Any time after the sixteenth, I think that's what she said when he phoned the other day. She didn't even seem interested. And Tommy will be home on the twentieth. It would be wonderful if she could be a few days early and get it all over by Christmas.'

As the door of the lift opened on the ground floor they got out, a feeling of freedom gripping them as he took her elbow and steered her towards the street. Then, with the smile that time had no power to change, he said, 'Now we'll go adventuring, Mrs M.' It seemed to draw a line under all that had gone before, Fiona and her moods, the layette that was to be delivered before the shop closed that evening and all the other paraphernalia that would come the following day. Now they were free, these next few precious hours were their own.

Instead of driving miles into the country, they headed back towards home, then turned coastward to Chalcombe where they knew they would find a good pub lunch at the Lobster Pot. The log fire was a welcoming sight and they had a leisurely meal. When an inner voice told both of them that this was a day they would remember, they looked around them and at each other and believed those were the unforgettable moments. But the day had more in store for them and their first suspicion of it was as they turned into the drive of Newton House and saw the doctor's car parked in front of the building.

'Oh my dear Lawks, I'm that glad to see you,' Mrs Cripps said as she rushed down the front steps of the house before they'd even come to a stop. 'It's all stations go here, you'd not been gone above an hour when the poor child gave a scream such as I've never heard. And they're still at it up there with her, the midwife and the doctor too.'

Peter was already out of the car and rushing into the house.

'Is everything going all right?' Zina asked anxiously. Then: 'Oh heavens, we haven't got so much as a vest or a nappy in the house until the order arrives. Tell Peter I've gone to the village shop in Myddlesham. Straight there and back, I won't be many minutes but I must get something to wrap the baby in and a packet of nappies.' As she talked she had moved over to the driver's seat and switched on the engine. Then with a skid of tyres on the gravel drive, more akin to Peter's driving than her own, she turned the car and was gone.

Indoors Dr Hutchins had heard their arrival and, as Peter started up the stairs, was coming down to meet him.

'How's she doing?' Peter greeted him, superstition making him ask full of hope, for surely if he gave a hint of how his heart was pounding it would be akin to losing faith. 'Is everything going all right? She's a month early.'

'I've already phoned for an ambulance. The child must be delivered by Caesarean section.'

305

'Has something gone wrong?'

This wasn't the first time Ernest Hutchins had had to prepare a family for what he feared was ahead, but he had never seen even a young husband look more distraught than the father of young Fiona Marchand, as he still thought of her, having brought her into the world and known her until she went off to make a film star of herself when, in his opinion, she would have been better at school. But you couldn't tell these stage folk anything.

'She isn't able to help herself at all; she's barely conscious.' And at that the doctor led the way into the dining room, and closed it firmly behind them. 'She's young, she's always been a healthy girl, I would have expected her to go through a confinement as nature intended.' For a second he hesitated, then feeling in the pocket of his white coat he pulled out four new-looking but empty packets of painkillers. 'These are not to be taken lightly. The dose is no more than four in twenty-four hours. Four packets, all of them empty and I'd swear they have only just been opened, you can see they've not been handled.'

'You mean . . .? Christ, but she can't . . .?' Peter stood gripping the back of a dining chair. 'She must have had them for headaches or something. They can't be new! What are you saying?'

'Was she anticipating motherhood with fear? With eagerness? With horror?'

'She was frightened. But wouldn't any girl be frightened the first time? Zina says that once it's over she'll be her old self.' Peter clutched at a

306

thin straw of hope, but the doctor's expression did nothing to give him confidence. Dr Hutchins would have given much not to be faced with what he had discovered and was thankful when he heard the siren of the ambulance.

'I hear the ambulance. Can you contact her husband? Not my place to ask but I've known you all a long time. Is everything well between them? Is he happy at the prospect of a child?'

'Extremely. There is nothing wrong in their marriage, he was simply committed to being back in the States and he agreed that while Fiona waited she would be better here with Zina.'

'Good, good. Now the sooner she is in hospital, the sooner she can be helped. She's in no physical state to help herself. You'd better destroy these empty packets. I found them on the floor by the side of her bed.'

By the time Zina arrived back with a packet of newborn nappies and a small and very soft blanket, which was the best Myddlesham had to offer, Fiona was already on her way to Deremouth. Such a short time ago she had thought that this was a day that would stay with her always, but with memories so very different.

The baby was delivered but it was too late for it to bring the healing to Fiona's mind that Zina had hoped, for under the anaesthetic she had drifted from unconsciousness to eternal sleep. The news was brought to Zina and Peter as they waited on the bench just inside the entrance to the maternity department.

Peter said nothing, simply sat like a statue, his

face an expressionless mask. Zina knew it had to be up to her to ask, 'And the baby?'

'A little girl. Six pounds one ounce, so even though she was early she isn't very below the average weight. She is perfect.'

Zina nodded, frightened to trust her voice. But she knew the strength had to come from her, so she made herself ask, 'Does she have to stay here or can she be taken home? Are there things we have to do here?' To her ears the voice didn't sound like her own and, from the look of Peter, he was travelling into realms known only to himself or perhaps himself and Fiona.

Looking back later she had but a hazy picture of the next hour. Hour? Half hour? Few minutes? Time had no meaning. They were taken to see their grandchild, such a tiny bundle cocooned in warmth in a crib behind a glass screen, then – or was it before? Nothing was clear in her mind – they were led to a room where Fiona had been moved to a hard, flat bed, covered with a sheet which was pulled back so that her pale and expressionless face was visible. That moment was indelibly printed on Zina's mind, just as the cold and impersonal feeling of the colourless cheek as she bent to touch it with her lips. She took Peter's hand, not letting herself look at him as she drew him towards the lifeless figure . . . Fiona, their little girl, their daughter. Most vivid of all, and something that would stay with her till the end of her days, was Peter. He might have been a sleepwalker. He showed no emotion, and as he bent forward towards Fiona, she found herself praying with all her strength that he would hang on to his unearthly calm. She wanted just to get him away, somewhere where they were alone.

The baby was left in the care of the hospital and without a word passing between them, she and Peter got into the car, he not seeming to notice that it was she who went to the driver's side. They were about a mile from home when she felt rather than saw a change in him; it was as if something had snapped. Taking a quick glance at him she was frightened by what she saw: from head to foot he was shaking, his mouth half open as he fought for breath, silent sobs seeming to choke him. Pulling to the side of the empty road she stopped the car, wanting to take him in her arms, but a sports car with a gear stick between them made it impossible. So she got out and went round to his side and opened the door then, with little comfort or elegance, squatted down so that she was at his level. Was he even aware? She didn't know and she had never felt so helpless. Then his face crumpled and, like a child, he howled. She felt relief. Now surely she could help him.

As he cried, he gradually became aware of his surroundings and of her.

'Why did she do it? Why? Why couldn't she have known that we wouldn't let her down. The baby could have stayed with us. Why didn't we tell her so? Zee, we failed her. All she wanted was for everything to be as it had been before, and so it could have been if we'd understood and told her we wouldn't let her down.' Crying as he was, it was hard to understand all his words, but the first ones were clear in Zina's mind.

'Why did she do what?' she shook Peter's arm as she asked. 'Peter, we didn't fail her, I won't listen to rubbish like it. But what did you mean by "Why did she do it?"? She did nothing, for months all she did was run away from the truth.'

Tears seemed to have drained his strength as he turned to look at her, really look at her. Then he wriggled to find something in his jacket pocket and produced four, squashed flat, empty boxes of painkillers.

'Dr Hutchins found these by her bed.' He managed a whole sentence before his next trembling gulp. 'New packets – you can see they were new – but they were empty. She'd taken them all. Is that why she wouldn't come shopping? Why couldn't she have talked to us?'

Zina looked first at the evidence of what had happened and then at Peter. Gone was her determination that she must be his prop, she felt stripped of all hope as from her squatting position she sank to kneel on the hard ground of the empty lane and lent forward, her head on his lap. She had made herself strong to help him and yet now his strength came from her own weakness. She felt his fingers moving gently on the back of her neck.

'Our little girl,' she whispered through her tears, 'such a happy child she'd been. And Tommy . . .' She raised her face and they looked at each other in helpless misery. 'What's this going to do to Tommy?' Somehow the thought of Tommy helped them face what had to be faced, for how could they think just of their own grief when, surely, for him it would be as if something of himself was lost.

Somehow they got through the days and weeks that followed. The Ivor who flew from California for Fiona's funeral was a different young man from the happy one who had brought his bride to England only half a year before. He arrived the day before the funeral and returned the day after, this time Peter driving him to Heathrow and then returning to Devon. The nameless baby had to be registered and it was Ivor who, in the short time he was with them, borrowed the car to drive to Deremouth to register the birth. And so it was agreed that for as long as he wanted, and permanently if he would give his consent, little Ruth (after Ivor's own mother) Fiona Tommi (which to Peter and Zina didn't seem like a proper name at all, although they were glad Tom hadn't been forgotten and believed Fiona would have been pleased) was to live with her grandparents at Newton House.

When just before Easter Ruth was baptized in the village church at Myddlesham, Ivor asked Tom to be her godfather, and arriving from the States brought two friends who had agreed to be godmothers. Their presence made the day a hard one for Peter and Zina, and for Tommy too, although he was less certain why he resented them. But Peter and Zina knew exactly what made their presence so hard: both women were good-looking, but that was only the start. Their make-up was superb, its application an art form;

their clothes were up-to-the-minute fashion – in fact ahead of the minute – their attire exaggeratedly glamorous. All that, the Marchands were prepared to accept, perhaps Peter more easily than Zina, Jenny and Derek or even Tom, who was of the visitors' generation. Yet, somehow their presence seemed to make the thought of Fiona alien, for they were examples of what she had craved. It was a difficult occasion and Newton House (this included unchanging and unchangeable Mrs Cripps) breathed a sign of relief when the taxi carried them all off to Exeter station.

'So, here we are,' Zina said as, the visitors gone, the family sat down to dinner. Jenny and Derek had gone home; there were just the three of them left. 'A new chapter and you with a new responsibility, Tom, godfather to Fiona's little girl.'

Tom nodded. 'Will you be all right, Mum? She seems to yell a lot in the night.'

'A habit babies have.' Zina was determined not to let it show how much she longed for a night of sleep. 'But it's not for long. Think what it was like when there were two of you shouting for attention.'

'You were younger then,' Peter said. 'And I seem to remember you used to tell me that having a baby prepared your body for looking after it – or *them* as in our case.'

'I've always thought so. But I'm fine and Ruth and I are getting along very nicely.'

'Be that as it may,' Peter said, watching her with concern, 'you're twice the age you were when the twins were born – added to which she's getting heavier all the time and I'm not going to risk you putting any strain on your shoulders. We must get a nanny to live in.'

'Oh Peter, no. Don't you remember what it was like after my accident. The house didn't feel like our own with nurses underfoot. I'll be OK, honestly I can cope.'

He shook his head. 'Perhaps you can, but you're not going to. I shall stop off at the agency on my way back to London – back to London on my own. With a nurse – once she settles in and we know Ruth takes to her – you can come with me sometimes like you used to.'

Zina didn't argue. And so a new thread became woven into the pattern of their lives, a girl of about twenty, not one who'd undergone training as a children's nurse and had a certificate to prove it, but one who had learnt through experience having lived with an aunt who had been happy to add to her family about every eighteen months. The girl's name was Clara Hawthorne. Fair but not strikingly blonde, blue-eyed and rosy-cheeked, not one of the day's slender fashion plates although it wasn't so much that she was over-weight as that her bones were well-covered and her bust rounded. Altogether she was a comfortable girl and she slipped into her role as if it were tailor-made for her. It seemed a case of history repeating itself, for her own mother had died when she'd been born. Her father, rector of a country parish, completely out of his depth with a baby, had looked for someone to care for her. Some seven years later the 'someone' had become her stepmother and four years after that her father had decided to take a missionary post in Africa. She had been sent to live with her Aunt Lou who already had four children and was soon to be brought to bed with the fifth. So Clara had gained first-hand experience of how to care for a baby, experience that had become more useful with the years as, by the time she was twenty and applied for the post at Newton House, her aunt had given her six more cousins. And Clara had no doubt about a career; looking after a baby was her idea of paradise.

On the surface, water closed over the gap that had been left by Fiona's death. Only the family knew the void, the grief and the guilt too that they had let her sink to such despair without realizing.

It was a summer morning when Ruth was about eighteen months old when Zina went into the garden where Clara was standing watching the little girl.

'I ought to go and get her,' she said as she saw Zina. 'Mr Marchand has a script with him, he must have come out to work. But just look how she's chasing him.'

They watched as, with the uncertain steps of the young, Ruth was following Peter as he made for the seat under the horse chestnut tree. She was calling something, no doubt words that meant something to her if not to anyone else. He heard her and turned round, then held out his hand so that she took it as soon as she reached him. Looking up at him she appeared to be having a lot to say, and he was certainly answering although how much he had understood only he knew.

'Give them a few minutes. It'll do him more good to have her for company than that script,' Zina said. 'You know, it's like looking back through the years. As soon as Peter was home, Fiona would follow him like a shadow.' From her tone Clara knew something of the happiness there had been in the house. 'Life can be so cruel.'

'"The Lord giveth and the Lord taketh away, blessed be the name of the Lord." That's what my father used to try and make me believe when I was small and things got broken or I was sad about something. But it's a hard pill to swallow, isn't it?'

'The Lord taketh away and the Lord giveth. Can it work that way round, I wonder? Was losing Fiona part of a pattern so that Ruth would be given to us. Not that any child is given, they grow up so quickly and move on to live their own lives. Just look at the two of them on that seat; I believe she really thinks she's having a conversation with him.' Then, changing the subject, she added, 'I'll probably go back to London again with Peter this week if you've got nothing special lined up for your day off? Would you mind having a longer break next week instead? Are you quite sure you're happy enough in the house with only Ruth for company – and Mrs Cripps in the mornings?'

'Of course I am. I've never minded being on my own here. It's funny, isn't it, how some places give you such a warm, safe feeling.'

'That's a nice thing to say. It's how Peter and

I felt when we first found it and I wouldn't want to live anywhere else – except the odd weeks in London, but that's certainly not for the sake of the place, just that over the years Peter has been away so much that it's good to have some time together.' She said it without thinking and then wished she hadn't. It wasn't her nature to let folk into her innermost thoughts.

'Truly, I'm perfectly all right with just Ruth – and Mrs Cripps, of course, she's a dear. I'd better go and get Ruth, or poor Mr Marchand will go to rehearsal without knowing his lines,' Clara said with a laugh and immediately started towards the couple on the seat. Ruth saw her coming and climbed onto Peter's knee, her arms tight around his neck.

Ruth was fighting her corner, clinging to Peter and shouting. Clara would have none of it. She lifted the child off him, said something to him and they both laughed then, carrying her yelling charge, started back towards the house. But Ruth had learnt when she was beaten and when screams would be wasted, so looking back at Peter she waved her hand and called what she imagined to be 'Bye Gramp.'

The next morning, with a feeling of freedom, Peter and Zina set off for London.

'We were so lucky the day Clara came to us,' she said contentedly. 'Lots of young girls wouldn't want to stay in a house alone with a baby.'

'Yes, we were lucky finding her,' he agreed, his mind already on something else. 'I shall be pretty tied up this week, early rehearsals usually mean long days. Perhaps you'll find some concerts

316

to go to. If you can't you'll have to amuse yourself going shopping. Remember before we went
to the States how you spent all the week at the
shops kitting yourself out for competition.' His
words surprised her or, more particularly, something gentle in his tone as he looked back at what
had been the beginning of such a dreadful time.
He was half smiling as he remembered. 'You
looked stunning, I remember how proud of you
I felt.'

She laughed, not so much because of what he
said as the relief it was that they could talk about
it.

'That's more than Fiona did,' she recalled, but
at this distance in time there was nothing but
affection in her tone as she remembered. 'I was
Queen of Frump in her sights. But to be fair,
Peter, some of those glamorous creatures must
have been older than I was and yet the bodies
they flaunted gave no sign of it.' She gave him
a quick glance, frightened that even after all this
time he wasn't ready for such reminiscences.

'She was a child, bless her, a frightened,
worried child. Why couldn't she have talked to
us then, right at the beginning, Zee? Did she feel
she couldn't trust us? Did she really want that
wedding?'

What a relief it was to talk about it. Through
all this time while they had grown ever fonder
of Ruth, they had shunned facing the reason for
her existence. Perhaps the first raw pain had
dulled into an aching shadow of sadness that lay
constantly at the back of their minds. Now their
memories of Fiona weren't of the morose girl of

her final months but of the happy child she had been. Except for brief visits when they had gone to the States, usually separately, they found themselves overlooking the Hollywood period. They had played no part in her years there, even though they had been left in no doubt that she'd been living her dream.

'She may not have wanted a wedding, but I am sure she was in love with Ivor, or at least thought she was,' Zina answered him, uncertain whether she spoke the truth or whether she said it to take away some of the pain of Peter's memories.

They joined the motorway, mingling with the flow already on it. Monday morning and it was crowded, lorries pulling out from the slow lane to the middle one and sending ever more cars across to the third. Peter was concentrating on the road and for a while they were silent. In fact the nearer they came to London the less chance there was for conversation.

For both of them Devon was home but, sure that Ruth was in loving hands with Clara, during the weeks of rehearsal, gratefully they slipped into a routine of both heading for London early Monday mornings and returning Friday evenings. The curtain was due to go up in the last week of September and it was at the beginning of that month when they arrived home after Friday midnight to find Tom's car parked in the drive.

'Lovely! Look who's here, Peter! I didn't think he had any engagements down this way. The lights are still on, so he's waited up for us.'

'Great! He's a good lad, he manages to get to

see us so often.' Then, not showing any sign of getting out of the car, he added, 'Does he talk to you about a social life? He ought to be meeting people, people in the music world. He's got off to a great start, but any career is helped by personal contacts.'

'You'll never make a party animal of Tom – and in that he's not so different from a good many in his line. I suppose it's different in the acting world; music is *personal*. I can't explain, but I promise you, Tom's fine. He never has needed to surround himself with people.' Neither of them mentioned Fiona, Tom's other half.

There was no sound as they let themselves in but they could see a narrow shaft of light showing under the drawing-room door so expected that was where he must be, surprised that he hadn't heard the car. But the drawing room was empty with the French doors open leading onto the back terrace where they could see a table laid, complete with their candelabra from the dining room and a bottle of something on ice.

'At last!' he greeted them, coming through the French door. In his usual way he shook hands with his father and hugged his mother, then he turned to the candlelit terrace where they could see a shadow of someone hovering.

'This is quite a reception?' Peter said, a question in his voice.

'Is it something special? An exciting booking?' Zina came straight to the point, her eyes shining with love and pride.

'A very exciting booking,' he answered, going

back towards the mysterious shadow on the terrace. 'Don't hide yourself away, chump.' Hardly the way to speak to a visitor holding his professional ladder! Peter looked at Zina with eyebrows raised, to be answered by a slight shrug of her shoulders.

Whatever, or whoever, they were expecting, it wasn't Clara, dressed in a pretty floral summer dress (the kind of dress that would have made ex-Hollywood Fiona look on her with scorn) and with stars in her eyes.

'Mum, Dad, you must be blind if you hadn't realized. But one thing I'm sure: you are going to love the daughter-in-law I'm giving you.'

Peter was the quicker of the two to recover his wits, or at least to half recover them. 'Well, I'm damned! But when did all this happen?' Then seeing the uncertain way Clara was looking, first at him then at Zina, he held out his arms to her. 'What do you mean "we are going to love her", she feels like part of the family already.'

Zina hugged first Tom and then Clara; everyone talked at once. That it was already well after midnight mattered not a jot. For them all, the warm summer night might have been mid-evening. Clara had prepared supper, Tom uncorked the champagne, Peter went to the cellar to fetch a second bottle (a good thing Jenny hadn't been there to cast a jaundiced eye on his overexcited foolishness).

'What was it you said about a booking?' Zina asked as they sat at the table where, despite the mild night, there was the first hint of autumn decay in the scent of the garden; but it was masked by the smell of the citrus candles aimed at keeping any remaining midges at bay.

'Mother, how dim can you be?' Tom laughed. 'This booking isn't for one evening of glory, it's for life.'

Perhaps it was the showman in Peter that couldn't be denied. He stood up and raised his glass. 'I want us all, all, not just Zina and me, to raise our glasses to the future of the next generation of Marchands.' For a second he paused, casting a glance at Zina before he went on: 'May you two be as blessed as we have been, and still are, bound by an invisible cord that grows stronger with the years. And may your years be long.' Just for a second his gaze held Zina's and they read each other's thoughts and felt Fiona's presence very close.

By the time the meal was over, two bottles of champagne consumed, the dishes packed into one dishwasher and the glasses into a second, they knew it would be a short night before Ruth shouted for attention.

'We ought to toss for which of us collects her and takes her to bed for a cuddle in a couple of hours or so when she decides that it's morning.' That was Tom's idea and watching them, for the first time, Zina recognized what she ought to have seen months ago. Why else had Tom made the journey so often? As far as she and Peter were concerned, he never changed, but they had remarked on his frequent visits and been too blind to see. Perhaps Clara wasn't the sort of girl they expected him to lose his heart to, taking it for granted that he would look for someone from the musical circle where he fitted so comfortably.

'Love is a funny thing,' Peter said as he finally got into bed. 'Is she what we would have expected for him? She's nice, she's a sweet girl, wholesome might describe her – but not the sort young chaps would be queuing up for.'

'I feel extraordinarily happy about it. I believe she is good enough for him, and for me to say that of any girl is an accolade. Lovely evening, wasn't it?' She snuggled closer to him wrapping one leg across his. 'Peter, what you said, did you really mean it or was it just that it made a good toast?'

'You need to ask? If their marriage is as complete as ours then, come what may, nothing – and I mean that, *nothing* – can divide them.' Perhaps they'd all had a little too much excitement and champagne, and that may have had something to do with the way he raised himself, leaning on one elbow and looked down on her. 'Zee, when I'm away, when you're not with me, it's as if I'm not complete. It's more than just that I love you, and I do with all my heart and soul, but it's something apart from that. How could I ever be all that I am without you – and how could you be all that you are without me?'

She nodded, feeling the burning sting of tears and their wetness on her cheeks (and again perhaps the champagne had something to do with it, not with the truth of what they said but of their willingness to put into words the love that was so much part of their daily life). Gently he smoothed her tears away as wordlessly he eased

322

himself above her and wordlessly she drew him close. There were so many facets to their love-making, from joyous, sensuous lust and pure carefree physical pleasure to something akin to ending their day in a moment of thankfulness at where life had brought them, but whatever form it took it was always spurred on by the love that bound them.

Tonight as he entered her he raised himself so that, by the light from the bedside lamp, they looked at each other. There was no wild passion in what they did, it was like a re-avowal of all they had pledged nearly a quarter of a century ago. This could have nothing to do with their shared grief when they had lost Fiona, and yet for both of them it was as if they were touched by the hand of peace. As long as they had each other, as long as they shared all that they were and the love that had brought her into the world, then surely they would never lose her.

Early the following year Tom and Clara were married. It was a quiet wedding in the village church of Myddlesham. Clara's Uncle Teddy gave her away, her Aunt Lou took the place of the bride's mother, but none of their many children came. It would have been a case of all or none and Teddy and Lou decided on none and gave themselves the rare treat of a few days away from home staying at Newton House while Lou's elder sister moved in to look after the family. It was seldom they had time to see each other as anything but parents.

'This is such a happy day,' Lou said to Zina

as they sat by the log fire, while upstairs tomorrow's bride and groom were bathing Ruth and putting her to bed. Tomorrow, by this time in the evening, they would be on a plane for their honeymoon in Italy. 'She is a dear girl, true gold all through and she and Tom are just right for each other. She loves music. Until she came to live with us she had piano lessons, but with a brood like we seemed set on producing we couldn't contemplate letting any one of them have more than any of the others.' Then with a laugh that spoke of contentment, she added, 'So all of them learnt to do without. But soon after she came to live with us she asked if she could join the church choir and they always gave her the solo parts – you know, the first verse of a hymn, that sort of thing. She has a nice voice.'

'Does Tom know that? He's never said.'

Lou Caldecott chuckled. 'I shouldn't think so for a moment. When you fall in love with a man on his way to becoming an internationally known violinist you don't boast about having sung in the church choir.'

'I'd boast about it if I had and I'd been given the solos. But, yes, she is a sweet girl and Peter and I are delighted. We shall miss her. When they come back from their honeymoon she will move around with him, going wherever he's playing and living in digs or hotels, but I don't know where they will choose for a base. Somewhere mid-England, I suppose.'

But it didn't work out like that. For the fortnight of their honeymoon Zina took care of Ruth, interviewing two unsatisfactory candidates for a replacement for Clara and going to bed each night more tired than she cared to admit. Then the couple came home to be greeted by wild excitement from the toddler. Apart from her, only Zina was there to greet them.

'Up me, Unc Tom, up me,' she shouted tugging at the leg of his trousers. He 'upped' her and was rewarded with a bear-like hug before he passed her over to waiting Clara. And when it came to time for her bath and bed it was as if Clara were still her carer.

'We've been talking while we've been away Mrs Marcha—' Clara started when she and Tom came down from settling Ruth for the night.

'You must break that habit,' Zina interrupted her, laughing. 'Call me Mother, Mum or Zina, I'm easy which you choose.'

'Then can I say Mum the same as Tom does? I'd really like that. I called my stepmother by her Christian name, and then there was Aunt Lou, and she was just like a mother to me but she was still Aunt Lou and I always envied the others being able to say Mum.'

'That's settled then, and Peter will be Dad – unless, having a father of your own you'd rather say Peter.'

'I'd like to say Dad. I've always called my father Father, the same as his flock did. But, Mum—' as yet the name didn't come naturally, she would have to work at it – 'we've been talking about Ruth now that we have come home. You go on, Tom, you tell her what we were wondering.'

So Tom put the proposition forward that they should make Newton House their base, and Clara would help looking after Ruth. Most of his engagements were either in London or the Midlands, and most of them were in the evening so he would have plenty of time to drive from home the same day, sometimes even returning after the concerto.

'You know this place is always here for you, but oughtn't you to be looking for a home of your own. That's what every bride wants surely.'

'I know, but it seems to me right that Clara and I make ourselves responsible for Fiona's child. I don't mean that to sound horrible, Mum, it's not because we're younger or anything like that, but you know how it always was with us when we were kids. It sort of makes her not being here easier if I am surrogate Dad for her child.'

Zina nodded. 'I understand how you feel about Ruth. But in time you'll be sure to move on to a place of your own and if you feel like that about her you'll want to take her with you. I don't want Peter to be hurt any more than he has been; watching them together I think he sees Fiona in her.'

'Can't we just let time take care of all that. I suppose I'm not being very assertive in wanting us to live here but, Mum, this is a sort of family home, the Marchand headquarters, eh?'

And so it was agreed. The only thing Peter insisted was that the young couple should have a sitting room of their own. 'We all get along very well,' he told them, 'but if this is to be your base you must have somewhere to call your own. I suggest that you take the morning room for your living room – it's a good size and gets almost no use. That's right next to the lobby leading to the back door. How about if we get some plans drawn up to turn most of what is now the lobby into a bathroom for you and have a new back door and porch? What do you say, Zee?'

Her expression gave him the answer he wanted. Plans were drawn up and the work put in hand. Apart from having first the builders, followed by interior decorators, life went on much as it had when Clara had been a nursemaid for Ruth. The furniture from the morning room was sent to the saleroom, so that the young couple could be surrounded by their own things. But how different it was from the time when Zina had been left with the task of breaking up their home to go to California; now there was a new feeling of hope. Most weeks Tom was away for at least a day and a night, and when he was at home he spent hours of each day in the music room just as Zina used to. She knew she was being selfish, for his hours of practice each day were nothing new, but she had always thought of the music room as especially her own and since she had had to give up the violin she had worked hard on the piano. Now she realized his time was more important than hers and waited until the young ones were out or Tom was away at a recital or concert before she let herself indulge. That was the only thing that marred the arrangement. Of course the bonus was that with Clara still there she was a free agent and often travelled back to London with Peter on Monday mornings.

It was about six months after Tom and Clara married, the new routine was running on oiled wheels, when he wrote to Ivor telling him of the general situation and asking that he would agree to Clara and him legally adopting Ruth. By return came Ivor's reply. Although Zina had sent him the occasional photo of Ruth, except for a Christmas card, they had heard nothing. Now though he wrote to Tom saying that he and his wife, Isabel Cornwall (and had they been filmgoers her name would have been familiar, but as they weren't her fame passed unnoticed) would be coming to England shortly and would discuss plans for Ruth.

'Shortly' turned out to be some months away, in fact so distant that they all supposed he intended to leave the arrangement as it stood. Then, about a year after Tom and Clara's wedding, there was a phone call from Ivor. He and Isabel were in London and intended to spend a couple of days in Devon so that arrangements could be made regarding Ruth's future.

'You'll stay here, of course,' Zina said, taking it for granted that that was what he intended.

'No. That's sure kind of you, Mrs Marchand—' (on his previous visits he had always called her Zina) – 'but we'll just call by for an hour or so. I want to show Isabel something of your country and we shall be in Devon I guess Tuesday or Wednesday of next week.'

'Try and make it Tuesday, Ivor. On Wednesday morning Tom will be on the road heading north. He has a concert in Manchester that evening.'

'Our plans are a bit fluid at the moment, but I surely would be disappointed to miss him.'

At Newton House there was a feeling of

328

excitement; even Mrs Cripps was told about the hopes and plans that appeared to be coming to fruition and when Tuesday came Clara, Tom and Zina found themselves repeatedly drawn to the window waiting for the arrival. But the day ended with no visit. The next day Tom waited as long as he could before setting off northward, but he'd barely been gone more than an hour when Ivor pulled up by the front steps. Standing back in the room Zina watched them, thankful that Peter wasn't at home. So this was the wife who had replaced Fiona. At first glance she appeared to be much the same as any other of Fiona's acquaintances Zina had met, made-up to perfection, dressed for the catwalk. It was only as Ivor introduced her, a ring of pride in his voice, 'This is my wife, Isabel,' and the girl took Zina's hand in hers, that she felt she saw behind the mask of perfect grooming.

'I've wanted to meet you, Mrs Marchand. Fiona and I were buddies, we sort of got sucked into the Hollywood scene at about the same time, both of us kids trying to believe we were fully-fledged growns.' How well it suited the description of Zina's own impression.

'I'm glad Ivor has brought you,' Zina said, making sure her hospitable tone did nothing to give away her thankfulness that Peter wasn't here to have to play host to Fiona's replacement.

'We wanted to come before this, but you know how it is. First I wasn't free, then it was Ivor who couldn't make it, then there was all the refurnishing to get sorted and staff . . . well . . .' She cut short what she was saying, warned off it by a sharp drawing down of Ivor's brows.

329

Zina noticed their quick exchange of glances and felt a stab of unease. Yet why? Isabel was clearly a woman who liked to chatter but perhaps he was more aware than she was that this had been Fiona's home and it might not be tactful to chatter about the details of his life with a replacement wife.

'Ah,' she said, a smile lighting her face, 'here comes Clara with Ruth. Such a shame you couldn't manage to get here yesterday, Tom wanted to be able to talk it all through with you. But I'll go and rustle us up some coffee and leave you all to get to know each other. Clara's going to make a perfect mother.'

'She's pregnant?' Isabel misunderstood Zina's meaning and, accustomed as she was to the demands of Hollywood concerning the perfection of a young woman's figure, supposed that the jolly-looking girl who came into the room at a pace to suit the toddler, had a natural excuse for her waistline.

'Here we are!' Clara announced with a friendly beam of welcome to the visitors. 'I'm so glad you've come at last.'

'Sure and it is last, too. We fly away almost before dawn cracks tomorrow,' Isabel told them. 'My, but aren't you the cutest little body I ever did see?' Ruth looked at her with suspicion, her bottom lip trembling. 'Come on now, honey, what about giving me a big smile?'

Zina and Clara shared a quick glance, neither quite sure what it conveyed, then Zina escaped to the kitchen to make the coffee.

'They've come at last, I see.' Mrs Cripps

330

greeted her. 'Him and that "hotlips" he's wedded to. What does our little Ruth make of them, eh? Oh and are they going to stay to eat with you? Is there anything you want me to be getting on with out here while you chat with them?'

'No, it's just a quick visit. They fly home first thing tomorrow.'

Mrs Cripps sniffed, her action louder than any words. 'Sooner it's all done and settled the better for the poor little mite. But what about all the paperwork? Or because her father is a Yankie will it mean Tom flying over there to get it sorted? Surely not. The little lass is pure English, same as you and me.'

'I should think papers will have to be sent back and forth. But I expect it will be very straightforward.'

''Tis to be hoped so. Tell you one thing, Mrs M, when I saw them get out of the car – I don't mind admitting when I heard it come I stood on the chair so that I could have a dekko – I was glad the poor master couldn't be here to welcome them. We women got more steel in us than the men, come to the crunch, and he would have been real upset seeing Ivor with another wife. Now then, that coffee's been brewing long enough. Time we stopped this chatter.'

Carrying the tray up the basement stairs the sound of raised voices in the drawing room warned Zina that all wasn't well. For a few seconds she stood outside the door listening. That was when she felt the first grip of fear. Then, taking a deep breath and standing straight, she pushed the door open and carried the tray to the table.

331

'Mum!' Clara seemed to have lost control of her voice as her words tumbled out. 'Tell them they can't do it. They want to take her back with them. She's always been here. You can't just move little children as if they are – are – parcels. She's a proper person. You can't do it to her. She's not a tiny baby, she knows where she is here, she's loved here.'

'Hey, hey, Mrs Tom.' Ivor spoke before Zina had had a chance to gather together her scattered wits. 'You wouldn't be saying she won't be loved back home where she was created? If you could just see the nursery she's got waiting for her. And her bedroom looks like every little girl's idea of fairyland. Sure shc'll be happy.'

Zina felt utterly helpless. Fight these two and inevitably she would be the loser; he was Ruth's father, surely no law could be on their side. She thought of Peter and what losing Fiona had done to him. His salvation had come from Ruth, from her dawning intelligence, from the way she followed him as if she knew the special bond that had always been between Fiona and him. If Ruth went, all the wounds would be open and, worse, there would be the constant fear for her happiness.

Turning to the visitors she didn't even try to hide her anguish, indeed she felt it was her only hope.

'Please, *please*,' she begged, 'don't take her away from us.' Then, ashamed that she could sink to such depths and yet knowing she did it for Peter's sake, she continued, 'After Fiona died – I just can't tell you what it did to Peter. I believe he will be scarred by it for the rest of his days, but his salvation has been Ruth. To watch them together is almost like looking back down the years. If you take her away . . .' She heard the croak in her voice and held her jaw stiffly, frightened to speak.

'It's hard, Mrs Marchand,' Isabel said in her slightly southern drawl, 'but at least Peter does have memories. I guess Ivor would like the chance to come first with his own little girl.'

It was Clara who seized what she saw as a way to tip the scales. 'But there will be other children, children from your own marriage. And when that happens, don't you see, Ruth must always come second for you, you wouldn't be human if your own didn't seem closer.'

The silence seemed tangible and then, speaking almost uncertainly, Isabel said, 'I didn't mean to say anything about this, but I guess it's only fair that you have the whole picture. I said just now that Fiona and I were buddies, we really were sort of soul mates. I was away on location when you and Peter came out, that's how it was we didn't meet up. We were real kindred spirits and one of the things we were hundred per cent agreed on was that we didn't mean ever to get pregnant. Neither of us was married, but we knew that wouldn't make any difference, no husband would change our minds. I had an operation just to be on the safe side and make sure there couldn't be any slip-ups, but she was real chicken and said she'd stick with the pill – and you know what happened. Ivor wants to be a father, well he is a father but you know what I'm saying, it's Fiona who has given him his child. But, like I say, she and I were two peas in a pod. If our positions had been reversed and she'd had herself put out of danger's way and I'd forgotten to take the wretched pill, then she would want to take the baby home same as I do. There! Now you can see why we aren't going home tomorrow without her. We're truly sorry for you and I hope your Peter will take it on the chin, but it's right that she comes back with us. Fiona was hundred per cent happy out there, she only ran home because she couldn't face being fat amongst all those beautiful people.'

As she stopped speaking Ivor took up the tale: 'She'll lack for nothing, I promise you.'

'Things don't matter, it's love she needs.' Still holding her jaw stiff Zina heard her tone as aggressive.

'Love has to be earned, but she'll earn it right enough and get it in spadefuls.' Ivor was getting restless. They had a long drive ahead of them and he wanted to get started. 'Look, Zina, nothing you can say will make me change my mind about this, but I promise faithfully that she will grow up knowing about Fiona and you folk here, I'll send you pictures and maybe one day you'll come and see her for yourself – or we'll bring her here. Do you reckon that coffee's still warm?'

Clara and Zina looked at each other in miserable silence. They knew they could do nothing but accept.

'You pour the coffee, Mum. I'll pack a bag for her,' Clara said trying to spare Zina.

'All we need is enough till we get home.' There

was relief in Isabel's voice; a few minutes and they'd be on their way.

'All her toys are upstairs, doll's cot and doll's pram, things that will have to be crated and sent by sea.' Zina tried to put expression into her words, but she felt numb with misery.

'No, don't bother with any of that,' Ivor told her. 'As long as you put enough in a bag for us to get her home, then you should just see what there is waiting for her.'

But still Zina couldn't give up the fight. 'Have you young brothers or sisters?' she asked the glamorous Isabel. 'Have you had experience of young children?'

'No, but honestly you don't need to worry. We've got it all worked out. On the way back to London we are calling in to collect a real English nursemaid, a proper trained one, uniform and all.'

Ruth staggered across the room carrying a picture book. Then tugged at Ivor's trouser leg. 'Ook,' she said hopefully with a smile that was enough to touch any heart, let alone that of her natural father. 'A 'tory. We read a 'tory?'

Clara disappeared upstairs to pack the case, a change of clothes, nappies for the night (with enough for tomorrow night in case they hadn't been on the list of essentials awaiting her arrival) nightdress, dressing gown and slippers, then on the top, despite being told that nothing else would be needed, she packed Rupert, the teddy bear that many years ago had belonged to Fiona.

'Truly, Zina, we'll keep in touch. And she'll have a splendid life.' Now that the difficult part was over and in a few moments they'd be on

335

their way, Ivor wanted to help her through what he knew couldn't be easy. 'And don't you think Fiona would be glad if she could know Ruth was to grow up where she had been so happy?'

But it wasn't Fiona Zina was thinking of, nor even herself; in her mind she held an image of Peter walking across the grass holding the tiny hand, giving her all his attention as they were deep in what Ruth considered conversation. It wasn't fair! Hadn't he suffered enough? This would break his heart.

Ten minutes later she and Clara stood at the head of the front steps watching the car disappear down the drive. They waited in silence until they could no longer hear the sound of the engine.

'We couldn't stop them,' Clara said, as if the knowledge that they'd had no power to prevent Ruth going might somehow make it more bearable.

'No,' Zina answered, one word spoken so quietly it was barely audible. Then, seeming to square her shoulders and raise her chin, she glanced at her watch. 'Clara,' she spoke with new determination, 'I'm going to drive up to town. I can't tell Peter on the phone, I must be there with him.'

Clara nodded. 'Poor Dad. There's no easy way of breaking it to him.'

'No. I dread it. It's not fair,' and she heard the dangerous break in her voice. 'It's going to rake over all the ashes. I know they are within their rights – and they'll love her and give her a happy home, but . . .' Helplessly she turned to dear, understanding Clara. They might have found

336

solace in crying together, but reason told them both that this was a moment for action.

'I'll bring the car round to the front while you pop up and get your things,' Clara said, feeling the need to do something to help.

And so it was that only minutes later she stood alone at the head of the front steps, this time waving Zina goodbye as she headed for London and Peter.

Stepping out of the lift Peter noticed a line of light shining under the door of his apartment. Imagining that he must have gone out without switching the light off, just as he put his key in the lock the door opened and there was Zina.

His spontaneous reaction was delight, but one look at her and he knew something was wrong. He drew her to him, holding her close.

'What is it? Something's wrong.'

With her face burrowing against his neck he could feel the movement as she nodded. Then, kicking the door shut as he still held her, he led her back into the room.

'. . . had to come.' Hardly more than a whisper as she pulled back from him and forced herself to meet his worried gaze. 'Ivor and his new wife came this morning.'

'Yes you told me he was coming. Hell, darling, I wanted to be there with you. It must have been so difficult – Ivor – with a new wife.'

She shook her head. She'd come all this way to break the news of what had happened and now that she was with him she couldn't find a way to ease the pain, either for him or for herself.

'. . . gone. They've taken her. I tried to stop them, but there was no way. He's her father.'

'Taken her? Fiona's little girl?' He whispered, barely audibly. Releasing his hold on her he turned away and when he spoke again he'd lost control of his voice, it was loud and harsh. 'Bloody man . . . Fiona's baby . . . all we have of her.' As if all power had deserted him he flopped onto the settee. He turned towards Zina, seeing her expression and in it reading her misery and helplessness. 'You drove all this way to tell me.'

She nodded, using all her willpower to keep her voice firm. '. . . wanted to. Wanted to be with you, just us.'

He nodded, taking her hand and drawing her down to his side. But instead of sitting, she sank to her knees burying her face against him.

'. . . wouldn't take her things. Not clothes, not toys. They said they have everything ready for her.' Zina didn't cry easily but now she was at rock bottom, and it took all her determination to form the words.

'Fiona's baby . . . all we had left of her . . .' What he heard had brought back all the anguish of losing the daughter who'd been so precious to him. Perhaps even he hadn't realized how he had clung to the love he had for Ruth feeling it gave him a link with Fiona, a future with something of her still with them. Silently he wept, she knew it from the jerky, trembling of his body as kneeling in front of him she drew him close. '. . . all we had of her . . . gone . . . all we had of her . . .'

'No darling,' Zina answered, doubting if he even heard her, 'we have memories, memories we can never lose.' It took every bit of her will-power to speak gently and calmly while inside she was as torn as he. 'Ruth'll be loved and cared for – and I believe she's being taken to where Fiona would want her to be brought up.' Was that the truth? Did she really believe it? All she cared about was helping Peter get through the shock and hurt of losing his beloved Fiona's legacy. From his misery she had to find her own strength.

'Fiona . . . now her baby . . . how much more are we supposed to bear?' His words were disjointed and barely audible. 'Like seeing her all over again . . . Fiona . . .' Uninvited the thought came to Zina that all this time he must have carried this misery in his heart, the wound of losing Fiona still as open and raw as in the first weeks.

With her face pressed against his she gave up her own battle for control. Perhaps he loved Ruth because she was a legacy from Fiona; Zina loved her simply for herself. But on that night neither of them looked beyond the emptiness left by her going.

Eleven

Zina took the pile of envelopes the postman passed to her and walked across the grass to the seat under the horse chestnut tree which, at this hour of the morning, was in sunshine. She haggled open the top one without so much as glancing at any of the others. Her face wore a half-smile of anticipation. To read one of Clara's letters was like hearing her voice. 'Wholesome' had been Peter's description of her when they'd first learned that she was to be Tom's wife and after all this time nothing changed her, the description was still as apt. With the folded sheets half in and half out of the envelope it was temptingly easy for Zina to let her mind drift back down the years. The junior Marchands hadn't been altered by time or success, perhaps a character trait Tom had inherited from his father. These days Tom and Clara were not so junior; but despite his rise to become one of the country's – and much further afield – foremost violinists, their feet stayed firmly on the ground. It was some twenty years since they had left Newton House, at that time taking their nine-month-old son Christo (or Christopher to give him his full name, which nobody ever had) and moving to a house with a garden sloping down to the river near Henley-on-Thames. Deirdre, their next child, was three years behind Christo and then after another three years had come Kate. All three grandchildren were very dear to Zina and Peter and through the years, if Peter had been at home between commitments during school holidays they always enjoyed 'borrowing' them to stay at Newton House. Just as long ago Tom and Fiona had when they were young, so the next generation loved to go adventuring with Peter. Then, last year, when Clara had already passed her fortieth birthday, the forth member of the Marchand Junior family had arrived and now at six months old baby Stephen was the delight of the whole family. Looking forward to the chatty letter that Zina knew it would be, she took it out of the envelope and started to read.

'Anything worth reading in the post? Who's that one from?' Peter's voice surprised her. So deep in memories had she been that she hadn't noticed him crossing the grass towards her.

'I haven't looked at the others. This one's from Clara,' she answered as he picked up the envelopes on the seat by her side and lowered himself to sit down. His sigh didn't go unnoticed and, making no comment, she cast a quick and worried look in his direction, changing it to a smile when he turned towards her. 'You check through the others,' she said, then as she returned to her reading, she exclaimed, 'Peter, listen to this! She suggests that they should all come here for your birthday. I suppose they see seventy-five as a milestone.' The letter seemed temporarily forgotten as she imagined them all and from there let her mind go to herself and Peter. 'The years go by so fast – but do you feel different? Do you

341

think of yourself as old? I expect that's how they see us, they must do, especially the grandchildren. But I don't, do you? We must have changed – oh I don't mean things like hair going white – or in my case a sort of messy-looking grey – I mean the essential *us*.'

He looked at her with a tolerant smile, the envelopes in his hand forgotten as he weighed up her question which, in truth, hadn't been a question as much as a comment on the passage of time.

'Does it feel like almost fifty years that we've been married?' He asked the question of himself. 'In some ways it has gone so fast, frighteningly fast; and yet it's as if there was nothing before, nothing that has left an indelible memory. Remember when they were children . . .' With his head back he gazed unseeingly at the blue summer sky. He too was lost in memories. 'Remember how you used to insist when I was home that I took them out without you?' He smiled as he closed his eyes, seeming to see the picture his words created. 'We used to go adventuring.' Then, not needing to spell out where his thoughts had taken him, he added, 'Her life's adventure was so short.' He fell silent, remembering the child who had held a special place in his heart.

'Joy, sadness, excitement, tragedy, it all gets carried along on the tide of time,' Zina mused. 'You know what I think, what I really *believe*? There's a purpose behind everything that happens. We may not see it at the time but, if we learn to trust, then later on we see the purpose. Think of little Ruth, what a dreadful time that was when Ivor and Isabel took her away from us. But, from this distance in time, imagine if she'd stayed. What would she have been doing now? She was just a baby, and we had no means of knowing where her dreams would be. With us would she have wanted a career in films like Fiona did? Out there she grew up in the industry. Our life has been so different here; you've never let your career colour our home and the life of the family. What would have happened if you'd signed that contract and we'd all moved over there? Would it have changed us?'

'Thank God we didn't take the chance. Yet would Fiona still have been here if we'd always been with her through her developing years?'

She took his hand in hers, struck by how cold it was despite the sunshine. Again his eyes were closed as he held his face towards the sun, so she was able to look at him without his knowing. Still a handsome man, but youth was behind him, of course it was, he was approaching his seventy-fifth birthday. She was barely six years behind him, but she still felt energetic, interested in life. The thought of retirement had never entered his head as the film idol of his youthful years had been overtaken by his love of stage with no more than the occasional film, sometimes only a cameo role with a character that interested him. Such was the advantage of success and longevity in the industry; he could play just the parts he chose to play. But lately something had altered him, something more than the natural passage of time. It was as if some of the joy of living had gone

343

out of him. Even after so long did it have roots in that dreadful time when they had lost Fiona? No, they had faced that together, a time she tried not to dwell on. Perhaps it was the inescapable fact that soon he must give up the work he so loved; was that what had taken hope – and, she believed, confidence too – away from him? She linked her fingers through his and felt his grip tighten.

'Perhaps you're right,' he said, 'about Ruth, I mean. Right there in the heart of the film world it must have seemed a natural progression for her to move into the business. And if Fiona knows, she must be so proud of what the girl has achieved. Yet, had she stayed here, who knows.'

'That, my darling Peter, is because, thank God, you never let yourself become anything but the real person you are. I bet not many in the profession stay as untouched by celebrity.'

'There are plenty,' he answered. 'And now, for me, that word celebrity is hardly applicable. Thinking of Ruth, or Rebecca as she so quickly became when she left here, do you think it would have made it any easier when they took her away from us if we'd been able to see into the future and know that she would have filled the role Fiona had made her own?'

'Of course it wouldn't, not for us. But she has been remarkable. She has captivated hearts right from her first film when she was only six through to today and, no doubt, beyond. That's a clever transition. Ivor and Isabel guided her well. I hate to remember the day they took her – and knowing how well it has worked out for her has never

344

made it any easier.' Then, changing the subject, she asked, 'Is there anything else interesting in the post?'

'Business envelopes, nothing pers . . .' His voice sounded strange, and faded into silence before he finished the word.

'Peter! Peter! What's the matter? Wake up, Peter.'

His head had flopped forward but he couldn't be asleep, for when she raised it she saw that his eyes were open. His breathing was shallow and he seemed to be staring straight ahead and yet when she moved her hand in front of his eyes he wasn't aware. She kept talking to him, chaffing his cold hands, silently pleading that he would properly wake and be normal even while reason told her that there was nothing normal in what had happened. A minute or two ago they had been talking quite naturally, he had been well. Or had he? Had that been just the impression he had meant to give.

Please, please, she silently begged. And then, speaking her thoughts aloud as, just as suddenly as he had drifted away, so now he appeared once more to be aware. 'Thank God. Peter, what happened to you? Do you feel ill? Why couldn't you have told me?'

'What?' He sounded puzzled. 'Ill? No, of course I'm not ill.' He sounded completely mystified by her concern. It was as if the minute or so he's stared so vacantly at nothing had never happened.

He seemed perfectly normal after that one episode, so much so that she almost persuaded herself it had never happened. In the afternoon they donned anoraks and drove the few miles to the coast where they walked for an hour or so. Life was good.

When they reached home they found a note by the telephone, a message Anna (the live-in maid who had come to them after Mrs Cripps had succumbed to pneumonia about ten years previously) had left on the hall table. There had been a call from Isaac Roache the film producer and friend of Peter's for many years. He had left no message but asked that Peter ring him back. While he made the call, Zina went to the kitchen to make some tea and, in her natural way, have a chat with Anna.

'I can do that, Mrs Marchand. You go and sit in the sunshine, I'll bring the tray out when Mr Marchand finishes his telephoning. I just made a few little almond biscuits. The recipe was in a programme on the TV yesterday evening. I had a try to taste them and they're pretty good even if I say so myself. I thought the master would like something a bit different and I remember he always likes almonds. He's all right, is he?'

Fear stabbed at Zina again but she made herself keep her voice bright as she answered, 'He says he is. I thought he looked tired, but I guess, Anna, we can't expect always to have the energy we had years ago.'

'Ah. I hear his step. He must have finished the call. Yes, he's outside, looking for you, I expect. You hop off and see him, I'll bring the tray out in just a jiff.'

So, sitting on the terrace and pouring their tea,

Zina was told the reason Isaac had wanted to talk to him.

'It seems I'm not on the scrap heap after all,' he said, trying without success to talk seriously and not let his smile tell her the excitement he felt.

'You'll never be on the scrap heap. But tell me, what did Isaac want?'

'He was sounding me out about a film.'

Before she could hold it back, she frowned. Film work was so demanding. Early mornings on the set, long days of work, probably hours of standing around. Even a stage performance would have been better.

'And are you interested?' Silly question, she told herself. Just look at him!

'It may be my swan song, but yes, I want to do it. Maybe there will be more after this, but for me this is special, *important*. There's to be a film of *King Lear*. Now you can see why I mean to do it.'

'Are you sure, Peter? Sure you want it, I mean? It won't be like acting it on the stage. While you're filming you'll have time for nothing else, desperately early mornings—'

'Zee.' He reached across the garden table and took both her hands in his. 'Zee, Lear saw my return to the stage. You know how I felt about playing him then. Then or now, in my heart no character has lived as he has. Yes, I want to do it. On the stage perhaps I was able to put flesh and blood into the king for theatregoers in the capital. Think of the people who might be moved by him if we can put that same emotion on the

347

screen, if he can be made to live for the audience.' As if he pulled a curtain down on his inner feelings he dropped her hands and stirred his tea despite the fact the cup was half empty and in any case he never used sugar. So seldom did he let his driving passion for what he did find expression even to Zina.

'OK,' she agreed, 'I can understand how you feel. *King Lear* has always been very special. So, Peter my sweet, what we shall do is rent a cottage, house, flat, anything, near the studio and I shall come with you.'

They looked at each other very directly, saying nothing. Zina was filled with purpose, she would see he was cared for, make sure if he had to have early mornings then he would have early nights. She wasn't happy about it, but it meant so much to him and perhaps what she saw as tiredness came from frustration because he wanted to work.

'You'll come with me?' he repeated and she looked down rather than let him suspect she had seen his eyes fill with tears.

'Next week the youngsters come, neither of us can go anywhere until after your birthday.'

'No. Shooting won't start yet. But tomorrow I shall drive up to talk about it, possibly to sign the contract.' Then it was he who changed the subject. 'While I'm gone you ought to take Mother-in-law out while this weather holds. Has she phoned today?'

'Yes, she checked in this morning. She really is amazing. Sounded as bright as a button. May we be as good when we get to be ninety-three. Even so I'm glad she agreed to have someone living in the house with her seeing that she was so pig-headed about not selling up and coming here.'

Peter half-smiled remembering Jenny and what Zina saw as her pig-headed refusal to give up her own home when Derek had died. 'She's a great lady is Mother-in-law, made of stout stuff. For all that, I'm glad she at least liked the idea of having a live-in companion to help her. Given a free rein even at ninety-three she'd still be mowing her own grass.'

Jenny looked at him with affection. 'You know something, Peter Marchand? You're a hundred per cent nice guy. She's ridden rough shod over you many a time and you never hold it against her.'

'You know why? Because I know exactly why she resents me: because she's more sensitive than you give her credit for and, right from the early days, she has known that you and I are – are – how can I say it? Some couples, even married happily, remain two separate characters. We don't. You and I are "us". Come what may, happiness, sadness . . .' He paused, reaching again to take her hand. 'No earthly separation can ever divide us.' This time it was Zina who felt the sting of tears. 'Now then, enough of all that. What did you say Anna had put in the biscuits because she knew I like it?'

'Almonds. You might guess, she's put one on the top of each.'

'Ah! So she has. Indeed I'm a lucky chap,' he said, in a tone that mocked himself. 'Women just fall at my feet, you know.' Then chewing on the biscuit, he said, 'I say, Zee, these are seriously good.'

Peter's birthday was more than just the evening party where friends of many years from stage, screen, production and management attended. The celebration lasted from breakfast until they staggered off to bed. Newton House was bulging at the seams with Tom and his family home and Jenny with her companion there all day and then staying the night. Celia had been on her own for more than ten years, the inevitable result of loving a man so many years her senior, so alone she came to the party. Still as eccentric in her dress, she was just as dear to all of them as she had been for years and, rather than drive home, she too was staying the night after the party ended and the hotels in Deremouth filled up.

'Quite a day, wasn't it, Zee,' Peter said as they finally lay down in bed.

'Lovely, every minute of it. The caterers did well, didn't they? I drank so much champagne I ought to fizz.'

'I want to make you fizz. Oh God but I want it.' For a few seconds they were silent, then moving his fingers around her hardened nipples and hearing that small sound he loved in her throat, he whispered, 'Zee, Zee, help me. In my mind I want to love you, sometimes I can think of nothing else. Help me. Tonight it's got to be good. Such a bloody failure.'

'You never fail me, you never have.'

'I fail us both. Look at me!' And he threw the

bedcovers back to expose the hopelessness. 'Yet, Zee, if I don't have you I – I – I can't think of anything but how much I want—'

'Tonight will be wonderful,' she whispered, her mouth almost touching his. Then she moved to kneel bending over him, kissing his forehead, his mouth, then slowly down to his chest, moving her tongue on his stomach, then down. She heard his sigh and didn't raise her head, there was no need, the sound was message enough and then, just as he'd longed, her mouth held him, her tongue caressed.

If only he could relax into certainty, but he was frightened, terrified that without warning all tangible sign of his desire would disappear. So often lately at the last moment, while his mind was filled with need and his body ready, suddenly hope would be stripped from him. But tonight it would work for both of them, it *must*. 'Now Zee, yes, yes, please God yes . . .' If she stopped what she was doing and he moved onto her, would he be no use again? As he made his first movement she bent over him, pushing him back to lie flat while she straddled him and lowered herself. He lay quite still, frightened to move in the wonder of what was happening. They looked at each other in the soft light of the bedside lamp and she felt that never in all their years had they been closer than at that moment.

For her the miracle was quick. She clenched her teeth in her battle not to cry out in this crowded house and, lying beneath her, Peter watched her as she was transported to a wonder beyond imagination, never once losing eye contact with him. Then she leant down against him, out of breath and filled with thankfulness. For him it wasn't over and for that she sent up a prayer of thanks. When she started to move again she knew from the sudden change in his breathing that his moment had come. So often lately this had been denied him but this time he climbed his mountain, not feebly but with strength that held him on the peak as he writhed under her. Remembering that rooms both sides of theirs were in use she held her hand over the mouth he didn't have the control to close, holding back his cries. Then, at last he lay still, breathless and filled with joy and thankfulness. Then, looking at each other, their expressions said it all. In their joy they laughed.

'What a perfect way to end a birthday,' she said a moment later, snuggling down in bed.

'Um, yes, perfect. Only one thing I want now.'

'Not a pee?' she chuckled.

'No. A cuddle. Wriggle closer.'

The success of the end of his birthday seemed to have done him good, for when they saw their overnight guests off next morning he looked brighter than he had for days. Tom and his family weren't going back until after lunch so the morning was a leisurely time, a game of tennis on the court that was marked out every summer now that there were young people to use it again.

'Dad seems very bright and fit, Mum,' Tom said when he wandered over to where she was deadheading the roses. 'When we got here I thought he was looking tired, different somehow. A bit drawn.'

'Perhaps he was dreading getting to seventy-five. Now he's there he knows it's no different from being seventy-four. And I think he's excited at the prospect of getting under the skin of his dear King Lear again.'

'I bet he is. But he'll find it frustrating, filming it out of sequence.'

'He won't let his beloved Lear down. He knows it so well even after all these years; he will be wonderful. And I know he is flattered and grateful that the part has been offered to him. We've found a funny little cottage. No, not funny – quaint. It's on the edge of the village, surrounded by fields. Someone has obviously bought it for holiday lets and had mod cons – up to a point – put in. A rather ugly electric water heater over the bath, no shower, but it does have a flush loo. Where it flushes to I didn't enquire, I suppose a septic tank somewhere. We shall be fine and I can keep an eye that he gets a proper meal at the end of the day and goes to bed early to make up for the crack-of-dawn starts. There's no television or radio but we shall take a portable radio and a record player.'

'You'll come to see us while you're there, won't you? Maybe he'll get a few days free of filming sometimes. But I expect if he does you'll want to get back here to check on the Marchand Headquarters. But come whenever you can, won't you. I'm playing the Bruch G minor in Oxford on the twenty-eighth. Any chance of your getting there?'

'One of my very favourite concertos. Every chance, I should think.'

But no one is master of his own destiny.

It was halfway through the morning of the twenty-seventh that the phone rang. Most days during his waiting moments Peter called her, often more than once during the course of the day. He never used to in the days when he left her at Newton House and was away for a week or more at a time, but having her so relatively near the studio it seemed natural to both of them that they should speak more often even though the calls were brief.

'Hi, Peter, you're early today. Not much on?'

'Mrs Marchand?' the voice of a stranger enquired.

'Yes?' An affirmation and an enquiry in one. With a mother in her nineties that was where Zina's immediate thoughts flew.

'I've been told to phone you. We found your number in Peter's pocket. He has been taken ill. I'm so sorry.'

'Ill? But he was fine when he left here. How do you mean, ill?'

'He collapsed. We're waiting for an ambulance. Can you come?'

They had considered bringing just one car, but never had she been so thankful that they decided on two as she was as she sped towards the film studio. She arrived as the ambulance was just driving away.

'They're taking him to Oxford,' Isaac Roache, the director, came to open her car door. 'I'll get my car and tell you as we drive.'

354

'No, I must take my own car in case they say I can bring him back. I can look after him if they say he has to stay in bed for a bit.' She wouldn't admit to the thought of anything worse.

'Yours is all right where it is. I'm driving you. This is mine. We'll talk as we go.'

She seemed to have lost all power of resistance and felt shaken and uncertain, frightened to let herself think and yet incapable of keeping at bay visions of every tragedy, as she followed him to his car. It was as they drove towards Oxford that he told her how Peter had seemed perfectly normal as shooting started, then just for a moment had looked bemused as if he didn't know where he was or what he was doing.

'When I spoke to him it was as if he didn't hear me, wasn't on the same planet. Frightened me for a minute. Then, just as suddenly as it had happened, so it was over. He picked up just where we had been before.' She remembered that other time in the garden. 'It was about ten minutes after that; the camera just panned in on him for a close-up and, with no warning, down he went, out cold.'

'How long was he unconscious? How was he when the ambulance people came?'

'He hadn't come round. Zina, the medics couldn't get a response. They'll be trying now, on the way to the hospital.'

With every fibre of her being she pleaded silently that he wasn't ill, seriously ill. Perhaps he was overtired; perhaps he would have to accept retirement. After all most men had been retired ten years or more when they reached his age. So she silently bargained, pleaded, even clutched at hope as they approached the hospital.

But it wasn't to be. For a while they waited and then she was called into the Senior Nurse's office where the news was broken to her. Peter had suffered a massive stroke and had died without regaining consciousness. There were formalities to be got through, and somehow, like a zombie, she gazed at the staff as they talked to her, shook hands with the doctors who had signed the certificate, made arrangements for his body to be carried back to Devon. How much of the organizing was her doing and how much Isaac's she could never remember afterwards, the whole sccnc was like a living nightmare, one from which she knew there would be no waking.

Isaac drove her back to the cottage where there were two cars waiting. One was her own which, unbeknown to her, Isaac had had brought back while they were at the hospital; but in her state of numb misery she wasn't surprised that it should be there. And neither did she feel any emotion when she recognized the second one and knew Tom was waiting for her, having had a phone call from Isaac. Yet she hadn't even been aware at the hospital of what he was doing or that he was making phone calls. It was probably he, too, who made an announcement to the press and the media.

That same evening at Myddlesham where Jenny and her companion Edith Hume listened to the ten o'clock news, they heard the announcement.

356

'I can't believe it! There was never anything wrong with him.' Jenny was torn between genuine concern and pity for Zina, a feeling of shame for the hundreds of times she had tried to score points against Peter and, perhaps even stronger than that, she silently acknowledged the truth that he must have been aware of how she tried to slight him and yet he never seemed to hold it against her.

'Poor, poor Zina. They were such a united couple. Whatever will she do?' Edith muttered as Jenny turned off the television. The rest of the news and tomorrow's weather forecast had lost interest for them.

'She'll do the same as you did and I did,' Jenny answered, 'she'll pick up the pieces and make the best out of what is left to her.'

The next day there wasn't a newspaper that didn't find a space on the front page. Peter had been a household name for forty-five years, from handsome young matinee idol to master of the classical stage. In Myddlesham where she was now the mother of a grown-up family, the erstwhile local baker's young daughter who used to have his pictures pinned to her bedroom wall was one of thousands up and down the country who, even if they had never met him, felt something had gone out of their lives.

The following year, on a July evening, Zina sat in the garden watching the sun sinking. It was that moment just before dusk when the world is hushed. She closed her eyes and yet, still looking into the sun, the world before her was filled with a red glow. Was it simply the brightness from the sun seen through her closed eyelids? She felt it was a glimpse into that timeless, endless space where surely his soul still lived. A smile touched the corners of her mouth.

When she felt a hand on her shoulder she raised her own to cover it.

'Were you asleep, Mum? Sorry if I disturbed you.'

In a second she was back in step, her moment of wonder gone and yet leaving her less lonely, less frightened of the stretch of empty days without him.

'No, I was awake,' she answered with the smile they all expected, 'I was just enjoying the last rays of the sun.'

'Glorious, isn't it. Seems a shame to drag you in, but Clara said to tell you it's food time.'

Together they walked back to the house where comfortable, pregnant Clara was just bringing the tray through to the dining room. The changes at Newton House had been Tom's idea. It was about six months ago when he, Clara and little Steve had moved in. For their older children too it was a base, 'home', although they had officially moved on and were busy with their own lives. At that time it was just becoming apparent to the most observant that at nearly forty-four Clara was again pregnant. But nothing fazed her and now, with the baby due to arrive, she plodded happily through her days, loving where life had brought her.

When Tom had suggested to Zina that they should come back, she had been frightened that they were proposing it because they didn't like to think of her being alone. But she had been wrong, at least in part.

'This has always been home, the place to come back to,' he told her earnestly, then added with a smile that said more than any words. 'We wouldn't get underfoot, Mum, and it worked when we were here way back. When I remember how it was for Fiona and me when we were kids, the Marchand Headquarters. I want it to be like that for Steve and this next one.' And any day now that new life would join them, the latest Marchand to find the magic that had been there for all of them.

And so Newton House once again became a family home, the garden a place for children at play, today's, tomorrow's or the ghost of yesterday's.

For Zina there could be no way back to the life she had known; her own capacity for joy had been lost with Peter. But as time passed she found peace. Perhaps it stemmed from the sound of the two little children playing, such an echo of the time that was gone; or from Clara's never failing good humour; from her own pride and love for Tommy as they made music together, she on the piano and he the violin; from the peace Jenny found as at nearly ninety-four she came to her final hours.

These things must have made the backdrop for her certainty of what would one day come to her, but she found her strength in something more. Sometimes, usually when she was half awake and half asleep it was as if Peter were with her, she seemed to hear his voice; brief flashes of time belonging just to them. She said nothing of this to anybody, not even Tom.

CPSIA information can be obtained at www.ICGtesting.com
Printed in the USA
LVOW08*2149050516

486934LV00003B/22/P

9 780727 872777